Jack

by

Phillip Boleyn

Outside of a dog, a book is probably a man's best friend.

Inside of a dog, it's too dark to read.
Groucho Marx

Copyright ©2021 Phillip Boleyn, sweetkoshka@gmail.com

No part of this document or the related files may be reproduced or transmitted in any form, by any means (electronic, photocopying, recording, or otherwise) without the prior written permission of the publisher.

ISBN 9798726035642

This is a work of fiction. Names, characters, places and incidents either are the product of the author's imagination or are used fictitiously, and any resemblance to actual persons, living or dead, business establishments, events, or locales is purely coincidental.

For Aphrodite Pelagia
The white rose shall not fade

For Koshka
My Other Heart

And to the memory of Veronica Franco
(1546-1591)

Contents

Prologue v
To Begin 1
Isaac's Story 53
Le Chat C'est Mort 140
Sleazebag 205
Comings & Goings 248
To Conclude 290
Epilogue 294
Acknowledgments 298
About the Author 301

Prologue

OH NO. NOT *THIS* AGAIN.

I have wandered into the kitchen in the reasonable expectation of having dinner. After all, it's 7 pm, and I've usually eaten by now - though truth be told Veronica can be extremely scatter-brained and I'm sometimes forced to remind her, with a nudge or a pointed look, to serve me. Today, I haven't eaten anything since lunch, and I'm hungry.

But as I round the corner towards where my food bowl sits, I am confronted by the sight of a naked man kneeling, head down, on the kitchen floor. The man, whose name is Donald, is facing away from me, which means his ass - which is rather substantial in area and is in addition spectacularly hirsute - is staring at me, like a hairy cyclops. At this particular moment, Donald is being made to put his face into my food bowl and eat whatever's in there, which I can tell from the smell was supposed to be my dinner.

Donald's specific kink is that he wants to be treated as if he were a dog. This involves, among other things, being led around the house on all fours with a leash and collar, and obeying random commands to *sit, stay, shake,* and *roll over*. The latter is particularly disturbing: I mean, trust me, the image of a middle-aged man - fat, naked and hairy - lying on his back with all four limbs in the air, with his tongue hanging out while he makes inarticulate woofing sounds, is not something you quickly forget.

Seriously, with all the things I've seen between these four walls, it's a miracle I'm not afflicted with PTSD. Veronica, who is towering over Donald in thigh-high boots and a black corset, turns and notices me. "Oh, sorry Jack," she says. "I'll get to you shortly." Then she adds, "Good dog!" - though it's not clear whether that's intended for me or the naked man who's currently noisily slurping up Alpo *Beef Chunks In Gravy*.

I wander back into the living room, lay down and sigh. I guess dinner will have to wait.

Oh well. It's the price I pay for living with a dominatrix.

To Begin . . .

"It is a truth universally acknowledged, that a single man in possession of a good fortune, must be in want of a wife." - Jane Austen: Pride and Prejudice

IT IS A TRUTH - admittedly not very universally acknowledged - that a single woman in possession of a good bullwhip, who beats the crap out of men for a living, must be in want of a wolf.

Or, failing that, a medium-sized pit bull.

I, the unconventional narrator of this tale, am said pit bull. Yes, I'm a dog. Allow me to introduce myself: my name is Jack, and I am almost four years old. Four legs, 60 pounds, mostly blond with some cute little white bits here and there.

I live in the city of Seattle with a 29-year-old woman with the surpassingly lovely name of Veronica Delacroix. Actually, it's not her real name, but we'll get to that in a moment.

We've been together for a little less than three years. Veronica and I share a comfortable house on a quiet tree-lined street in the pleasant and currently very hip neighborhood known as Capitol Hill. The tidy little house is about fifty years old: two bedrooms, two bathrooms, wraparound porch, sizeable mortgage.

Unfortunately the nice, tidy little house is also occupied by a cat. This one, like all cats, is both particularly annoying and perpetually on the verge of being irate, yet for reasons that defy understanding Veronica seems to actually like him. By the way, the cat's name is Bonkers, which tells you pretty much everything you need to know about his personality.

I see you trying to form an image in your mind, a natural thing to do when a character is first presented (I'm talking here about Veronica, not the cat). Her name suggests breeding and sophistication, you think: a woman named Veronica Delacroix must be tall and refined, with expensive clothes and well-groomed hair that is carefully arranged, perhaps held in place with a tasteful silver pin. Your mind's eye is already magnifying this small detail: the pin is of Celtic design, purchased from a tiny artisanal jewelry shop in a quaint village on a small, windswept Scottish island (Iona? Orkney?)

Or perhaps - since I have told you her name is false - that is all pseudo-baptismal bluff. Perhaps Veronica is a fraud: short and squat, with crooked teeth and ill-kempt mousey hair. Perhaps she is one of those girls who hides a heart of gold beneath the cheap sweaters she buys for a few dollars from Goodwill, but she is otherwise a forgettable, beige human being to whom you would not give a second glance if you passed her on the street. Full of vague dreams, destined to be forever timid, forever disappointed.

Or is she something else entirely?

Well then, herewith a brief portrait for you. To begin, Veronica is indeed reasonably tall: five foot nine inches in her bare feet, rather more in the spike heels that she favors and frequently wears. She is slim, with long, shapely legs and a bosom that is appropriately sized for her frame: her breasts are large enough to be confident but not so big as to be preposterous. She has what most would admit is a classically beautiful face: high cheekbones and large green eyes set above a graceful, aquiline nose. Full lips, a fine jawline, a slender neck.

Will that do for now?

What's that, you say? O yes, but I have omitted a key detail: her hair. Ah, her hair. Her hair is her glory.

And it is also, in a way, her name. For Veronica's real name is Holly. Her mother named her after a tree: Holly the pagan evergreen, the tree with fruit of fire, like the glorious red of Veronica's hair.

Veronica is my human, and I am her dog.

And the other detail you should know - as I hinted to you in my shamelessly parodied opening line - is this:

Veronica is a professional dominatrix.

Etymology

I like many things. Dog things, of course - long walks (off-leash), treats, chasing squirrels, sniffing other dog's asses, peeing on everything, and ripping small rodents into messy little chunks. The usual stuff. But I also like some human things, including words. Words are important. Dogs have a language of sorts, but it's pretty basic, probably because when your race's overwhelmingly favorite topics of conversation center on food, urination and bushy-tailed rodents, it doesn't give you much to work with. So, lacking a refined language of my own, I find human words - their use, their origin - a constant source of fascination. You could say that words are my hobby - well that, and eviscerating small animals.

Regarding the word *dominatrix*, Miriam-Webster has this to say by way of a definition:

> *Dominatrix* \?dä-mi-'na-triks\, noun. A woman who controls and hurts her partner during sexual activity in order to give her partner sexual pleasure. First known use 1971.

Although Webster is not entirely correct. The word has been in use much longer, although not in the modern sense: in 1561, a chronicler described Rome as "dominatrix of nations", meaning a dominant female entity (-*trix* being the Latin female suffix). The current meaning - the one which conjures up images of a tall woman wielding a good-sized bullwhip in a black leather corset and thigh-high boots - is quite recent. By the way, the plural is *dominatrices*.

So what exactly is a dominatrix? Simply explained, a professional dominatrix - *pro domme* for short - is a woman to whom men pay money in exchange for certain erotic services of a rather unorthodox nature. A dominatrix is not to be confused with a prostitute - although admittedly the stimulation of the male nether regions is a task common to both professions. But whereas a prostitute delivers pleasure, it is a dominatrix's job to inflict, in various creative ways and to greater or lesser degrees, pain or discomfort upon those all-important body parts. Among others.

I shall ignore for now the perplexing question of why a man would pay a woman a substantial sum of money to make him wear high heels and a corset and force him to run back and forth across a room with his balls chained to his ankles while his ass is repeatedly whacked with a wooden paddle (yes, dear reader, I assure you that this happens). I shall ignore this mostly because - frankly - I'm a dog and I have no idea why you humans do half the things you do. But as our little story unfolds you will meet some of Veronica's clients, and maybe you can figure it out for yourself.

Anyway, this is how Veronica earns her living. And since it keeps her in heels and me in dog food, I'm not one to complain.

Hero Dog

For some time after we met, my human was under the gravely mistaken impression that I am an attack dog, a fiercely loyal protector who could be trusted to defend her from muggers or rapists - or secretly sociopathic clients.

This unfortunate delusion originated on the day we met, and indeed in the manner of our meeting.

On the evening in question, Veronica was taking a short cut across Volunteer Park to her house on Capitol Hill. As she later breathlessly related the story to a friend, she had stopped in a local café on the way home to purchase a roast beef sandwich and a latté. So there she is, about to take her first bite out of said sandwich, when a man jumps out from behind a tree and blocks her path. He's holding a rusty but obviously quite serviceable kitchen knife, and is telling her to *Give me the fuckin' purse, lady, or else!* Veronica drops the latté and screams, the guy grabs her, and all seems lost.

But then - cue the cavalry bugle calls! - suddenly here comes, like a shot out of the dark, Hero Dog! Barking wildly, Hero Dog runs full-speed into the man and sinks his teeth into his forearm. Not surprisingly, this causes him to drop the knife, howl in pain and rapidly beat a retreat into the night. Yay Hero Dog!

To say that Veronica was grateful to her unexpected canine rescuer is about as much of an understatement as saying that Kim Kardashian is not a nuclear physicist. After the guy had disappeared, there was a protracted interlude involving praise, petting, hugging, kissing, more praise... repeat.

After a couple of minutes of this, and when things had settled down into a somewhat less effusive emotional state, Veronica suddenly noticed that I was not wearing a collar. "Aw, don't you have a home, doggie?" (No). "Where's your owner?" (What owner? Dogs don't have owners, we have humans.) Are you lost? (No, I may not have a GPS but I'm perfectly aware of where I am, thank you). And then the magic words: "Would you like to come home with me?" (No shit, lady, wag wag wag).

So off we went together, the crime victim and her intrepid attack dog. Over the next few days, I became for Veronica's friends the star turn in the oft-repeated story of the mugger in the park. "God, he was so *brave*! I don't know what I would have done without him!" More petting, hugging, kissing, et cetera. More praise (more treats, yay!).

Except - and I am embarrassed to admit this now - it wasn't like that, really. I've never told her this, but the reality was that I hadn't eaten a thing all day, and when I threw myself at the mugger and sank my teeth into his arm it was only because he happened to turn at just the wrong moment.

I was actually going for the sandwich.

Guard Dog

Look, here's the thing about pit bulls: despite everything you've heard, we're actually total crap as guard dogs. Well, not entirely. If the burglar breaking into your house happens to be a squirrel, I can assure you we'd take care of the situation - and other than shredded intestinal tract and other grisly little squirrel bits generously distributed across your living room floor in the aftermath, you'd have no worries.

Actually, a squirrel *did* get into the house once. Demonstrating extremely poor squirrel life choices, the creature in question made the fateful decision to enter the dining room through an open window on a warm afternoon in late spring. Unbeknownst to the squirrel, my day bed lay directly under said window, and, compounding big mistake with HUGE mistake, he landed directly on my head.

It is difficult to overstate the epic nature of the chaos that followed. Indeed, Dante himself could not have better scripted the ensuing 90 seconds. Rapidly comprehending the extreme nature of its plight as it bounced off my cranium, the squirrel took off at an appreciable fraction of the speed of light and shot through the house with a 60-pound dog in hot pursuit, both of us bouncing off walls, chairs, couches, tables, beds, the fridge, the stove, the armoire, a couple of wardrobes, and that nice and unfortunately placed porcelain vase at the top of the stairs. Meanwhile, Veronica was frantically running after us from room to room, screaming at the top of her lungs and repeatedly yelling utterly pointless commands - "Come! Come!! COME!!! *NO!!! STOP, YOU FUCKING MORON!*" Presumably this torrent of imperative was aimed at me and not the squirrel, but in fairness to myself she was lamentably unspecific.

Finally, in its desperation to find a way out, the squirrel made the fatal mistake of running into the bathroom and launching itself towards what it optimistically believed to be an open window. A second later, its graceful flight was rudely terminated as it thudded into the inconveniently placed insect screen, and fell to the floor. And there, with a well-aimed lunge, a satisfying crunch and a toss of my head, I efficiently broke its little rodent neck.

It was, unquestionably, the greatest moment of my life.

So - squirrels, no problem, you're golden. Ditto miscellaneous other rodents. But humans breaking into your house for rape and pillage - sorry. We really don't give a crap.

Isaac

In the immediate aftermath of what came to be known as The Squirrel Incident, I was temporarily *canina non grata* with Veronica, who continued to utter random curses as she followed the trail of destruction the squirrel and I had left behind us. I was secretly rather hoping that she'd be proud of me and have the squirrel stuffed and prominently mounted on a wall somewhere - deep down I'm an incurable optimist - but instead she picked it up by the tip of the tail and carried my hard-won trophy out to the trash, holding it at arm's length and maintaining an unnecessarily extreme expression of distaste the entire way. *Sic transit gloria mundi.*

Anyway, it was abundantly clear that I was not going to be getting any treats for a while. I suppose I could have followed Veronica around and tried my best to look adorable (which I am) and repentant (which I wasn't), but it all seemed like way too much effort. So instead I went to visit Isaac.

Isaac is my best friend. Contrary to what you will inevitably assume, Isaac is not another dog, but a human. He is 78 years old and lives in the house next door. That is, the next door to the west - the house to the east of us is occupied by a paranoid little twerp named Leroy, who you will meet in due course.

Isaac is American, although he spent much of his childhood in England - his father was a diplomat who was posted there for many years - and you can still hear traces of that accent in his voice.

Isaac's house is where I usually go when I am on Veronica's shit list. But I don't need to be in the metaphorical doghouse - by the way, what a stupid expression - to visit. I go there often, for the pleasure of Isaac's company. Because, like me, Isaac is at heart a philosopher.

How do I, a mere dog, know this? Because - and I'm sorry, but this is where things get really weird and you accuse me of being a fruit loop of the first order - well, because Isaac and I talk. Well, he talks, I think... and somehow he knows what I'm thinking and we carry on a conversation like this. I know it sounds weird - okay, I grant you it IS weird, unequivocally - but it actually feels very natural when it's happening. Neither of us understands how this works, but it does.

I discovered that Isaac could read my mind the first time I met him, which was the day after Veronica adopted me. I wandered into his yard that sunny afternoon and found him sitting in an Adirondack chair reading a newspaper with a glass of white wine by his side. Either he didn't immediately notice me, or he pretended not to. He continued reading.

Now, when a male dog meets someone or something new - beit human, canine or anything else - our first thoughts always, without exception, involve the following analysis:

HUMAN			DOG				OTHER LIFEFORM			
Does he/she look scary?			Is it male or female?				Is it smaller than me?			
Yes	No		Male		Female		Yes		No	
Avoid	Does it have food?		Is he smaller than me?		Is she in heat?		Is it furry and runs away?		Does it have scary teeth?	
	Yes	No	Yes	No	Yes	No	Yes	No	Yes	No
Wag tail, look cute	Ignore it or hump it	Exert dominance	Sniff ass politely	Hump	Hump	Kill it	Kill it anyway	Avoid	Chase?

The elderly man in the chair looked like a generally friendly person. At any rate, he wasn't leaping up to chase me with a carving knife, which is, I find, generally a good sign. Consequently, my thoughts turned to whether he had any food. He did not, it seemed. Oh well, I thought, *I guess I'm not getting any treats from you,* and turned to leave. At which point the weirdness happened.

From behind the newspaper, the man's voice suddenly said, "No, I'm afraid I don't have any treats out here, but if you'll wait a moment I'll get you something."

I stopped and turned back to look at the man, who had put down his newspaper and was gazing at me with large, kindly eyes. Was this mind-reading or just coincidence? The latter, of course - dogs are dogs, always on the lookout for food. This isn't rocket science - we're pretty simple creatures.

The man rose from his chair and addressed me again. "What would you prefer? I don't have dog treats, exactly, but I think I can find some cheese or ham in the fridge. Or perhaps a saucer of milk?"

Well duh, I thought - ham of course. I'll eat pretty much anything that once walked around on four legs. The man laughed. "Very well," he said, "ham it is."

And with that he walked up the three steps to his back door and disappeared into the house.

He returned a few moments later with a small plate of ham and placed it before me. I tried to eat it gracefully, but it smelled so good that the act of consumption was rather like a Ferrari going from a standing start to 60 mph: slow for the first fraction of a second, and then - *zoom!* - full-on acceleration straight to, well, in this case inhalation of pig parts. It was delicious.

Thank you, I thought.

"You're very welcome, I'm sure," said the man.

I stared at him and examined his face more closely. It had not been a young face for many years, but it was full of character and kindness. He had dark eyes, large ears and a prominent but rather graceful nose. Clean-shaven. And he smelled good - which I can assure you, is not the case for all humans. I still can't believe the bewildering array of perfumes, aftershaves, deodorants and all the other artificial crap you apply to your bodies. Sometimes I wonder if you roll around in toxic chemicals just for the fun of it.

I wondered how old the man was.

"I'm seventy-five," he said. "I'm not sure how that translates into dog years."

Wait, I thought, *you really* can *read my mind, can't you?*

"Yes, it seems so," replied the man simply.

Whoa, this is super-weird. How does that work exactly?

The man considered for a moment. "Actually, I have no idea. But somehow it seems very natural." And it did.

Well, huh, I thought.

"Huh indeed," said the man. There was a pause while we gazed at each other and both took in the weirdness, which - weirdly enough - was becoming less weird by the moment. Finally the man spoke again.

"It seems we are destined to be special friends," he said. "I am Isaac, and I am very pleased to meet you."

And I you, I thought. *Really pleased.*

Isaac smiled and patted me on the head. "Now, what's your name?"

Well, funny you should ask. That's a problem I've been wanting to talk to someone about...

A Rose By Any Other Name

The morning after I accidentally rescued Veronica from the mugger, we were having breakfast in her kitchen. I had just finished wolfing down an entire can of dog food that she'd bought at the supermarket the previous night, and she was sitting in a chair in a floral bathrobe, sipping a cup of coffee and idly picking at the almond croissant on the plate before her. She was clearly pondering something. Her long legs were crossed, and her thick red hair tumbled over her shoulders in gloriously anarchic disarray. Red hair is not a requirement for a dominatrix, but apparently it helps with the overall image.

She turned to look at me, and smiled thoughtfully. "So, doggie, what do I call you? You need a name."

Uh-oh.

You humans think we dogs don't understand our names. That a name is just a meaningless sound that we learn to recognize because it is consistently associated with food, petting, punishment, reward and various other acts and commands that the sound usually precedes or follows. Well - as usual - you're wrong. We know *exactly* what it means. And, dear reader, if you honestly think that your beloved pet will ever forgive you for permanently saddling it with a name like Burrito, Fifi, Fufu, Fluffy, Ketchup, Piglet, Pooper or Mister Weenie... then you have, as they say, another think coming. You should hear some of the names we make up for you in retaliation.

So, on this sunny morning in November, Veronica and I had arrived at a critical moment in the dog-human relationship. At this juncture, the human can choose to honor or humiliate her faithful companion with an appellation that is either a noble epiphet or a screaming embarrassment. One that - either way - the dog will carry for life. This matters, because other dogs also know what your name means, and some breeds will tease you unmercifully about it at every opportunity (for some reason, this is a particular trait of Jack Russells. Don't ask me why - it's in their twisted little genes).

Veronica proceeds to tell me that she is deciding between two names: the relatively inoffensive and actually kinda cute *Jack*, and - ogodpleaseno - *Savior*. She explains to me that she was so impressed last night with my bravery and *intrepidness* - I don't think this is a word, actually, but Veronica seems to think it is so I let it go - and she wants to recognize that.

Look, I understand that she was trying to be nice to me, and she thought that this name was an honor, but it's terminally dopey and pretentious. (I can already hear the next Jack Russell I meet: "Oooh, *Savior*! Come *save* me, you're so big and strong and brave! Come on, *Savior*, whaddya waitin' for?" God, I hate Jack Russells). Above all, it's just not me. And then of course there's the minor issue of the truth behind my infamous act of intrepidness. If she wanted to truly memorialize the event, she should have named me *Sandwich* (oddly enough, I'd be okay with that).

I raised the issue with Isaac the following day, right after we'd established that we could somehow magically converse. He laughed sympathetically. "I'm sorry," he said. "I wish I could help, but at my age going to your next-door neighbor and telling her that you've been speaking with her dog is the sort of thing that gets you locked up for good. But let me think about it, and perhaps I can find a way to tell her without her calling in the men in white coats."

JACK

As it turned out, the naming problem solved itself the following day, without the need for neighborly intervention.

Veronica was having coffee with her best friend Anna DeVere. Like a number of Veronica's friends, Anna is a prostitute. She is tall, willowy and sleek, with long legs, large breasts and a very pretty face framed by short, stylishly cut dark hair. Because of these attributes - and less obvious skills that I have not been privy to - rumor has it she commands $600 an hour for her erotic services. Anna is 32. She has an IQ of 160 and a Ph.D. in history - which, according to Veronica, makes her "the most educated whore in the 206 area code". That she is an escort by profession and not a historian is due to the simple fact that - as Anna puts it - a Ph.D. in history and a quarter will get you one-sixteenth of a latté at Starbucks, whereas a couple of hours on her back bought her the high-end espresso machine that now reposes regally on her kitchen counter.

I like Anna - she's a lot more thoughtful than most of Veronica's friends, and she has a healthy cynicism about humanity that is manifest in often quite clever sarcasm. She's not the huggy, cuddly type who automatically turns into a mass of blubbering idiocy when she sees a pet; but I know from the way she treats me and talks to me that she is fond of dogs, and would like to have one of her own.

"So," Veronica began, sipping her latté, "I have to name my new dog here." She gestured to me, lying on the rug at her feet. I was attempting to look cuter than usual.

Anna looked down at me and considered. "Hmm. So what are your choices?" she asked.

"Well," said Veronica, "I was originally thinking something really guy-like, because he seems like a very practical down-to-earth dog. Something like *Jack*."

Anna nodded. "Yes, I can definitely see him as a Jack." I wagged my tail in the vain hope that it would reinforce the wisdom of this option.

"But then I thought, he's so *brave* and he practically saved my life last night. So I think I'm going to call him *Savior*."

Anna isn't Isaac - no one is - so I couldn't exactly ask her to tell Veronica that she was out of her freaking mind, but I did look up at her as pleadingly as I knew how in a desperate attempt to communicate my distaste for this terminally stupid name.

Anna returned my gaze, then raised her eyebrows and gave Veronica her best cynical look. *"Seriously*, Vee?"

"What?"

"Oh, nothing. I just didn't realize you wanted the entire planet to know that you have such a deeply meaningful relationship with Jesus Christ that you named your dog after him."

Veronica groaned and put her head in her hands. "O *God!*"

"Precisely."

And that, thank heaven, was the end of that. Suddenly and irrevocably, I was Jack.

Needless to say, Veronica does not have a close personal relationship with Jesus. Nor do any of her friends.

In fact, if the Old Testament is correct, they're pretty much all going to Hell.

Client

Talking of Anna - praises be heaped upon her name - she was responsible for providing Veronica with one of her most devoted regular clients, a middle-aged man named Norbert Tucker. Norbert is in his mid-50's, a balding, paunchy man who reminds me of a lumpy potato shoved into a pair of trousers.

He had originally hired Anna as an escort. The relationship began with a couple of sessions of regular sex that was sufficiently dreary and unimaginative that Anna had to reach deeper than usual into some past theatrical training to pretend to be enjoying it. But then he began requesting that increasingly irregular acts be performed upon him; and when one day the act in question involved tightly tying up his testicles with fishing line, she realized that what Norbert needed was not a prostitute, but a dominatrix. Besides, Anna has never been very good at knots. And so she referred him to Veronica.

Despite his physical shortcomings, Norbert is actually a highly paid top executive for a certain gigantic, world-swallowing local computer company, the name of whose famous founder rhymes neatly with *masturbates*. Amusingly, this gives Veronica added incentive to dish out the suffering which Norbert clearly craves, because Veronica has long had issues with the confused, counter-intuitive mess that passes for a menu system in said company's premier word-processing software. Although Norbert works in the behemoth's anti-piracy division and has nothing whatsoever to do with writing code, he gallantly pays the price for those who do: more than once, Veronica has hit him with a switch harder than usual while demanding to know *Why the fuck do you keep changing the goddamn menu when it took me six months to learn the last stupid version?* (Thwack!)

Thus does Veronica vent her frustrations, and for his part Norbert takes it like a man; the arrangement works well for both of them.

Although Veronica regularly subjects him to a variety of increasingly humiliating acts, Norbert's favorite thing is hair removal. And good lord, does Norbert have hair to remove: naked, he can do a passable imitation of a bipedal shag carpet. The first time I saw him I found myself wondering whether werewolves were really creatures of myth after all. However, the specific hair which Norbert begs Veronica to pluck is that which grows abundantly on his scrotum. For this procedure, he is usually strapped to an X-shaped St Andrews cross, legs and arms spread wide and firmly secured to the frame at all four corners. His balls are tied tightly at the base of his penis with twine or fishing line, or sometimes a thin leather thong. These days Veronica gags him before beginning, because the one time she didn't he screamed so loudly that a basset hound in a house halfway down the block started howling.

Thus immobilized, Norbert suffers blissfully while Veronica pulls out his scrotal hair, singly or in chunks, until the hair is all gone and his poor crimson balls look like a plucked raw chicken. For this exquisitely tortuous depilation service he pays Veronica a thousand dollars a session. He sees her on average around once a month, which is about how long it takes for the hair to grow back to pluckability length.

By the way, his name really is Norbert. One would think that this appellation was given to him by Veronica as part of a degradation exercise, but this particular humiliation was visited upon him at birth by his parents.

I mean, seriously, who names their kid Norbert? No wonder the guy's screwed up.

Leroy

And talking of screwed up: meet Leroy, our other next-door neighbor. Not a pleasant fellow, but one who nonetheless has a minor role to play in our little story.

It's not entirely clear how Leroy Fawkes came to live in Seattle; or, more to the point, why he stays. Being a right-wing Republican in this town is broadly equivalent to being a Satanist in the Bible Belt - you don't really fit in with the locals. This is especially true on Capitol Hill, where a rock thrown randomly in any direction is more likely than not to hit someone gay or socialist, or a person whose biggest regret in life is having been born too late to experience the 1960's. So you would think that a person who abhors liberals, hippies and sodomites would move before they drowned in their own bile; but Leroy remains here nonetheless, a five-foot-six towering rock of fundamentalist Christian conservatism awash in a sea of sinners.

Veronica's knowledge of Leroy's biography is scant, largely because after their first conversation she vowed to avoid him at all costs. Unfortunately, this is not easy to do when the object of your avoidance lives next door, and when the person concerned has made it abundantly clear that one of his greatest goals in life is to one day copulate with you.

Every time Leroy sees Veronica he invariably says, "Hey, baby... yer lookin' *real* good today." And, every time, he somehow manages to convey this observation the way a really hungry guy would who's just caught sight of a large pork chop.

I know rather more about him. This knowledge comes from eavesdropping on conversations he has with friends - he actually has a couple - or neighbors, or any of the random passers-by whom Leroy traps with a friendly greeting and then, when they are unwise enough to respond, proceeds to regale with the tale of his life.

Leroy is from a small town in Alabama, just north of Birmingham. I mean, *small* town. One where the installation of their first and only traffic light became both a cause for protracted controversy and a story good for front-page headlines in repeated editions of the local newspaper. This is the *Times-Picayune*, circulation 341 souls.

According to Leroy, his mother Lilith was a well-bred debutante from Montgomery who was seduced by his father's caddish good looks and by his empty promises that he was headed for a life of luxury and accomplishment (I'm paraphrasing here - Leroy's version is much cruder and is related largely in words that trend heavily towards the monosyllabic). Said life never materialized, and his mother found herself stranded in this little hick town in the back of the southern beyond.

Her campaign to make something out of her dismal situation was not helped by producing Leroy. Despite his mother's commendably persistent attempts to cultivate culture and breeding in her only son, he instead enthusiastically embraced the life of a rural redneck. Leroy showed little interest in learning, confined his reading to lurid pulp fiction, and spent as much of his free time as possible out in the woods, murdering the various animals that found themselves on the wrong end of his shotgun.

Whether Lilith ever accepted the fact that she had raised a moron is not clear. But if there was a single moment when she became resigned to this sad fact it was probably when she took Leroy to Paris in a desperate attempt to civilize her dolt of an offspring via the culturally transformative experience of European travel.

To which Leroy proved happily immune. For there in the City of Light, upon seeing the Eiffel Tower for the first time, he casually announced to her that he didn't think it was half as good as the one in Vegas.

After that, his mother more or less gave up. She continued to feed and clothe him, but apportioned upon her hapless son no more affection or effort than the minimum required by maternal instinct and the law. Instead, her energies were redirected towards charitable causes of a Christian (and strictly Republican) nature.

For his high school graduation, she gave Leroy a car with a vanity plate which read UNGR8FL. That the sardonic point of this was entirely lost upon her son merely confirmed in Lilith's troubled mind her abject failure as a mother.

After high school, he wandered through random employment before moving to Seattle on some sort of construction job. That was five years ago. He's still here.

Since then, Leroy has become increasingly obsessed with conspiracy theories, which, like his life story, he broadcasts to anyone who will listen. These take many forms, but his favorite topic in the dark imaginary world that he inhabits is how the government is secretly putting female hormones in the water supply to turn everyone gay. Although to be fair, you could be forgiven for finding this notion vaguely credible here on Capitol Hill.

So there you have it, a picture of our immediate neighborhood: kindly old telepath on one side, leering paranoiac on the other. It's a mini-universe in balance, yin and yang, with us occupying the fulcrum squarely in the middle.

Dis/Belief

If you are worrying over the perhaps more perplexing question of how a dog can be telling you this - or any other - story... Well, I'm afraid you're just going to have to suspend your disbelief for a while. As you will discover within these pages, not everything can be explained, even in this modern world of ours.

In this book, as in life, it is most important that you believe in Magic.

Pedigree

I am not, to be strictly accurate, a pure-bred pit bull. Truth be told, my mother - an American pit bull terrier, which by the way is the smaller, less scary kind - had a brief and distinctly unromantic dalliance with a cattle dog in the alley behind a Mexican restaurant one night. This was in the town of Yakima, in eastern Washington state.

As my mother related the story, she was minding her own business rooting through trash bags filled with leftover burritos and other south-of-the-border culinary delights when around the corner comes this quadrupedal Casanova. Upon seeing my mother, the dog skidded to a halt, inhaled the incomparably glorious scent of a female in heat, and started barking and woofing at her suggestively.

There are exactly fifteen different sounds that boy dogs make in their efforts to persuade a girl dog to copulate. But all of them mean exactly the same thing which, roughly translated into human terms, is: "Hey baby, wanna do it?" Subtlety among male dogs is not exactly a strong suit.

She gave him a cursory glance, then ignored him and returned to a largely uneaten chicken taco that she had just dug out from beneath a dumpster.

Apparently the fact that my mother did this instead of sinking her teeth into his neck - or balls - was taken by the male as a sign of, if not exactly enthusiasm, at least assent; and the next thing my mother knew her face was slammed into some two-day-old guacamole as she was mounted in a frenzy of humping.

The unsolicited dalliance lasted all of five minutes. Her lover's deficiencies in the area of romantic subtlety were partly compensated for by his surprising lack of fleas, or so she said. She never knew his name, and he didn't leave a phone number. And two months later she gave birth to four of us.

So I am a mutt. From my mother I inherited pragmatism, an affectionate nature and an unusual fondness for Mexican food. My anonymous father gave me brains and bat-like ears. And a tendency to think far too much for my own good.

Most of the time I sleep the sleep of the innocent, untroubled by worries, or guilt at the many rats I've despatched to rodent heaven. But lately I've found myself lying awake at night contemplating the reason for my existence. More specifically, why I'm walking this earth as a dog. Don't get me wrong - I *like* being a dog. But my incarnation in this particular form instead of something else seems somehow so... well, improbable.

It's an issue.

Prehistory

Of my early life, I have only sporadic memories.

My mother was a stray, and therefore so were we, her kids. This is not an easy thing for a dog to be in eastern Washington: the place is oppressively hot in summer and glacially cold in winter - not to mention the fact that some of the human inhabitants are brain-damaged rednecks who think that shooting stray dogs is a fun way to spend a Saturday afternoon.

Together with two brothers and a sister, I was born on Hallowe'en night. My mother told me that some kids found us while they were out trick or treating; and after spending an appropriate amount of time in the cooing adoration of our mother and her four tiny, adorable puppies, they scooped us all up and conveyed us to the care of a teenage girl who was the daughter of a local farmer. The farmer refused to allow us into the house, but after much pleading by his daughter - as any parent knows, whining teenage girls can be very persuasive - he consented to letting her house us in his barn.

That barn was the only reason we all survived through the ensuing months of winter. I remember all of us curled up in a five-dog ball in the hay while the wind howled outside and the snow piled high against the barn walls. Luckily for us, the daughter regularly sneaked us food.

At first a reluctant host, the farmer himself became more enthusiastic about his new tenants after he began to find the increasing number of half-eaten rat carcasses with which we decorated our humble dwelling. My mother was an excellent ratter, you see; and in due course my sister and I developed into pretty good pupils. On some nights, the rat carnage was spectacular. If God turns out to be a rodent, there's little doubt that I'll be spending eternity immersed in some exceedingly deep excrement.

But all good things must come to an end - isn't that what you perpetually pessimistic humans say? - and the following spring a fire damaged the barn. Besides, it's one thing hosting a dog and four cute little puppies; but by now the family had turned into five medium-sized and very rambunctious dogs - which was rather more doggage than the farmer had bargained for.

So we were once again homeless. We managed to eke out a living in Yakima over that summer, relying on our mother's experience and common sense to find good foraging places, and to avoid capture by the local Animal Control.

Then it was September, and the return of winter was just a few weeks away; and we had no idea how we were going to make it through to the following spring.

Enter Fate, which takes many strange and wond'rous forms. On this particular evening of early autumn, it was manifest in the shape of a freight train that had stopped at a railway siding on the edge of town. My mother and I were hunting rats by the tracks.

She flushed a particularly large, juicy rat from a hole beneath the rails. It ran away from her and towards me; then, comprehending its predicament between two obviously highly motivated dogs, abruptly changed course and scurried up the side of a boxcar, shot through the open door and disappeared inside.

Without thinking, I leapt to the platform and entered the car. The panicked rat was running around in circles along the edges of the interior, desperately seeking an exit. In five seconds I had him... lunge, toss, crunch. Dead rat.

Carrying my prize in my jaws, I walked back to the open door, when suddenly the train began to move. Having no experience with trains, I had no idea what this meant or what I should do. So, instead of jumping down to the ground as common sense would dictate, I just stood there at the door, a dead rat hanging limply from my mouth. I stared blankly at my mother, who stared back at me as the train picked up speed and separated us forever. I never saw her again.

The train traveled its jerky, lumbering way for several hours, and did not stop until it reached the center of Seattle. There, I finally alighted in the middle of the industrial district and surveyed the new neighborhood that Fate had chosen for me.

I didn't know it at the time, but one of Seattle's nicknames is *Rat City*, and the smell of rodent was the first thing that hit my nose as I walked across the tracks away from the train. They were everywhere.

I loitered in the industrial district for a few days, feeding on rats and mice and sleeping in abandoned buildings. But after being chased out for the third time by homeless drunks who did not, apparently, care to share their temporary abode, not even with a cute and friendly dog, I decided it was time to seek greener pastures. And after some random wandering, I somehow ended up on Capitol Hill, where our story continues.

I often wonder what my mother thought that day as her kid rode off into the sunset. We didn't have time to say goodbye, or for me to thank her for bringing me into the world. I will always remember the look on her face as the train pulled away, and in my sentimental mind I imagine that she was bidding me a fond farewell.

Goodbye, son - and good luck! Write if you get work.

Things You Don't Know About Dogs

There are a number of things I guarantee you don't know about Dogkind. I'm definitely breaking the Canine Secret Code of Silence by telling you this stuff, but it's necessary to my little story that you have this knowledge.

First of all, many dogs can comprehend English perfectly well. They understand everything you say to them - or to other humans. If they don't seem to, it's because they either find what you're talking about of absolutely no interest, or because they're choosing to ignore whatever you're ordering them to do at that particular moment. We respond only to a small set of commands - the inevitable *Sit, Stay, Come, Shake, Touch, Roll over* et cetera - and lead you to believe that anything else is beyond us. In reality, it's a convenient deception, one that allows us to keep chasing that squirrel when you're screaming at us to stop, or to stare at you with a look of well-practiced incomprehension when you tell us "For the *thousandth* time, stay *off* the couch!" (Huh?)

I say "many dogs" can understand, because it's also true that many can't. As even humans appreciate, dog intelligence varies widely among breeds. For example, the entire world clan of Irish setters are collectively as dumb as a bag of hammers, and not nearly as useful. The rest of us honestly sometimes find ourselves wondering how they manage to put one paw in front of the other when your average setter doesn't seem to have more than a couple of brain cells lodged somewhere deep in his cranium (doggie joke: Q. What do you call an Irish setter with his nose in another setter's butt? A. A synapse).

Second, dogs can talk to each other telepathically. No, really. We can't just randomly mind-read - we have to specifically *direct* a thought at another dog - but it all works pretty efficiently, more or less. You hear the thoughts in your head, much as if the words were spoken. This is essentially what I do with Isaac too, which I guess makes him some sort of honorary dog.

Third, dogs dream about one thing and one thing only: chasing squirrels. Seriously. When you see us whimpering in our sleep with our legs jerking around like we're having a *petit mal* seizure, we are always, always, dreaming about running down a squirrel. Strangely, we never ever catch it. Go figure.

Fourth, you know those times when a dog spends forever sniffing around looking for just the right spot to poop while you stand there, staring at us impatiently and telling us, *Oh for heaven's sake, get on with it!*? Well, although sometimes we really *do* need a very specific spot or smell to stimulate our pooping reflex, half the time we decided where to plop one down two minutes ago, but we keep sniffing around just because it's so much fun to watch you slowly going nuts. Especially if it's raining.

What else? Oh, that look of utter dejection and abandonment that you get when you leave us behind in the house - the one that says, *How can you go out without me when I live to love you?* - we practice that in the mirror when you're not home.

There are a few other things that will come up in due course, but that's enough for now.

By the way, cats can communicate with dogs too, but they never do. Like everything else, it's beneath them.

Talking of which...

Etymology

Cat, noun. Old English *catt* (c. 700), from West Germanic (c. 400-450), from Proto-Germanic kattuz, from Late Latin cattus. The near-universal European word now, it appeared in Europe as Latin *catta* (c. 75 C.E.), Byzantine Greek *katta* (c. 350) and was in general use on the continent by c. 700, replacing Latin *feles*. Probably ultimately Afro-Asiatic (compare Nubian *kadis*, Berber *kadiska*, both meaning "cat"). Arabic *qitt* "tomcat" may be from the same source. Cats were domesticated in Egypt from c. 2000 B.C.E., but not a familiar household animal to classical Greeks and Romans. The nine lives have been proverbial since at least the 1560s.

Cat, noun. A small domesticated carnivorous mammal which, if not properly cared for, is liable to revert to a feral state.

To which one can only add - as Dorothy Parker allegedly said when they told her Calvin Coolidge was dead - how can they tell?

Off the Menu

I have been made to understand that I am not allowed to eat the cat. No explanation was given.

Look, trust me on this - cats are nothing more than furry parasites. You amuse each other by discussing their aloof natures, and you make jokes about them being little royalty who own you rather than the other way around.

You don't know the half of it.

I continue to be amazed that many people - Veronica included - harbor grand delusions that cats are actually capable of feeling affection, or indeed anything other than utter contempt, for the humans whose presence they barely tolerate in exchange for food and shelter. The fact is that every cat, no matter how pampered, thinks it has been given a bad deal, and deserves more.

I blame the ancient Egyptians. Four thousand years ago, some pharaohnic twit by the Nile conceived the seriously batshit idea that cats were gods. The Egyptians began venerating them, complete with statues, offerings and mummification. For catkind, it's been all downhill ever since. I mean, when was the last time you heard anyone say, "Sorry, I can't make brunch today - Fluffy just died and I have to go mummify him"?

But somehow this ludicrous expectation wormed its way into feline genes, and every single cat born in the four millennia since has come into the world pissed off at being deprived of what it sees as its divine birthright.

The good news is that it's ridiculously easy to mess with the mind of a creature that is so confused about its place in the universe, because virtually *everything* you do will provoke an annoyed reaction. With Veronica's cat Bonkers, my favorite approach is crude but effective. I wait until he is sound asleep, then I carefully sneak up to him and apply my tongue to his face, trying to cover as much of it as possible before I hastily retreat as he awakens in a rage and tries to claw my eyes out.

This simple act never fails to provoke an extended bout of furious cleaning, as Bonkers tries to rid himself of every trace of this foul creature who has dared to pollute the immaculate purity of his fur. A casual lick is good for at least five minutes of outraged ritual purification, and I can get it up to ten or fifteen if I remember to lick my ass first.

Try it sometime. As Veronica once said to Anna for some strange reason, pussy licking never gets old.

Psychic

Isaac and I have been discussing the not-unremarkable fact that we can communicate freely with each other. As I noted before, our conversation - him reading my thoughts, me listening to his responses - seems very natural to both of us. I regard it as a mark of respect that Isaac has never actually commented on what is, to humans, the other extraordinary phenomenon here: that, as I noted above, a mere dog can be perfectly fluent in English. I don't know how this is possible either, but I cannot recall a time when comprehension of the language was not a feature of my life.

By the way, unlike other dogs I can also see in color. Go figure. And my favorite color is green - I knew you secretly wanted to know that.

Anyway, Isaac takes my intellectual capabilities for granted, which I appreciate. And he never comments on the fact that this dog with whom he has extended philosophical discussions occasionally interrupts such elevated discourse to lick his own genitals or bolt after a passing squirrel. He accepts me as I am.

Today I proposed that a psychic might be able to shed some light on our relationship. After all, these people are supposed to be in contact with the spirit realm. Or to possess an understanding of the greater mysteries of life. Or something. So perhaps one of them could explain why Isaac and I are uniquely and unusually connected.

Isaac was skeptical. "I don't know, Jack - I suspect these people are usually frauds. Or at least they're deluding themselves that they can do anything supernatural."

I understand what he means. I once knew a German shepherd who claimed he could read other dogs' minds, but then that isn't exactly difficult to do. Making a pronouncement such as *"I am sensing that Randy wants to mount Fifi"* is about as solid a bet as predicting that the next thing that comes out of Donald Trump's Twitter feed will be idiotic.

Well okay, but may I just point out that you're calling into question psychic powers when what you and I do in our discussions would probably fall squarely into that category by most definitions.

Isaac nods. "Good point," he concedes with a smile.

Thank you. Anyway, it's worth a try, don't you think? If nothing else it might be good for some cheap entertainment.

Isaac shrugged. "Very well. But I have no idea how to find a 'good' psychic. I suppose I'd better consult the Great Guru Who Knoweth All Things."

You mean another psychic?

"No - the Internet."

Ah, that. Not being capable of using a keyboard, this source of information is literally beyond me. I understand the concept, though judging from Veronica's browsing habits 90% of the Internet consists of lurid pornography and stupid cat photos.

After ten minutes at his computer, Isaac announces that he's found a psychic here on Capitol Hill whose talents are sanctioned by that unimpeachable arbiter of quality, Yelp.com. "Her name is Madame Lulu and she has nine reviews, most of which give her five stars."

Huh. And the ones who don't?

Isaac scrolls down to the one-star reviews. "Well, this one says *Money-grubbing bitch who wouldn't know an aura from an anus*, but I'm not sure I'd put much stock in that - from their other reviews they sound like a deeply angry person."

Well okay. What does she do, anyway?

"Well," replies Isaac, reading. "Her blurb says that she can - let's see - communicate with dead loved ones, provide advice on romance and employment, assist with diagnosing maladies, and generally - I'm paraphrasing here - help you sort out your psychic ills."

Nothing about communicating with dogs?

"It doesn't say anything about pets."

Hmm. Shall we give her a try?

Isaac calls and makes an appointment for later that afternoon, and at precisely 4 pm we find ourselves outside a red brick building which has steps leading down to what appears to be a rather dingy basement apartment. One would think that a genuine psychic would have used her talents to play the stock market and thus be living in rather more luxurious accommodation, but perhaps she's just a simple soul at heart.

There is a rather crude painted sign above the steps which says *Madame Lulu, Psychic. Secrets Revealed.*

The sign has a depiction of a crystal ball, with a woman leaning over it who looks remarkably like Joan Rivers.

Hopefully it isn't a portrait of Madame Lulu.

We descend the steps to a door with a large glass panel at its center, the view through which is obstructed by a thick velvet curtain. The window announces, in large gold letters, that the inhabitant beyond the door is

MADAME LULU
KEEPER OF SECRETS

Isaac rings the doorbell. Thirty seconds go by, and he is about to ring it again when the sound of shuffling feet and jangling metal can be heard on the other side of the door. The curtain is drawn back to reveal a small woman in her mid-50's. She has a mass of unkempt curly brown hair that is spilling out from beneath a purple velvet hat, and she is wearing what appears to be a velvet kaftan. At least half a dozen strings of beads are hung around her neck. She has silver rings on all ten fingers, large hoop earrings, and so many bracelets on her forearms - hence the jangling - that it's a wonder she doesn't topple over from the weight. Fraud or not, she certainly looks the part.

Opening the door, she sees me for the first time. The sight prompts a grunt from Madame Lulu, who announces curtly, "No dogs!"

"Ah," says Isaac politely, "that's unfortunate. You see, my dog is the reason I'm here."

Madame Lulu looks skeptical. "Your dog? Do you think he's possessed by evil spirits or something?"

"No, I --"

"He looks like he might be."

Excuse me?! Madame Lulu is giving me a quite unwarranted look of suspicion.

"No, no... well, really I have no idea," Isaac replies. "I mean, no, he's not possessed by evil spirits. But, well, you see my dog and I can communicate. I mean, we talk openly, and..." Isaac trails off, looking awkward. He didn't expect to be embarrassed revealing this confidence to a nutcase who thinks she can talk to dead people.

"Your dog *talks?*" Madame Lulu is clearly skeptical.

"No, no... he doesn't actually speak, of course. But I can read his mind, and he understands everything I say perfectly. We have conversations and..." Again his voice trails off and he looks embarrassed.

Madame Lulu is now looking at Isaac with an expression that betrays her obvious belief that the elderly man standing before her is in the advanced stages of dementia. "Look, I don't mean to be rude, but..."

Isaac, collecting himself, interrupts. "Madam, I can certainly understand how you would find this unbelievable. But perhaps I can demonstrate?"

She grunts again. "And how would you do that?"

Isaac looks down at me. I stare back intently, hoping to communicate to Madame Lulu the kind of deeply meaningful relationship that does indeed exist between us. "Well," says Isaac. "How about if I go up around the corner here, and you bring out some object to show to the dog - his name is Jack, by the way - and then put it away. He'll tell me what it is, and I'll come back and tell you."

Lulu folds her arms and thinks for a moment. Then she raises her eyebrows and sighs. "OK," she says finally. "I suppose I have nothing to lose, and this could be amusing." She flutters her hands towards Isaac in a shooing gesture, initiating another bout of metallic cacophony. "Ok then... off you go."

Isaac smiles and disappears up the steps and round the corner. Meanwhile, Madame Lulu retreats into her apartment, bangles a-jangling, and a few moments later emerges with an object which she holds out to me with one claw-like hand.

"OK, doggie. Tell your friend what I've got here."

I stare.

I stare more. It doesn't help.

The truth is, I have absolutely no idea what the hell that thing is. It looks like a penknife and indeed it has a series of blades that are hinged together at a single point, but which Lulu has pulled out and arranged in a fan shape so that I can see them all. One of these protruding parts is clearly a regular knife, but the other four each have a weird triangular blade at the end that is perpendicular to the shaft - or whatever you call that flat bit it's attached to. The triangles are of different sizes, arranged in order smallest to largest. Finally, there is a thinner metal piece that ends in a sort of hook. The object as a whole is brass, I think, and it looks old.

I'm communicating all this to Isaac in a sort of psychic *Charades* in the desperate hope that it'll make some sense, or that he will come back and say something like, "I don't know, but it's like a penknife, but isn't" and that this will be a sufficiently accurate description to satisfy Madame Lulu... who suddenly closes all the blades and takes the mysterious object back into her apartment.

She returns a moment later empty-handed. "Okay," she shouts. "You can come back now."

Isaac comes down the steps. He's smiling. "Well," he says, "you certainly set my friend here with a hard problem. He doesn't know exactly what you were holding..."

"Ha!" exclaims Lulu in triumph, "I knew it!"

"...but," continues Isaac, undeterred, "from his description I would guess you were holding a fleam."

Madame Lulu's face suddenly loses its color, and she is visibly stunned. "That's... that's correct," she stutters. "And that's... truly remarkable."

Forget the remarkable. What the hell is a "fleam" when it's at home?

Isaac smiles and looks down at me, ignoring the profanity in the question. "It's an old medical device, used for... well, for blood-letting."

Blood-letting? Charming. Didn't they use leeches for that?

"Well yes," replies Isaac, "they did use leeches, but this was another method for draining blood from a patient. It goes back a long way actually - probably to Anglo-Saxon times."

A fleam, I repeat, *a fleam. Strange word.*

"Yes. The origin of the word is likely from *phlebos*, meaning 'vein', and *tome*, 'to cut'."

Hmm, interesting. Greek?

"Yes, it's Greek" says Isaac. "Very good."

A clearly mystified Lulu is looking from Isaac to me and back to Isaac as we have this exchange. She speaks haltingly. "You were... actually having a conversation with him right then, weren't you?"

Isaac shrugs. "Jack likes words," he says simply, as if that explains everything. "Anyway, may we come in?" Still stunned by what she has just witnessed, Madame Lulu steps aside and motions for us to enter her inner sanctum. With slight hesitation borne of wondering why our loopy hostess would own a blood-letting device, and hoping the answer doesn't involve animal sacrifice, I walk with Isaac through the front door.

Madame Lulu's apartment is one giant psychic cliché.
It is dark, cluttered and messy, and there is an overpowering smell of incense. Books are piled on several surfaces and sit side by side with candles of varying sizes, colors and stages of burning; I can only imagine what the local fire marshal would have to say about this hazardous juxtaposition of flame and paper. At one end of the room there is an altar of sorts, upon which sit yet more candles and an eclectic collection of statues. These include Buddha, Ganesha, Pan, Aphrodite and, well, something unidentifiable and buxom that looks disturbingly like what you'd get if you crossed the Virgin Mary with Pamela Anderson. There is a well-worn bunch of plastic flowers in a gaudy purple vase on Madame Lulu's heavy oak desk, and next to this is a set of Tarot cards, and the inevitable crystal ball. The latter rests upon a brass stand that is supported by four stylized cat's feet.

And in one corner, perched regally on a plump velvet cushion, there sits a real cat. It is a large, long-haired white Persian with a smooshed-in face and eyes that come straight out of a horror movie. With tedious predictability, the cat stands up on its cushion, arches its back and hisses at me.

I ignore him. Like any self-respecting dog, I love to scare the crap out of cats; but I also recognize that there are rules of etiquette that prevent me from murdering one in someone else's house. So, despite the fact that this absurdly pampered parasite would be no match for the bone-crushing jaws with which generations of selective breeding have endowed your average pit bull, I content myself with a suitably intimidating growl and sit down next to Isaac. The cat hisses again and slowly lowers itself back onto its cushion, eyeing me warily.

Madame Lulu hands Isaac a clipboard. "Fill out the form," she commands. Attached to the clipboard is a ballpoint pen with *Mike's Lube & Service* stamped on it. As the dog of a dominatrix, I can't help wondering if this comes from something other than a mechanic's shop.

Isaac dutifully fills out the form, and recites the various parts of it as he does so. "Name... ok. Address... yes. Star sign... um, Aquarius..."

"Ah," says Madame Lulu, nodding, "Aquarius. Of course." This is evidently so self-evident that she doesn't see fit to explain.

Isaac continues to read aloud. "Reason for visit... Need to contact departed loved ones... Advice on romance, advice on work, advice on family, financial problems, incontinence..." Isaac looks up. "Incontinence?"

Madame Lulu shrugs. "Some people don't respond well to the meds," she says.

Isaac returns to the form. "General psychic malaise, dream analysis, aura adjustment... Um, there doesn't seem to be anything here that covers our situation."

"Just put down 'Other' and give a brief description", she says.

Isaac writes something and hands the clipboard back to our hostess, who is sitting behind her desk. Madame Lulu clasps her hands together, inhales dramatically and closes her eyes in what appears to be rapt concentration. She holds this position without explanation. After about ten seconds Isaac and I look at each other, and I wonder whether she is summoning spirits. In response, he gives me a *Who knows?* kind of shrug. Then suddenly the silence is broken by an enormous fart, and the tension leaves Madame Lulu's face.

"Sorry," she says, waving her hand in the air just in case. "Refried beans," she adds by way of explanation. "Now, tell me about this remarkable... connection that you have with your dog."

Isaac explains the basics: he talks, I think, he reads my mind, it's all very natural. He mentions Veronica in passing and notes that she - and, by extension, I - am his next-door neighbor. At Madame Lulu's request, there are additional demonstrations of our connection, including one in which Isaac turns away, Lulu holds up an object, I tell him what it is and he tells her.

"It's remarkable," repeats Madame Lulu. "I've never seen anything like it."

She and Isaac continue to discuss the details of our communication, and finally Isaac says, "So we're wondering if you have any way to find out how - or why - this is happening. We really didn't know who else to ask."

"Yes," says Lulu. "I must... *consult*." She enunciates this last word with emphasis. Lulu doesn't explain exactly who or *what* she is going to consult, but she again closes her eyes and puts her hands together in a gesture of prayer.

Isaac braces himself for another fart, but it doesn't come. For the next minute or so, Madame Lulu appears to be carrying on a conversation of sorts with an invisible entity - though her side of the exchange mostly consists of her nodding and saying "Uh-huh... uh-huh... yes, yes I see". We wait patiently for her to return to Planet Earth.

Finally she opens her eyes, breathes deeply, and lowers her hands to her lap. "Very interesting," she pronounces. "Very, *very* interesting."

"Yes?" says Isaac. "So what can you tell us?"

Madame Lulu inhales one more time and shakes her head rapidly, as if she's trying to clear some ectoplasm that's gotten stuck up her nose.

"Well," she says at last, "my spirit guides tell me that the two of you were together in a previous incarnation, and this is why you have such a remarkable connection today."

"Really?" says Isaac. "Go on."

"You were very close," she continues. "And in that life you were both human. The guides did not explain why he has fallen into a lower state of being in this one."

A "lower state of being"? Excuse me? She's talking about me, isn't she?

Isaac ignores my reaction to this offensive remark and asks her a question. "When did this all take place exactly?"

"Well," says Lulu, "The spirits do not give dates, but judging from the costumes you were wearing in the vision they granted me, I would say sometime in the early 19th century.

Seriously? And what the hell have we been doing since then?

Isaac recognizes that this is a valid question, and repeats it, albeit more politely.

"Oh," replies Lulu, "Spirits can linger in the Netherworld for decades or even centuries before taking form again. Or you may have passed through other lives I am not permitted to see. I can catch only glimpses of your prior incarnations amid the Eternal Darkness Of Time." These last four words are clearly capitalized.

"I see," says Isaac, and while I can't actually read his mind I'm pretty sure he's thinking that this is the biggest load of crap he's ever heard. "Are there... other details of how we were... back then?" he asks.

Lulu shakes her head. "I'm afraid not. I know only that you were together." She pauses, then adds, "It's not even clear which of you was the wife."

Wait - the WHAT??

"O yes," says Lulu, seeing the looks of surprise on both our faces. "Didn't I mention? In your past life, you two were married."

Stardom

Isaac and I laughed most of the way home. But looking back, we should have realized that revealing our little secret to someone as invested in the promotion of the supernatural as Madame Lulu was a mistake. As it turned out, the self-styled Keeper of Secrets decided that this one was just too good to keep to herself.

It took three days for the consequences of Lulu's indiscretions to be manifest, and the manifestation came in the form of a knock on Veronica's front door at 10 a.m. She had been heading to the door anyway to let me out, since I needed to pee. I mean, *really* needed to pee. Veronica had conducted a long session with a client the previous evening, and as a result she was late getting up that morning. I had also drunk far too much water before going to bed, so by the time she had dressed, brushed her teeth and put some coffee on, I was ready to burst. We have a dog door at the back, but Veronica locks it at night to stop raccoons from partying in the house, and she'd forgotten to unlock it.

Pace pace pace, stop, look imploringly at human, repeat. Finally Veronica - she can be really dozy in the mornings - got the hint. "Oh, do you need to pee, Jack?" *(Mmmphh, pace pace pace ow ow ow).* So we were on our way to the door and some desperately needed urinary relief when the knocking happened. As anxious as I was to relieve myself, I stayed back in the living room to watch through the front window... after all, you never know what's going to be on the other side of a door, and as I warned you earlier I'm crap in the guard dog department.

Veronica opened the door. On the other side were two men who were apparently from some kind of television station. One of the men was shouldering a large and obviously very expensive professional video camera. The other - who looked as if he must spend a good portion of every morning attending to his ridiculously coiffed hair - loosely held a large microphone in his right hand.

"Are you Veronica Delacroix?" asked the microphone guy. He pronounced it *Dela-croicks*.

"Delacroix," Veronica corrected him, irritated. "Yes. And who are you?"

""I" - there was a studied pause - "am Digby James." He waited, evidently expecting a reaction of recognition, but to his disappointment the very attractive woman in front of him stared blankly. "I'm a reporter," he dutifully explained, "and this is my cameraman Jimmy." Apparently Jimmy was too insignificant to merit a last name. "We're from the Investigations Channel."

At this, Veronica's heart skipped a beat. She had no idea what the "Investigations Channel" was, but it sounded ominous. Instantly her mind conjured up a paranoid scenario in which a TV station was conducting a detailed investigation into either prostitution or the professional bondage scene. This had been a recurring nightmare of hers ever since she had become established in the business, and she knew two escorts who had been outed publicly. And now it was happening to her! Obviously they had somehow identified her as a dominatrix and were here to harass her in an effort to get her to reveal sordid secrets about herself and her clients. O God! She would be on TV! Maybe the show would be nationally syndicated and her mother would see it! O God, not her mother!

Despite the rising panic that her vivid imagination had stirred up, she tried her best to remain composed. "Okay," she said calmly, "and how can I help you?"

"Well," said Digby, "we have just uncovered a fascinating little item involving you for one of our shows." O God! Her mother!

"Look," she said, "I'm a... a consultant and... an entertainer... and..." Her voice trailed off as she desperately tried to think of what else she could say to disguise her true profession. Deep down, she had known that this moment would come some day, and she really should have prepared for it.

"That's nice," interrupted the reporter. "But quite honestly we really don't care what you do."

"You don't?" said Veronica, confused. "Then what do you want with me?"

"We don't want *you*," said Digby curtly. "We're here to interview your dog."

Relief

The reporter's doorstep pronouncement was followed by a confused pause. Veronica's brain was having trouble processing the information that her ears had just faithfully relayed to it.

Various responses occurred to her, but she finally settled on a simple "Excuse me?" It would be an understatement to say that, as she said this, Veronica's eyebrows were raised; indeed, they almost levitated, and if they had not been attached to her face they would probably have ended up hovering several feet above her head.

"Your dog," repeated the reporter. "You know - the one who talks to people. You *do* have a dog, right?"

Veronica's eyebrows once again attempted to escape from her face. "Yesss," she replied slowly. "I do. But I can assure you he can't talk. You must have the wrong address."

Digby refused to be put off. "His name is Jack, right?"

Veronica's brow furrowed. "Yes," she said, again slowly. "How did you know that? And for God's sake what the fuck is all this about?" Now that she knew that this was not an investigation into her, she had recovered her composure and was in no mood to indulge idiocy.

"We have it from a... source... that you have a dog named Jack who can talk to people."

"A *reliable* source," interjected Jimmy-the-cameraman, who was apparently allowed to have an occasional speaking part.

"A *reliable* source," mimicked Veronica sarcastically. "And - if I may enquire - which mental institution is your reliable source currently inhabiting?"

"She's not in an institution," huffed the reporter, then added hurriedly, "I mean, *they're* not in an institution." Apparently Digby was feeling guilty that he had just indiscreetly revealed the sex of his source, as if by narrowing down her identity to half the population of Seattle he had committed an unforgivable breach of professional etiquette.

"Look," said Veronica with as much patience as she could muster, "I have no fucking idea what you're doing here, and I know that here on Capitol Hill we have more than the usual quota of nutcases roaming the streets. But a talking dog? *Really*? I think someone's having you on."

"Our source is not alone," persisted Digby. "Several people have witnessed him talking."

Seriously? Either Madame Lulu was inventing imaginary friends to bolster her little tale, or she was counting her spirit guides as witnesses. Which, come to think of it, is pretty much the same thing.

Veronica sighed heavily. She was quickly tiring of this self-important little twit, and was mentally imagining him naked, bound and gagged in her dungeon with hot wax being applied to his genitals. Fantasies of this nature occurred to her quite frequently when she was forced to think about or deal with people she didn't like. Justin Bieber and Dick Cheney featured prominently in some of the more lurid ones; once she imagined the two of them tied together - an image that made even Veronica shudder.

Suddenly Jimmy-the-cameraman yelped with delight and pointed to the window. "There! There's the dog!"

"Aha!" exclaimed Digby, as if Veronica had denied having a dog. "Look, can we *please* talk to him?" It was obvious from his tone that pleading with one of the mere mortals whom he regarded as cannon fodder for his various TV shows was something he felt compromised his dignity.

Veronica considered for a moment. Apparently these morons weren't going to give up until they had satisfied themselves that this was a wild goose chase, so she reluctantly saw no alternative but to let them in and get this over with as quickly as possible.

She sighed. "Okay, come in and interview my dog... and much good may it do you. This is epically stupid." Eagerly, the dynamic duo entered the living room. They stared expectantly at me, as if I would suddenly begin reciting the Gettysburg Address. Evidently Madame Lulu had omitted to mention the minor detail that, while I could communicate freely with Isaac, I didn't actually *speak*.

"Well, go on," taunted Veronica. "Here's your interviewee. I'm sure he's just dying to discuss current affairs. Or maybe the sex life of squirrels," she added sarcastically.

Jimmy pointed the camera at me while Digby thrust the mike in front of my face. "Um," he said, not very professionally. Apparently he hadn't given much thought to what he was going to actually say now that he had me on the other end of his microphone.

I stared at him blankly. I needed to somehow convince this guy that I was nothing more than a regular dog, doing regular dog things - so of course I turned around and casually licked my balls. Veronica snorted with amusement.

Digby was not going to give up that easily. Attempting to turn the situation to his advantage, he said, "Tell us why dogs do that."

Come on, dude, seriously? It's the old joke: because we can. I continued to lick, and tried to act as if he wasn't there - which wasn't easy, because he was wearing a strong and particularly revolting cologne whose name - I'm just guessing here - was *Chanel Number 69, Turkish Whorehouse*.

"Look, dog," he insisted, his frustration increasingly obvious, "we know you can talk. Think of how famous you'll be when you're on TV. You could end up doing every commercial there is and make a fortune for your owner." He said this in a rather self-conscious tone, as if the absurdity of believing that a dog could actually talk was finally beginning to worm its way into his normally impenetrable self-confidence.

I continued to apply my tongue to my nether regions (it's great, you should try it sometime). But when the reporter rudely thrust his microphone between my mouth and my genitalia, I realized that this had gone on too long. Clearly a dramatic gesture of some sort was called for.

I stopped my genital grooming and looked around, hoping to find some inspiration. And there it was... Bonkers was curled up on his bed, wheezing happily; the minor commotion going on in the living room was disturbing his sleep not at all. That's the thing about cats: they can be unconscious for a good 21 hours a day - and incredibly annoying for the other three.

Now I will freely admit that my increasingly desperate urinary situation may have blinded me to the obvious disciplinary consequences of my next act, but I didn't care. By that point, it felt like the level of fluid I was unwillingly retaining had backed up and was now sloshing around my cranium. I honestly would not have been surprised if it had started to leak out of my eyes.

So, with as much dignity as a dog with a full bladder can manage, I calmly walked over to the cat, cocked my leg, and peed on his head.

Etymology

pandemonium (n.) 1667, Pandæmonium, in "Paradise Lost" the name of the palace built in the middle of Hell, "the high capital of Satan and all his peers," coined by John Milton (1608-1674) from Greek pan- "all" (see pan-) + Late Latin daemonium "evil spirit," from Greek daimonion "inferior divine power," from daimon "lesser god" (see *demon*).

Transferred sense "place of uproar" is from 1779; that of "wild, lawless confusion" is from 1865.

banshee (n.) 1765-75, a spirit in the form of a wailing woman who appears to or is heard by members of a family as a sign that one of them is about to die. Irish, *bean sidhe* "woman of a fairy mound".

Rodeo

Pandemonium would indeed be a reasonable word with which to describe what happened next, although to be strictly accurate there was only one demon involved.

It took Bonkers a few seconds to wake up and discover that what was happening to him really wasn't some hideous dream, but once that grim realization had set in he went - to use the correct psychiatric term - batshit crazy.

I swear to god his entire head - his wet, dripping head - opened up, and from that infernal maw came a screech that could have woken the dead. Seriously, even I was impressed: if there was such an event as the Annual Screaming Banshee Contest, Bonkers would have nailed first place. Come to think of it, the analogy is pretty appropriate: a banshee predicts a death in the house, and Bonkers left very little doubt whose death he had in mind.

As this Cry of the Damned echoed through the house and froze the blood of numerous small rodents living in the neighborhood, I realized that I should probably remove my genitalia from within the immediate reach of the banshee's claws. Said organs being, you will recall, immediately superior to the banshee's head. I jumped aside just in time to avoid a vicious swipe - one that would probably have done serious damage to my chances of ever fathering puppies - and took off across the living room.

I say "took off", but I wasn't in any particular hurry - which turned out to be a major error of judgement on my part. Having pissed off Bonkers on many occasions, I complacently expected the incident to all blow over pretty quickly; after all, he's a quarter of my size and, as cats go, more of a pampered house pet than a feral beast. However, I hadn't counted on the depth of his rage at being turned into a furry urinal.

In my memory, it all happens in slow motion: there is another blood-curdling screech, I turn, and there - flying high through the air towards me in a slow, graceful arc, mouth opened to the max, legs spread-eagled, and every last claw unsheathed - is Demon Cat.

I have to give Bonkers his due: his trajectory was perfect. He landed dead-center on my back and immediately dug his claws into my side. This action, and the shock that accompanied it, had the unfortunate side effect of causing me to empty the remaining contents of my bladder onto Veronica's carpet. I yelped in pain and this time *really* took off. And for the next thirty seconds, Veronica's living room was host to an insane tableau, the chaos of which rivaled The Squirrel Incident. I'm peeing, howling and galloping around the living room with a psychotic cat riding me like a horse, and Veronica is chasing us both and swearing profusely. From my point of view, it's like a rodeo: I'm bucking up and down trying to dislodge Bonkers, but he seems to be glued to my fur. Yes, he is a *very* determined cat.

Finally, Veronica hurls a small cushion at us. It's probably more luck than skill, but this unorthodox projectile catches Bonkers squarely in the head, and he loosens his demon grip just long enough for me to shake him off. I retreat behind a chair; Bonkers continues to hiss and spit in my general direction, with a couple of homicidal looks at Veronica thrown in for good measure.

Veronica sighs heavily and runs a hand through her rather disheveled hair. "Jesus *CHRIST!*" she exclaims, exasperated. Then she turns slowly to the two television boys, fixes them with her most malevolent glare, and says, "And you two - get the *FUCK* out of my house!"

Interlude

Half an hour later, after I had been understandably banished together with the camera crew, I was sitting in Isaac's kitchen relating the story of what had just happened next door. Isaac was laughing so hard he was holding his stomach, and tears were running down his face.

"O my God, Jack," he finally managed to say between bouts of more laughter, "you really *peed* on the cat?"

Well, it killed two birds with one stone. I did really need to pee. And I have to say it's strangely satisfying to wake up a sleeping cat with a urine bath. I outdid myself this time - he'll probably still be cleaning himself this time tomorrow.

Isaac - who knows about my pussy-licking habits - erupted in laughter again.

Not to mention that it served the original purpose, which was to get rid of the TV people.

"So what did they say, anyway?"

You mean after the cat had tried to surgically excise my genitals with his claws?

More laughter. "Yes."

They didn't get to say anything. Veronica threw them out.

"No more psychics," Isaac said. "I don't know what she told them, but we were foolish to let our secret out. We must be more careful in future - I don't want to create trouble for Veronica. Or you."

Yes. And remind me to pee on her cat if I ever see him again.

"Well, anyway," said Isaac, after he'd stopped laughing. "Thank heaven that's the end of *that*." But of course it wasn't.

Viral

It was too much to hope that the Demon Cat Incident, as it became widely known, would be the end of our brush with public notoriety. Alas, not for us just fifteen minutes of fame.

Because of course Jimmy the cameraman had filmed the whole thing. And while he had no intention of airing it on TV - there was not a single three-second segment which did not feature Veronica systematically running through her impressively large inventory of invective - he of course couldn't resist sharing it with his family that evening. And of course his family had to include a teenage girl named Emily who almost peed herself laughing when she saw the video.

And of course Emily immediately shared it with her two hundred Facebook friends, who subsequently sent it to *their* friends, and so on. And inevitably somewhere along the way someone posted the video on Youtube... and that's where things really got out of hand.

Within the first 72 hours, the Demon Cat video had logged over one hundred thousand hits, and by the end of that week it had become an international phenomenon. Even Chinese state television picked it up: they devoted an entire news segment to it, though it turned out that they did this not because it was funny but because it served as yet another example of the pathetic frivolity of capitalist culture.

A few days later, the visits began.

It's not entirely clear how people discovered Demon Cat's address. Evidently one of our neighbors recognized either Veronica, Bonkers, me or all three of us and posted a terribly helpful comment beneath the video that said, *"I know where Demon Cat lives!!!!!!!!!!"* complete with our street address. Following this, members of that ubiquitous subset of the general population, Pathetic Losers Who Have Nothing Better To Do With Their Lives Than Look At Cat Videos, began to appear on our front doorstep at irregular intervals, hoping to meet Demon Cat in person.

The first to materialize were a pair of teenage girls named Tiffany and Lo. They weren't around long enough to establish what "Lo" was short for - though judging by the fact that Lo was clearly a shameless little whore, dressed as she was in a red miniskirt and a tank top at least two sizes too small for her burgeoning teenage breasts, I'd say it was *Lolita*. Educated guess.

"Hi," they announced in unison when Veronica opened the front door. "I'm Tiffany."

"I'm Lo."

"Yes?" said Veronica. "And?"

The pair giggled. "Well," said Tiffany, "can we, like, meet your cat?"

"What?" replied Veronica with a glare.

"Your cat," repeated the one called Tiffany, with another giggle. "We, like, saw him on Youtube." Veronica gave the pair an exasperated look. In addition to the obvious issue that the appearance of these two bimbos heralded the fact that someone had somehow discovered her address, Veronica had a particular abhorrence of teenagers whose vocabulary was so poor that they peppered every sentence with *like*.

"You '*like*, saw him on Youtube'?" she mocked.

"Yeah."

"Well, *like*, fuck off." she said, and slammed the door.

This instruction to go forth and copulate was one which was heard a lot over the next few days, as members of the impromptu Bonkers Fan Club appeared at all hours. They were mostly young and mostly local, teenagers and

20-somethings who thought that seeking out the Youtube Demon Cat would be a hilarious break from their usual occupations of playing video games or hanging out at the local mall. Most were female, some were male, and they almost always appeared in groups of two or three.

There was a small handful of older devotees, exclusively female. And a few individuals from out of town who were in Seattle for some other reason and decided to include Bonkers in their Emerald City sightseeing: Pike Place Market, Space Needle, Chihouly Gardens... crazy cat. All received the same frigid reception, and all were summararily sent packing.

Then there was the woman who claimed to have traveled all the way from Trenton, New Jersey for the sole purpose of meeting her new feline hero. "But I brought treats!" she shouted plaintively through the mailbox after Veronica had slammed the door on her.

After a week of this, Veronica posted a notice on said front door:

If you're here to see a cat you saw on Youtube, this is NOT where that cat lives. There is NO cat here, I have been the victim of a tasteless prank. Please respect my privacy and leave. Thank you.

She was tempted to include below the text an image of a shotgun pointed at the reader, but decided that this was too aggressive and that people would respond better to a simple courteous request.

This was placed above a long-standing notice aimed at the pests who frequently canvassed the neighborhood pedaling politics, charity, religion, magazine subscriptions or various other unwanted products and services:

NO SOLICITING
(Yes, this means you)

I already give money to charity
I don't need home improvements
I don't want a subscription to *Guns & Ammo*
I don't believe petitions make any difference
And I think your God does a really lousy job

So have a nice day... elsewhere. Thank you.

P.S. My dog eats Republicans and Jehovah's Witnesses

The cat notice did indeed work for a few visitors: Veronica's video security system recorded them walking up to the front door, reading the notice, looking disappointed and turning away. But ultimately its efficacy was fatally compromised by the glaring contradiction between the part of the notice stating unequivocally that no cat inhabited the premises and Bonkers' frequent habit of sunning himself in the window immediately to the right of the door. This resulted in gleeful ejaculations of "There he is!", followed by variations on "Hey, Demon Cat! Hey, kitty kitty!". Usually this was accompanied by rapping on the window to get Bonkers' attention, though all this served to do was to provoke the look of contempt with which he regarded everyone.

Eventually these periodic visitations by feline pilgrims became too much for Veronica, and she decided that she needed to leave the house for a while.

She called Anna. "Sweetie, is there any chance I could crash at your place for a week or so? These morons are driving me crazy."

"Of course, Vee," Anna replied. "But I'm afraid my apartment complex doesn't allow dogs. You can bring Bonkers, but I don't know what you're going to do with Jack."

It has always pissed me off to no end that rentals ban dogs while permitting cats. Dogs don't claw the furniture, shred the drapes or deposit nasty little hairballs in places where you inadvertently squish them with your bare feet in the middle of the night.

"Oh, shit," said Veronica. "I hadn't thought of that." She thought for a moment. "Maybe Isaac can take him for a while." She paused, thinking. "Actually, he and Jack seem to get along *amazingly* well."

If only she knew.

Favor

Isaac opened his front door and smiled at the sight of me and Veronica standing on his porch. He was actually very fond of Veronica, and it didn't hurt that she was an exceedingly attractive specimen of the female sex. He'd made a comment about this one day, and I'd responding by rather impolitely asking whether a man of his advanced years still maintained an interest in girls.

Isaac had fixed me with a wry smile. "Jack, I may be old, but I can still appreciate a beautiful woman. Just because I can't paint doesn't mean I don't like looking at a work of art. I'm not dead yet." I had to admit that the comparison was not entirely inappropriate: the longer I lived with Veronica, the more beautiful she seemed.

"Hi, Isaac," Veronica said. I was sitting obediently beside her, tail wagging, looking terminally cute.

"Good morning, Veronica, " Isaac replied. "Good morning, Jack." He bent down to pat my head.

JACK

Good morning to you too. Veronica is here to ask if you'll take care of me for a while. These morons are driving her crazy. Isaac nodded surreptitiously to acknowledge that he understood.

Oblivious to this exchange, Veronica continued. "The thing is, Isaac... These morons are driving me crazy. I'm really sick of them showing up at my front door trying to see Bonkers. I'm going to go crash with a friend for a week or so, but her apartment doesn't allow dogs. So I was wondering if I could ask you a huge favor?"

"Certainly. What is it?" he asked, knowing full well.

"Is there any way you could perhaps take Jack for a while? If it's not a hassle for you." Isaac smiled broadly. "Of course, I'd love to. He's a great dog and I enjoy his company."

Veronica breathed a sigh of relief, but then she frowned. "That's great... but I don't know if I'm going to cause you trouble with this. I mean, if people see Jack at your house they're just going to start bugging you. I really don't want that."

Isaac considered this for a moment. "Hmm. Yes, you're probably right. These people are very persistent, aren't they? Though I do have to admit the video was hysterical."

"You saw it?"

"Of course. I think half the planet has seen it by now." Veronica groaned.

"O God. Tell me about it."

"I'm sorry, Veronica. I didn't mean to be flippant."

"No, it's okay," she sighed. "I can now grudgingly admit that it's funny. I just wish it had happened to somebody else. I don't know what Jack was thinking when he did that."

Isaac of course knew exactly what I was thinking when I did that, but he resisted the urge to comment. "Well look," he said. "I don't know if I've ever told you, but I have a house on Lake Chelan. I was actually thinking about going out there for a week or so anyway. Change of scene, you know. It's very relaxing there, and I think Jack would really like it. He can swim, and there are woods to run around in. Plenty of squirrels," he added with a smile.

At the mention of this magical word, my ears immediately went up. Of course I understood everything that Isaac was saying, but I'm aware that dogs are supposed to visibly react to certain key words - *walk, treat, squirrel*. People find this endlessly cute, so I was merely fulfilling expectations. Veronica saw the ears go up and laughed, right on cue.

"God, that would be great. Are you sure it's not an imposition?"

"O no, not at all. I love having Jack around. It will be fun for me. Good canine company at the lake."

"That's wonderful. And to be honest, I think Bonkers could use a break too. He hasn't been the same since Jack peed on him."

I could see Isaac desperately trying to suppress a guffaw. "Yes, I'm sure he hasn't."

"Thank you *so* much, Isaac. I'll bring his food and dog bed." And so it was arranged.

Bedfellows

By the way, it's true that I have a bed of my own, though I rarely use it at night. Instead, I sleep with Veronica. She wasn't sure about this in the beginning and made some token attempts to evict me, but I'm so adorable as a bed partner that it was inevitable she'd give in.

Crawling under the covers to sleep against her legs, warm and comforting, quiet as a mouse.

Emerging in the morning from under those covers to snuggle up close, my back against her body, my head on the same pillow.

Delivering a few gentle, affectionate licks to her nose as she's waking up.

I mean, seriously, what's not to fall in love with?

Retaliation

It's the following morning, and I'm looking forward to heading out to Isaac's lake house. But first things first: breakfast.

After making herself coffee, Veronica cooks up a special treat for me: beef liver. She hates cooking the stuff, but she knows it's my favorite. I suspect she's making a batch now because she's feeling guilty at packing me off with someone else for a few days. Whatever, I'll take it.

The smell as it cooks drives me crazy, and I'm slobbering onto the kitchen floor. Finally I decide to go outside and pee while the process finishes, so I squeeze through the dog door at the back and hunt around for a suitable spot to do my business.

This is not something to be hurried. The street contains numerous canine calling cards on which I can void my bladder, most of which I recognize. Among others, there's a chihuahua from the next block, the bloodhound from down the street, and a German shepherd who belongs to two gay guys who live somewhere in the neighborhood. After much sniffing and careful consideration, I decide to give equal time to each of these, and distribute accordingly.

By the time I come back into the house, my meal is ready: the delicious dish is waiting for me on the kitchen floor.

I notice that Bonkers is sitting on the kitchen counter watching me, swishing his tail. He's not supposed to be up there, but Veronica has all but given up trying to stop him.

Anyway, I can't wait to eat; I haven't had beef liver in ages. But as I approach my dog dish, my sensitive little nose picks up another scent mixing pungently with the divine fragrance of braised cow organ. A strong, acrid smell, replete with ammonia.

And as I stare into my dog dish at my favorite food, I realize what's going on. Bonkers has peed on my breakfast.

Margo

A couple of hours later, Isaac and I are driving along State Route 20 towards Lake Chelan. It's quicker to take Interstate 90, but Isaac prefers the more scenic route through the northern Cascades. Either way, it's a little over a three-hour drive from Seattle, but we're in no hurry: it's a gorgeous day, blue and shining, the kind of day that is common in summer. The kind that is the reason everyone here suffers through the dark, soggy season that is winter in the Pacific Northwest.

Furthermore, we're driving in style in Margo. Margo is a 1970 Oldsmobile Ninety-Eight convertible. She's a magnificent machine: sleek, extravert-red and so big you could easily host a small cocktail party in her expansive interior. Margo drives so smoothly it's like we're riding on air, and she's the perfect car for a summer drive through this beautiful mountain scenery. Although Isaac will be the first to admit that she's not exactly economical: the huge V-8 Rocket engine gets all of 8 miles per gallon, and he jokes that if you listen closely while we drive you can hear the world's fossil fuel reserves being slowly drained.

I am riding next to Isaac in the front, sitting up on the plush bench seat. I am thoroughly enjoying the smell of the warm summer air rushing past, with its multitude of scents: earth, pine, flowers, squirrels. Between the classic car and the cute dog riding shotgun, we get a lot of appreciative honks and waves from other drivers.

Margo is named after an ex-girlfriend of Isaac's, back when he had girlfriends. As he puts it with a smile, "Like her namesake, that girl was large, loud and expensive to maintain."

What happened to her? I ask.

"Oh, I don't know," he replies. "We only dated for about six months - it was never serious. Last I heard she had married some executive - probably someone who could keep her in the style to which she desperately wanted to become accustomed. That wasn't me."

Actually, I know remarkably little about Isaac's past, and now I'm curious. *Isaac, were you ever married?*

"No Jack, but I was once very much in love." He pauses, and to my great surprise, I see him begin to tear up.

Isaac, are you okay? What happened? Did she die?

He smiled ruefully. "It's okay, Jack. She... she disappeared, long ago. She could not... stay."

She disappeared? You mean she left you?

"Not exactly." He paused. "It's a long story, and complicated. Perhaps I'll tell you when we're at the lake. Actually, truth be told I haven't spoken to anyone about her in years - it might do me good to tell you."

I gazed at him, surprised at this sudden change of mood. The day was as bright as ever, but somehow a shadow seemed to have crept into the landscape.

Do you miss her? I asked, after a pause.

He looked at me and sighed. "Jack, there is not a day goes by when I don't think about her. Yes, I miss her. Very much. And not only her."

There was someone else too?

He nods, and a single tear rolls down his cheek. "I'll tell you later. Soon."

Rachel

Chelan, a lake in Washington State, third deepest in the United States and 28th in the world. From the Salish Indian words *Tsi-Laan*, "deep water".

We arrive at Isaac's place an hour or so later, after a brief stop at a supermarket to pick up some food and other items. Lake Chelan is long and skinny, snaking its way through a lush mountain valley in the North Cascades over a total length of more than 50 miles. Isaac's house lies close to the southern end, a short distance northwest of the small town of Sunny Bank and just outside the boundary of a state park. Perched on a bluff and set back from the water's edge by a few yards, the cabin is hidden from anything behind it by a dense cluster of fir trees, but nothing obstructs the magnificent view across the lake. Isaac tells me it was built by his father in the 1930's, a few years after construction of the Chelan Dam raised the water level by more than 20 feet.

Isaac parks Margo under a car port on the side of the house and we get out and stretch our six legs. It occurs to me that this makes us, collectively speaking, an insect of some sort, but I quickly dispel the Kafkaesque image.

"Welcome to Camp Fishless," says Isaac, his arms outstretched in an exaggerated gesture. He explains that the name was coined as a joke by his mother, who knew full well that whenever Isaac's father said he was going to the lake for a few days to fish what he really meant was that he wanted to get some peace and quiet away from the family so he could do the only thing that really mattered to him in life, which was to be left alone to read. He never brought back a single fish.

We enter the house, which is tidy, simply furnished and full of light. The living room has large picture windows which look out over a spacious deck and, just beyond, the lovely emerald waters of Lake Chelan. There are bookcases along most of the walls, and everything smells of pine and cedar. I've been here only a few minutes and I love this place already.

While Isaac is unpacking the various items he has brought with him, I ask if I can explore the woods. "Sure," he replies. "Just don't get lost."

I promise not to, and head out down a path through the trees, enjoying the many smells that Nature has to offer around me.

I have been wandering for about twenty minutes, sniffing happily at the base of trees and peeing on random objects, when I enter a small clearing. It's maybe a couple of hundred yards across, evidently the result of some isolated logging; there are a few tree stumps here and there. Clusters of pretty sun-loving wildflowers adorn the edges, and birdsong fills the air all around.

I am enjoying this peaceful idyll when suddenly a squirrel shoots across my path with a look of terror in its beady little eyes. I am about to spring into action and take off after it when I see another dog bearing down upon me in a blur of legs, fur and murderous intent. The dog is female, and on first look I guess that she's a mix of ridgeback and something smaller. She's a little taller than me, a short-haired blonde with a powerful whip of a tail. She is sleek, toned, built for speed.

"Out of the way!" she commands, and a split second later passes like a bolt of lightning right in front of my face. I've never seen a dog move this fast: she is rapidly gaining on the squirrel, who is desperately trying to reach the sanctuary of a large pine tree at the edge of the clearing some twenty yards away. And he makes it, with the dog now only a few yards behind. As fast as his little legs can carry him, the squirrel shoots up the broad trunk: three feet, five, seven. Safety coming closer with every inch.

But, just as I expect the other dog to screech to a disappointed halt, I watch in awe as she adroitly adjusts her stride; then, in one magnificent act of flawless coordination, she leaps a good ten feet into the air and plucks the hapless rodent off the tree. She lands with perfect stability on the ground, and shakes the squirrel just once to break its neck. Then, without a second's pause, she takes off again with her prize in her mouth.

I find myself having to catch my breath. *No!* I think, my thoughts and heart racing. *Don't leave! We just met!*

Wait! I yell to the rapidly retreating figure. *Wait! What's your name?*

"*Rachel*," she replies, without so much as turning her head. And then she is gone, a gorgeous vision of ruthless efficiency and canine beauty swallowed up by the trees.

A little later, I wander back into the house, still dazed by what I have witnessed. Isaac looks up from a comfy armchair in which he's reading a book. He raises his eyebrows in a quizzical look.

"Jack, are you okay?"

No, I reply, coming over to sit by his side. *No, I'm not.*

Isaac looks concerned. "What's the matter? Has something bad happened?"

Yes. Yes it has.

"Jack, what's wrong? Did you hurt yourself?"

I pause, still reeling.

Worse, I say. *Much worse. I think I'm in love.*

Summer

Despite regular excursions into the woods, including to the clearing where I first saw her, I do not see Rachel again for three days.

Isaac and I pass the time with walks, or just hanging out together on the deck. He reads, I soak up the sun, and we occasionally share some snacks. The weather remains glorious.

On our second afternoon at Camp Fishless Isaac leads me down to a secluded little beach just below the house, and I watch as he flips over a small wooden boat that has been sitting upside down under a tarp. He drags the boat to the water's edge and invites me to get in. I do, and he pushes the boat out into deeper water, hopping in just as it begins to float freely.

It's my first time in a boat, and I watch, fascinated, as Isaac sets a pair of oars in the rowlocks and with slow but rhythmically sure movements takes the small craft out into the lake.

I love the movement, and the breeze, and the whole lazy serenity of this day.

A few hundred yards from the shore, Isaac hauls the oars and we drift. Neither of us feels the need to say anything, to intrude into a silence broken only by the gentle lapping of the water against the side of the boat, and the occasional call of some distant bird carried faintly on the intermittent breeze.

The day is hot under the sun, and after a while I am baking and panting. Isaac strips off his shirt, and I see that there is a tattoo right over his heart: the single word *Tashka*. I am about to ask about this, but Isaac forestalls the question with another topic.

"I'm sorry," he says, "I forgot to bring water. But if you're hot perhaps you'd like to go for a swim. Actually, it occurs to me now that I don't know if you *do* swim?"

I do. In fact I love the water. Veronica sometimes takes me to Lake Washington to swim there.

"Oh, well then. Good. Can you jump out of the boat, or do you need me to lower you into the water?"

I can jump. And I do, launching myself off the port side and making too large a splash as I hit the surface. The cool water feels wonderful, and I am immediately refreshed. I shake my head to clear some water out of my ears, then start to swim away from the boat.

Isaac laughs. "Have fun." He pauses. "Oh, and avoid the alligators."

The what? Holy crap! I start paddling frantically back towards the boat, but when I get there and look up I see Isaac laughing.

"Sorry, Jack. It was a joke. There are no alligators within a thousand miles of here."

That's not funny, I say. Although actually it is.

I swim for awhile, moving in slow circles around the boat. Then when I'm ready for a break Isaac grabs me by the scruff of the neck and somehow manages to haul me back inside.

We drift some more, each lost in our own thoughts, enjoying the beauty of the day. I gaze out towards the mountains, standing clear against a summer sky of cornflower blue. There is a timelessness to this place, as if the very hills themselves were engaged in a slow contemplation of the ages, or were locked in the resolution of some ancient mystery, whose unraveling required centuries of undisturbed thought.

This notion puts me in a contemplative mood, and I decide that it is a day for philosophizing. And for talking about something that has gradually become a quiet obsession in my muddled little doggie mind.

Isaac? Can I ask you a question that's been bothering me for a long time now?

"Of course, Jack. What is it?"

It's just that... well, I keep wondering something.

"Yes, what?"

This is going to sound weird.

"Weirder than a dog and a man having an abstract conversation on a boat in the middle of a lake on a summer day?"

Yeah, maybe.

"Go on then - tell me. What are you wondering?"

It's just... well. Isaac, why am I a dog?

Isaac pauses to take in the question. "What do you mean?" he asks.

I mean, why am I a dog and not a human? Or, for that matter, a bird or an antelope or a mountain gorilla? Or a fish swimming below us in this lake? Or any one of the gabillions of other life forms on this planet? And let's not get into bacteria or viruses. Or spiders - especially spiders. I shudder.

I hate spiders; it's a little-known fact that dogs can have full-fledged heeby-jeeby arachnophobia just like some humans. That's me. If a tarantula dropped on my head I'd keel over from a heart attack.

Isaac laughs. I ask him what's so funny.

"I'm sorry, I don't mean to be flippant. It's just that when I woke up this morning I didn't expect my immediate future to include a deeply philosophical discussion with a dog who's having an existential crisis."

He smiles, and affectionately strokes my head.

"This is really bothering you, isn't it?" he asks.

Yeah, it is.

"Well then, we should go back. This is a discussion that requires some alcohol. At least," he adds, "it does for me."

Gossip

In fact, we stay out on the lake for a while longer, agreeing that it is too lovely a day to waste inside. I swim some more, and we drift, laze, and gossip about people we know. At the mention of Leroy, Isaac grimaces.

"Leroy is a troll. I have no idea why he isn't back in the South and in the 19th century where he belongs."

I notice he never talks to you, which is strange because he seems to assume everyone else is fair game for his life story and conspiracy theories.

Isaac chuckles. "That's probably because I said something to him once that I figured would make him keep his distance."

You did? What did you say?

"I told him I was gay. And that he had a beautiful rear end. If I recall, I actually licked my lips as I told him that."

You did not! Seriously?

"Well, I knew he was a homophobe, so I figured it was either that or tell him I worship the Devil. The gay thing seemed a surer bet."

Very clever. Veronica would love to find something that would have him avoid her - she can't stand him, and he's always hitting on her.

At this, he tells me that he likes Veronica very much, and wishes she would find a worthy boyfriend. That he sees various men coming to the house, but that they never seem to stay for more than a few hours.

Um, well... there's a reason for that. They're not exactly boyfriends.

Isaac gives me a quizzical look, and I ponder whether I should reveal the nature of my beloved human's self-employment.

You must promise not to say anything, including to Veronica.

"Of course, Jack. Though I think I know where this is going. Is she a... well, perhaps I shouldn't presume. But is she... a prostitute?"

No, though several of her friends are. She's actually a dominatrix.

Isaac utters a little exclamation of surprise. "Really? Good lord, I would never have guessed. You mean she..." He pauses, trying to articulate the question. "Well, I don't really know what I think she does in that... profession."

She beats the crap out of men for money. Among other things.

Isaac's eyes widen. "Wow. I mean, I knew such women existed, but I never thought I'd end up meeting one. Let alone live next to one. She really beats men up - and they *pay* her for this?"

Yes, and they pay her very well. You'd be amazed. I have seen things... man, have I seen things. Things that cannot be Unseen.

"I'm afraid to ask. I must say Veronica manages to be very discreet about this - though come to think of it, I did think I heard screams coming from your house once."

Oh, that was probably Norbert.

"Norbert?"

I tell him about Norbert. He is both amused and fascinated as I relate the details of some of Veronica's clients and their particular erotic predilections.

Anyway, I say, *as you might imagine, Veronica doesn't exactly have a normal social circle, and it's very hard to find a guy who doesn't freak out when his date tells him that she tortures other dudes' genitalia for a living.*

Isaac nods. "Yes, I imagine that would make dating rather difficult. Well, I hope she finds someone one day. She's a lovely person. Although," he adds after a pause, "that seems like an odd thing to say about a dominatrix."

Actually, that's the tagline on her website: "The sweetest bitch you'll ever meet."

"She has a website?"

Of course. You can't be in that business and not advertize on the Internet.

"Oh my. I'm afraid I've been living a rather sheltered life."

Yes well, there you have it. I am the dog of a dominatrix. Your next-door-neighbor has a dungeon in her basement. And despite being smart and beautiful, she can't get a date.

"That's sad," Isaac says. "She deserves a good man."

It's a pity she's too young for you, I say. *You'd be a wonderful boyfriend.*

Isaac laughs heartily. "Me, date a dominatrix? It would probably kill me. Although," he adds after a moment's thought, "I can certainly think of worse ways to go."

We drift with a breeze that has sprung up while we were talking. Isaac looks towards the shore. "I suppose I'd better start rowing before we end up halfway down the lake. Let's go back to the house, and try to figure out the reason for your existence."

Philosophy

An hour later, we are sitting on Isaac's deck. He is drinking some white wine and eating a couple of cream puffs - Isaac *loves* cream puffs - and I've just finished scarfing up some beef liver that he was nice enough to cook for me.

"So," he says, "tell me your troubles. What's this big problem about being a dog?"

Well, I begin, *it's not exactly a problem as such. I like being a dog. Presumably you like being a human too. But given the number of creatures on Earth, from bacteria to beavers, it seems to me that the chances of you being a human are ridiculously small.*

"That's true, I suppose. Did you know that there are over 350,000 species of beetles alone?"

Seriously?

"Seriously. The biologist John Haldane was once asked what he'd learned from studying nature. Supposedly he replied that 'God has an inordinate fondness for beetles.'"

Well, there you go then. Probability says you should be a beetle.

"But if I were, I probably wouldn't be having this discussion, or be able to think about this stuff."

It might be fun being something else. A lion, or a whale. I'd like to be an eagle and fly. In a pinch, I'd be a cockroach, if only because I think it would be kind of fun to crawl out from somewhere at an inopportune moment and creep people out. I'd like to try being lots of things. But, I add, *I draw the line at a cat.*

Isaac laughs. "Cats aren't *that* bad."

They're evil.

He takes a sip of his wine. "So what do you suppose are the implications of all this?"

I don't know, I reply. *That's what I'm trying to figure out.*

"Do you believe in reincarnation?" Isaac asks after a pause.

I don't know, I reply. *But - no offense - I'm not sure how I feel about being married to you in a previous life.*

Isaac laughs. "Ah, Madam Lulu," he says. "But don't you think I'd have made a good husband?"

Who says you were the husband?

"Well, okay. But the idea of being hitched in a past existence to a dog is weird enough - I don't think I could handle switching genders too."

Fair enough, I say. *But do you believe in reincarnation?*

"Well," says Isaac after some thought, "I'd certainly like to. The idea that all we get is this one time around isn't very satisfying. Although," he adds, "the idea of having to go through puberty over and over again fills me with dread."

Is it that bad?

"O God, Jack, you have no idea. The insecurities, the social awkwardness. The peer pressure from other adolescents who are just as messed up and horrible as you are. Trying to fit in and figure out who you are, and all the while hormones are surging through your system and poisoning your brain. It's the worst. I don't suppose dogs have to deal with all that nonsense, do they?"

No, we don't. Though we get the hormone poisoning too - it just happens faster, like everything else in our lives. One day you're still a puppy, and the next you're suddenly hit with this overwhelming desire to hump everything in sight.

Isaac laughs. "That's not very different from your average teenage boy," he replies.

Why did you ask about reincarnation?

"Because that's another issue of probability, like being a human instead of a beetle or a bacterium."

How exactly?

"Well, think about it. Humans in their present form - *Homo sapiens* - have been around for about 200,000 years, or so scientists currently believe. That's maybe ten thousand generations, and thousands of lifetimes. What's the probability of my being here, alive and sentient and aware, *now*? Not a hundred years ago, not a thousand or a hundred thousand, but *right now*? If consciousness is snuffed out when we die and we get only this one time around the block, it seems awfully unlikely that I'd be living my short little life at *this* time and not in any of the many stretches of three score years and ten in the very extended past that came before. Doesn't it?"

Yes it does, I suppose.

"Which rather implies that there's some sort of reincarnation."

Well yes - and that's another thing I worry about. What if next time around I'm reincarnated as something weird or vile? What if I come back as a bunny?

"What's wrong with bunnies? They're cute."

Yeah, they're cute - and very tasty. I mean, everything *kills bunnies. I kill bunnies. I definitely don't want to come back as prey because of - what do you call it? - karma. Karmic retribution.*

"Then maybe you should stop killing bunnies." He smiles, and pauses. "Want to hear another improbable?"

Sure, though my little doggie brain is already hurting.

He smiles. "There's this foundational idea in modern physics called the Anthropic Principle. It's complicated, but essentially what it says is that conditions in the universe must be such that they allow an observer to exist and thus observe the cosmos."

Okay... I think.

"What's improbable about this is that if any one of many characteristics of our universe were even very slightly different, life could not exist and we would not be here to observe things."

Such as what?

"Oh, there are many examples. If what's called the strong nuclear force was even two percent stronger than it is, it would fundamentally change the way that hydrogen works. And since the fusing of hydrogen into heavier elements is what powers the stars, and stars create the conditions for life to evolve, then that change would pretty much rule out life - and there would be no one here to observe the universe, and we wouldn't be here discussing it."

Isaac drinks some more wine. "Likewise, there are other parameters that are exactly right in this universe, but if they were changed just a little we wouldn't exist. Taken together, the probability of all those things being exactly right for the evolution of life is extremely small."

And yet it exists, as you say. And as we do.

"Yes. For many scientists, this says that our universe is just one of many - perhaps an infinite number of universes, all with different characteristics. If you accept that idea, then it makes sense that in some of them the conditions for the development of life will be favorable, no matter how remote the probability of all those various factors lining up in just the right way. In a cosmos of multiple universes, a few will work out just right."

Or maybe God exists and made everything that way?

"Well yes," he replies, "I suppose one can't rule out the possibility of a Creator in some fashion. After all, the fact that the universe exists at all is hard to explain. *Not* existing would be a lot simpler - if there were nothing. Everything else back to the Big Bang can be explained - and some cosmologists don't seem to have a problem with the ultimate origin of everything even before that. But to me, it seems difficult to accept."

He pauses, then adds, "Once or twice a year I'm sitting out here on the deck at night with no artificial light around, and I look up at the night sky and it scares the crap out of me - the fact that it all *exists*. And yet most people seem to just sleepwalk through life without ever thinking about the implications of that, or even noticing. The whole universe is arrayed above them - a giant banner screaming the improbability and wonder of existence, and yet they walk home happily unawares, and go back to their soap operas and reality shows."

So do you believe in a God?

"Well, not in any of the forms that humans conceive of. I accept the *possibility* that something supernatural that we don't understand may have been behind the existence of the universe, long, long ago. What that was, and whether it still exists, I have no idea. And the idea that God is male and loves only Christians - or Moslems, or Jews - it's ridiculous."

Why? My knowledge of human religious practice is pretty scant.

"Well, take the Bible. It was written by a bunch of goat herders maybe three thousand years ago. They knew virtually nothing, and their whole world was based on superstition. Yet millions of people today are convinced that this old book is the sacred word of that ancient deity, and that everyone else on the planet is absolutely wrong. The same is true for all the other major religions - they're all rooted in mediaeval superstition and ignorance."

You don't believe in any of them?

"No, Jack, I don't. Christians will tell you that Jesus Christ is the son of God and that anyone who doesn't believe that is wrong and will be condemned to some terrible damnation for eternity. The idea that this dogma might just be connected to the fact that almost all of them were brought up in a Christian culture never occurs to them. And in another part of the world, millions of people grow up in a Moslem culture where they're taught that Allah is the only god and that the Christians are all terrible heretics. And if you were born in India you believe there is a whole pantheon of gods and that Christians and Moslems are all wrong. It's just stupid - none of these people think about it objectively. If they did they'd realize just how ridiculous the whole thing is."

He smiles. "I'm sorry - ignore me. I'm a crotchety old man. It's just that religious belief has created so much conflict and suffering in the world." He pauses. "I don't suppose dogs believe in a god, huh?"

No, but beef liver comes pretty close as an object of worship. It's every dog's absolute favorite. Isaac chuckles.

"Ok," he says. "Hint taken. I'll get you some more."

Philosophy II

Isaac has a fresh glass of wine and another cream puff, and I have finished a second plate of beef liver.

Simple pleasures.

So why are we here?

"Beats me, Jack," Isaac replies. "People have been asking that for thousands of years - though as far as I know you're the first dog to do so."

It's all very mysterious. You could go nuts thinking about it - at least I could.

"No, you're right. But sometimes I wonder..." His voice trails off.

What do you wonder, Isaac?

"I've always been struck by the great profligacy of Nature. A tree or a plant produces hundreds or thousands of seeds, and perhaps two or three successfully germinate. Humans and many other animals produce literally millions of sperm just so a single one succeeds in fertilizing an egg. Everywhere in Nature you see huge numbers, all designed to ensure a very limited but all-important success."

Where are you going with this? I ask.

"Well, look at the universe. Our galaxy, the Milky Way, has an estimated one hundred thousand million stars. In the observable universe there are believed to be two trillion galaxies. So the number of stars in the universe is literally and figuratively astronomical. It's hard to see that extraordinary profligacy and not wonder whether it's all designed to ensure that *something* happens - with the rest being just disposable... well, disposable waste, I suppose. Glorious waste."

What happens?

"Well, that's the question. Something important? Who knows? Perhaps the something is related to life, or perhaps life has nothing whatever to do with it."

Isaac drinks some more wine. "There's a funny short story by an old science fiction author named Fredric Brown. It's about a man who is a solipsist."

What's a solipsist?

"It's someone who believes that everything in the universe exists only in his or her imagination, that he or she is the only thing that's real."

Interesting idea.

"Yes, it is. Anyway, this man has a really terrible week - his wife leaves him, he loses his job, he gets into an auto accident - and there he is lying in a hospital bed depressed. And he suddenly becomes a practicing solipsist, and everything around him - the room, the hospital, the Earth - disappears. But when he tries to wish himself out of existence, a voice in the void speaks to him. He asks who the voice is, and it says that he's the one who created this whole universe that the man has just wished out of existence. And now that that's happened, he can finally rest."

So what happens next?

"The voice disappears, and the man realizes that there's only one thing he can do. He creates the Heaven and the Earth. It takes him seven days."

I ponder this for a moment. *You mean he had to do that in the hope that eventually someone like him would come along and wish it all out of existence so he could himself disappear?*

"Exactly. It's a cute story. And I find myself wondering whether everything in the universe is just there as part of some grand experiment to produce some all-important end result - one whose creation requires vast numbers, and an unimaginable scale of space and time."

We are both silent for a while, and I think about everything Isaac has said.

This is all too weird for me, I'm afraid. I'm just an ordinary dog.

"Jack, you are very far from being an ordinary dog. But yes, it's very weird. Perhaps one day we'll find out the answers - and I suspect that they are more bizarre and more profound than any of us can imagine."

I think I need a nap, I say. *Sleep is strange too, isn't it? Sleeping and dreaming - they're like visiting another world.*

Isaac nods. "How are we to know whether dreams are the reality, and this life is just a dream? There was once a Chinese philosopher named Chuang Tzu who said, 'Once I dreamed I was a butterfly. Now I do not know whether I was then a man dreaming that he was a butterfly, or that now I am a butterfly dreaming that he is Chuang Tzu.'"

That's cute.

"It's an interesting spin on reality. For that matter, who is to say that as a person dreams, their dreams are not at that very moment being enacted by some anonymous characters on the other side of the world, or in another universe?"

You mean someone is chasing squirrels in another universe?

Isaac laughs, and pats my head. "Maybe. Or maybe you're the one chasing the squirrels in someone else's dream."

All About Ewe

Rachel, a female name meaning "ewe", a female sheep (Hebrew). In some interpretations, a more lengthy meaning is given: "to journey as a ewe that is a good traveler". In the Old Testament, Rachel was the wife of Jacob and the mother of Joseph and Benjamin.

The next morning, I am again running around in the woods in the hope of finding Rachel when I hear a dog barking in the distance. It's definitely a female bark - yes, we dogs can tell - and it sounds like it could be from a dog about the size of Rachel, so I run off in that general direction to investigate. Whoever is barking has something cornered (yes, we can tell that too).

A minute or so later I emerge into the same clearing where I met Rachel for the first time, and there she is! She is standing at the foot of a tree and staring up into it. Closer inspection of the scene reveals a large cat sitting on the lowermost branch, glaring down at Rachel and hissing at her every time she barks.

Hello Rachel, I say. I try not to show how pleased I am to see her.

She glances at me. "Oh hello... whatever your name is."

Jack, I say. *It's Jack.*

She looks up at the tree again, which is currently playing temporary host to one very pissed-off feline.

Treed the cat, huh? I say, by way of conversation.

Rachel gives me a look that clearly says she finds my attempt at repartée less than scintillating. *"Do you always state the obvious?*

Mostly, I reply, hoping that the self-deprecation will win me a smile. It doesn't. I try another tack. *Can I help?*
"That depends. Can you climb trees?"
Well, no.
"Do have another way to get a cat out of a tree?"
No.
"Well, then - you can't help, can you?"
Unfortunately, her logic is unassailable. And it's becoming apparent that if I have any intention of taking this girl a-courtin' it ain't gonna be easy.
Why do you want the cat out of the tree? I mean, are cats just fun to mess with for you, or are they a menu item?
Dogs can't quite raise their eyebrows contemptuously the way humans do, but if she could, she would.
"If you must know, I haven't eaten today."
Really? Hasn't your human fed you?
"My human can't always feed me, so I have to find my own food. THAT" - she motions with her muzzle to the tree - "was supposed to be breakfast, but it got away."
What do you mean, your human can't always feed you?
"It's complicated."
Where do you live?
"Here. In this wood. I live here."
You mean you're a stray?
"No, I'm not a stray." Clearly Rachel doesn't care for this term. "I choose to live freely, out here."
What about your human?
"Are you always this nosy?"
Pretty much. Look, I'm just curious. You seem like a nice dog and it bothers me that you're homeless.... or whatever it is you are.
"Don't worry about me. I can take care of myself."
I recall my first encounter with her. *Yeah, I imagine you can. You certainly nailed that squirrel a couple of days ago.*
"Squirrels are easy."
No they're not. They're fast little suckers.
"Maybe you're just too slow."
I'm not slow. And of course I've caught squirrels.
I am not being entirely honest here. I omit the minor detail that it was actually *squirrel*, singular, and that it wasn't exactly a fair contest given that the rodent in question accidentally landed on my head and was subsequently pursued within the confines of a house.
"Okay, Jock..."
Jack. It's Jack.

JACK

"Okay, Jack, the intrepid squirrel catcher, since this stupid cat is obviously not coming down any time soon, I have to go find something else to eat. Nice talking to you." She says this last part with not the slightest trace of sincerity, and turns away, obviously about to take off.

Wait, I say. *Look, come with me to our house and I'll get you something to eat. It's the one on the lake just up there.*

"Thank you," she replies, rather more sincerely this time. "But I can't. Maybe later. Right now I have to go and make sure Alice is okay."

Alice?

"She's my human."

But you don't live with her?

"No."

Why not?

Her expression changes to one of disgust. *"Because,"* she says, "Alice lives with a moron."

Isaac's Story

JACK

MUCH TO MY DISAPPOINTMENT, Rachel did not appear at the house later. Isaac and I went for another boat ride, and divided the rest of the day between short walks and lazing on the deck. He read a book on eastern philosophy, I lay in the shade and thought about Rachel, squirrels and the meaning of life - but mostly about Rachel.

That evening, we were sitting on the deck again enjoying the last glow of a protracted summer sunset. The full moon had risen above the mountains, huge and yellow in the eastern sky. Isaac was staring at it, deep in his own thoughts.

Isaac, can you tell me the story of the woman you mentioned the other day? The one you loved?

He started slightly, as if my words had suddenly summoned him back from a dream. He sighed. "You must be a mind-reader," he said. "I was just thinking of her."

I think mind-reading is your department.

He smiled and softly caressed the top of my head. "Yes, I'll tell you. I've never told the full story to anyone, actually."

Really? Why not?

"It's complicated. Many people knew us, of course - we were together for a couple of years. But no one ever knew..." He paused. "No one ever knew the true nature of our relationship. They would not have believed it. Some days even I question if it really happened. But I will tell you."

I still have no idea what he is talking about, but I am flattered by this confidence.

Why me? Why not another person?

"Because by the very fact that you and I can communicate in this... unusual way, I think you accept that not everything can be explained by reason. That magic - or call it what you will - must in some sense exist in the world."

Yes. Yes, I suppose I do.

"Very well then. I shall tell you everything, and hope you don't think I'm crazy."

You're actually the sanest human I've ever met.

"Thank you, Jack. That means a lot, coming from you."

He glances once more at the moon, and for a moment seems to be lost in thought again.

Beautiful moon, I say.

"Yes. Yes it is. And appropriate that it is full tonight. The moon has much to do with my story."

He sighs. "I wrote about her, you know. I suppose it was part writing exercise and part therapy. Perhaps, instead of just telling you about her, I should read the story."

I'd like that.

"Good. Then let's retire to the living room."

We go back into the house, and Isaac busies himself making a cup of tea. When the kettle has boiled, and he has poured the steeped tea into a mug, he walks over to one of the large bookshelves that line the room. From the top shelf he takes down a box the size of a large book, and brings it to the coffee table in front of the fireplace. The top of the box is beautifully decorated with an illustration of a mermaid.

Opening it, he carefully removes a sheaf of papers.

"It's been a while since I've looked at this," he notes. "I wrote it long ago. I hope it reads well." He settles into an armchair, and I lay by his side.

"Are you sitting comfortably?" he enquires. I say that I am. "Good. Then I'll begin." He sips the tea, and clears his throat.

"Once upon a time, long long ago, there was a young boy..." And with that, he begins to read.

Prologue: The Wood

THE BOY WAS BORN BY THE SEA. The memory of its vastness, its voice, still haunts his dreams. He knows that he will return to the ocean one day, that there his future lies. But not now.

Now he lives inland, in a large rambling house that seems sprung from the downs on which it lies, as if by enduring for so long it has somehow earned the right to become a part of the landscape. At the back of the house, a lawn runs unevenly down to a small brook. On the brook's far bank, dark and imposing like an unspoken threat, is a wood.

In the weeks that he has lived here, the boy has become fascinated by the wood, although it frightens him in a way he cannot explain. The wood draws him to itself, he thinks, and he has found himself spending more and more time there. First patrolling its perimeter, gazing up uneasily at the eaves. Listening, contemplating, wondering. Imagining.

He spent two weeks like this, suspended on the margins of the wood. Then one day, on a sudden impulse, as if heeding a silent call, the boy crossed the threshold. Some instinct told him to do it quickly, reflexively, in one swift and irreversible movement, before reason intervened and stayed his will. As he passed between the first trees, as sunlight was transmuted into shadow, he could hear nothing except his own heartbeat, echoing in his ears like a series of hammer blows.

Fifty yards into the wood he stopped. As he stood beneath that great canopy and gazed into a silent world of dappled green, it seemed to him as if the earth was holding its breath. And he sensed that by this one simple, innocent act of entry he had committed himself to something he could not name.

That was a month ago. Now the boy rises from his bed and silently dresses himself in the darkness. Passing his parents' bedroom, he hears the muted sound of his father's snoring through the heavy oak door. Descending the staircase, he feels the soft touch of the carpet under his bare feet, then the grave-cold stone floor of the kitchen. Quickly he gathers the things he has prepared. Then, as the grandfather clock in the living room solemnly chimes the beginning of a new day, he opens the back door and steps outside into the warm June night.

He pauses briefly to look up at the moon, a pale orb which hangs suspended like a sentinel in the southern sky. Then, with a deliberate step that is neither slow nor hurried, the boy walks down the garden towards the wood. There is no change in his pace as he reaches and crosses the tiny stone bridge that spans the brook, then vanishes into the trees beyond.

Within the wood, silence. A soft breeze like a whispered benediction. Trees with stars in their hair, bright Arcturus glittering high above the world. And a young boy kneeling as he carefully lays his small burden on the forest floor. There is a plate with bread and a small pile of salt. A glass of wine. A single white rose.

Satisfied that these tokens are pleasingly arranged, the boy stands. Hands clasped in front of his chest, he stares into the center of the wood, and bows his head. Then softly, very softly, he utters two words to the darkness.

I believe.

Nothing changes, nothing moves. With a brief glance at the rose, the boy turns and slowly walks back through the trees to the world beyond the wood. Passing over the bridge, he ascends the garden towards the welcoming silhouette of the house.

But as he moves away, a small figure under the summer stars, something from within the darkness of the trees watches him go, and sighs.

Interlude

Isaac pauses his reading and takes a sip of tea. Outside, dusk has turned to night, and the air is a little chilled.

It's a really interesting story so far, but I have to tell you I'm a little creeped out by it. What was the thing - the person, the whatever-it-was, in the woods?

Isaac smiles. "You'll have to wait to find out. A good storyteller never reveals everything at the beginning."

Well, fair enough. But if I'm going to have nightmares about something creepy and supernatural, I'd kinda like to know ahead of time.

"Don't worry, it's nothing bad. Quite the opposite, actually."

Okay. But who was the boy?

He takes another sip of tea. "The boy was me, Jack."

Really? This actually happened to you when you were a kid?

He looks at me askance.

Okay, okay. I'll try not to get ahead of myself. Go on.

"Thank you. Now, to continue the story, we must move on from the first scene, traveling through time to a point some fifteen years later. Got it?

Grown-up you. Check.

He drinks a little more tea, and continues.

"Now I'm going to introduce you to my father. And to the only woman I've ever loved."

Rowan

My father lived to read. There were times when I felt that all of his other activities, including us, were simply spaces to be filled between books. He loved language above all else save my mother, who had stolen his heart, and the Sea, which was for him the beginning and the end of all glorious things. He felt for English a passion that I have seen equaled in very few romances. I would sometimes come into a room and find him walking to and fro, or perched on a stool by one of the great bookcases that filled the house, reading softly aloud to himself for the sheer pleasure of hearing the words spoken.

I think of my father when I think of her. Strange that I should link them, two such different people. So removed from each other in time and in perspective, and my father normally so intolerant of the young. Yet not so strange. For she too loved books, and language, and the beauty of words. And she charmed him as she charmed so many others.

My father fell to her instantly, and utterly. I doubt that he ever recovered from the surprise of it; his only similar experience had involved meeting my mother for the first time, and the immediacy and intensity involved with that event was not something he had expected to repeat, especially so late in life.

I remember every detail of the moment. We had just arrived at the house after a long, meandering drive from London. Anxious to introduce her to my father, I took her into the library, where I knew I would find him. But before I had even had the chance to announce our presence - for my father, as usual, was engrossed in a book and oblivious to our appearance - she walked directly to a particular bookcase, as if drawn by something she knew was there. Standing on tiptoe she reached up and with great care took down a volume of Dante. She looked down at its cover and briefly smiled, as if fondly thinking of the innumerable hands, eyes and minds that this venerable old book had engaged during its long life. Then, unhesitatingly opening it as if she had already selected a passage and knew precisely where it lay, she began to read aloud.

My father looked up, astounded. Her Italian pronunciation was flawless - a fact that was not lost upon him, polyglot that he was - but it was not that which captivated him. Rather it was the sound of her voice, fluid and warm like a stream in summer, and the extraordinary skill she possessed in rendering words their due. In anyone else, the act would have seemed pretentious. But in her reading he recognized the love of language that he knew so well, conveyed without the slightest trace of vanity.

When she finished, I was amazed to see tears on my father's face. Deeply moved, and yet deeply discomfited, for a moment he could not speak. So great was his shock that he, the master of words, was speechless.

Slowly, he recovered his disheveled wits. Shaking his head as if to awaken himself, he smiled self-consciously and asked, "Your name... what is your name, child?"

And she, smiling that glorious smile that lit up even that dark and musty old room, echoed the repetition in his question, saying, "Rowan. My name is Rowan."

~

Rowan. Her name was Rowan. Rowan the mountain ash, the tree with berries bright as blood. As bright as her red hair, which flowed like a mane over her shoulders and seemed - depending on the time of day, the light and her mood - like fire, or roses, or sunset.

She was of modest height, a little more than five foot seven in her bare feet, with a light step and a feline grace in her movements. Slender hands with long, delicate fingers. Skin as pale as the moon. And an angular, almost vulpine face in which were set clear, bright eyes, startlingly green. This face, the face I came to love, was much of the time quietly serious; and her smile, when it came, was always a surprise.

We remained at the house for almost two months, pressed by my parents to stay. That they enjoyed having me so close to them for such an extended time I never doubted, but I knew that behind their insistence lay also a desire to prolong the pleasure that they took in Rowan's presence.

When I think of those days, I see a hot, flaxen summer whose brilliance memory has softened rather than dimmed. The spring had been miserable, with long days of rain, and even the annual miracle that clothed anew the world in green was overshadowed by the unbroken gloom of the sky. But what spring withheld, summer gave ungrudgingly. The weather was exceptional, the days long and the nights candled by stars.

Indeed, the weather was so good that a few people could not help but voice their concern. "It's not natural," grumbled old Granny Cook one day when we met her on an afternoon walk. Infused with the superstitious pessimism that is the birthright of the British, she seemed to feel that such an abundance of sun was a gift mistakenly sent, to be paid for at a later date with some ill fortune.

"Oh, Mrs Cook!" laughed Rowan, touching her arm affectionately. "Enjoy it while it lasts!"

"Ay, Rowan, I can do that as well as the next folk," she replied, shaking her head. Then she added, "But it'll end one day, you'll see!" She delivered this prediction as if its accuracy was anything but inevitable.

Over the slow, languid weeks of that summer we watched the gradual progression of the moon as it waxed huge and yellow, then faded to the slimmest arc of silver above the patient trees. I was made to pay more attention than usual to the lunar cycle by Rowan, who followed it with a quiet obsession. Every evening I would find her sitting on the grass in the garden, hugging her knees to her chest, silent and pensive as she gazed up as if in reverence at the moon. I once asked her why she did this, but she would say only that it was a habit that was important to her, one that reminded her of a memory, the substance of which she would not disclose.

"Tell me," I urged as I sat beside her and put my arm around her, holding her close. She shook her head and gently squeezed my hand in hers. I felt the cool brush of her hair as she leaned her head on my shoulder, yet not for an instant did she take her eyes from the moon. I did not press her, sensing that in this nightly ritual some private sadness lay hidden. As indeed it did.

I have come back to the Greek island where it all began. To write and to remember. I have returned here, to Kalliste, jewel of the Sea, for the first time since those days, now almost a decade past. I have rented a little house at the edge of the clifftop. A middle-aged woman named Maria is the caretaker, and she dutifully comes by each morning to wash the salt from the walls. Having no language in common, we confine our interactions to a nod or the occasional smile. She pities my solitude, I think; but in truth I have no need of company.

Outside, there is a small terrace with a table and a single chair that is comfortable enough, and from here I can look out at the sea below and give myself to the sunlight and the wind. And to memory.

The wind reminds me of her. Everything reminds me of her.

I have come like a man seeking a lost limb. One that cannot be seen, because it is no longer there, but which he still feels, keenly, as a part of himself. Yes, I am haunted by absence.

I cast myself back along the silken thread of memory to those days, and try to set down, in the permanence of black ink, a portrait of her. Was she real? Did they really happen, those extraordinary events that I now try to capture in elusive words? I must of course be careful in my rendering of the past - for we all select memories as we choose photographs, passing over those which show us in unflattering light or poses.

Well then, let us begin, on a hot day in the capital...

Interlude

Isaac stops reading and looks down into his empty mug. "I need more tea," he says, and puts down the manuscript.

You can't stop reading now! I have so many questions.

"And I have answers for you, but all in good time." He busies himself at the stove.

This is sounding like an Emily Brontë novel, I say. *Very tragic.* "Wuthering Heights" is one of Veronica's favorite books, so I've heard about the three sisters from Haworth.

Isn't there a Cliff Notes version?

"Don't you like my writing?" Isaac asks, with just a trace of hurt in his voice.

I love your writing. It's wonderful. But dogs don't live as long as humans - "life is short" has a different meaning for us. So you have to forgive a little impatience sometimes.

He smiles. "OK, here's the short version: Boy meets girl. Boy falls in love with girl. Girl loves boy, but girl is not what she seems. Girl has to leave. The end."

I pause for a moment to replay in my head what Isaac just said to make sure I heard him right. *Wait... 'Girl is not what she seems' - what?*

"Do you want me to continue the story? I promise to finish before you turn fifteen."

I sigh. *Yes, okay.* I wag my tail to show my appreciation, a gesture that does not pass unnoticed. *By the way, does this story have a title?*

"Ah yes, it does. I should have mentioned that. It's called *Glamour*."

Glamour? Was Rowan a fashion model or something?

Isaac laughs. "No, she wasn't. Although in different circumstances she could well have been, I suppose. She was certainly beautiful enough." He pauses. "Actually, she looked a little like Veronica. Red hair, classic looks. Veronica reminds me of her sometimes."

Well if she wasn't a model, why "Glamour"?

"It is a rather different meaning of the word, one which is much more ancient than the sense used today." My own love of words has not yet stumbled upon this particular nugget, and I'm at a loss.

So what does it mean, this other sense?

"Guess what I'm going to say now?"

I sigh again. *That I'm just going to have to wait to find out?*

"Bingo."

You're a tiresome old man sometimes - you know that, right?

Isaac grins. "Privilege of the aged."

Oh very well. Please go on.

He settles back into the chair with a fresh cup of tea. "Okay then. Next part: how we met."

Kalliste

Athens in July. Streets blasted with noon heat. Rippling air, baked and anhydrous under a cerulean sky.

Not a single street dog moved anywhere, and the whole city felt like a potter's kiln.

I had come to Greece a month before, intending to stay for two or three weeks. To visit some islands and move on. I knew I wanted to visit Damascus, but from there I had no clear destination or plan, other than a desire - articulated with vague insistence by my heart - to move ever eastward.

My traveling was rather haphazard, and if I am honest I must confess that my itineraries were set largely by the romance of names and the images and histories that they conjured. Damascus, the Jasmine City. Istanbul, clothed in centuries of echoes from Constantinople, from Byzantium. Cairo, al-Qahirah, "the Victorious". And beyond these in the wide world, so many more. Zanzibar and Dar-es-salaam: the sails of Arab dhows at sunset reflecting purple in the Indian Ocean (O! Where are they bound?). Samarkand and Tashkent - the Silk Road, the Pamirs marching to the Tian Shan and the High Himalaya, and on and on and on below a pale, ethereal sky, forever distant.

So much history, so much romance. Islands, bays, peninsulas, each with a name and a hoarded store of events large or small, historic or long-forgotten. The great rivers of the world: Danube, Volga, Nile, Congo, Amazon, Indus, Yangtze, Amur; their waters flowing ceaselessly hundreds or thousands of miles past countless settlements, a Babel of languages, and millions of lives, each with their small, unique stories of joy and sorrow, triumph and loss, hope and disappointment. Passing ever onward through the changing lands and out to the great rolling oceans beyond.

Names drove me... I suppose there are worse ways to plan one's travel.

The year was 1965, and I was twenty-five years old. I had hitch-hiked my way across the continent of Europe, drawn ineluctably to the Mediterranean's shores. And so I landed in Athens one bright day in June. I checked into a youth hostel, spent a couple of days paying homage to the usual tourist sights, then boarded a ferry for Hydra, one of the Saronic Gulf islands a couple of hours from the capital.

And long before we arrived, I had fallen in love with Greece and knew I would stay. As the ferry cut through the sparkling azure water, I stared transfixed, and recalled what Henry Miller had said of the country when he first arrived: "A world of light such as I had never dreamed of, nor ever hoped to see". He was right: Greece was a dream - wide and shining, the sunlight infusing optimism into everything.

JACK

It was everything England was not - that gray, sodden prison of the emotions with, as someone once said, its narrow towns and narrows roads and narrow kindnesses and narrow reprimands.

Upon my return to Athens, I rented a small one-bedroom apartment in Thiseion, which in those days was a peaceful backwater neighborhood under the Acropolis. Not needing a job, I passed my days wandering the streets, and writing bad poetry in local tavernas and cafés. I wanted nothing more, and in that sunlit world I was happy.

But now the city heat was too much. I needed air that moved, and islands cooled by the sea wind. And so early one morning I packed a few things in a rucksack and rode the ancient tram to Piraeus, the weary old car screeching and protesting the entire way. I walked down to the harbor; and there, on a whim, I took the first island ferry I laid eyes on, determined to go wherever it was bound.

I liked this capricious act of committing myself to a random and unknown destiny. It was not the first time I had practiced this; in fact I had given myself over to Fate in this way a number of times. I once boarded an overnight train in Marseilles that was bound for a place called Irun; I had no idea where that might be, other than (I assumed) somewhere in Europe. In the morning, I awoke to see the Pyrenees stretched out under a clear blue summer sky, with the train heading into Spain. On what path had that random choice placed me? Who would I meet, what would I experience? How would the direction of my life be different now than if I had gone to Rome, to Vienna, to Paris, or to any of a thousand other destinations? Of course I would never know - we cannot rewind our lives - but I loved the complete surrender to chance that the act involved.

I stepped onto the old steamer, rocking gently at the Piraeus dock, having no idea that this particular act was to change my life in the most profound way - and for the bargain price of just three dollars for the one-way voyage.

The boat, it turned out, was headed for Santorini, that incomparable jewel of islands. I remember I literally gasped when, some nine hours after we left, I awoke from a nap, walked to the ship's rail and caught my first sight of those towering volcanic cliffs, high above an impossibly blue sea. As we came closer and Santorini became clearer, I was held spellbound by this gorgeous insular vision; I had never in my life seen a place so beautiful.

I was so overwhelmed with the experience and all it represented - the freedom of travel, the reaffirmation of my choice to eschew security and instead seek the beauty of the world - that, remarkably, I began to cry. As tears slid down my cheeks, I shook my head in wonder and joy, and whispered to myself, "Santorini!" Invocation of a dream.

"Kalliste." A woman's voice, next to me.

I turned, wiping the tears from my face and feeling embarrassed, but she was smiling.

"The island was once called Kalliste. It means 'the most beautiful.' I suspect you would not disagree." I laughed, though I remained rather flustered.

"You're right," I replied, gathering myself. "I've never seen such beauty. It's astonishing."

I paused to take in the appearance of this unexpected witness to my sudden emotional response. She was beautiful, this girl: fairly tall, slim, with red hair and green eyes, and a fine, kindly face. She spoke with an accent that could have been English, but was strangely difficult to place. She looked to be in her mid-20's, yet there was something about her that seemed ageless. The eyes were not young. A paradox.

"Kalliste was the name of one of the Haliae, the sea nymphs," she continued. "She was the daughter of the sea-god Triton. Legend tells us that her father presented her to one of the Argonauts in the form of a clod of earth, and when that was washed overboard during the voyage it formed the island of Santorini."

I wanted to speak, to say something intelligent in response to this unsolicited lesson in mythology, but I was struck dumb, enchanted by this lovely girl and her mellifluous voice. I wanted to implore her to continue speaking, about the island, about anything at all.

"Really?" I finally managed to get out. "She was a sea nymph?"

"Yes," she replied. "The Haliae were beautiful maidens. They rode through the sea on the backs of dolphins."

She paused, and we both gazed out to sea, lost in our own thoughts. Suddenly she clapped her hands with unfettered delight. "Look!" she exclaimed, pointing. "Dolphins!"

And there they were, as if summoned by her voice: a school of dolphins rushing towards us, surfing and jumping in the waves created as the ship cleaved the bright water.

"It's an omen!" I suddenly blurted out. "They came for us! It must mean we are meant to be friends."

"Yes," she replied, smiling, and her gaze moved from the dolphins to me. "We are indeed, Isaac."

"Wait - how did you know my name?" I asked.

She gestured to my rucksack, which lay on one of the ship's benches, next to the rail. "It's on your name tag," she said simply.

Of course; although for some unaccountable reason I had the strange feeling that she was not telling me the whole truth.

"I see," I said. "But since you appear to have no luggage, and since you have me at a distinct disadvantage, I must insist that you tell me your name."

She laughed, and nodded. "Yes," she said. "That's only fair. Well, Isaac, I'm Rowan. My name is Rowan."

She smiled, a smile as warm and beguiling as that Mediterranean afternoon.

I remember thinking in that singular, blessed moment that this was surely the most perfect day of my life. I was young, I was free. I was in Greece, approaching an island of legendary beauty. And I had just met the prettiest girl in the world, and her name was Rowan.

We conversed easily for the remainder of the trip. She was an artist, she said; I was an engineer. I recounted my biography: born in the United States in 1940, an only child. Transplanted to England at ten when my father, a diplomat, was given a long-term posting there. A boys' grammar school, an engineering degree at Cambridge, then back to the U.S. for graduate work. With the modest income that came from an invention that I had developed and sold during my Masters work, I was, at least for a couple of years, financially independent. And so I had returned to England - where my parents still lived at that time - with the intention of taking time off to travel, and I had no particular date by which I felt the need to cease my wandering and settle down. She listened to all this with interest, occasionally interposing a question about how I had liked this, what was such-and-such place like, and so on.

About her own origins Rowan was coquettishly evasive, turning my questions into a flirtatious game. My normal curiosity was piqued by my inability to decipher her accent.

People are betrayed by their voice. I had something of a talent for distinguishing - and imitating - accents: I could usually correctly place someone at least to their country, and with anyone English I could localize their accent to a specific region or even city. But I found myself at a loss with Rowan. Her English was idiomatically fluent, yet something told me that she had not been born in the British Isles, or at least had spent significant parts of her life elsewhere. There were clear hints of a romance language in the softness with which she uttered her vowels, but in her Rs lay a very occasional trace of Slavic. Finally I gave up trying to figure it out, and asked her outright where she was from.

She smiled flirtatiously. "I couldn't possibly tell you that," she said. "We only just met and I have no idea who you are. You could be an axe murderer or one of those serial killers I'm always reading about in the newspapers. You could end up stalking me and feeding me to a wood chipper." She looked at me with feigned studiousness. "Do you own a wood chipper, Isaac?"

I laughed. "I do not. I'm not even entirely sure I know what one looks like. Do I really look like a serial killer?"

"Oh, you never can tell. I read that serial killers are often highly intelligent and charming."

"I'll take that to mean that you think I'm intelligent and charming. I suppose that's a start."

She glanced at the island, which was looming ever larger in our view as we approached. "Are you a serial killer?" she asked.

"No, I'm not."

"Well of course that's exactly what a serial killer would say." *She paused, then smiled.* "Where do you think I'm from?"

I sighed. "I honestly don't know. I'm normally good at placing accents, but yours has me mystified. I don't think you're English," *I added.*

"You're correct. I'm not."

"But you must have spent a great deal of time there?"

"Yes, I have."

"What's your first language?"

She smiled. "Guess."

"I honestly don't know," *I said, genuinely flummoxed.* "Not French."

"Non, monsieur, je ne suis pas française," *she replied. The French accent was flawless.*

"Not Italian either."

"No, io non sono italiano. Anche se io amo l'Italia." *I'm not Italian, but I love Italy. Again, the accent perfect.*

"Spanish? No."

"No, señor. No soy española tampoco." *Not Spanish either.*

"Portuguese? Greek? Turkish?"

"Não. Ochi. Hayir."

"Good lord - how many languages do you speak?"

"A few." *A Mona Lisa smile.*

"And you have occasional traces of... well, I think Slavic in your accent."

She smiled again and nodded. "Very good - you have a good ear. I've indeed spent much time in eastern Europe."

I sighed. "Okay, I surrender. I am forced to conclude that you're actually a very cleverly disguised Chinese."

She laughed, putting her fingers to the corner of her eyes to make them slanted. "Yes, you're right. I confess."

Laughing with her, I asked, "So, you're not going to tell me?"

"Not just yet. I'll leave you wondering. I've always fancied myself as an international woman of mystery."

"Well you certainly have me mystified. And charmed," *I ventured, knowing that I was openly testing the limits of what I optimistically felt was a developing intimacy.*

"Why thank you, kind sir. I will admit to being rather charmed myself."

I smiled. "Well, if you won't tell me where you're from, at least tell me how old you are."

She feigned shock. "One does not ask a lady her age."

"Apparently I just did."

"Indeed. Well, I am whatever age it pleases you for me to be."

I shook my head and sighed. "Okay, woman of mystery. Have it your way."

We ceased talking for a while, both of us perfectly comfortable in the silence, and enjoying the breeze off the water. Soon the vessel was entering the caldera from the northwest, passing through the narrow channel between Thirasia and the main island of Thira. On our port side, the brilliant whitewashed buildings of the tiny village of Oia clung precariously to the margins of the black and blood-red cliffs high above us.

I turned to Rowan, who smiled warmly; there was a silent acknowledgment of our mutual captivation by the beauty of the island.

"Where are you staying, if I may ask," I enquired.

"Actually, I don't know," she replied. "I haven't arranged anything. I came here rather on a whim."

"Me too," I said.

"Do you suppose we could find two rooms in the same hotel?"

My heart leapt at this suggestion of intimacy, or at least of continued companionship. "I don't know, but I would be delighted to try."

"But it has to be a hotel on the edge of the caldera," she said. "One cannot come to Santorini and not awaken to that view."

I nodded. "I agree. And I must admit that when I boarded this ferry in Piraeus I never imagined that I would make the acquaintance of a woman like you, Miss... I'm sorry, but I don't know your last name."

"Latana," she replied.

"Latana," I repeated. "Hmpf! That's not very Chinese. I'm beginning to think you're a fraud."

"Not true!" she exclaimed with mock offense. "My mother was Chinese, but my father was a Zulu warrior."

We were approaching the dock at the island's little port of Athenias, our journey almost over. "Ah yes," I said, smiling. "Yes, that would explain it."

As we stepped off the old ferry the sight that greeted us was one that had changed little in decades. Standing there on the dock were fifty men of various ages, youthful to ancient. Each one wore a cloth cap of identical design, distinguishable solely by patterns of stains or wear, or the fading that came from long use under a relentless sun. Beneath each cap, a face - every one tanned to a rich brown. These were not men who expended the limited currency of their days indoors.

And next to each man, waiting with a weary patience long learned from servitude, was a donkey. There were no cars, indeed there was no road back then. A long path of steps ascending snakingly up the cliff face was the highway, and the donkeys were the transport. They greeted every ferry, and made the long ascent to the town of Fira twice a day in summer.

I paid the minimal tariff for both us, and Rowan and I mounted two of the beasts, who suffered the accustomed burden in silent acquiescence.

Partway up the path, Rowan's donkey stumbled briefly. His owner evidently viewed this as a transgression to be punished, and struck the animal on its hindquarters with the crop that he had been waving around idly in the air. He shouted something in Greek that sounded like a curse and hit the donkey a second time.

He was raising the crop for a third blow when Rowan turned towards him and beckoned him to come closer. When he did, she spoke to him in Greek, and I could not tell from her tone whether she was upbraiding him for striking the donkey, or conversing about a completely different topic.

To my great surprise, the man took off his cap and bowed to her, then said in broken English, and with genuine contrition, "Yes, Miss. I sorry. He good animal. I no do it again."

Rowan smiled and thanked him, then leaned down and appeared to whisper something to the donkey, who immediately raised his head, swished his tail and picked up his pace.

"What did you say to him?" I asked. I made no attempt to conceal my amazement at what she had seemingly just achieved with both man and beast. "And did you really just say something to that donkey?"

Rowan smiled. "I just explained to him that it was unnecessary to hit the poor creature. And that animals respond better to kindness than discipline."

"And the donkey?"

"Oh, it was just some nonsense to comfort him."

Or was it? As ridiculous as it was, I had the distinct impression that Rowan had not only said something very specific to the beast, but that he had understood her perfectly. I dismissed the irrational thought from my mind.

"I wouldn't want to be a donkey here," I said. "Poor creatures - what a hard life, up and down these cliffs every day in the hot sun."

"Yes," Rowan replied. "The islanders believe that the donkeys contain the souls of the dead who are languishing in purgatory and paying for their sins."

"Really? Remind me to be better behaved in future, just in case."

Rowan spent the rest of the journey chatting amiably with the donkey's owner, whose name was Costas. In response to my query, she told me that her Greek had been acquired some years before and was rather poor, although that was not evident from the seemingly fluid conversation that was taking place next to me.

She paused occasionally to smile at me or to point out something in a view that was becoming increasingly spectacular with each turn in the path.

"Costas says his cousin has a place on the rim in Firostefani a little out of town," she said. "He'll take us there. I've no idea how it is, but the way he describes it makes it sound like the best establishment in Greece."

"Of course it does," I said. "I just hope there's a good view - and no bed bugs."

JACK

In fact, the cousin's hotel - while hardly the luxurious establishment of Costa's description - turned out to more than acceptable. It was a Class B hotel, where for a few dollars a day you received both bed and board, and a private bathroom. The receptionist gave us adjacent rooms that were simple but clean (no bed bugs were evident). Most importantly, both had a small balcony overlooking the sea; the view was breathtaking.

After unpacking, we sat on Rowan's balcony. I opened a bottle of local white wine that we had stopped to buy on the way up; it was made from the ancient assyrtico grape. I poured some into two glasses that we had borrowed from the hotel. They were ancient, mismatched and water-stained, but it didn't matter. We sipped that cold, fragrant wine, fruit of the soil and the sun of Santorini, and submerged ourselves in the unmatched beauty that lay unfurled like a painting below us.

I would not have been anywhere else in the world at that moment, and rather impulsively told Rowan so. She smiled, and said simply, "I agree. I'm glad you're here to share this."

We remained on the balcony until the bottle was drained, talking idly and continuing to gaze, entranced by the magnificent panorama before us.

Finally Rowan said, "Let's go inside. It's a little too bright out here in the sun."

We rose and went into her room. I was not sure where I should sit in the small room, but she motioned for me to join her on the edge of the twin bed.

I sighed.

"Why the sigh?" she asked.

"Oh, it's a good sigh. A very good sigh. You cannot imagine how happy I am right now."

"Yes, I can," she replied, and reached over to take my hand in hers.

I shuddered with the pleasure of her touch, of this unexpected intimacy. It was the first time she had touched me, and I suddenly felt a surge of... of what? Emotion? No - rather it was as if I had, with that touch, been connected to something I had not known existed, but which had been until that moment missing from my life.

Who was this extraordinary girl, this beautiful and mysterious young woman who spoke lord knows how many languages and who could, it seemed, charm donkeys and their irascible Greek owners with equal ease?

"Rowan..." I began.

She put a finger to my lips. "No questions," she said, as if reading my mind. "International woman of mystery, remember?"

"Yes," I protested, "but..." A thought suddenly occurred to me. "O God," I said, "please tell me you're not married?"

She laughed. "Heavens no," she replied. "I'm quite unattached."

She sighed. "Isaac, I'll try to explain at some point, but for now let's just enjoy the moment. Besides," she added, "mystery is the essence of romance."

I raised my eyebrows in surprise. "Is this a romance then?"

"Isaac, look out there," she replied, nodding towards the sea. "We're in a great romance - Santorini is the romance." But she smiled with a coy turn of her head, as if acknowledging the evasion. "Now," she continued, "tell me a story."

"About what?" I asked.

"About anything. Something nice. Just a good story."

"And will you tell me a story in return?"

"Yes," she said. "I will." She was still holding my hand.

"Very well," I said, and drank the little wine that remained in my glass. "Let me think."

She lay back on the bed, her head propped up on her arms. "I'll begin the story for you, shall I?" Without waiting for a response, she said, "Once upon a time, there was a girl on a boat in the middle of a bright blue sea..."

Telling a story with a random beginning is much like boarding a ship with no knowledge of its destination; and so of course I have always loved this leap of literary faith. My father would tell me a story every night when I was a boy, and I always had to supply the first line. Somewhere along the way I picked up the talent myself and our roles reversed: he providing the opening, me spinning the tale. I never knew whether the next one I began would be mediocre, good or - as they sometimes were - enthralling. My father was a kind literary critic and always had a good word for my efforts when the story was done; but I lived for those occasions when he would clap enthusiastically and pronounce "Well done! That was a good one."

If you are fortunate and your mind is suitably engaged, the story unfolds as the tale is told. You find yourself amazed to hear your own voice describing characters who have sprung up, unbidden and from you know not where, and engaging in the most surprising acts.

The girl in the boat is named Elspeth, you say. Why Elspeth? You do not know - the name just appeared in your mind a second before you uttered it, as if it had been there all the time, waiting to be summoned into the light.

You keep talking, with no idea of where your story is headed, yet somehow you keep it going, keep creating new images, new ideas, new twists in the plot. So.

Elspeth is clothed in a blue dress, the exact color of the sea around her. The boat has a mast and a small white sail, and, borne on a wind from the south it moves slowly on, conveying Elspeth to an unknown destination - or perhaps to nowhere at all. A bird flies with the boat, sometimes behind, sometimes making slow circles above the mast. The bird is pure white, with long tail feathers and wings like a scimitar.

Warmed by the sun, Elspeth becomes drowsy, and drifts into a dream; and when she awakens, the sun has gone and the sky is full of stars, stars beyond count. The Milky Way blazes above her, a river of light flung with glorious haphazardness across the sky. It is, she thinks, like diamond dust scattered across the light years.

The white bird still flies above her.

The sea is calm - so calm that the brilliance of the night sky is perfectly reflected in the water. Stars above, stars below. Elspeth feels as if she is no longer in water but adrift in the middle of the universe, and that she could step out of the boat into those stars. Indeed, so entranced is she by this notion that, heedless of her peril, she stands and, as if hypnotized, places her right foot on the gunwhale of her boat. She seems to be about to make the leap into space.

But just as she is about to commit herself irrevocably to this act, Elspeth hears a sound like the distant chiming of tiny bells. The spell broken, she looks up to see a star falling slowly from the great firmament above, leaving behind it a trail of incandescence that glitters faintly and then is swallowed by the blackness of the night.

The star comes ever closer until with a soft splash it falls into the sea a short distance ahead of the boat. The star does not sink, nor fade, and Elspeth steers the boat towards it. As the star comes alongside, she carefully scoops it out of the warm water and holds it before her, gently cupped by her two hands. It pulses and glows within the cage of her fingers.

The white bird alights on the mast, and says to Elspeth, "The star has fallen. You must return it to the sky."

"But how?" asks Elspeth.

"You must climb the mast," answers the bird.

"But the mast is not high enough," Elspeth says. "It cannot reach the sky."

"Have faith," says the bird. "Do you believe in magic?"

"Of course," replies Elspeth. "Magic is real. Everyone knows that. Or they should," she adds.

"Then climb, and believe."

And so, carefully placing the glowing star in the pocket of her frock, Elspeth ascends the mast. As she approaches the top, she wonders how she can possibly reach the sky this way. But then she stops. Closes her eyes. Thinks about magic.

"I believe!" she says.

She opens her eyes, and finds that - magic! - the mast has transformed into a ladder that continues high above her, so high that she cannot see the top. It is a ladder without end, she thinks. A ladder to the stars.

And up, up, up Elspeth climbs. The star glows in her pocket, and now far below her a dolphin leaping from the water sees the silhouette of a little girl climbing into the sky.

It is a long journey, for the sky is very far, but she does not stop. She climbs ever upward until, looking down, she can see the curve of the Earth below her, and the outline of islands in the faint first light of dawn.

Finally, as the sun's rim breaks the distant horizon to begin a new day, and just before the stars begin to fade, Elspeth reaches the top of the ladder. She takes the star from her pocket; and as she fixes it to the sky, there is a sound like the ringing of every bell in the whole world.

"You're welcome," Elspeth says to the sky.

And with that, on an impulse, she casts herself off the ladder into the universe, and finds herself falling, falling, falling... And then suddenly, magically, flying, effortlessly descending through the air in an exhilaration of movement, with the white bird at her side. Falling, falling into drowsiness and dreams...

She awakens in her bed with sunlight streaming into her room and her mother calling her to come to eat. "Oh my," says Elspeth as she stretches and yawns. "That was a wonderful dream."

Just then her mother enters her room. "Come on, Elspeth," she says, "Your breakfast will be getting cold." Her mother gazes down at the bed, her eye caught by something she sees there. "Where did that come from?" she asks.

Elspeth turns her head and looks where her mother is pointing.

And there, on the pillow next to her, is a beautiful feather from a white bird.

When I finished, I looked at Rowan to see if my impromptu tale had met with her approval.

"I hope you liked it," I said simply, and rather sheepishly. The story seemed silly now.

In response, she gently pulled me down next to her, then raised herself onto one elbow and gazed down at me, shaking her head and smiling. A single tear rolled down her cheek; I had, incredibly, moved her.

"It was a beautiful, beautiful story," she said. "A gift. Thank you."

For no reason I could have articulated, I suddenly felt - somehow *knew* - that my whole life hung upon that moment.

"Rowan -" I said, though in truth I had no idea what I was about to say.

"Shh," she said softly. And then her hand was in my hair, and she leaned down, paused for a second to smile, and pressed her mouth to mine.

Never to be forgotten, that first kiss, magnificent and vertiginous. More than anything, it felt like falling. I felt as if I were swooping down in air like Elspeth, free of fear and gravity. Down, down, long and far into an other-world of passion... passion undreampt-of, new-found and explosive, bursting as if upon unbruised lips, the kiss long and lingering and ripe with the honeyed taste of endless summer.

When it finally ended, I was shaking with the thrill of it.

She smiled and stroked my hair. "Are you okay?" she asked. I was moved by the genuine tenderness with which she posed this question.

I closed my eyes, the taste of her mouth still fresh on my senses. After a long moment I said, "I am a bell."

She cocked her head to one side quizzically. "A bell?"

"It's a line from a writer I love. 'I had been my whole life a bell, and never knew it until that moment I was lifted and struck.' That's how that kiss made me feel." I shook my head in disbelief at the intensity of what I had just experienced.

Rowan nodded slowly. "O my," she said finally, and nestled against me, her head on my shoulder. "That is indeed a beautiful analogy." She stroked my hair, then said, "Then I must be a bell too."

I kissed her on the forehead and shook my head again. "My God," I said. "Where did you come from? What great good did I do in a past life to deserve meeting you?"

She smiled. "You may find it was something you did in this life," she said, rather mysteriously.

"In this one? What would that be?"

In answer, she said nothing, but smiled and kissed me again. The kiss slow at first, then deeper and insistent, then frenzied. And suddenly we were undressing each other, our hands greedy with discovery as clothing was removed and discarded, our mouths devouring, trying to slake an urgent, unquenchable desire.

I mounted her, and she cried out as I entered her body, clutching my hair and pulling my face to within an inch of hers as I slid into her as far as I could. I wanted to lose myself in her. There was a sharp intake of breath from both pairs of lungs at the same moment, and we froze for a second, staring into each other's eyes with an intensity and a passion that was at that moment utterly focused, utterly undiluted.

Then she kissed me again, roughly, almost harshly, and said, breathlessly and with the delicious openness of a willing surrender, "Isaac, I'm yours."

The next day we rose late, unwilling to relinquish the warmth of the embrace in which we had slept for the better part of the night. Eventually Rowan managed to quit the bed and, still naked, wandered sleepily to the balcony to greet the morning. I joined her a moment later after slipping on a pair of shorts; I was rather more modest - or perhaps fearful.

I walked out to see her with her arms stretched wide, as if trying to enfold the whole of the caldera into her embrace. The view was magnificent, the water sparkling under a sun that was slowly ascending into a cloudless blue sky. I slid my arms around her belly and held her tightly, kissing her neck.

"Good morning, Miss Latana. If you're not careful you'll get arrested."

She placed her hands over mine and I could feel her smile. "I don't care. There are few places in the world I'd rather be imprisoned."

We remained silent for a while, taking in the incomparable beauty of the island view. Pressed against her naked body, I was already aroused again, and wondered whether I could persuade her to come back to bed.

She turned, held my face in her hands, and kissed me. "I'm afraid you'll have to wait awhile. I'm hungry."

I frowned. "You knew what I was thinking?"

She laughed. "Of course. It's not difficult to read the minds of men. Besides," she added, running the tips of her fingers teasingly across the front of my shorts, "I could feel your... interest."

"Very well," I sighed. "But you should know that I plan on taking you to bed for a good part of the day."

"Hmm," she replied, her index finger slowly tracing the outline of my lips. "Well, I might be amenable to such an arrangement. If you're a good boy. Now let's go and eat."

We dressed quickly, she in a white summer dress imprinted with a pattern of forget-me-nots and yellow roses. I had honestly never seen a prettier girl in all my life.

On the way to the terrace where the hotel served meals, we enquired at the reception if we could cancel our two single rooms and be moved to a double. The middle-aged woman behind the desk exhibited no surprise as she effected the change, and commented only with a frown. Romances apparently bloomed easily in the intoxicating atmosphere of this most beautiful of islands, but she clearly disapproved of our salacious liaison. Greece at that time remained a culture rooted in traditional morality, and while this conservatism was slowly being eroded by a promiscuous wave of 1960's western youth, it would be a good decade or more before it finally succumbed. Indeed, outside the islands and mainland areas where tourists now swarm, it never has.

Breakfast was a simple affair: fresh bread, thick yoghurt, olives, sliced tomatoes and a rather salty local cheese. There was fruit juice, and the powered caffeinated beverage which had been marketed so successfully in the country that Nescafe had entered the Greek language as the word for instant coffee. The view was predictably spectacular.

Afterwards, we walked arm in arm down into the main town and poked around the little shops. After an hour of this idle wandering we stopped at a small café at the edge of the cliff and ordered two Greek coffees. They came, as all beverages did in Greece, with a plate of mezze: some olives and almonds, small rectangles of bread with a little feta cheese, and a couple of Saloniki peppers. The quantity of this food was not trivial; indeed, for the minimal price of a drink in those days, you could eat for free.

We sipped the coffee and picked at the mezze, gazing out across the turquoise water to the uninhabited island in the center of the sunken caldera. I asked Rowan if she knew whether it was volcanic in origin.

"Oh, all of Santorini is volcanic," she replied. "But yes, that is the center of the new activity. It's called Nea Kameni - the name means 'new burnt'. There was some Roman historian - I forget his name - who described its first appearance sometime in the first century."

"I suppose this is a dangerous place to be in the long run."

"Yes, though it's been a long time since the catastrophic eruption that's supposed to have destroyed Minoan civilization on Crete."

"You're remarkably well informed. Though I suppose you could be just making all this stuff up."

She laughed. "I'm not," she said. "I'm horribly honest even when it's perhaps not such a good idea. And I read a lot."

"So, honest woman, tell me about yourself."

Her face instantly took on a serious look, and she took my hand in both of hers. "Isaac, I can't. Not right now. Please trust me and don't ask questions yet. I'll explain when I know you better, but I have my reasons for... for not telling you certain things."

She saw my frown, and added, "Don't worry - it's nothing bad. I'm not a serial killer fleeing from justice or anything like that. But I need you to trust me and just let it go for now, if you can do that. Please."

This last word was uttered in such a sweetly imploring tone that I found myself moved. I could not imagine why Rowan was hiding behind all this mystery; but on this brilliant Greek morning, a few hours after making love with this enchanting young woman, I decided I could afford to be patient.

"Okay," I said. "No questions, I promise."

"Thank you. Now," she added, "I am remiss."

"How so?"

"I promised you a story last night."

"Yes. Yes, you did."

I knew that this was an attempt on her part to change the subject, but I didn't mind. "I have a rather large supply of stories. My family specializes in them." I was about to ask about her family, but caught myself. No questions.

"Well," I said, "I can think of nothing better in the world at this moment than to sit here looking out at all this ridiculous beauty, and hear you tell me a story."

Rowan smiled. "Good. Now, give me a subject."

I considered. "The Sea," I said, simply.

She nodded, and looked down at the water below us. "What do you see there, Isaac?" she asked, pointing to the bay beneath us.

"Waves," I said, simply.

"Yes," she said. "Waves unending. Now I want you to imagine a coastline," she began. "Not this one - a shore somewhere on the very edge of the Atlantic Ocean."

I thought for a moment. "Okay... I'm on the coast of Cornwall in England, say somewhere near Lands End. Will that do?"

"Yes," she said, nodding. "That's an excellent choice. A perfect choice."

She took a deep breath, and closed her eyes. There was a pause, as if she was preparing herself, or somehow entering a different state. Finally she spoke, and the change in tone was astonishing. Her voice took on a richness, an almost hypnotic quality.

"It is a bright day," she began. "The sun is shining, but the wind is high. Very high. It rises with every hour. A gale is sweeping in from the Atlantic, raging at the high cliffs on which you sit. The great westerly wind... It ransacks the trees, sends waves rippling wildly through the cornfields. Tonight this gale will peak - mercilessly it will assault the land, driving stars and light of moon before its face, and heaven will shake with the fury of it.

"But now... now you are sitting in the sunlight on the edge of the cliff, buffeted by the wind. It is fresh and clean, and it carries within it the scent and the taste of salt. Next to you are clusters of sea pinks - they are brave little flowers, tossed as they are this way and that. Above you seabirds wheel and whirl in the anarchy of the sky, their cries borne upon the wind. For what do they call? For danger? For sorrow? For the racing exhilaration of flight on such a day of madness as this? You do not know.

"Below you, a huge wave crashes into the rocks. It rolls in from the sea, then suddenly arcs and curls, rearing up like a great tiger. It flings itself with massive force against the hard land. As it strikes, the wave detonates: tons of water split and shatter, rising up, up, up in a glorious eruption that ascends the cliff face, reaching halfway up the obdurate rock. It peaks... hangs for less than a second... then falls back to once again become one with the raging sea.

"It all happened in one brief, explosive instant and then was done. And yet, and yet..."

She stops to drink some water. At this pause, I suddenly find to my surprise that I am perched on the edge of my seat. I am transfixed. It is not just the remarkable beauty of the language she uses, which is lyrical and cut from whole cloth as if she were reciting a text long prepared instead of weaving a story from nothing. It is the sound of that voice. It was made for storytelling, like no other I have known before or since. Remarkably, I felt as if I was in the story: the world could have dissolved around me while she was speaking, and I doubt that I would have noticed.

She saw my expression of rapt concentration, and smiled. I guessed that she was used to this sort of reaction.

"And yet..." she repeated.

"And yet this violent meeting of land and sea is merely the very end of a story, the last moment of a great journey that began far away, three thousand miles across a boundless ocean.

"There, where the sea touches the verdant margins of another continent, another world than this, there a wave was born. Born of wind, child of a storm in latitudes remote from these northern climes, the wave was despatched to take aim at a distant shore. Growing stronger as it gathered speed, the wave rolled on. Soon it left behind the shallow waters of the continental shelf, as the seafloor below it plunged into the void.

Ever northwest the wave rolled, high above the limitless abyssal plain and the darkness of the deep ocean.

"It began in warmth, in tropical water replete with painted fish. But the wave cooled as it moved north. Colors flashed upon it and within. Green with depth, blue from the sky, and sometimes the gray reflection of leaden cloud that heralded an impending storm.

"On the wave rolled, sweeping through schools of flying fish bursting in bright colors from its surface like faery children. Dolphins surfed gleefully down its face, and the wingtips of seabirds sliced into its crown. When the sun set, starlight fell upon its waters, and one night a golden path was painted upon it in rippling moonglede.

"Halfway through its journey, for one night, the wave echoed with the songs of whales.

"Three thousand miles, on and on. Over seamounts rising from the deeps, over lightless valleys far below in which no bird would ever sing.

"And as the wayfaring wave at last surges across those last few miles and flings itself with all its might into the land, so it ascends the cliff on which you sit on that bright autumn day, and a little of the spray is borne higher upon the wind and is cast gently into your face. You feel the sharp taste of salt, and the brief, refreshing chill of the cold water as it strikes the warmth of your living cheek.

"And in that moment you become, for just one fleeting second, a part of that history, of that long journey. There on that windswept clifftop, you are conjoined to that far-off land, marked by a watery world, and anointed with the blessing of a vast and restless sea."

The story had been quite short, but during the few minutes in which Rowan spoke I had been transported to another place. For much of the tale my eyes had been closed, and in my mind I had seen, vividly, the images of the wave that she had conjured. Indeed, so adept was her voice at immersing the listener in her story that I could have sworn I had felt the spray in my face as the wave ended its journey and broke upon the rocks below.

My eyes remained closed for a few seconds after she finished speaking; then I opened them to see her smiling. I leaned forward and took her face in my two hands, and kissed her lips.

I shook my head in wonder. "How did you do that?" I asked. "I saw everything so clearly as you were speaking. It was as if..." I searched for the right words. "As if the story was happening inside my head."

She smiled again. "You're a good listener - a receptive listener. Not everyone is. But I learned to tell stories from my mother, who learned from her mother, and so on. It's an old tradition in our family."

"Well thank you," I said. "I almost feel like I should pay you for that experience."

"Oh, my stories are free," laughed Rowan. "But you can buy me this coffee if you like."

She stretched, and turned to once again take in the view. The sun was high now, and Santorini was beginning to bake in the noon heat.

She took my hand. "It's hot," she said simply. "Too hot to be outside. Besides," she added, "you promised to take me back to bed."

Interlude: A Guessing Game

It was quite late when Isaac put down the manuscript. Like Rowan, he stretched, and rubbed his eyes.

Outside, the moon had risen full and yellow above the lake.

"Well, Jack, I think that's all I have the energy for this evening. I hope I haven't bored you."

On the contrary, I'm really enjoying the story. Maybe too much - I'm not sure it will be easy to go to sleep tonight with all this mystery about Rowan swirling around in my head.

"Yes well, I'm afraid you'll have to wait to find out about her - as I did. We can continue tomorrow if you want."

I know - she's a spy.

"No, she's not."

A hired assassin?

"That's more or less the same thing. And no."

She's running from a jilted lover who wants to kidnap her.

"Again - no. And you can guess all you want, but you're going to have to wait to find out."

Hmph. I lay down with my front paws together and my head on them, the way dogs do when they're trying to look long-suffering. For maximum effect, we stare poignantly up at our human.

But Isaac is having none of it. "Is that well-practiced pathetic look supposed to make me change my mind?" he asks.

I lift up my head. *O have it your way. But I think I deserve some more liver for putting up with you.*

Isaac shakes his head. "Nope - we're all out. I'm afraid it's just not your night."

JACK

That Bitch Again

The following morning Isaac is up before me. I think about leaving the bed, but the truth is I was out hunting rats until late and could use a little more sleep. I hear Isaac busying himself in the kitchen: the kettle boils noisily - he's making tea - and there is the sound of a plate being pulled from a stack in one of the cabinets. A little while later, the toaster pops up; apparently he's having a bagel for breakfast.

I continue to lay in the absurdly soft and comfortable king-sized bed, wondering what the day will bring.

I don't have to wait long for the answer.

I hear the back door being opened, and Isaac saying, "Well hello there!" I wonder whether one of our neighbors has come round to borrow a cup of sugar - isn't that what human neighbors do? I decide it's unlikely. Isaac's nearest neighbor lives a few hundred yards down the shore, and it's awfully early for someone to visit unannounced.

A short while later, Isaac comes into the bedroom.

"Jack, you might want to rouse yourself. There's someone here to see you."

Rachel!

I leap off the bed and scurry to the back door. She's sitting patiently on the step, looking around.

"*Don't tell me you were still in bed?*" she asks with more than a hint of contempt.

I didn't sleep a lot last night. I was out hunting.

"*Hunting? What for? You have a human to feed you.*"

I'm feeling slightly defensive. *Yes,* I say, *but one can hunt for pleasure.*

"*Oh, one can, can one?*"

Yes. If you must know, I was out hunting for food for you.

Rachel doesn't seem particularly impressed. "*Really? And did you catch anything?*"

Yes, I did. I slip past her and retrieve a rat from a spot under the house. I drop it in front of her.

She sniffs it and turns it over onto its back with her paw. "*It's very small.*"

There's a saying that dogs have which is remarkably like the human expression about a bird in the hand being worth two in the bush. It's perfectly relevant here, so I decide to remind Rachel of this in an effort to underscore the depth of my largesse in provisioning her.

A rat in the paw is better than a cat in a tree.

"*Yes, and beef liver in a bowl is better than either. I know you have some - I can smell it on your breath.*" She was salivating; as I said before, beef liver is the ultimate treat for pretty much any dog.

Well I'm afraid I ate the last of it yesterday. I say this with some small sense of satisfaction - screw her if she doesn't want my rat.

"You mean you ate it all and didn't save any for me?"

Well, yes, but -

"That's very inconsiderate of you," she interrupts.

How was I supposed to know you'd come over here this morning?

"Because you invited me yesterday. Do you have a memory problem or something?"

You're impossible.

"I know, Jock."

It's Jack.

"I know."

You know?

"Yes."

Then why do you keep calling me Jock?

"Because I like messing with you."

She wags her tail. *"Thank you for thinking of me, Jack. It's a very nice rat. Now can we please go inside and eat some canned dog food?"*

Breakfast

We enter the house; Isaac is still in the kitchen.

"So this is your human? He seems very nice."

Actually no. My human is back in Seattle. But this is my best friend. His name is Isaac.

"How come he has you here?"

It's a long story involving... well, a psychic, a cat and a television crew.

Rachel is pondering this and I can tell she is about to ask what on earth I'm talking about, when Isaac looks over at us and smiles. "Hello," he says. "You must be Rachel."

Rachel turns and gives me a confused look. *"How did he know my name?"*

I told him.

"You told *him?"*

Yeah.

"Wait - you talk *to this guy?"*

Yep.

"You're joking, right?"

Nope.

"How can you talk to humans?"

I dunno. I just can. Well, not all humans - just this one.

Rachel looks very skeptical, so I decide to provide a demonstration.
Tell me something - anything. What's your favorite color?
"My favorite what?"
Oh, that's right - never mind. I always forget that other dogs see in only black and white. *Okay, tell me something else... besides beef liver, what's your favorite food?*

Rachel considers. "I don't know - I guess marrow bones. Why are you asking these stupid questions, anyway?"

I turn to Isaac. *Do we have any marrow bones? Rachel likes them.*

"No, Jack, I'm afraid we don't have marrow bones. But I can go to the store and get some later." Rachel's mouth literally drops open, something I've never seen in a dog.

"You have GOT to be kidding me!"
Au contraire, ma cherie.
"What's that?"
It's French.
"What's French?"
Never mind.
"Do it again. Tell him... I don't know... tell him he has nice eyes." I relay this to Isaac.

"Thank you Rachel. You have very nice eyes too."

"Holy crap! You CAN talk to him!"

I am now enjoying this immensely. But then I remember that Rachel must be hungry.

So, would you like some breakfast? I ask.

"Yes - yes, that would be nice. Thank you. I still can't get over this. It's amazing."

I ask Isaac to open some dog food and he takes a can from the cupboard. "Beef stew okay?" he enquires. Rachel says that sounds great, and I duly relay her answer. Isaac spoons out half the can into a bowl and sets it down on the floor. Rachel devours it like she hasn't eaten in a week.

"Oh my," says Isaac. "You *were* hungry, weren't you?"

I explain Rachel's situation to Isaac - at least as much of it as I know, which I realize isn't very much at all.

That she lives wild in the woods, and that her human is a little girl who lives with a man Rachel hates.

"I'm sorry to hear that," Isaac says, as he empties the rest of the can into the bowl. Rachel could clearly eat more, and she does.

When she has finished, Isaac asks, "What's so bad about him? Is he the girl's father?"

Rachel sighs and looks up at Isaac, then turns to me. *"That,"* she says, *"is also a long story. Though it doesn't involve - what was it again? - a psychic, a cat or a television crew."*

Etymology

Meiosis, (n.) A specialized type of cell division that reduces the chromosome number by half. The process occurs in all sexually reproducing single-celled and multicellular eukaryotes, including animals, plants, and fungi. From Greek *meiosis* "a lessening," from *meioun* "to lessen," from *meion* "less," from root *mei-* (2) "small". First use in this sense 1905.

Moron, (n.) 1910, medical Latin, from Greek *moron,* neuter of *moros* "foolish, dull, sluggish, stupid," probably cognate with Sanskrit *murah* "idiotic." Latin *morus* "foolish" is a loan-word from Greek. Adopted by the American Association for the Study of the Feeble-minded with a technical definition "adult with a mental age between 8 and 12"; used as an insult since 1922 and subsequently dropped from technical use.

Moron

DNA recombination is a funny thing. It is life's first and ultimate roll of the dice. One which determines, from the conceptual outset, whether the resulting offspring will be magician or madman, monster or mediocrity. One shuffling of the parental genes gets you Beethoven, another delivers Hitler... or, most of the time, something much less memorable in between.

As his name would suggest, the waste of space and natural resources that was Salvatore Kaufman sprang from Sicilian stock on his mother's side and German on his father's. The miracle of genetics at conception could have produced the best of both ethnicities, the romance and culture of Renaissance Italy commingled with the work ethic of the Prussian.

But no. The genetic dice rolled another way, and that fateful meeting of sperm and egg delivered instead a man whose personality was in large part defined by Mediterranean laziness and a distinctly Teutonic brutality. Had Sal Kaufman been disgorged from his mother's birth canal in Sicily, he would have grown up to become a low-ranking mobster, the uneducated thug dispatched by his boss to beat protection money out of old ladies and shopkeepers. In Germany, in another age, his destiny might well have seen him clothed in the uniform of the SS.

My own opinion of this disgusting specimen of humankind is formed later, after I've had the displeasure of meeting him. But on this sunny morning at Isaac's cabin, Rachel describes the basics of why she would not - as she puts it so eloquently - pee on him if he were on fire.

She tells us about Alice, who is eleven years old. It's a tragic story: her parents died in a car crash six months ago, and unfortunately a court appointed as her guardian her only living relative, Sal Kaufman. Remarkably, there were no kindly grandparents or good-hearted aunts and uncles to take Alice in. So - thanks to a legal system that invariably gives preferences in such matters to blood relatives, no matter how unfit - instead she got stuck with a redneck cousin with missing teeth and a fifth-grade education.

Rachel had been Alice's dog when her parents were alive, but things went badly with Sal pretty much from the beginning. Sal made it clear he didn't much care for dogs, and when Rachel barked at him the first time he yelled at Alice, he reacted by hitting her. Alice had never liked her cousin - indeed, until her parents died, she'd only ever seen him twice - and his abuse of Rachel planted in her a seed of resentment which quickly blossomed into the dark flowers of a bitter hatred.

A month later, when Sal made it clear one day that he was going to punish Alice for "being sassy" by spanking her, Rachel planted herself squarely between the two of them and growled menacingly. That was too much for the redneck, who swore profusely at both girl and dog, then retrieved a baseball bat and announced that he was going to "enjoy beating that fucking dog to death". Alice screamed, ran to the front door and threw it open, then bodily pushed Rachel out and told her to run. Which she did, reluctantly, disappearing into the woods with Sal Kaufman's curses and threats polluting the air in her wake.

Since then, Rachel has lived in the woods. She returns to the house whenever she can, when she knows Kaufman is not there; otherwise, she and Alice have clandestine meetings in the woods or on a beach that they both frequent. Alice sneaks food to her whenever she can; otherwise, Rachel survives on the strength of her wits and her remarkable athletic ability.

It's worth noting in passing that while every dog on the planet dreams of catching squirrels - and never gives up the hope of doing so even into old age - most never succeed even once. It takes smarts and speed to actually apprehend one of these bushy-tailed little hors d'oeuvres. But Rachel nails them with impressive regularity.

Isaac takes all this in as Rachel tells her tale through me. He sits attentively in an armchair, his hands pressed together beneath his chin. When she has finished, he looks sad, and I detect anger in the face of this normally light-hearted, pacific old man.

"Well, Rachel, I wish we could do something. But it sounds from what you're saying that his treatment of Alice doesn't quite rise to the level that would justify a call to Social Services - you know, the government department that investigates child abuse."

He ponders for awhile. "It's clear that you can't keep living in the woods though. It's fine now, in summer, but you won't survive once the weather turns colder. They get a lot of snow out here."

Rachel says that she won't abandon Alice, that she has to stay to keep an eye on her and protect her if Kaufman's abuse reaches a point where she's in genuine danger.

"Are you sure?" asks Isaac. "You could come and live with me in Seattle. We could check up on her from time to time. Maybe we could get her a cell phone that she could use to contact me."

No, Rachel replies, she won't leave Alice on her own here.

"Well then, at the very least you should stay here at the house for now, while Jack and I are here. And I'll try to fix up a kennel or something outside that you can use when we leave."

What about food? I ask.

"I can manage," Rachel says. I repeat this statement for Isaac's benefit.

"I'm sure you can," says Isaac. "But we should figure out some way for you to be fed so you don't have to go decimating the local squirrel population."

Rachel finds this amusing. *"Trust me, there's no way I can make a dent in that. There are a gabillion squirrels in these woods. I could hunt them from now until this time next year and the place would still be crawling with them."*

Isaac thinks some more, and then smiles. "I think I have the perfect solution," he says. "Can you arrange for Alice to come down here today or tomorrow?"

Rachel says she'll try, and I ask what he has in mind.

"Easy. We'll buy a lot of dog food and I'll leave her the spare key so she can feed Rachel here. They can use the house as a meeting place - and of course as shelter for Rachel."

I am so overwhelmed with the kindness of my friend that I suddenly leap into his lap and lick his face all over. He laughs under this emotional onslaught, and pretends to protest.

Rachel too wags her tail and presses her face against Isaac's leg. Isaac pets us both, and I sense Rachel's pleasure at his touch. And I suddenly realize that she must be lonely much of the time. In the end, dogs need humans as much as humans need dogs.

Well, *some* humans, anyway.

Boating for Beginners

Rachel spends the morning with us, then goes off to check on Alice. She returns a couple of hours later to say that Alice is okay, and that Kaufman is out hunting squirrels - or anything else he can find. Rachel is disgusted by the fact that he kills for pleasure rather than food, and frequently discards the animals whose lives he cuts short with such casual brutality.

"At least when I kill a squirrel, it's put to good use," she says.

We spend the rest of the afternoon together. Isaac pushes out the row boat and we drift around on the lake for an hour or so.

Boating is a new experience for Rachel, and she's not sure what to think of it. She's ungainly at first, tripping and galumphing about, and upsetting the balance of the small craft with her frenetic, uncoordinated movements from side to side. But eventually she gets the hang of it, and settles in a spot on the bow, where she perches regally like a figurehead as we glide over the smooth water.

She's a good swimmer, and we have fun in the water together, racing each other to see who can be the first to reach a stick that Isaac dutifully throws for us over and over again. Usually she wins.

You cheated, I say after she gets there first yet again. *You splashed so much I couldn't see at the start.*

"You're just slow," she replies. "No wonder you can't catch squirrels."

I think about bringing up The Squirrel Incident in response, but on second thought I decide that it probably wouldn't do much for my reputation.

Finally we head in to shore and dry off on the deck in the hot sun. At around five o'clock, after being fed, Rachel heads out again to check on her young charge.

Are you coming back tonight?

"I'm not sure," she replies. "It will depend on what's happening at the house."

I hope you do. You can sleep with me.

"Don't flatter yourself," she replies, and disappears down the path into the woods.

Rachel does not return for the night, and I find myself worrying about her.

"Oh I wouldn't worry, Jack." She's survived very well so far, and she's a clever dog. She'll be okay." We are in the living room, and Isaac is having his usual evening cup of tea. "Would you like me to distract you by reading to you some more?" he asks.

Yes please. With Rachel around during the day, I had almost forgotten my curiosity regarding the Rowan story. *Is this where you tell me what's going on, finally?*

"Maybe," he says with a smile. "Let's find out, shall we?"

Love

We remained on Santorini for a week, lost in each other and oblivious to all else. We walked the high cliffs hand in hand, inhaling deeply of the crisp sea air. We swam in a turquoise sea, and made love on deserted beaches of black volcanic sand. I will confess I did so warily lest we were discovered in the midst of our coupling; but Rowan never seemed to worry, and gave herself always to me with an incautious abandon that I envied.

One day we rented bicycles and visited the inland villages, eating a simple lunch in a tiny café under the curious eyes of old men with weathered faces, and older women swathed in the black of perpetual mourning.

Everywhere we went Rowan engaged strangers with an effortless charm, and I rode happily in her wake. And always there were stories. I tried as well as I could to entertain her, weaving tales from the foundational thread of the first line she always provided; and for her part she was a gracious listener, and through her eyes or her kisses always showed a genuine appreciation for my efforts. But I could never match her skill at this art.

There were tales of the land: the mountains, the rivers, the woods. Especially the woods. Tales of reality and tales of magic. Nature was often a character in her stories: the trees were the keepers of history, the wind had a voice, even the clouds looked down upon the world below and stored what they saw in droplets of rain that fell and nourished the earth with stories.

Listening to her, as with her first story of the wave, I was always captivated, and behind closed eyes my mind would submerge into the details, as if I myself were a part of the tale.

And with each story-telling, I fell ever more ineluctably under her spell.

I think it is true that I had been in love with Rowan from the first time she spoke to me on that ferry, framed as the moment was in the glorious beauty of the island and the Sea. I was not aware of it then, but as the days passed under that Greek sun the depth of my feeling for her became increasingly obvious to me.

And one evening, as we sat together on the terrace of the hotel watching the full moon rise over Nea Kameni, her head on my shoulder and my hand in hers, I knew – with more certainty than I had ever known anything - that I loved her. Would always love her.

I stroked her hair and looked into those green eyes. "Rowan," I began.

She smiled, and kissed me. "Yes," she said, nodding. "I know. I love you too."

When did I know? When did my heart first begin to suspect the truth about the lovely mystery that was Rowan?

It was not simply the secrecy, the insistence that I ask no questions about her life or her past. Every day I discovered in her some new thing, some new gift or act or memory that collectively betrayed a depth of learning and experience that could not possibly, I thought, be possessed by one so young. Not that I knew her age, for even that she would not reveal.

Or her nationality. At one point I briefly considered snooping through her belongings for some clue to her origins; but I knew that this would be a terrible betrayal, and with difficulty resisted the urge to do so. But it was true that I had never seen any identity document; as far as I could tell, this woman - whose many travels had obviously taken her across Europe and perhaps beyond - did not possess a passport. I assumed it must be stored elsewhere.

She was fluent in several languages, as I have said. She had a familiarity with the geography of Europe that went far beyond what could be learned in books, or by endless poring over maps; in her stories she described the smallest details of woods, of streams, of villages, of people, with the certainty of someone who had, surely, been there. And the breadth of her knowledge of history and of ethnography was that of someone who had studied these subjects over many years. Indeed, there seemed no topic on which she could not contribute some interesting fact.

Either she was the wisest, most gifted young woman I had ever known, or... or what? I could think of no alternative explanation. Perhaps she was a savant.

But even savants cannot read minds, and I was beginning to believe that, at least at times, Rowan could read mine. This was ridiculous, I knew; yet there were regular instances when she anticipated what I was about to say, or articulated a thought that had entered my mind ten seconds before, or answered a question I had not yet asked.

I had been about to tell her that I loved her.

"Yes," she had said. "I know. I love you too."

And so I was increasingly mystified. But my journey to the truth, the extraordinary, impossible truth: that began some time later, far away, in the silence of a wood.

England

After a week, we returned to Athens. There, I found waiting for me a telegram from my father. It had been delivered two days before, and conveyed the sad news of the sudden death of a university friend. He had been killed in a car accident in London. The funeral was in three days.

I turned sadly to tell Rowan, whose face reflected concern. "What is it, Isaac?" she asked.

"A friend of mine died. I must return to England."

She hugged me tightly and kissed me on the lips. "I'm so sorry. How did he die?"

I told her the details – the little I knew. I sighed. "God, I hate to leave you."

She ran her fingers across my cheek. "You don't have to. I'll come if you want me to." My face must have lit up, because she smiled.

"Really?" I said. "You'll come to England?"

"Yes," she replied. "Except I'll have to come separately, a little later. I have something I must do here first." I knew better than to ask what. Besides, I was so happy that she would join me that I had no desire to risk ruining the moment with a poorly timed question.

I left the following morning on a British European Airways flight to London. I offered to buy Rowan a ticket; she thanked me but said it was unnecessary.

"Well at least get word to me on when you're arriving. I can meet you at the airport. I mean, are you going to fly?"

"I'm not sure," she replied. "Just give me your address, and I'll let you know when I'm arriving." We took a bus to the old airport at Glyfada, where after checking in I held her for a long time.

"Goodbye, my love," she said, finally. "Keep close." A lovely expression.

Somehow I managed to tear myself away from her to board the flight, turning at the last moment to see her smiling and blowing me a kiss. And then I was on the plane, wishing I wasn't, and we were on our way.

The old De Havilland Comet landed at Gatwick at noon. Predictably, it was raining; English weather has an ability to deflate even the most optimistic spirit, and suddenly all the joy of Greece evaporated and left me in a dark mood.

After clearing Customs, I telephoned my father to tell him that I would be arriving on the afternoon train. He met me at the small rural railway station which served a collection of villages on the South Downs. It was part of the legacy of a golden age of rail travel, before motorways had desecrated the landscape of England; British Rail made periodic attempts to close the station, a threat that was always met with fierce resistance from local residents, and – at least to date – had been successfully rebuffed with the help of their prominent Member of Parliament.

I stepped off the train and saw my father waving from down the platform. No railway staff were in evidence.

We drove to the house in the old Austin Morris that he insisted on keeping despite repeated protests from my mother. He described the old car as 'reliable'; citing its many breakdowns, she disagreed and yearned for something more modern. There was always a hint of the society girl in my mother, as practical and down to earth as she was in her daily life; had she been allowed to, I suspect she would have gone out and bought herself a sports car.

My father filled me in on the details of my friend's tragic death. Then, in an attempt to switch the conversation to a more cheerful topic, he asked how I was enjoying Greece. I told him how happy I was there. I described my little flat in Athens, the beauty of the light, the culture, the food, the people. I discoursed at length on the volcanic miracle that was Santorini.

I talked of everything, in fact, except Rowan.

As we drove up to the house, I pondered this silently. Why was I afraid to tell my parents about her? Part of me was bursting to confess that I was in love, and with an extraordinary woman – indeed, one I knew would impress my father, which was not an easy thing to do. But I withheld this major development in my life. The mystery surrounding Rowan left me discomfited, and deep down I wondered whether I should worry that she would not fulfill her promise and come to England after all. And I realized with rising panic that I had no way to contact her, or find her should she disappear; there was no address, no phone number. If she chose to, she could become a ghost.

Three days later, my anxiety had deepened. Still I had received no word from her, no indication that she was on her way. My parents noticed the change in my mood and enquired if everything was alright; I lied and said that I had been affected by the death of my friend. And by the funeral, which had indeed been a dismal affair of poorly sung hymns and unnecessarily suppressed grief.

But then – joy! – Friday brought a telegram from Rowan informing me that she would arrive in London the following day, and would I meet her?

I borrowed the car from my father, and excitedly told my parents that I was going to pick up a friend – a female friend – and that I was eager for them to meet her. I told them nothing about her, not even her name; they would just have to wait to see. Pleased by the sudden lifting of my mood, they resisted the urge to enquire further.

I left early to ensure I was not late, and despite this was driven to near-madness by the crawling traffic on the M25 motorway that skirted the west of London. But finally I arrived at Heathrow. I was early – she had told me she would be standing outside the Arrivals hall at 1 pm, and it was well before that – yet there she was at the kerb. I honked and pulled over, and virtually leapt out of the car. In my haste to greet her I almost knocked over a small child, and received an irate look from the child's mother as I mumbled a hasty apology.

And then she was in my arms, warm and real and there, with me. And suddenly nothing else mattered.

Interlude

Isaac yawned. "I think that's all you get for tonight," he said.

What? But we didn't find out about Rowan! You promised we would!

"I promised no such thing," he said. "I said we'll see... and we have duly seen." He grinned.

You have to tell me! Here I am, wide awake and worrying about my girlfriend –

"She's your girlfriend?" interrupted Isaac. "Does Rachel know this?"

Well no, not yet, I admitted. *But she will be soon. I hope. Anyway, I'm worried about her and I can't sleep and now I* really *won't able to sleep thinking about Rowan.*

Isaac laughed at my patently exaggerated concern. "Oh very well. I'll read you the next part. But then we should go to bed. It's late."

I wagged my tail and tried to look appreciative.

A Murder

I have already described my father's delighted reaction to meeting Rowan. My mother's response was rather more muted, but there soon developed between them a warm feminine companionship. They cooked together some evenings, with Rowan contributing recipes or ideas that involved spices unfamiliar to the dreadfully bland English palate of the 1960's, a time when people joked that Britain had created an empire that conquered half the world for the sole purpose of finding a good meal. Sometimes she would venture into the woods or the surrounding countryside, and return with herbs or mushrooms.

Inevitably my parents enquired, out of politeness and genuine curiosity, about Rowan's origins. I told them that she was an artist, from a family that had lived in various places in Europe. They somehow settled on the assumption that she was of English and Italian descent, and neither she nor I said anything to dispel this belief. I provided few other details - I had none to give - and, sensing a desire for privacy that they must have found a least a little perplexing, they politely did not press either of us for more.

I had intended to return to Greece a few days after the funeral, but with Rowan's instant acceptance into my family circle, we decided to remain in England for a while. Besides, the day after I brought her to the house, the weather suddenly changed. Summer swept in that morning on a southerly wind and firmly installed itself in the English landscape; and the national mood was lightened overnight.

It was a gloriously idle summer, full of the heady joy that is the possession of youth, and of love. Youth is a time of endless beginnings, before the shadow of mortality creeps in to forever compromise one's enjoyment of life. And while - as Bernard Shaw famously said - youth is wasted on the young, it was certainly not wasted on me in those days. I was fully aware of how precious my time with Rowan was; I woke up every day grateful for her presence at my side, and lived in a state of continual astonishment at my good fortune.

There were walks and little rural explorations. There were long conversations about everything and nothing, with good food and drink, and the occasional bonfire, as their accompaniment. There was warmth and sweetness, and endless love-making in a large, creaky double bed. My parents tactfully ignored the sounds coming from our bedroom, and at breakfast each day never commented on our frequent and probably very obvious coupling.

Rowan's storytelling continued, but no longer to an audience of one. Like me, my parents were enthralled by her tales, and we soon instituted a nightly ritual in which we all gathered at the bottom of the garden to drink wine or tea, the three of us sitting on lawn chairs or on the grass to listen to whatever story she decided to spin that evening. She sat on the grass cross-legged, holding forth like Scheherazade herself.

Some evenings I would tell a story of my own, always with Rowan providing the first line. Occasionally my father would contribute the recitation of a poem from the vast collection curated in his prodigious memory, and every now and then we persuaded my mother to sing a folk song or something whimsical from the music hall. She had a lovely voice, but was shy and never quite believed the praise that always followed her impromptu performances.

Each day Rowan would go to the wood. I took her there the first time, telling her how, as a boy, I had been afraid of the place. She showed no such apprehension, and needed, it seemed, no guide within the shadowed green world among the trees. I recalled how many of her stories were set in forests.

After that first time, she often went alone to the wood. She would kiss me, say simply, "I'm going to the woods", and that was that. I understood that I was not being invited to join her, and I did not press the matter. An hour later she would reemerge; she always seemed more relaxed and centered as she walked across the lawn towards the house, smiling as she saw me sitting on the bench beside the little pond my father had constructed years before.

One day, though, I decided on a whim to join her. She had gone down to the wood perhaps twenty minutes before, and I had watched as she crossed the little stone bridge over the brook and disappeared into the trees. It was a hot day, and I thought how pleasant it would be to walk with her in the cool air of the wood. And I knew of no reason I should not go.

I crossed the bridge and walked towards the wood's edge. But suddenly I stopped. I found to my surprise that I was gripped by a sense of unease, one which recalled the nervousness of my very first entry, years ago when I was a boy. Why? I knew and loved this place; it was familiar and comforting to me, a place of beauty, a sanctuary. And yet my heart was beating fast, as if it knew of some danger of which I was unaware.

This is silly, I thought, and forced myself to move forward on the path.

I continued along the main path, wondering where Rowan was. Suddenly I became aware of crows cawing somewhere ahead of me. Instinctively I followed the sound, moving as quietly as I could. The cawing was louder now; wherever the crows were, there were many of them.

I traveled perhaps another two hundred yards, my sense of unease rising with each step. Finally, I came to the edge of a small clearing in the trees.

And there, as I stood hidden by the trunk of an old elm, my breath was caught in my throat, and my heart seemed to stop.

In the middle of the clearing, Rowan stood with her arms raised. Before her, perched on almost every branch of the many trees ahead, were crows. Scores of crows, all of them cawing, all of them with their black eyes fixed on Rowan.

For some reason — trivially so given the significance of the strange scene before me - I recalled that the collective noun for a group of crows was a murder. Here was surely the ultimate murder of crows, and with my lover as the focal point in their midst.

Rowan bowed her head for a few seconds, uttering words in no language I knew. Then she raised her head again and brought her arms together in front of her, palms joined.

There was a pause in which nothing moved; then a large crow with a single white feather in its tail flew down from its perch high in an oak tree. With practiced grace, it alighted on Rowan's hands. It gave a single caw.

Carefully she withdrew her right hand, the crow deftly stabilizing itself on her left. She brought the crow towards her, and gently stroked its head. Again she spoke words in that strange language. The crow responded by bending down and rubbing its beak against her wrist.

The whole extraordinary tableau probably took less than a minute, during which I was transfixed. I was paralyzed with shock, with fascination, and with disbelief.

And then suddenly, as if awaking from a dream, I recovered myself and, almost involuntarily, took a step forward into the clearing and called out Rowan's name.

The effect of my intrusion was dramatic. A hundred crows exploded off the branches, rising in a storm of black wings, their voices rupturing the air. They wheeled in the sky above and scattered, gradually disappearing in all directions over the trees. Finally, they were all gone, and silence once again descended upon the wood.

Rowan, meanwhile, had turned at the sound of my voice. She smiled at me, then looked up to watch the crows dispersing. When they were gone, she walked over to me.

"Isaac."

"Rowan." *I honestly did not know what else to say.*

She smiled again, but ruefully. "It's ironic," *she said.* "I was going to tell you very soon – this week. But I will tell you now."

"Tell me what?" *I felt my heart beating fast again.*

"The truth, about me. Though I fear you may find it impossible to believe."
I shook my head, still in disbelief at the events of the past few moments.
"After what I just saw," I said, "I suspect I would believe almost anything." I paused, dreading to ask the question that screamed within my head.
"Who are you, Rowan? What *are* you?"
She took both my hands in hers and looked me directly in the eyes.
"I am Fay," she said, and nodded, as if acknowledging a truth to herself. "Yes, I am Fay."

Interlude

Isaac put down his manuscript and smiled at me.
"So now you know," he said.
What? I don't know anything.
"You wanted to know about Rowan. Now you know that she was Fay."
Fay? What on earth is "Fay"?
"Ah," said Isaac with a sly smile, "I see your confusion. Well, if it's any consolation I had no idea what she meant at the time either."
Please don't tell me you're not going to tell me.
"Oh, I'll tell you. Or rather, Rowan will, in her own words. In the next bit. Tomorrow. Or whenever."
You're enjoying this, aren't you?
"I confess I am, rather."
You do remember that dogs bite, right?
"Oh, I don't think you'd bite the hand that feeds you," he said, still grinning. "I think I'm safe - at least until the day you learn to use a can opener."

Pervert

The following morning, to my great relief, Rachel shows up on the deck at 7 am. I am already up this time; I was worrying about her and didn't sleep very well.
I run to her and give her a lick on her muzzle.
"That was very presumptuous of you," she says.
Seriously? This from someone who routinely greets a stranger by sticking her nose in his ass.
"I actually don't do that."
Come to think of it, I don't think we've ever done that with each other.
"So?"
Well, do you want to do it now?
"Not particularly."

I'm just saying... you have a very nice ass and I wouldn't mind smelling it.
"What are you - some kind of pervert?"
It's not perverted - it's just a basic dog thing. Everyone does it.
"I don't".
What, were you out sick the day they taught Canine Behavior 101?
"No, I just don't want your muzzle lodged up my rear end."
I wasn't going to lodge *it. There will be no lodging. I was just offering to have a quick sniff.*
"You *are a pervert.*"

Just then Isaac appeared. "Ah, good morning Rachel. What happened last night? Jack and I were hoping you'd come back here." He smiled mischievously, then added, "Jack was *really* hoping you would." It's lucky that dogs don't blush or I would have turned a deep shade of crimson.

"He was, was he?" said Rachel, looking at me. *"How sweet."*

That's me - sweet. Ask anyone. I paused. *So what did happen last night?*

Rachel's expression changed and she became serious. *"He was drunk again,"* she said. *"There was a lot of yelling. I decided to stick around in case anything bad happened."*

Was he yelling at Alice?

"No, just at the world in general. He does that a lot - drinks and goes off on these tirades about things he hates. Lots of things. He finally drank himself to sleep at some point during the night."

So do you think you can get Alice here today?

"I'll try. We usually meet at the beach in the morning." I relay all of this to Isaac, who nods.

Rachel says she'll attempt to lead Alice here by barking to emphasize the importance of the matter, and trying to get her to follow her. But Isaac has a better idea.

"Why don't we all go to your beach? Then I can explain to her what's going on."

"That sounds good," says Rachel approvingly. *"Just try not to look like a pervert."*

I relay this to Isaac. "Okay, I'll try my best," he promises.

Rachel turns to me. *"I was talking about you,"* she says.

Alice

Alice, a female name meaning "noble". Variant of the old French name *Adelais*, a form of *Adelaide*, and the Germanic *Adalheidis*.

After breakfast - fried eggs and bacon for Isaac, Purina Beef 'n' Vegetables for us - we all troop down the path to Rachel's beach.

It's another beautiful summer day, and Rachel and I muck about in the water while Isaac sits patiently on a log, occasionally getting up to throw a stick for us.

We've been there for around half an hour, and I'm beginning to wonder whether Alice is going to show up, when suddenly a little girl comes running down the path out of the woods. Rachel barks and runs up to her, and the two of them greet each other with what is obviously enthusiastic affection. Alice drops to her knees as Rachel jumps around her, tail wagging and tongue delivering random licks to the girl's face. It's a heart-warming sight.

Alice is a pretty girl, with startlingly blue eyes and rather unkempt blonde hair falling over her shoulders. I guess she's about average height for an eleven-year-old, but she has a lithe body beneath her simple white frock, and from her tanned skin I can see that she spends a lot of her time outdoors.

While I'm appraising her, she looks up and notices for the first time that she and Rachel are not alone.

"Hello," she says simply to Isaac.

"Hello, Alice. Nice to meet you. I'm Isaac."

Alice frowns. "How did you know my name?" she asks.

"Well," Isaac replies, "that's a long story, and one that I'm afraid you're going to have a very hard time believing."

Alice looks increasingly suspicious. "What's the story, then?" she asks.

Isaac pauses, and looks down at Rachel, who has come over to sit by his side. "Well, what would you say if I told you that your dog Rachel here told me all about you?"

She thinks for a moment. "I'd say you're nuts. And how d'you know my dog's name?"

Isaac nods. "Yes, that's entirely understandable. And I know Rachel's name because, well, she told me that too."

Alice is pretty clearly beginning to wonder if she should run from this aged nutcase. Sensing this, Isaac presses on.

"Alice, I'm just going to tell you the whole thing, and all I ask is that you listen to me. Then afterwards I'll do something to show you that this crazy story is in fact true."

Alice shifts uneasily and is obviously trying to process this and decide whether this guy represents a danger to her. But just then, Rachel stands up, jumps, and puts her paws on Isaac's chest; he bends down a little, and she licks his face, then drops to the ground and walks over to Alice, her tail wagging.

"Rachel, what are you doing?" she asks her dog.

"I think Rachel's trying to tell you that I mean well and that I'm here to help you," says Isaac.

Alice pets Rachel, whose tail is still wagging.

"Okay," she says, "my dog seems to like you. So go ahead - tell me your crazy story."

"Thank you," says Isaac. "I'll try to make this clear to you."

"So Rachel *talks* to you?" asks Alice skeptically.

"No," he replies. "Rachel can't talk to me."

"Yeah, tell me something I don't know."

"Rachel can't - but Jack can. This is Jack." He points to me, and I wag my tail encouragingly. "Rachel talks to Jack, and Jack tells me."

"Oh yeah, well that makes *much* more sense," says Alice, with sarcasm beyond her years.

Isaac sighs. "I suppose we should demonstrate." He thinks for a moment. "Why don't you whisper something to Rachel - anything you like. Then Rachel will tell Jack, and Jack will tell me."

Not surprisingly, Alice looks very dubious. "Okay, she says - but put your fingers in your ears."

Isaac does as he's told, and Alice bends down to whisper something to Rachel. Rachel licks her face, then relays this to me, and I in turn relay it to Isaac.

Isaac laughs. "You had Cornflakes for breakfast and you have a piece of cheese for Rachel in your left pocket."

Alice reaches into the pocket and produces the cheese, which Rachel accepts gratefully.

"I still don't believe you," she says. "I see magicians on TV who do this sort of thing. I don't know how you did it, but it's way easier than believing you can talk to my dog."

"Fair enough," Isaac responds. "So tell Rachel to tell me something that I couldn't possibly know, something that's a secret just the two of you share."

Alice thinks, then whispers to Rachel again. The relay happens, and Isaac raises his eyebrows sadly. "The night your guardian tried to kill Rachel, you sneaked out of the house very late and found her in the woods. You gave her some leftover chicken that was the only thing you could find for her to eat, and you lay on the ground under a tree with her and cried while she ate it."

A tear runs down Alice's cheek. "Yes," she says. "Rachel was so hungry, and I was so sad. I didn't know what was going to happen."

"Look, Alice," says Isaac, "I know all about your situation. About Sal Kaufman, about your parents. I'm really sorry. But I think I can help you at least a little. Rachel's a very smart dog, but she can't live here in the woods when winter comes. I offered to take her back to Seattle with me, but she won't leave you."

Rachel looks up at Alice, who hugs her close.

"I love her," she says simply, and another tear forms in one of her eyes. "She's my best friend, and I don't know what I'd do if something happened to her." There is a hint of desperation in her voice.

She looks at Rachel. "So you can really understand everything I say? And this other dog can talk?" Rachel barks and wags her tail - the doggie equivalent of a nod.

"I know it's very weird," says Isaac, "and I honestly don't know how it happens. But it's true. Somehow I can read Jack's mind."

As Alice takes this in, Isaac continues. "So here's the thing, Alice. I have a house just down the shore there. I'm not there all the time, but I can give you a spare key and you can use it whenever you want. Rachel can stay there. I'll buy a lot of dog food for her so you don't have to worry about her going hungry."

"Really?" she says. "That would be so awesome."

Isaac smiles. "No problem. I just ask that you keep the place fairly clean, and don't throw any wild parties while I'm away."

Alice snorts. "Yeah, that's not happening. As you may have noticed, this place isn't exactly the social hub of the planet."

Isaac laughs. "Yes, you're right, it isn't. Now, would you like to see the house?"

Alice hesitates. What she's being asked to do obviously runs counter to everything she's ever been told about what not to do with strangers. "I don't know..." she says.

But then Rachel takes her hand in her mouth and gently tugs her forward. She releases the hand and walks a little way down the path that heads in the direction of Isaac's house. She stops and looks back at Alice, wagging her tail.

Alice looks at her. "You really think this is okay?" she asks the dog.

Rachel barks and wags her tail again.

"Well okay," says Alice, and begins to follow her. "If you say so."

Home Sweet Home

We arrive at the house shortly after, with Rachel and I in the lead. Alice hesitates at the front door and looks uncertainly at Isaac.

"You don't own a wood chipper, do you?"

Isaac laughs. "No," he says, "I don't. But it's funny - someone else once asked me that." He smiles wistfully at the memory of Rowan on Santorini, so many summers past.

"What happened to them?" Alice asks.

"Well, they didn't end up in a wood chipper, if that's what you mean," Isaac replies. "Don't worry," he adds, "I'm not a serial killer, if that's what you're thinking."

"That's just what a serial killer would say," Alice responds.

He grinned. "That's what my friend said too."

Isaac opens the door and Rachel immediately goes inside. Alice hesitates for another second, then follows her, with Isaac and I close behind.

Alice looks around. "It's beautiful," she says. "Oh - and you have so many books!"

"Do you like to read, Alice?" Isaac asks.

"O yes!" she says with genuine enthusiasm. "I love reading more than almost anything. But," she adds, "well... it's just that we don't have many books, you know, up at the house. Cousin Sal's not exactly an intellectual."

"Well, you're welcome to read whatever you like here. Most of these books belonged to my father - he was a great reader. He'd come out here sometimes for a few days just to sit by the lake and lose himself in a book."

Alice is slowly walking along the bookshelves, perusing titles. "What's your favorite book?" she asks Isaac.

"My favorite? Wow, that's a tough question - there are so many."

"But what's your absolute favorite that you love more than anything else? Say you're stranded on a desert island and before the ship sinks you can only grab *three* books before you get into the lifeboat. What would you take?"

"That's a wonderful question," Isaac says. "I'd have to think about it."

"You can't think about it. The ship's sinking! You have two minutes to decide."

Isaac laughs. "Good point," he says. He thinks. "Okay... I'm going to take a book of poetry... and Virginia Woolf's novel *The Waves*..."

"What's that?" asks Alice. "And I like poetry too," she adds.

"*The Waves?* It's a wonderful novel. It's the story of six people's lives, from childhood to old age, but beautifully written - it's rather like poetry actually. I don't think any other novel is quite like it."

"What about your third book?"

"Ah, that would have to be Tolkien's *Lord of the Rings*," he says.

"I love that book!" Alice exclaims. "That would definitely be one of mine. Definitely."

"It would also be one of Jack's, I suspect," he says, laughing and looking at me. "I read it to him last winter." He did. Isaac and I would settle by the fireplace every evening and he'd read to me. It took about four months, and I loved it - even though there are no dogs in the book. You'd think Tolkien could have come up with at least *one* canine character among all those orcs and elves.

"You read books to Jack?" asks Alice, her eyes wide. "Really?"

"Really," he smiles.

Isaac walks over to one of the bookshelves and pulls down a volume. "This is a first edition of the first book, *The Fellowship of the Ring*." He hands it to Alice.

Her mouth is open - apparently she knows what a first edition is. With care that approaches reverence, she opens the book and turns the first pages. She looks at the flyleaf and her eyes widen.

"Is this - ?" She looks at Isaac.

He smiles. "Yes," he says, "that's Tolkien's signature. He signed it for my father in 1954, when the book first came out."

"Wow," says Alice. "Is it very valuable?"

"Yes, it is, actually. It's worth a great deal of money."

She carefully hands it to Isaac. "You'd better take it. I'd hate to, you know, spill coffee on it or something."

"It's okay," he says. "I trust you. You obviously love books and take care of them." Alice nods.

"Now," says Isaac, "would you like to see the rest of the house? And then maybe we can have some lemonade on the deck."

Isaac leads Alice on a tour, showing her where he keeps the canned dog food and telling her he'll buy more later today. They discuss the fact that Rachel will need a way to go in and out by herself, since Alice won't always be able to come down to open the door for her. Isaac tells her he'll install a dog door that she can use - one that's opened by a magnet on the collar.

"Why do you need a special collar?" Alice asks.

"Because otherwise *any* animal can get in. I don't want you to come down here one day and find twenty raccoons having a convention inside."

"O yeah, okay."

The tour over, we retire to the deck. Isaac and Alice drink lemonade, and he gives Rachel and I a marrow bone each with which to occupy ourselves.

Alice stretches out and lays back in one of the Adirondack chairs, and puts her hands above her head, basking in the late morning sun. She smiles and says, "I think this is the best day ever."

Isaac smiles. "I'm really glad," he says, and takes a sip of lemonade. He is clearly enjoying the day too. Some time later, Isaac looks over at Alice. Rachel is lying next to her, still working the marrow bone, and Alice has her hand on her head.

"Alice, do you have a cell phone?"

"No," she replies. "I used to. But Sal won't pay the bill for it and says I don't need one. He's so cheap," she added.

Isaac thinks for a moment. "Okay, well I'm going to send you one. I want you to have some way to contact me if anything really bad happens, or if you just need something."

"Really? That would be amazing!"

Isaac smiles. "I'll have it delivered here so you can pick it up. But either hide it or keep it here so he doesn't find it."

"Okay, I will," she says gratefully.

"Oh," Isaac says, reaching into his pocket. "I almost forgot. This is the spare key." Alice takes it, and thinks for a moment.

"Is there somewhere we could hide this? I don't want Sal finding it and asking questions - or taking it away from me. That's just the sort of thing he'd do."

"Hmm, good point. Let's think." Isaac gets up and takes Alice outside; and, after some thought, he removes a brick from the path and slips the key underneath it. "Will that work?" he asks.

Alice nods. "Yes! I promise I'll remember which brick it is," she says.

"Good," he replies. "Well Alice, I think you're all set. And remember - no wild parties." Alice giggles.

"And listen Alice - you really can't tell anyone about Jack and I - you know, that we can talk. You'll probably get me locked up if you do."

"Okay," she says, "I promise not to say anything to anyone."

Then her face takes on a more serious look and she gazes up into the old man's eyes.

"Thank you, Isaac," she says. "Thank you for being so nice to Rachel... and to me." And she reaches up and puts her arms around Isaac's neck, and kisses him sweetly on the cheek.

Demi-Gods

We stayed at the house for a few more days, and slipped into an easy routine. Alice would come down in the morning and spend as much of the day there as she could. Isaac asked her if Sal questioned her absences, but she said he didn't care enough to be suspicious.

"He's happy to not have me around," she said. "I told him I made a friend nearby, and he's dumb enough to believe me."

"Well, let's hope it stays that way," Isaac replied.

Rachel started spending the night at least some of the time, with both of us sharing the bed with Isaac. He never complained - I think he liked having two dogs curled up next to him all night - though I discovered that Rachel was a dreadful bed hog. Quite how a 65-lb dog can manage to stretch out and occupy three-quarters of a king-sized bed is one of the smaller mysteries of Nature.

It was all rather wonderful, and I was finding myself enjoying Rachel's companionship more and more. But one day Isaac received a text from Veronica saying that she needed to move back into the house, and was going to do so in a couple of days. No doubt because, for a dominatrix, an empty dungeon doth not income create.

"Well," said Isaac, "I suppose we'd better head back on Friday and return you to your rightful mistress."

I sighed (yes, dogs sigh). *I hate to go, especially leaving Rachel here,* I said. Then added, *I wish we had a reason to stay out here for a long time, and bring Veronica.*

Which turned out to be a huge mistake.

It's a little-known fact that somewhere up there in the clouds there are demi-gods sitting around bored out of their tiny minds. And, having nothing better to do, these annoying little pricks listen very closely to everything that's said below and - if the wish isn't written in rigid contractual language and accompanied by a lawyer's letter threatening dire legal consequences in the event of abuse - they will interpret those wishes in the most perverse way possible and then make them happen. As pretty much everyone has found out at some point or other, Fate is a capricious mistress with a very sick sense of humor.

In other words: always be careful what you ask for - because you just might get it.

Interlude

That evening, Isaac cooked some beef liver for Rachel and I, while he enjoyed a pizza, a glass of red wine and the inevitable cream puffs for dessert. Rachel pretty much inhaled the liver.

We sat on the deck for awhile, gazing at the moon. Isaac sipped his wine, lost in his own thoughts.

Are you thinking about Rowan? I asked.

Isaac nodded. "Yes, Jack. The moon always reminds me of her."

Rachel was lying on the floor next to me; she raised her head. *"Who's Rowan?"* she asked.

Long story, I said. *She was someone Isaac was in love with. I'll fill you in later if you want.*

Rachel seemed satisfied with this, and put her head back on her paws.

Can you read some more? Please?

Isaac smiled. "Yes, Jack, I will. Gladly. And this time I promise you'll learn all about who she is."

The use of the present tense confused me. *Is? You mean you still know her?*

"I mean she still exists, but not here."

Not here? What does that mean?

He sighed. "It's complicated. I'll try to explain."

Fay

In the middle of a wood, in silence, I faced the woman I loved and searched her green eyes for answers.

"Fay? What... what does that mean?" I knew the word, of course, but could not conceive how it could apply to Rowan.

Rowan sighed. "Come," she said. "Let's sit." She led me by the hand to a fallen tree and motioned for me to sit beside her on the old moss-covered trunk.

I stared at her, unable to articulate my thoughts; indeed, I could make little sense of them myself.

"Let me tell you a story," she said.

I continued to stare.

"Once upon a time, there was a boy. A boy who walked into a wood at midnight on a warm summer's night. He carried with him an offering – a white rose and some wine, some bread, some salt..."

Finally, I found my voice.

"How could you know that?" I asked. I made no attempt to mask my astonishment. "I've never told anyone."

"I was there, Isaac. I saw you."

"You were there?"

"Yes. I watched as you placed your offerings on the forest floor. And when you stood there and said 'I believe', you touched my heart. Ah, those two words! Just two words, but they were everything. The unquestioning belief, the utter sincerity behind them. You cannot imagine how important that was to me, to find someone in your world who believed, who never questioned his faith in the possibility of magic. It was a gift - more so even than the offerings, as sweet and as thoughtful as they were."

I was reeling. None of this made rational sense.

"How could you have been there? And how could you have known what I meant when I spoke those words?"

"I knew, Isaac. Just as I know that part of you is still that small boy, the one who still believes." I slowly absorbed the implications, vague as they still were at that moment.

"So you are Fay? Fay," I repeated. "Does that... does that really mean what I think it does?"

"Yes my love, it does. It means what you knew it meant when you were a boy."

I put my head in my hands and sighed deeply. Rowan placed a hand upon my knee.

"So... so this girl I love, she is a..." I couldn't bring myself to say the word, so preposterous was the idea.

"She is Fay – what you would call a faery. Although," she added, "your people have a very misguided understanding of what that means in reality."

I laughed grimly. "Reality? I no longer know what reality is."

She nodded. "I understand. It's a lot to take in."

I looked at her. "Yeah, that's one way to put it. I'm in love with a faery. Whatever that is in 'reality'."

She stroked my hand. "Are you angry?"

I shook my head slowly, but in truth I had no idea what I was feeling at that moment. I suppose my predominant reaction was emotional shock, compounded by confusion.

"So tell me," I said. "What is the reality? What does it mean to be Fay?"

She sighed. "I'm not sure where to begin. It's a long story."

"You're good at stories," I said, and I admit there was an undertone of sarcasm in my voice. "Try me with this one."

"Perhaps it would be easier if you asked me questions."

"Perhaps," I replied. "But I'm not sure I would know what to ask."

She nodded. "Yes, I understand. Okay then. I am a member of an ancient people..."

I interrupted her. "When you say ancient, do you mean the people – the group, whatever they are – are ancient, or that you are as a person?"

"I mean my people. Although I myself am not young by your standards."

I raised my eyebrows. "You're not? How old are you?"

She hesitated. "Do you really want to know?"

"Yes – though I admit I'm rather terrified to hear the response."

"I was born twelve years before Queen Victoria died."

I remembered the date of the old queen's demise from history class at grammar school – 1901. I did a quick mental calculation, and stared at her, stupefied.

"You're 77 years old?"

She smiled. "Yes. Though quite young for one of my people."

The absurdity of my situation was just now beginning to sink in. Suddenly I laughed and shook my head.

"What's so funny?" she asked.

"Well, it's a bit much to take in, as you said. I mean, I've always fantasized about sex with an older woman, but this is ridiculous."

She laughed too.

"You don't look like any 77-year-old woman I've ever slept with."

"And how many is that?"

"One to date - though I just found that out." I paused, and stared at this beautiful and seemingly young woman. Suddenly the breadth of her experience and knowledge made sense.

"So, go on. Tell me more. What else do I need to know about my septuagenarian lover? Are you immortal?"

"No, I'm not. But my lifespan is much greater than that of humans. Hundreds of years. Though," she added sadly, "it can be diminished."

"How?"

"By exposure to your world." She opened her hands and gestured to our surroundings. "By being here." I wanted to ask why, but this was just one of a hundred questions that jostled for space in an amorphous, disorganized mass inside my head.

"Can Fay be killed?"

She raised her eyebrows. "I hope that's a rhetorical question." I nodded. "Yes, we can. And often were, long ago. Ours is a sad history, as I shall tell you in due course."

"Do I seem like a child to you, since you're so much older?"

"No, you don't. Not at all."

"Let's see... can you foretell the future?"

"No. Though we do have a strong sense of some significant impending event sometimes."

"Such as what?"

"Death. We can sense its approach in a person, sometimes."

"That's creepy. I'm not sure I'd like to have that power."

"I've only felt that a couple of times - and you're right, it's not a pleasant sensation."

"I rather thought you'd be able to tell the future. The Fay sound like gypsies."

To my great surprise, Rowan's expression suddenly changed, and she spat.

"Don't ever compare us to those people!" she said, the vehemence in her voice obvious and startling. "The gypsies are thieves and liars. Many humans have this ridiculous idea that they live some sort of terribly romantic nomadic existence, but in reality they're just parasites who spread crime and discontent wherever they go."

"I'm sorry, Rowan. I didn't mean to offend you... I really don't know much about this. Obviously."

Her face softened. "I'm sorry," she said. "But the gypsies have often been complicit in the persecution of Fay. There is no love lost between our two peoples."

We were silent for a while, and then I thought of a question which I knew was silly, but couldn't resist asking anyway.

"Can you fly?"

"Fly?" She laughed. "No, I cannot. You must be thinking of those quaint little fairies you find in children's books."

I nodded. "Arthur Rackham and his ilk," I said.

"I thought so. Victorian illustrators have a lot to answer for. Anyway, no – Fay cannot fly, though we can move through space in ways you cannot."

"Really? How?"

"It's complicated. But there are paths - portals - between your world and ours, and by moving into mine and then choosing a different exit I can travel across great distances here with ease."

I thought about this. "So you didn't take a plane here then?"

"No."

"You just whizzed from one world to another. Dropped into your world in Greece and came out through a back door that plopped you down on the kerb at Heathrow Airport."

"Something like that, yes."

Suddenly another mystery made sense.

"You don't have a passport, do you? That's why you couldn't come here with me?"

She nodded. "Fay don't have passports," she said. "We have no nationality in your world. Actually, I can cross borders, but not... officially."

"Really? What – do you make yourself invisible or something?"

"Not exactly. Let's just say we Fay can make ourselves... well, un-noticed at need."

"You say Fay as both singular and plural." It was a question, and one which immediately struck me as absurdly trivial. To enquire about a fine point of grammar seemed inane given the import of everything else I had just learned.

"Yes," she answered simply.

"What else do I need to know about the Fay?"

She considered, then said, "We never lie."

"Never?"

"Never. We can allow people to believe an untruth if it proves necessary, but they must come to that untruth themselves."

"Interesting. So how many languages do you speak?"

"Nine or ten with reasonable fluency, a smattering of others. Languages come easily to Fay."

"But you have your own language too?"

"Yes," she said. "It is called Faïnna. It's an ancient tongue whose roots go back thousands of years."

"And it's not related to any other language?"

"Actually it is, at least superficially. It shares some roots with Euskara, the language of the Basques."

This surprised me. "How is that?"

"All European languages share a common ancestry - except Basque. Euskara is a holdover from a time before what historians call the Indo-European invasions. All these tribes came in from the east, starting around six thousand years ago. They forced out the original human inhabitants and replaced their languages with the ones we know today - or rather the ancestors of those. The Basque tongue was one of those originals, and it alone survives. As I said, it has an ancient ancestry that has a common root - albeit a long way back - with Faïnna. I've never learned Euskara, but it would not be difficult. Many of the words are remarkably similar. So is the grammar."

I was silent for a while as I processed all this information. After weeks of mystery, this felt like a flood. "Can you read minds?" I asked after a moment. "I've often felt you knew what I was thinking."

"No," she said, "I can't. However, Fay are often very... I think you would say intuitive. We have a strong sense of what a person is feeling - all the more so if it's someone we love." She smiled. "That is often confused for mind-reading, but really it's just knowing a person well and being tuned in - sort of a receptacle for their emotional responses. And," she added, "you and I have become so close, despite the short time we have spent together."

I looked around the clearing, and became aware of the sound of birdsong.

"So what was with the crows, anyway? It looked like that Alfred Hitchcock movie in here." The Birds had come out a couple of years before.

"I'm afraid I don't understand that reference," she said. "But.... well, I have an affinity with some animals. Crows have always been friends to my people. We have a long history together. We have both been persecuted."

I sighed. "I can see we need to spend a great deal of time talking about all this. I'm not sure I can believe any of it."

"You believe it, Isaac. You have always believed – you just didn't know the details."

She laid her head on my shoulder. I was still confused, and would remain so for some time. But curiosity and fascination were rising fast within me, and – I realized suddenly – excitement. I was being allowed entry to a supernatural world that, I assumed, few humans were ever allowed to know.

As this thought went through my mind, suddenly Rowan raised her head, gripped my shoulders and gave me a serious look.

"You cannot tell anyone this, Isaac. No one, not even your parents. This is very, very important. No one must know what I am. I have cast myself at your feet in telling you this."

"At my feet?"

She withdrew her hands. "It's an expression we have. It means to place complete trust in someone, to tell them a secret that cannot be shared."

I put my hand on her cheek and looked into her eyes. I saw great concern there.

"Oh Rowan, I would never betray your trust. Never. You have my word."

She sighed, and the tension left her body like a breaking wave. "Thank you," she said, and kissed me. "Do you still love me, Isaac?"

I smiled. "I have loved you from the first moment I saw you." I said it without a second's hesitation.

Tears rolled down her cheek. "Thank you, my love." She let out a great sigh. "I'm so glad to have told you. It has been such a heavy burden to keep that secret."

We were silent for a while. I held her in my arms, inhaling the sweet fragrance of her hair as thoughts swirled around in my confused mind. Finally she raised her head from my shoulder.

"I know you have many questions," she said. "I will answer them all – I owe you that. You have been so very patient with me all this time. But for now I would ask two things of you. First, hold your questions until this evening."

I nodded. "Okay. And the second thing?"

"I want to make love with you," she said. "For the first time with no secrets between us. Take me to bed."

Interlude

Isaac paused to drink some wine. He looked at me.
"So, what do you think, now that you know?" he asked.
I thought about my response. *This really happened?*
"It did, Jack. And now you can understand why I don't tell too many people this story."
And you believed that faeries exist, when you were a boy?
"I did. I don't know why. Perhaps it was necessary to my destiny - my path to Rowan. But somehow I just knew."
Well, the story is amazing. As Veronica would say, O my fucking God.
Isaac laughed. "Yes, she does swear a lot, doesn't she?"
Like a sailor, I said. *Keep reading.*

Etymology

fay (noun), late 14c., fairy. From old French *fae* (12c., modern french *fée*), from vulgar latin *fata* "goddess of fate," feminine singular of latin *fata*, literally "the fates".

faery (noun), also *fairy,* ca. 1300, "the country or home of supernatural or legendary creatures; fairyland," also "something incredible or fictitious," from old french *faerie* "land of fairies, meeting of fairies; enchantment, magic, witchcraft, sorcery" (12c.), from *fae* "fay," from latin *fata* "the fates," plural of *fatum* "that which is ordained; destiny, fate."

Wind and Shadows

We returned to the house and made love with a passionate intensity that surpassed anything that had gone before, like two people who had been deprived of carnal pleasure for a long time. Luckily, my parents were both out on a walk and were spared the clamorous complaining of the bed that accompanied our fevered coupling.

Later, after we had finished dinner with my parents, Rowan addressed the table.

"Time for a story," she said. "A special story tonight. For Isaac." She glanced at me and smiled.

"Wonderful," my father said. "Let's go to the garden. I'll open another bottle of wine – a special one for a special story."

The deep and genuine affection he felt for Rowan was obvious in the way he spoke to her. I wondered how he would react if he knew the truth about who she was.

Ten minutes later, we were gathered in the usual spot at the bottom of the garden, close to the brook. I and my parents reposed in comfortable wooden chairs; Rowan, as usual, sat on the grass on the slope above us, facing the wood. My father poured the wine, a glorious Premier Grand Cru Pauillac, dense and fragrant and the color of bruised plums. He raised his glass in a toast.

"To Rowan," he said simply. "Who graces us with her storytelling."

"Thank you," she said, smiling. "It is an honor to do so for such an appreciative audience as this."

We all took a moment to appreciate the wine - it was heavenly - and then gazed at Rowan in anticipation.

Her regular stories were a delight; the idea of a special tale from her lips was quite tantalizing.

As was her habit, Rowan placed her hands together and closed her eyes. She remained silent for perhaps ten seconds. Then she began to speak, and once again there was that enchanting, hypnotic voice, the voice that captivated her listeners and lulled them into a dream-like state in which the story became real.

"Long, long ago, when the tallest trees were but seeds on the branches of their forebears, when the mountains were high and unweathered, before the cities, before the taming of the horse, when forests marched across the earth, when men feared the gods and lit fires to assuage the darkness of a moonless night... there, in the distant unremembered past, lived creatures in human form..."

The spell was cast. And as she spoke these first words, I knew that I was about to be told the history of Rowan's kind.

They were known as the Faylinn, she said, the People of the Wind. Nomadic by choice, the Faylinn followed the great winds of Europe and western Asia in their movements. They had a special love for the Zhyrosh *- the wind humans know as the Sirocco - which blew warm and strong from across the Mediterranean Sea. Humans cursed this wind, which often brought dust storms and destruction, but the southern branch of the Faylinn exulted in its power, and used its appearance in spring to time their migration to more northerly climes.*

Elsewhere, other Faylinn tribes moved with different winds. The Bora, which chills the Adriatic in winter. The Khamseen of North Africa, hot and bone-dry. The three great northerlies: Elesian, Mistral and Meltemi. The Notios, born in the Sahara and blasting the Greek islands from the southwest. And lesser winds for which humans have no name.

The People of the Wind shared a common ancestry with humans, long ago, and for centuries the two peacefully co-existed and even intermingled. But as the centuries passed, humans held war and technology in increasingly high esteem, whereas the Faylinn clung to their traditional ways, choosing a life of movement and the quiet pasturing of animals. They loved the land, and the serenity of Nature; conquest and theft were alien to them.

Inevitably, this contrast brought them into conflict with humans. The Faylinn were persecuted, or at best marginalized, and increasingly they retreated into the safety of the woodlands.

And there, deep in the great forests that still covered the landscape of Europe, there happened the phenomenon that the Faylinn called the Trans-Realming.

Exactly how this occurred is not known; perhaps it was some genetic mutation within their kind, or simply an extension of their kinship with the natural world. But at some point in the past, perhaps five thousand years ago, a change occurred in the offspring born to the Faylinn. Some of the children possessed strange gifts that allowed them special powers with Nature: the ability to speak to beasts and birds, or to hide themselves at will. And some disappeared for days, only to return to their anguished parents and report that they had been to another realm, a wonderful place of warmth and bounty, where no humans could be found.

It began with just a few children; and at first the other Faylinn refused to believe their peculiar tales of visits to an enchanted world. But as these children grew up and bore offspring of their own, their strange abilities spread through the population until, within a few generations, all Faylinn were born with those powers, and the existence of the alternate reality they now called the Summerland was undoubted, and a part of every Faylinn's life.

Meanwhile, the conflicts with humans grew. The gradual destruction of the forests increasingly deprived the Faylinn of their traditional sanctuary; and humans witnessed with growing suspicion and fear the seemingly magical powers of these strange people.

And what humans do not understand, they seek to destroy.

For many years, the persecution was but local in nature, and sporadic. But with the rise of Christianity, and the particular intolerance which that religion held for anything that smacked of the supernatural, a campaign was forged to extirpate the Faylinn, and the Old Religion to which they had long adhered. In some places they were actively hunted, and terrible things were done to them and their children in the name of a cruel God they did not understand.

They retreated ever more often into their own Summerland realm. Many continued to visit what they called the Temporal World, but tried their best to remain unseen when they did so.

And so the People of the Wind became the People of the Shadows.

Yet many Faylinn yearned to return to the old home of their ancestral past, as changed as it had become. They missed the Winds, and they longed to hear the call of the Sea. And many wished still to experience the positive and even affectionate contact with humans that had once prevailed between the two peoples.

But their appearances in the Temporal World, and the strange acts they were sometimes seen to perform there, created dark legends among humankind. They became known as Fay, a race of supernatural beings. On dark nights, as people gathered around the fire and listened to the wind howling outside, they spoke in whispers of glamour, *Fay magic that could harm or - less often - help humans.*

And as their persecution increased with the insidious spread of Christianity, the Faylinn diminished in both real numbers and imagined form. Although they themselves remained the same size, the stories humans passed down from generation to generation represented the Fay as of smaller and smaller stature, until by the end of the Middle Ages they had become faeries - tiny beings who could in some cases fit neatly and charmingly into the bell of a flower.

It was a long tale, full of sorrow and yearning, but also bright with joy. As Rowan spoke, we knew the wonder of a life spent in the woods under the stars, the exhilaration of the wind, and the freedom of a people moving with the seasons across an ever-changing landscape.

"And so," she concluded, "here ends - at least for now - the history of the Faylinn, the People of the Wind and Shadows."

As her small audience was suddenly recalled back to their own world and time, all three of us sighed in unison. We none of us wished the story to end.

My father was the first to speak.

"Rowan, you have outdone yourself tonight. That was a remarkable story. I feel like I have just awoken from a faery enchantment. I'm beginning to believe that you are one of the Faylinn."

Rowan laughed. "Well," she replied, "perhaps I have a little Fay blood running in my veins."

Both my parents nodded and smiled. "More than a little, I think," said my mother.

Ah, if only they knew.

Glashtyn and Tana

We finished the wine, and with more words of thanks my parents kissed Rowan and myself and bade us goodnight. The moon had risen over the trees, and Rowan gazed at it pensively.

"That was an amazing story," I said. "Thank you for telling us - though I think it was meant largely for me."

Rowan smiled. "Yes it was," she replied, hugging her knees to her chest. "I wanted you to know the history. There is more, of course - much more - but that is the outline of a long and sad chronicle."

"It's very sad," I agreed. "Good old Christianity - you can always rely on Christians to persecute others." Rowan said nothing, but sadness briefly crossed her face.

I had many questions still. "You mentioned that there were different tribes of Faylinn," I said. "Is that still the case?"

She nodded. "Yes, it is. In fact some of their names have come down to you in human folklore."

"Really? Which tribe are you?"

"Ah," she said, "I'm a mongrel. My father was Glashtyn, my mother Tana. The Glashtyn were formerly a numerous people, good with boats and the Sea. But their range shrank dramatically with time, and by the end they were found mainly on the Isle of Man, north of the coast of Wales. If you read about them, the books will tell you that Man was their sole abode, but it's not true. Once they ranged from Ireland to the Danube, and south to the Pyrenees."

"And your mother's tribe - the Tana?"

"Yes. The Tana were always a small tribe, but revered by the Faylinn for their close ties with the natural world, and for their story-telling. Whenever a troop of Tana traveled through a settlement, the local Fay would beg them to stay and tell a story. Dozens would gather in the evening to hear the tale."

"Listening to you, my love, I can certainly understand why. But where were the Tana from?"

"Well, there was no 'from' for Faylinn. When the tribes lived in this world, they were nomadic, and the Tana were no different. Some traveled far, from the Atlantic coast of France to the Levant. But most were centered in the Balkan Mountains - many lived in what is today Romania. Our winds are the Crivăț and the Austru - though we know them by different names. The Crivăț is cruel, and brings terrible blizzards in winter, but we love it for its wildness and the way it screams through the valleys."

"Fascinating. What was the other one?"

"The Austru. It's a southwesterly wind that blows warm across the land, and brings with it the scent of mountain flowers."

"Mmm, lovely. By the way, what does your name mean?"

"Rowan? It's from the tree, the mountain ash. Humans once believed that it held magic power to ward off evil spirits or magical spells."

"So I'm safe with you, then?"

She smiled.

"What are your parents' names?" I asked.

"My mother is called Sylvane. It's a beautiful name - it means 'blessings of the forest'. It suits her - my mother loves the woods, as do I."

"And your father?"

"His name was Kailenn."

"Was?"

"Yes, he is dead."

"I'm sorry," I said, and frowned. "I thought Fay lived for centuries."

"They do - usually. But my father came to this world, and spent too much time here."

I asked the obvious question. "How... I mean, is that something bad for you?" I recalled that she had said earlier that a Fay's lifespan could be 'diminished' by being here, in this realm.

She nodded sadly, and sighed. "If we leave the Summerland, we are slowly... drained. I cannot think of a better way to put it than that. Our life force is depleted, and if we remain too long we can die."

"But why? You used to live here, before the - the Trans-Realming."

"Yes, but the lifespan of a Fay was then quite short - three or four decades at most. In the Summerland it became greatly extended. But if we return here then it reverts to the way it used to be. And while humans have lengthened their lives to the better part of a century, for the Fay - here - it remains as it was before we found the other realm."

"So why did your father come? Why did he stay?"

She sighed. "That is a long tale. But it was because of my sister. Eolande was her name." She paused, and sighed again. "Eolande, the Violet Flower - that was the meaning. She was beautiful, and my father adored her. But she entered the Temporal World, and never returned."

"And you don't know what happened to her?"

She shook her head. "No. As time went by and she still did not return, my father became distraught. He came here repeatedly, seeking news of his elder daughter. He hoped desperately to find her or - or at least to learn what fate had befallen her. He wandered far and wide, but brought back only rumors - rumors of no substance that led down paths with no ending. But," she added sadly, "he never gave up - and that was his undoing. One day after a long absence, he returned to us an old man, frail and gray. He passed away shortly after."

"He could not be... cured in the Summerland? Or revert to his lifespan there?"

"No," she replied. "For some reason that no one understands, time spent here is... Well, I suppose it is rather like the running down of a battery that can never be recharged. And worse, the aging clock actually moves faster and faster the longer we reside here."

With rising panic, I suddenly realized the implication of what she was telling me.

"But - but does this mean--?"

She nodded, her face a mask of sorrow. "Yes, my love - I'm afraid so. It means I cannot stay."

Talking Horse

It is not an exaggeration to say that I was devastated by this latest revelation. I had fallen deeply in love with this extraordinary woman, and now I was being told that she could not remain here with me.

"Well, this gives new meaning to the expression 'love 'em and leave 'em'," I said, with a flippancy that my heart certainly did not feel.

Rowan saw the look of despair on my face, and took my hand.

"The need is not immediate," she said. "I can remain for some time. As I said, the effect increases with time here. It seems to have little impact for awhile, and then gathers momentum."

"How long?" I asked. "How long do I have you for?" My heart was beating fast in anticipation of her answer.

"I don't know entirely. But a couple of years, perhaps longer."

"Do you have some warning when this begins to take effect?"

"Yes. A weariness sets in and gradually creeps through the body. It is called the Waning. Once it begins, the Fay must return to the Summerland immediately, else it slowly devour them."

"How many times have you been here?"

"Many," she said. But that's the other thing about this - for some reason, it does not affect the young. Up to the age of perhaps 20 years, we are immune. It is only after we reach maturity that it becomes a problem."

"But you are much older than that."

"Yes, which is why I have visited only occasionally."

"You were here when I was a boy."

"Yes. I came to see the Sea, and to walk in this wood." She sighed. "Oh, Isaac, this wood was once so beautiful, and so large. You can have no idea. Even in my youth it extended many more miles to the east and west. My grandfather knew it when it was but one part of a forest that covered much of the land, and gave refuge to wolves and bears. But that was long ago... it is just a remnant now."

"I'm sorry," I said. "But was it just coincidence that you were here that night when I came into the wood?"

"Yes it was. A very happy coincidence."

"Were you... were you invisible or something?"

"No, but it was dark and I willed you not to see me. I had no idea who this small person was, entering the woods so late. It was very unusual to see a human like that. I was about to leave, but then I saw that you were carrying some things - strange objects indeed for someone to be taking with them on a midnight walk in the woods. I was curious. And then you performed your ritual, and my heart melted."

This raised another question. "But our meeting on the ferry in Greece - that wasn't coincidence, was it?"

"No," she admitted, "it was not. I came to find you."

"Why?"

"Because I couldn't forget that night, and I knew - just knew - that we would have a bond, you and I. Fay believe that each person has a twin in spirit. We call it Tashka - it means "my other heart." You search for that person, that soul, your whole life. Many never find them. But when I saw you, I knew. I knew you were my Tashka."

I sighed. "So on that fateful night I set in motion events which have brought us here. You and I together, but unable to remain so."

She looked at me, and her face was full of concern. "Do you regret that this happened, Isaac?"

I shook my head. "No, Rowan - I could never do that, though I fear you've ruined me for other women now. And if you disappear from my life in two years or three - or tomorrow - I honestly don't know what I will do. I'm not sure my heart will heal from this."

She took my face in her hands. "Let's not dwell on that now. We have time, at least for awhile - let's enjoy it."

I sighed. "I suppose so. But if what you say is true, it's just postponing the inevitable." She kissed me, a tender kiss that barely brushed my lips.

"Many things may happen within the space of a year or two," she said. I said nothing in reply; I was brooding on the future.

"Let me tell you a story," she said. "This one does not come from the Faylinn - it was first told sometime in the Middle Ages."

I looked up at her. "Yes?"

For once, she did not begin by closing her eyes; the story commenced immediately.

"Once there was a thief who tried to steal jewels from the king. He was caught, and brought before the king for judgment. The king had no interest in clemency, and sentenced the thief to death. After pronouncing his doom, the king asked the thief if he had anything to say before he was led away to execution.

"'Yes, your Majesty,' said the thief. 'I beg of you to grant me mercy, and to delay my execution for one year. And, if your Majesty so desire it, to give me any one of your horses. If your Majesty grants me this, I swear that I will, within a year, teach the horse to talk.'

"The king was amused by this, and not a little curious. 'You will teach my horse to talk?' he asked.

"'Yes, my lord, I will,' replied the thief.

"'Very well,' said the king. 'So be it. I shall send to you one of my horses, and a year from now we shall meet again and see what you have made of your pledge. But if the horse does not talk, then you will not escape the gallows a second time.'

"The thief was set free, and led to the stables, where a horse was given to him. The stable hands enjoyed much laughter over his claim.

"And indeed, when he told a friend of the bargain he had made, the friend was astonished at his folly. 'Are you mad?' he asked the thief. 'No one can make a horse talk!'

"And the thief replied, 'My friend, within a year many things may come to pass. For within a year, the king may die, or the horse may die - or I may die. Or...' - and here the thief smiled - ' or the horse may talk.'"

I could not help but smile too, despite my gloomy mood. "That's a sweet story," I said. "I don't suppose we know how it turned out."

Rowan laughed. "We don't - but of course I for one hope the horse talked. Perhaps the thief was Faylinn." I shook my head in wonder at the bizarre situation in which I found myself. In love with a faery; not exactly the life story I had imagined for myself.

I kissed her. "You are an amazing woman," I said. "And I will never regret meeting you - no matter how this turns out."

She kissed me back, tenderly, and said, "Ya azhul t'vyezh."

"What's that?" I asked.

"Words in my own language - in Faïnna."

"What does it mean?"

She kissed me once more, and smiled. "It means 'I love you'."

Etymology

glamour (n.), 1720, Scottish, "magic, enchantment" (especially in phrase *to cast the glamor*), a variant of Scottish *gramarye* "magic, enchantment, spell". The word is said to be an alteration of English *grammar* in a specialized use of that word's medieval sense of "any sort of scholarship, especially occult learning," the latter sense attested from c. 1500 in English but said to have been more common in Medieval Latin. Jamieson's 1825 supplement to his *Etymological Dictionary of the Scottish Language* has *glamour-gift,* "the power of enchantment; metaphorically applied to female fascination." Perhaps related to Icelandic *glám-sýni,* "illusion," probably from the same root as *gleam.* (Sense of "magical beauty, alluring charm" first recorded 1840. As that quality of attractiveness especially associated with Hollywood, high-fashion, celebrity, etc., by 1939).

rowan (noun), the mountain ash, 1804. From *rowan-tree, rountree* (1540s), northern English and Scottish, from a Scandinavian source (compare Old Norse *reynir,* Swedish *Ronn* "the rowan"), ultimately from the root of red, in reference to the berries.

"There were those in this neighbourhood, long after the beginning of the present century, who believed that a slip of rowan tree carried on their person dispelled glamour, and rendered nugatory all the powers of sorcery and witchcraft." [Alexander Laing - Lindores Abbey and the Burgh of Newburgh, 1876]

Glamour

The next day was hot. In the absence of the slightest breeze, the air was baking and still. Even the birds stopped singing. It felt more like Greece than the south of England.
Rowan and I went to the wood in search of a cooler space. We sat on the same fallen tree where she had first told me who she was.
I still had many questions, which sprung up in my mind in seemingly random order. I asked one I'd been thinking about for a long time.
"I've been meaning to ask you: what did you tell that donkey in Santorini?"
Rowan laughed. "I didn't really tell *him anything. I whispered some words that are, well, they're what we call a 'soothing charm'. There's no real magic to them - but the sound of the words can have the effect of calming a person."*
"Or a donkey," I said.
"Yes. But I can't talk to donkeys. Just to crows - and some dogs." "Dogs? Really?"
"Yes. Dogs have always been close companions to the Faylinn... somehow along the way we learned to understand each other. But not all dogs. I don't know why."
"I'd like to be able to talk to dogs," I said.

She cocked her head and gave me a rather enigmatic smile. "Then perhaps one day you shall," she said.

"I doubt it. I'm a mere mortal."

"So am I, my love."

"Not quite the same, though, is it?"

"I suppose not."

There was a pause.

"So what do you say to crows?"

She laughed again. "You'd be surprised. Sometimes the conversation is about the most trivial things."

"What - like the weather?"

"Yes!" she laughed. "Crows have a particular fascination with weather, and they're very sensitive to changes. As far as I can tell, they're pretty much the bird experts on coming storms."

"You're serious?" I asked. I really didn't know whether she was making all this up as a joke at my expense.

When you've just learned that your lover is a faery, you're prepared to believe pretty much anything.

"I am!" she said, smiling broadly. "And why not, anyway? They're affected by weather, just like us - even more, actually. They don't have solid homes to shelter in."

"I just always assumed that if animals could speak to us they'd say all these profound things about Nature and the universe. Impart their animal wisdom, or something like that."

"No, it's not like that," she said. "Animals have everyday worries just as we do, and they talk about them."

"Hmm. Somehow the natural world just lost some of its mystery."

"Oh don't say that," she replied. "Animals have a relationship to Nature that far exceeds that of humans. You've strayed so far from anything resembling a natural path, what with your obsession with technology. An animal's voice is beautiful - you can hear in it a reverence for Nature. And also Nature's magic."

"Talking of magic," I said, turning to face her, "can you do some for me?"

"Magic? What do you expect to see?"

"I don't know. But you can summon crows and talk to animals, so I'm expecting something really good."

She pretended to frown. "Very well. Do you have a deck of cards?" she asked.

"What - you're going to do a card trick?" I asked, incredulous.

"No of course not," she replied, with a self-satisfied smile. "I just wanted to mess with you."

"Very funny."

"Look, we really don't do magic as such."

"Talking to animals, and crossing to another realm and living for hundreds of years - that sounds like magic to me."

"It's all about a strong connection to Nature, that's all." She paused. "Do you really want to see what you would call magic?"

"Of course I do."

"Alright." She looked around, and fixed her eyes on a tree. "Watch," she said.

Rowan walked over to a large oak tree at the edge of the clearing, and stood with her back against its broad, wrinkled trunk. She pressed her body against the wood, hands by her side. For a moment, nothing happened.

"So?" I said, my arms folded across my chest.

She put a finger to her lips; and then the extraordinary happened. As I watched, Rowan slowly melted into the tree. She merged with the trunk, gradually disappearing into the wood until no trace of her body remained. No matter how hard I looked, all I could see was the tree.

My mouth fell open. "O my God!" I said, astonished. "Are you really still there?"

Suddenly, the tree had a voice. "Yes, I'm here," it said.

"God almighty," I said. "How did you do that?"

Suddenly she emerged from the tree, stepping out of it into the clearing. She curtsied in courtly fashion, and smiled.

"Satisfied?" she asked as she walked towards me.

I was almost speechless. "Amazing," was all I managed to say. "You became the tree... how did you do that?"

She cocked her head to one side. "It's not difficult for the Fay," she said. "As I said, it requires a very close relationship to Nature, that's all."

"That's quite the party trick."

"Oh, it's much more than that," she said. "That party trick saved many a Fay when the Christians came hunting for them."

She resumed her place next to me on the old tree trunk.

"You must really hate them," I said.

"I pity them more. To live your life in hatred and intolerance of others, to be so mean-spirited in everything you do - it's very sad."

"Not all Christians are like that," I said. "Most aren't."

"I know, but many were, in the old days."

"Well, I'm afraid I can't find it in my heart to have compassion for such intolerance. To me they're just evil people. The funny thing is, none of them seem to have read the New Testament."

"What do you mean?" she asked.

"I don't believe in Jesus, don't believe he was divine. He probably existed, but just as one of a long line of self-styled prophets - one who happened to touch a nerve with both the Romans and the local Jews. But if you believe his teachings, he was more about tolerance and love than anything hateful.

Yet throughout history Christians have used the Bible to justify the most egregious crimes, including genocide. All in God's name."

"Yes," she replied, "I understand that quite well. Genocide is not too strong a term to apply to the Christian campaign to eradicate the Faylinn."

"How is it that we don't know about this?"

"Because they didn't leave too many witnesses, and the ones who survived retreated into the other realm."

"Still, I'm surprised there's no history of this."

"There are echoes," she said. "Much of the persecution was already complete during the Dark Ages, though it continued for centuries - and swept up others in its wake."

"Others?"

"The witch trials," she said. "Some of those women were Fay, though most were human. Innocent women who were different in some way, or living alone. Or just a person who someone had a grudge against. In some places - especially Germany - the local authorities would confiscate the property of anyone accused of witchcraft, so there was a strong economic incentive there that fueled the madness."

"All in the name of God."

She nodded. "The Church was very good at its holy work. Did you know that there is not a single original holiday in the Christian calendar?"

"Yes, I did, actually. My father has delivered that lecture more than once."

"Good for him. All the holidays, saints' days and so on - they're all originally pagan. The only one that's survived is Hallowe'en."

"Which is All Saints' Day," I pointed out.

"Exactly. It was brilliant, actually. How do you wipe out a rival religion? Persecute its followers, and appropriate everything in that religion to your own ends. Rename the festivals and the holidays, and in time no one remembers what they once were."

I sighed. "Well, this is a cheerful conversation," I said.

She nodded, and stood up. "Enough of depressing things. Let's go back," she said. "I want to make love again. And after that you can find me a pack of cards."

"Seriously?"

She smiled. "Yes," she said. "I happen to be very good at card tricks."

Interlude

Isaac put down the manuscript; I could see that there was a substantial portion that was as yet unread. I was still digesting these latest revelations about Rowan and his relationship with her.

So you knew you could talk to dogs? I said.

"I didn't - not until I met you. You were the first, and so far the only."

How do you suppose this happened?

"I have no idea, Jack. I don't ever recall her casting a magic spell on me or anything like that. I never paid any heed to the comment at the time - in fact I'd completely forgotten about it until I read it again just now. I mean, it isn't like I've been walking around for the last fifty years saying hi to every dog I met in the vague hope that one of them would say hi back. And then one day you walk into my yard and I find - to my lasting surprise - that I can read your mind."

Why did it take so long, I wonder?

"I don't know, my furry friend," he said as he picked up the manuscript again to resume reading. "Apparently you're just a very special dog."

Well yeah, I replied, *I know I'm special.*

Next to me, Rachel - who I had assumed was asleep - gave a loud snort of disdain.

Isaac smiled, then picked up the manuscript and resumed reading.

Moon

The following day we decided to go out for an evening walk together. We strolled arm in arm along a path that led across a field before winding slowly up to the crest of a nearby hill. The path was old, and I wondered how many lovers had trodden the ground here, walking hand in hand as they discussed their hopeful dreams.

We were chatting about nothing of importance, enjoying the fragrant evening air and the song of a thrush in a copse. Suddenly Rowan stopped and gazed at the sky above the hilltop. There, rising above the horizon, was the full moon. She stared at it, and seemed so lost in her own world that for a moment I wondered if she remembered that I was standing there beside her.

I gazed at the moon too, and made an effort to bring her back to me.

"You probably know this, but some cultures don't see a Man in the Moon. In Japan, they see a rabbit, and -"

I turned to Rowan as I was speaking, and saw tears on her cheeks.

I wiped a tear with my hand. "What's wrong?" I asked.

She was silent for a moment, then heaved a great sigh. She turned away from the moon and looked at me.

"Eolande," she said simply.

"Your sister?"

She nodded sadly. "Yes."

"What about her? Is she the memory you spoke of when I asked you why you gaze at the moon every night?"

JACK

Rowan nodded again. "Let's walk to the hill," she said, "and I'll tell you."

A few minutes later we were at the crest of the hill. The moon was now fully above the horizon; it was larger than usual, I thought, and a lovely pale yellow. We sat on the grass, and I took her hand in mine and waited for her to speak.

She brushed more tears from her face. "I couldn't tell you before," she said. "Before you knew the truth about me - that I'm Fay. But now I can."

I stroked her hand, but did not speak.

"Eolande was older than me - ten years older. Despite the age difference, we were very close. So very close." She looked down sadly and paused, as if recalling a memory. "She was my big sister, and I idolized her. She was beautiful and spirited and kind, and she always looked after me. She was not one of those girls who shun their embarrassing younger sisters - she made sure I was included in everything, and she was always the first to comfort me when I was sad, or applaud me when I did something good. She was my heroine, my champion."

"And did she love the moon?"

Rowan nodded. "Yes. She knew everything about its cycle, and all the legends associated with it. There are many in my culture." She paused, and looked up again at the yellow orb above the horizon. "When I was a little girl, Eolande would take me by the hand at night, and we would walk to a place where we could see the moon. We sat there together, she and I, gazing at it while she told me some story. The stories varied with the phase of the moon: sad stories for the new moon, stories of solitude for the crescent. And always tales of joy and hope when the moon was full, like tonight."

We were silent for a while, both gazing at the sky. Finally I asked, "When did she leave?"

Rowan did not speak for another moment, and another tear rolled down her cheek. Then she said, "When I was nineteen. She was such a free spirit you see. In love with life, always seeking adventure. She visited the Temporal World - your world - several times, and each visit was longer than the one before. She was in love with the Sea, she said. She used to joke that she wanted to become a mermaid."

I smiled weakly.

"But the last time..." She was again staring at the ground.

"What happened, the last time?"

Rowan shrugged. "She never returned." She paused. "But I had a premonition, I don't know why. I begged her not to go, but she hugged me and said she would be back when..."

"When what?"

Rowan turned to look at me. "She said she would be back when the moon was full - that I should look for her then."

She sighed again. "And so I do. Every month I watch the moon go through its course, and watch it as it waxes larger. And with every day some small part of me clings to a rising hope - a vain hope - that this time, this full moon, she will return."

I pulled her close to me and stroked her hair.

"But of course she never does," she said, and I felt her tears against my face. "She never will. Something happened to her here, and she is gone. Gone forever."

Tashka

We were silent for a while, our thoughts lost in sadness.

Suddenly, Rowan shivered and pressed herself closer to me.

"What's wrong?" I asked. It certainly wasn't cold.

Her head was on my shoulder, but I could see her staring into the air above. "There are shadows in the wind tonight - gray ghosts that chill the moonlight with their thin, unearthly cries."

"Ghosts, really? You're scaring me. What's out there?" Now I shivered at the image she had conjured.

"I'm sorry," she said. "There's nothing to worry about - they can't hurt us."

"But what are they?"

"They are beings from another realm. We call them mordreds, *but we have no idea what they are really. Their world intersects with ours from time to time - they appear as fleeting shadows on the wind as they pass through. They are invisible to humans, but Fay can see them, and hear them calling out. They can't hurt us," she repeated, "but their cries are haunting - so haunting. I don't know what they're saying, these beings, but to me their voices sound like they are consumed with loss and despair."*

She raised her head and looked out again. "They're gone," she said.

"How many realms are there?" I asked.

"Who knows? Many more than we imagine, I'm sure." She put her head back on my shoulder.

"Do you miss your father?" I asked after a pause.

She sighed. "Yes, of course. He was a good man, generous and loving."

"And this world killed him."

"Yes, it did, eventually."

"It's strange that the Summerland doesn't, well, cure - what did you call it? - the Waning?"

"Yes. It cannot do that. Ironically, it's different for humans who come to our realm - there their ills are healed and they become youthful again. No one understands how."

I started at this newest revelation.

"Wait - humans can enter the Summerland?" I said excitedly. "Then I could come with you!" Joy was rising within me, but I could tell from the expression on Rowan's face that it was premature.

She shook her head. "No, my love," she said. "I'm afraid it isn't that simple."

"So humans can't enter the Summerland?"

"Yes, they can," she replied sadly. "But only when they die."

I tried to take in what she was telling me.

"You're saying that you and I could be together again, after I die?"

"Yes, we could. Humans are sometimes allowed to enter the Summerland, although it is a privilege granted only rarely."

"So how does that work? Do I have to take a test or something?" I asked, flippantly.

"Yes, there's a written exam. It's quite long."

"You're joking, right?"

Rowan laughed. "Yes, of course. You just need an invitation." She kissed me. "One that I will be overjoyed to give, when the time comes."

"Well why not now?" I asked. "I could just hit myself over the head with a rock or something."

Her expression turned serious. "No, my love. I know you're joking, but suicides don't ever come to the Summerland. No one knows where their spirits go, but I suspect it's nowhere nice."

I mulled over this rather disturbing idea. "Maybe that's what the mordreds are," I said.

"Maybe. Not a pleasant thought. But no - whatever they are, they're neither human nor Fay. They are echoes from another world."

"So I get you here for a while, and then you disappear and I have to wait for a few decades before we can be together again?"

She nodded. "If that's really what you want. I know it's a lot to ask.."

"What about you? Would you honestly wait for me for fifty or sixty years?"

She looked up and met my gaze. "Yes, my darling," she said, caressing my face. "You are my Tashka, and I will wait for you for a thousand cycles of the moon."

Interlude

Isaac paused and looked at me.

How long is a thousand cycles of the moon, exactly? I asked.

"About 80 years, give or take."

That's a long time.

"Yes."

It's very sweet and romantic, I said, *but I have to say it isn't helping my philosophical problems.*

"How so?" he asked.

Well, all this talk of other realms... what if I get reincarnated in one of them? It's bad enough thinking about all the options here on Earth. What if I come back as a mordred? That doesn't sound like much fun.

Isaac shrugged. "I don't know what to tell you, Jack. It's all a big mystery.... maybe one day we'll know the answers."

Is there a lot more to the story? I asked.

"Not a lot," Isaac replied. "At least not that I wrote down. I'll try to read you the rest of it before we go to bed."

Is there anything new and creepy in the next part?

"No," he laughed. "But there is a major... development."

The Call of the Wind

It was a clear day in September. A storm had blown through the previous afternoon, bringing with it rain and wind that battered the roof of the old house for hours. But then the wind had veered with the cold front, and we awoke to a bright morning and a sky strewn with shreds of white cloud that scudded overhead.

Invigorated by the change of weather, we drove to the coast, turning off the old A2 at Dover and meandering along local roads that I knew well to a point at the top of the famous white cliffs. The coast of France was clearly visible across the English Channel, and spume flew off the crest of the waves in the gale. On the cliff, it was hard to stand still.

Rowan stood there at the edge, her arms across her chest and her eyes closed, and let the wind buffet her.

She inhaled deeply, and sighed.

"Strange," she said, opening her eyes. "This is the Levant. It is a southern wind - it doesn't normally blow this far north."

"How can you tell which wind it is?" I asked.

"The smell."

"It just smells of the Sea, like all winds here."

"To you, perhaps. But for me it carries the scent of mountains in southern Spain, and of the warm waters of the Mediterranean. I can even smell the flowers of Gibraltar in its breath."

"And does it speak to you?" I asked, only half-jokingly.

She turned and put her arms around my neck, and smiled. "Yes, my love, it does. It calls to me, as it does to all Faylinn."

"And what does it say, this wind?"

"That it is time to move, to begin again the endless migration of my kind."

"So, does this mean we're leaving here?"

She kissed me. "We don't have to," she said. "But it would please me if we did."

"Then we shall," I replied, surprised at my decisiveness. "Where will we go?"

"To the Mediterranean," Rowan said without hesitation. "Back to Greece, at least to begin with."

"My parents will be crushed."

"I know. I'll miss them - they're wonderful people."

And three days later, just like that, we were on our way. There were tearful goodbyes, and then my father drove us to the cross-Channel ferry terminal in Dover. He left, a saddened man, I boarded the ship... and Rowan - having no passport - simply disappeared.

I was to travel, alone, from Paris to Athens on the Orient Express, which at that time was so bereft of its former glory that it was no longer even classified as an express train under the European railway system. For three days I inhabited a cramped compartment with some French students who smoked Gauloises cigarettes without a break, leaving the carriage perpetually wreathed in a haze of blue smoke. But they were friendly and shared their food, and they put up with my fractured attempts to speak French.

When we finally arrived in Athens, I alighted on the platform and anxiously searched the sea of faces for Rowan. And there she was, the prettiest girl in the world, smiling and running into my arms.

We remained in Greece for a few weeks, wandering the islands and the Peloponnese in the warm late summer weather. But in early November the wind called to Rowan again - this time it was the Bora from the mountains of central Europe - and soon we were once more moving on.

For a month we wandered through the Carpathian Mountains, through valleys and villages disconnected from time. In that mediaeval world, I was quite the exotic wonder, and it was not uncommon for a small crowd to gather and follow us as we walked the dirt streets of small towns. But Rowan seemed completely at home here in the ancestral home of the Tana; she belonged there, a natural part of the landscape.

We traveled ever west, both of us ineluctably drawn to Venice, that most extraordinary and unique of cities. Before we had even arrived, we had decided to remain there for the winter.

We arrived on a Tuesday afternoon, and threaded our way from Santa Lucia railway station through endless alleyways and canals, emerging finally from between two palazzi to the Grand Canal itself, which opened before us like an impossible, faded dream.

"I love this place," Rowan said. "There's nowhere like it."

"Yes," I replied. "There is magic in our world too."

La Serenissima

We rented three rooms in a palazzo which overlooked the Grand Canal. It was certainly not cheap; but when you are in a city that affords such unique vistas, thrift seems foolish. There was a small balcony on which we often took a light meal, despite the cold, idly watching the gondolas and other traffic plying the waters below. Rowan loved to get up before dawn and take a vaporetto to Piazza San Marco, before the crowds overwhelmed the great square; for even in the winter of the mid-1960's, the city was host to plenty of tourists gawking at the wonders that La Serenissima - Venice, the Serene Republic - had to offer. In the tranquil silence of daybreak, broken as it was only by the distant cries of gulls over the Giudecca, you could hear the echoes of that long and once-glorious history.

At each full moon, Rowan would ascend the tower of the Campanile; because, she said with a smile, she wanted to be closer to the moon than anyone else in the city.

For four months, we immersed ourselves in the living romance that was Venice, getting lost in its back streets, shivering in the sea air as we traversed the canals, sipping coffee and reading to each other in waterfront cafés, and making love on an endless series of lazy, languid afternoons. It was the perfect place to be in love; and yet the melancholy that pervaded the city, especially in winter, reflected well the bittersweet reality, the perpetual caveat, that underlay our union.

We were, we knew, living on borrowed time.

Amatheia

One afternoon in late May, Rowan and I were sitting in a café that looked out over the Grand Canal. We were drinking espresso and talking about our plans to leave Venice for the summer, when suddenly I noticed that Rowan was distracted. She was staring at what looked like an adolescent girl seated at a nearby table. She was very pretty, with dark hair, prominent cheekbones and large, almond-shaped eyes.

"What is it?" I asked.

Rowan turned to me briefly, then continued to gaze at the girl. "That girl," she whispered, "I think she's Fay."

"How can you tell?"

Rowan shook her head. "I just know. She has the look."

At that moment the girl caught Rowan's gaze; her expression changed and she stared intently at us. Rowan spoke in her own language, giving a traditional Faylinn greeting that she later translated for me from the Faïnna.

"*La luna estrezha y'zhora nazh stryaitchu,*" she said. *The moon shines on the hour of our meeting.*

Immediately the girl rose and came over to our table.

"*Faylinn zara,*" she said, in a low voice. It was a statement, not a question. *You are Faylinn.*

Rowan nodded. "*Ya Rowan zhu. Ya Tana et Glashtyn.*" Rowan translated for my benefit, although it was obvious what she had said: she had told the girl her name, and her tribe.

"*Ya Amatheia zhu,*" the girl replied. *I am Amatheia.* She sat down.

"*Vertan triba zhara?*" *What is your tribe?* Rowan asked.

"*Ya Marinka zhu,*" she said. "*Vaina maya ama Rusalka zha.*"

"She is of the Marinka," Rowan explained. "They were originally from the area that is now Hungary. The tribe is named after a flower that grows in the mountains. But her mother is Rusalka - they lived on the coast and were closely associated with the Sea. The word is well known today, actually - it means mermaid in several Slavic languages."

"*Vai,*" nodded Amatheia. *Yes.* Apparently she understood at least some English.

"*Et zhenvat irau zhara?*" *How old are you?*

"*Ya verro zhu.*"

"She's fifty."

"Fifty?" I asked, and made no attempt to mask my astonishment. "She looks like she's twelve!" Rowan shrugged. "Marinka are known for aging slowly. No one knows why."

"*Zhenvat lunas izan Venezia?*" Rowan continued. *How many months - moons - have you been in Venice?*

"*Dva irau.*" *Two years.* "*Venezia aqua zha - et ya Rusalka zhu. Ya mazhda hemaya.*"

Rowan sighed. "She is in love with Venice because it is water and she is Rusalka. She says she must be here. But two years is a long time, and I fear the Waning will claim her if she remains too long."

"As it will you," I replied.

Rowan said nothing, but nodded sadly.

Amatheia and Rowan continued the conversation in Faïnna. Rowan introduced me as her partner, and if Amatheia was surprised at this unusual union of human and Faylinn she did not show this in her expression, but instead smiled at me briefly. Rowan occasionally translated significant items of information from their discussion, but for the most part I was left to contemplate the Grand Canal as the two women talked.

I studied Amatheia as they conversed. Here was clearly a confident woman of maturity and experience, yet my mind could not reconcile this with the childish nature of her appearance. She was beautiful, but her eyes betrayed an underlying sadness, as indeed did Rowan's. I wondered if this was a feature of all Faylinn, destined as they were to be exiles from the Temporal Realm that they once loved.

Finally, Amatheia said she was late for an appointment with a friend, and rose to leave.

We stood and bade her farewell. "Perhaps we shall meet again," Rowan said, but now she had switched to Italian.

"Forse, ma io non la penso così," she replied in perfect Italian. "Il destino di Faylinn in questo ambito è quello di essere soli." Perhaps, but I think not. The destiny of Faylinn in this realm is to be alone.

She and Rowan exchanged blessings, and Amatheia turned to go. But suddenly she stared at Rowan; she tilted her head and her face took on a curious expression. Then she stepped forward and placed a hand on her belly.

"T'vya dozhka bella zhana," she said.

Rowan frowned. I looked at her, questioningly. "What's wrong?" I asked. "What did she say?"

"She said..." Rowan paused. "She said that my daughter will be very beautiful."

"What?"

"Vaina ya ny hzaudun," Rowan said to Amatheia. But I'm not pregnant.

The girl smiled at us both, and nodded. "Yes," she said, now in accented English. "Yes Rowan - you are."

"But how can this be?" I asked. We were alone again in the café; Amatheia had gone, swallowed up by the aquatic anonymity of the city.

"It's rare,' Rowan replied, "but there's no reason Fay and humans cannot produce children."

"Do you believe her?"

"Yes," she nodded. "The Marinka have this skill, to sense pregnancy before it becomes known to the woman."

I was still reeling from this huge new complication in our situation. I did not know what to say, or feel. "So what do we do?"

Rowan took my hand and looked at me. "Do you want this child?"

"I would love to have this child, with you. But how is that possible? You're going to have to leave, sooner or later. And then what? Do you take the child with you, leave her here with me without a mother - what?"

She sighed, and gazed out over the water. "I don't know, my love," she said, finally. "But if you want this child, we must somehow make it work."

"And what about you?" I asked. "Do you want this?"

She smiled, and kissed me. "Yes," she said. "More than anything."

JACK

Gwynifar

After much discussion, we decided to stay in Venice. We were happy there, and we both rather liked the idea of having a Venetian-born daughter. Neither of us questioned that the child's sex was female, as foretold by Amatheia.

I told my parents the news, and they were overjoyed at the prospect of having a grandchild. There was, inevitably, an expectation that we would marry; but since Rowan had no papers of any kind, this was an impossibility - and anyway neither of us felt the need for a ceremony and a piece of paper to validate our relationship. My parents baulked at this at first, but eventually put it down to the changing tides of society - this was the 1960's, after all, when half of western youth seemed to living in sin.

"What shall we call her?" Rowan asked one day as we were drinking coffee on our accustomed perch on the balcony, listening to the gossip of the gondoliers below.

"Give her a faery name," I suggested. "We could name her Sylvane, after your mother."

Rowan smiled. "Yes, we could. Or Audrey, after yours."

"She should have a name with a nice meaning. Not one of those that mean something like 'consecrated to God' or some other Christian nonsense."

"Yes," she said, "I would prefer not to take a Christian name for our daughter. Christians have not been kind to my people."

I thought for a moment, then said "Gwynifar."

"I like that," Rowan said. "It's Gaelic, I think?"

"Yes, it's Welsh. There are a few variants - Guinevere is the one everyone knows. You know, wife to King Arthur, queen of Camelot."

Rowan nodded. "So why Gwynifar - what does it mean?"

"It depends who you listen to. In some renditions, the name means 'white phantom' or 'white shadow'. But I like the third meaning - 'white wave'. Like the first story you ever told me, on Santorini - the one about the wave. If I wasn't already in love with you by then, then I certainly was by the end of that story."

Rowan smiled. "Very well. She shall be Gwynifar, Gwyn for short."

"Gwynifar Sylvane LaTana Rosenberg. Now there's a mix of cultures for you. Welsh, Jewish and Fay - the poor kid will be completely mixed up."

"Or she'll have the best qualities of all of them."

"Perhaps," I said. "And talking of that... are we getting a magical daughter?"

"I cannot say," Rowan replied, and her face took on a serious look. "I have no experience with half-human, half-Fay children. No one I know does now - it's very rare. She may well be entirely mortal."

"Or," I replied, "she might one day disappear into thin air."

Gwynifar, my daughter. The white wave, the white phantom. She was born on a wild night of storm on Valentine's Day 1967. At the moment of her birth shortly before 5 a.m., the clouds suddenly opened to reveal a fingernail moon riding high above the city skyline. A new moon for a new soul.
And as she emerged into the world, howling like the wind beyond the walls, I thought her the most beautiful thing I had ever seen.
Green eyes and red hair, gift of her mother. What other gifts had been passed to her, I wondered?

Cry Sorrow

My parents came out to Venice to meet their new grandchild shortly after she was born. Then in May, they announced that they were returning to the U.S. to spend the rest of their retirement in the country of their birth. They gave various nostalgic reasons for the move, but in truth I think they were mainly tired of English weather.
My father enquired whether Rowan and I were going to stay in Venice - or would we like to have the house? We jumped at the chance to live by the wood where our story had begun, and so in June we sold or gave away most of our possessions and made our way to what I jokingly referred to as - parodying Shakespeare - the Septic Isle.
There was a frenzy of packing and organization as my parents prepared to uproot themselves for another continent; and then suddenly they were gone, and we were alone with the house and the wood.
The summer passed all too quickly, but we were as happy as the days were long. We watched in daily amazement at the growth and development of this tiny being we had brought into the world. Gwyn was an easy child, quick to laugh and quicker to smile, even at strangers; and she became a fast favorite of the various old ladies who would stop by the house on their daily walks. These visits were invariably unannounced, but Rowan bore them cheerfully, and always invited the women in for tea.
One of the "Coven", as Rowan collectively referred to the group, was a woman named Ailsa, who was almost 80 years old. She was Scottish by birth but had lived in the south for decades, marrying an Englishman against the wishes of her family and remaining here after his death left her a widow in the 1950's. We grew very fond of her, and she was always the most welcome of the old women. Ailsa possessed much wisdom and common sense regarding the raising of children - she had produced five of her own - and she was a great help to Rowan.

The weather turned cold early in the autumn, and November brought seemingly unending rain. On the evening of the 16th, the sky cleared just long enough for Rowan to acknowledge the full moon. Then, three days later, as that moon was on the wane, came the event we had dreaded for so long.

I returned from a trip to the local grocery store to hear her crying in our bedroom. I ran to her, and found her sitting on the bed, sobbing as I had never seen her do. I at first feared that something had befallen Gwyn, but saw that the child was asleep in her crib.

I asked what was wrong, and in response she held out her hand and displayed a sheaf of her hair. I frowned, and stared at her questioningly.

She gave a sharp intake of breath, wiped the tears from her face, and looked up at me. "It has begun," she said. "The Waning has come for me at last."

Parting

Time dulls, but does not heal, the keenness of grief.

I look back on that November day and remember every detail, as if the scene was still before me now. The clothes she wore, the gray of the sky, the smell of the old house. The frenzied beating of my heart. And, more than anything, burned into my memory forever, the look of utter hopelessness on Rowan's face as she said that she must leave me.

I knew it would come, that day, but there was no preparing for it. Part of me had never accepted the certainty of the Waning, or had at least believed that it would come later - always later, never now.

But now it was Now.

Losing hair was the first sign, she said. Next would come a graying of pallor, an aching in the bones, and then a rapid aging. She had seen it before, in her father.

"How long?" I asked. "When must you go?"

"Now," she said through her tears. "I must go within the day." She could heal in the Summerland, she said be whole again - but she had to return there immediately, before the process became irreversible. We lay on the bed, bodies entwined, and cried together.

"I will never see you again," I sobbed. I was inconsolable, as was she.

She fought back more tears, then looked at me.

"I can return," she said, "but only three times. More is not permitted. And I can never stay more than a day."

"I don't believe this is happening," I said. "I can't lose you."

"You're not losing me. I shall always be with you, and we will be together again one day."

"But not until I die," I said bitterly.
"Yes. Can you wait that long for me?"
"Of course. You're my Tashka, remember?"
She smiled through her tears. "Yes, my love."

We made love one last time, a lingering, tender act; one that broke both our hearts.

Then we rose, dressed, and ate a cheerless last meal together. She fed Gwyn, sobbing as she did so, her tears falling on the infant's face as she suckled her breast. She no longer made any attempt to conceal her anguish at having to leave her daughter behind.

"Do you want to take her?" I asked. It pained me to suggest this, but I had to at least offer.

"I want to take her almost as much as I want to stay," she said. "You cannot imagine how devastating this is for me, to have to leave her here. But I can't do that to you. I can't leave you alone here, or deprive you of your daughter."

"But what about you? I do know, Rowan - I know how much pain it will cause you to be parted from her."

She shrugged hopelessly. "It's the price I pay," she said.

One more hour, and then farewell.

We were clutching each other like two people who feared they would never again hold someone in their arms.

"I love you with all my heart," she said. "You know that, don't you?"

"Yes," I replied. "As do I you."

"We will be together again one day, I promise."

"That day cannot come soon enough."

She nodded, and wiped the tears from her face. "I must go," she said, and kissed me one last time. With more reluctance than I have ever done anything, I opened the back door; and then she was on the stoop. She put a hand to my face, and smiled through her tears.

"Azhur, maya Tashka," she said, then turned and walked towards the wood.

I watched her go, and silently repeated the words.

Azhur, maya Tashka.

Farewell, my Other Heart.

Away

I cried for the better part of two days, locked away in the house. Finally, I pulled myself together for Gwyn's sake, and busied myself as I could with household chores.

JACK

A week after Rowan left, the old widow Ailsa came by. I had been in no mood to receive visitors, and had politely put off a couple of other callers over the past few days. But I realized now that I could use some company from a woman I had come to regard as a friend.

I had no idea how I was going to explain Rowan's absence in the long-term. If anyone asked - and no one had, yet - I was going to concoct a story about her having to leave town to be with a sick relative. After showing Ailsa into the dining room, I mumbled something to this effect, that she was in Italy for a while.

"No, she's not, my lad," Ailsa said, surprising and discomfiting me despite the kindly tone in which she delivered this statement of disbelief. "She's what we call Away" - she traced out a capital A in the air - "Gone back to the Summerland where she came from."

She saw the look of astonishment on my face, and said, "Oh, you don't need to pretend with me, Isaac. I knew soon as I saw her, that she was one o' the faery folk. She had the look."

"You believe in faeries?" I said, still unsure of whether to admit the truth.

"Aye, I do. I'm from Scotland, Isaac - up there we believe in glamour. We're not fooled by modern times, nor any of that nonsense the Church would have ye believe."

I had no idea what to say, and told her so.

"You don't need to say anything if you don't wish to," she said. "But I imagine you're hurting something terrible now, what with her gone and the babe to care for an' all."

And suddenly, at this unlooked-for gift of sympathy from an old woman, I broke down and cried. I sobbed like a baby as Ailsa took me in her arms and consoled me, and then the whole story came pouring out like a wave. It was an immense relief to be able to confide in someone, to tell them this impossible truth that I had shared with no one, not even my parents.

"People will think me mad if they find out," I said when I had finally told her everything.

"Don't worry," she said. "Your secret's safe with me. But you'd best be making plans to go elsewhere afore folk start asking too many questions."

She was right, of course: I could not stay. Beyond the problem of how to explain the permanent absence of my partner - I could not bear the thought of people believing she had left me - I had no wish to remain in a place that was defined by the two of us, not by myself alone. We had met here, we had parted here. Now half of me had gone, and the house seemed empty and full of shallow echoes. As did the wood, the trees stripped of their leaves by the chill autumn wind. I tried to walk there once, but it was a winter wood, and my memories were all of summer. And every cawing of a crow reminded me of her.

But where to go?

The solution arrived one day in a letter from a friend with whom I'd been in graduate school in the U.S.. He was an enterprising engineer who had made something of a name for himself consulting to the oil industry, and now he was setting up his own business on the east coast. He invited me to join him as a partner, citing both my creativity as an engineer and - as he put it - my superior business sense. Having no other viable option, I accepted almost immediately and prepared to leave England.

My biggest problem was what to tell my parents. In the end, I deferred this and said I would explain everything when I arrived in the U.S. - although what exactly I was going to say I had no idea. After consulting with them, we agreed to sell the house. I left the sale in the hands of a real estate agent, and made plans to depart with Gwyn for a new, Rowanless life in America. A New World.

I made one last visit to the wood, on a still, overcast day in late December. I sat on the fallen tree in the clearing where Rowan had gathered the crows and had explained to me who she was. I had never felt more alone. Finally I stood up and placed a glass of wine, some bread and salt, and a white rose on the ground - just as I had done long ago. I bowed briefly, knowing that this time there was no unseen presence among the trees watching my ritual. And then I walked away, tears chilling my face in the cold wind.

The next day I closed up the house and headed for London and the airport, leaving behind me a flurry of gossip in the village, which Ailsa did her best to moderate. We had embraced warmly when it came time for me to leave.

"Good luck, Isaac," she said. We were both holding back tears. "You'll be with her again one day, you'll see."

"Will I?" I replied. I did not know.

Two days after Gwyn and I had arrived, I called my parents and told them the truth. Everything. I was aware that by doing this I risked them thinking me crazy, but I figured that if anyone was morally obligated to believe such an absurd story, it was one's father and mother. I never knew for sure if they believed me.

We had a long conversation, which featured many questions that I had answered as best I could. At the end, my father said, "I'm sorry, Isaac. She was an extraordinary woman, to be sure."

"Is," I said. "She is still extraordinary. She's just no longer here."

Return

Three times, she had said. There was no indication of when.

We had settled into our new home on the Massachusetts coast. I was preoccupied with the various details of setting up house and home anew, not to mention working with my friend to establish a consulting company. I was glad of the distractions all this work brought, and gave little thought to when - or even whether - the mother of my child would reappear.

Then it was February, and Gwyn's first birthday, which fell on a wet and gloomy Wednesday. I had arranged nothing to celebrate - one-year-old kids don't really appreciate the concept of birthdays. I was in the kitchen of our small house, making myself a grilled cheese sandwich which, sadly enough, was going to have to serve as dinner that evening. The sound of the rain on the roof made me glad to be indoors.

Suddenly I was surprised to hear a knock at the front door. I wasn't expecting a visitor, and I wondered who would be out on such a miserable night. Curious, I opened the door to find Rowan standing on the doorstep, dripping onto the welcome mat.

"May I come in, Mr Rosenberg? It's rather wet out tonight."

I almost screamed with delight, throwing my arms around her and holding her tightly, oblivious to the sodden state of her clothing. We stepped inside and she delivered a long, passionate kiss which, like our first, left me breathless.

Finally we separated. "Where in God's name did you come from?" I asked. "And what are you doing outside on a night like this?"

She smiled. "I've had to walk a way to get here."

"Why didn't you just materialize here in the house, or whatever it is that you do?" I still had no idea how Fay moved between worlds.

"Well, for one thing you can't just pop out anywhere. The portals come out at specific places, and the nearest one was a mile or so away. And I had to find the house first."

"How exactly did you do that, by the way? I mean, know where we were living?"

She grinned. "Faery secret. I'd tell you, but then I'd have to kill you."

"God, you're soaked. Let's get you out of these clothes."

She took everything off and then, naked, went to the crib to see Gwyn.

"My God," she said. "She's so beautiful."

"She has a beautiful mother."

Rowan gently picked up her daughter, who stirred and awoke, her green eyes casting around sleepily to see who had disturbed her repose. Groggily, they focused on Rowan, and then Gwyn smiled at her and made a small cooing noise. Rowan held her close, the child's head pressed against her neck, and she began to cry.

"God, I have missed her so much," she said. "It has broken my heart to leave the two of you like this."

I enveloped them both in my arms, and we stood there for a few moments, silently swaying, inhaling the scent of skin and hair. Finally Rowan laid Gwyn back in the crib and turned to me.

"Oh Isaac, I'm so sorry it has to be like this. You have no idea how much pain it has caused me."

"Of course I do."

"Yes," she nodded. "That was a stupid thing to say. Of course you do."

"How long do I have you for?" I asked.

"A day only," she replied sadly. "I must return by tomorrow evening."

"And then you can come back only twice more."

"Yes."

"Well then," I said, "let's make the most of it, shall we?"

Over the next 24 hours, we slept but little. We made love four times, each time more tender and more sorrowful than the last, until at the end we both cried through the entire act.

Rowan held Gwyn for much of the time in between, talking and singing to her in Faïnna; and as the hour of her departure drew near, I could see her holding the girl ever more tightly.

Finally, her time was up. We were both openly weeping now.

"I won't see you again for a long time, will I?" I said.

She shook her head. "No, my love. I will return when Gwyn is almost grown, perhaps."

"And will you take her away from me then?"

"Oh Isaac, I don't know. If she wants to come with me..." Her voice trailed off. "You have her now at least, which is more than I do. You will be at her side as she grows up, which I won't. There will be so many lost years - I will miss my daughter's entire childhood. Please don't make this harder than it is already."

I held her in my arms and stroked her hair. "I'm sorry," I said. "It's a truly awful deal for both of us."

"It will be better, one day."

I sighed. "I live in hope," I said.

Rowan held Gwyn close, and spoke a blessing in Faïnna. Then she kissed her, and said "Keep close, little one," and laid her back in her crib.

One more hug, one more kiss, one more tearful farewell. Azhur, maya Tashka, azhur.

And then she was gone, and I was once again left behind.

Sleight of Hand

And so we have arrived at the last chapter in my tale.

It has now been nine years since I last saw Rowan, and a life that was literally extra-ordinary has become routine - or at least as routine as any life can be that has been touched by supernatural events, and left to brood over memories of magic, and of love.

JACK

Every night when the weather is clear I sit on the grass and gaze at the moon, as she did. I am saddened always by this ritual, but I cannot give it up. It is my last link with her. I watch the phases slip from full to new and back to full again, a nightly reminder of the constancy of change. Is she out there somewhere, in her world, staring at this same moon and thinking of me? My heart knows the answer, and is glad.

And what of the child, Gwynifar, the white wave, this unexpected gift? I have not yet told her the full story of her mother, and who she was. Perhaps I should tell her now, while she is still a child, for to children all things are possible, and magic is unquestioned. But no: that conversation must wait until she is old enough to coldly analyze the reality, to gradually bring herself to accept the seemingly unacceptable and weave it into her life.

Until then, I watch her for signs of the unusual, for some hint that would declare her Rowan's child in more than just looks. She is lithe and graceful and she loves the woods; but then many children have these qualities. Recently she has taken an interest in, of all things, magic tricks. For a while I read much into this, but now I think it merely another joke played by a Fate that delights in the unbearably flippant. Still, she is remarkably adept at sleight of hand...

What glamour do I expect to see: a disappearing act, perhaps? God, not that. Not that!

It is selfish, I know, but there are many days when I hope that Gwyn is wholly mortal, wholly ordinary. That she knows nothing of glamour, nothing of the lure of the wood, of beauty under the moon. That she will not grow up to yearn for another world, and in it to seek the mother she has never known. But somehow I know this: if she is indeed part Fay, then all this will be as inevitable as the waning moon.

Am I destined to be left here not once, but twice?

Tonight the moon is full. Gwyn is in the house, practicing a magic trick, and on this fine summer evening I am left alone on the grass with my lunar contemplations. As I think of her, my precious daughter, and of all those chance events that brought her, improbably, into my world, I am suddenly and inexplicably struck with a sense of peace, of certainty.

Relaxed and content, I stand and walk towards the house. She will show me her magic trick, I will clap appreciatively, and then I will take her to her bed and read to her as I always do. A faery tale tonight, perhaps - why not? She will snuggle warmly against me as I read, and I will be comforted and lulled by the sound of her breathing, deepening as she slips into sleep. And I will be happy.

Yes, she will leave me, but I can always hope that she will return, or that we meet in another realm. For while a part of her comes from Rowan, the rest belongs to me.

Interlude

So Gwyn was Fay also, right?
"Yes, Jack, she was. Half Fay - but she possessed all the powers of her mother, though it took her a while to grow into them, so to speak."
When did you know for sure?
"I knew when she about Alice's age, eleven or so."
How did you find out, finally?
"Because of an incident that occurred with some other children." He paused, and I could see the sadness in his eyes as cast his mind back. "I didn't witness the incident myself, actually - I heard about it from one of the children involved, and then afterwards from Gwyn herself. But I wrote about it as if I'd been there. It's the very last part of my story."
Isaac sighs, and picks up the one remaining page of his manuscript.

The Wood

On a blue day in high summer, three children run laughing into a wood. They are hot from playing in the August sun, and the sudden change in temperature feels good on their skin as they slip into the cool shade of the trees. A few yards into the wood, the boy and one of the girls stop, their laughter suspended by a vague sense of unease at the silence within. But not the third child, the girl with red hair and green eyes whose idea it was to come here. She runs on, pausing only to look back and urge on her companions.

"Come on! Why d'you stop?"

"Gwyn, come back, it's spooky in here," *says the boy.*

"O Mark!" *admonishes the girl.* "It's not spooky - it's lovely here. It's my favorite place. Come on, let's play hide and seek. You two count to ten and I'll hide."

"Ten?" *says the other girl, suddenly forgetting her fear in surprise.* "You can't hide from us in just ten seconds. Don't you want twenty, or a hundred?"

"No, ten will do. You'll see. Cover your eyes, here I go! Bet you can't find me!"

They do as instructed, faces in their hands, two young voices ringing out the count. "One... two... three..."

As he counts, the boy's curiosity begins to grow. How could his friend possibly hide in so short a time? "Four... five..."

In fact, how could she even get far enough away from them?

"Six... seven..."

And why does he not hear her footsteps running away? Carefully, he spreads the fingers of each hand just enough so that he can peek out. For an instant he frowns in puzzlement, for the red-haired girl has not moved from where she stood when they began counting. She stands looking at them, arms folded and a bemused smile on her pretty young face.

"Eight... nine..." Only one voice is counting now.

Suddenly the boy gasps at what he sees from inside the dome of his hands. For the girl is disappearing before his eyes, merging seamlessly with bark and leaves behind her, until all he can see is the tree of which she has somehow become a part.

"Ten! Here we come, ready or not!" The other girl looks up, then around. "Which way shall we look?" she asks. Then, noticing the boy staring with mouth open, apparently at a tree, she says, "What's the matter with you?"

The boy continues to stare. "How did she do that?" he says.

Loss

Isaac put down the paper and gave me a smile, warm but poignant. He folded his hands and sighed.

"That's as much as I wrote," he said. "But of course there was more. We had wonderful years together, Gwyn and I, until... until she left."

When did she go? I asked. And why?

"She was sixteen years old. She knew what she was, of course - she had known of her strange abilities for a few years, and after the incident in the woods I finally sat her down and told her the truth about her mother. She very much wanted to meet her, and to experience the Summerland. And," - here Isaac sighed, sadly - "I knew that I couldn't stop her if she wished to go. Nor would I have wanted to."

So what happened? How did she leave?

"Rowan came for her, as I knew she would one day. It was her second return - the second of the three that she was permitted. There was no warning - she just appeared one day out of the blue. I was overjoyed to see her, of course - it had been so long. But I was also very sad, because I knew that Gwyn would probably leave with her. As she did."

That must have been so hard for you.

"It was. As hard as saying farewell to Rowan after the Waning set in. I had lost my lover, and now my daughter was leaving me too. It was a very sad day for everyone - there were many tears, but Gwyn was so excited to meet her mother, and I could see how much she wanted to be taken to the other realm. I could not deny her that."

But did she return?

"Yes, and quite regularly for a while. I had to concoct a story for public consumption, that she'd gone off to a private school in Europe, and then later had found work there. That she came back once a year for some time after helped bolster the credibility of the lie. But she is Fay, and Fay cannot linger indefinitely in this world - it's the price they pay for their powers. Eventually she stopped coming back, and it's now been more than ten years since I've seen her."

You miss her a lot?

"Of course," Isaac said. "But it's the price *I* pay - for loving a Fay."

Love Deferred

Tu m'as rendu fades toutes les femmes,
et mediocres tous les autres destins

(For me you have rendered all other women dull,
and all other destinies mediocre)

- Henri de Montherlant

We were silent for a while. Finally, Isaac sighed and stretchevd.

"Well, that's my story," he said. "Now you know everything, and why I've lived my life with a broken heart. But a heart that retains a measure of hope."

I'm sorry, I said. *It's a wonderful story, Isaac. But I can see how much she meant to you - how much they both did.*

He nodded. "If Rowan is right, then I will be with them both again one day - and not too long now, I'd guess, given my advanced age."

That's a long time to wait for love on a chance.

"I suppose it is. But she's worth the wait."

Isaac paused and took a sip of tea. He gazed into the mug reflectively for a while, then looked down at me. "So you see, Jack, why I never married. I dated other women, and I had a few relationships that lasted for months or even a couple of years in some cases. But it was never the same. It was all just a way to fill in the spaces of time. I could never have committed myself to another woman, knowing that my heart could never belong to her. It would have been dishonest."

He sighed sadly. "Rowan was - is - everything to me. There can be no other."

Le Chat C'est Mort

Cat in the Doghouse

We went to bed that night in a somber mood, but by morning Isaac was his usual cheerful self again.

We set off for home after breakfast, and arrived in Seattle to find Veronica reinstalled in the house, and Bonkers in the satisfying state of being *felina non grata*. This was obvious from the moment I walked in: I immediately detected a frosty atmosphere between my human and what I regard as her disposable pet. I didn't know what had happened, and Bonkers - who was sulking in the corner silently broadcasting more than his usual measure of disdain - wasn't about to tell me. I had to wait until later that day to overhear her telling a friend the story, and it was a cracker of a tale.

It seemed that on the previous evening Veronica had conducted a three-hour session with a new client named Oliver. Oliver - who, like half the current population of Seattle works for Amazon - was a very valuable client in terms of what he was prepared to pay for Veronica's erotic services. Oliver had the added advantage of not being very high maintenance in terms of what he desired from said services. Some bondage, some flogging, some orgasm denial... a little of this, a little of that.

After tying him up and administering various forms of corporal punishment to selected parts of his anatomy, Veronica made him swallow two whole Viagra pills. She then gagged him, and bound him securely to the St Andrews Cross in her dungeon. In which position he was left to stare at a wide-screen TV on which was playing a particularly shameful European porn movie involving two nubile blondes, a well-endowed black man and a surprisingly enthusiastic German shepherd. The idea was to deprive him of the ability to relieve himself for an extended period, after which Veronica would return and - if she deemed that he had been a good boy and asked her nicely once his gag had been removed - she would relieve him with her hands while he was still bound to the cross.

Oliver's erection was already fit to burst before she even left the room, his arousal heightened by having his balls tied tightly with a thin leather thong. Which item proved his undoing.

Having thus prepared her client for his ordeal of porn-infused denial, Veronica left the dungeon to relax for half an hour. She made herself a pot of fresh jasmine tea, then retired upstairs to her bedroom. She scrolled through the large music selection on her iPhone and decided she wanted to listen to something loud and energetic. Settling comfortably on her king-sized bed, she pulled up the *Best of Led Zeppelin*, put on headphones, and hit play.

Note to those in a similar situation: *don't* put on headphones when you have a client in your dungeon.

Because unfortunately Veronica had inadvertently failed to completely close the dungeon door.

Enter Bonkers. Like me, he is under a long-standing prohibition from entering this sacred space in the basement; and being a cat, this just makes him all the more determined to do exactly that. And so, with the preternatural radar cats have for detecting an opportunity to do something that their owners absolutely, under any circumstances, want them not to, Bonkers wandered down to the basement and, seeing the door slightly ajar, used his brainless little head to push it open just enough to create a cat-sized space.

Enter cat. Cat sees naked man strapped to cross, legs spread, penis erect. Cat looks man up and down. Cat sees leather thong dangling from man's balls.

You can see what's coming, can't you?

Yay, new cat toy!

A few seconds later, muffled screams emanate from the dungeon. Meanwhile, up in her bedroom Veronica is sipping jasmine tea and happily rocking out to Robert Plant singing *Communication Breakdown*, oblivious to the fact that, two floors below, her beloved pet is currently using a man's genitals as a scratching post. I'm sure that the poor guy's desperate flailing and the resulting jerking up and down of his balls - and with that, the attached thong - only compounded the problem, not to mention Bonkers' fun.

How long this went on for is not clear, but by the time Veronica finally went down to check on her new client Bonkers had apparently grown bored with this new game and had wandered off in search of other entertainment.

The aftermath was not pretty, and involved several bandaids - not easy to affix to a shrinking penis, by the way - a fair amount of Betadyne, numerous apologies and, worst of all, a refund of the hefty fee that her new client had paid for his inaugural and probably final session. Oliver remained stoically silent throughout, and left with a curt nod and a distinct limp.

I would just like to point out that, while I will concede that the Squirrel Incident involved the replacement of a broken vase, I have never cost my human $2,000.

I hope she remembers that come Christmas.

Diversion

It was the ever-resourceful Anna who finally figured out a way to deal with the stream of people coming to the house in the hope of meeting Demon Cat. The stream had diminished to more of a trickle while we'd been away, but the demonic feline was still good for a few demented pilgrims every week.

"It's ridiculous," Veronica complained one evening as the two of them shared burritos and some appropriately ethnic Mexican beer. "Bonkers even has his own Instagram site now where people are encouraged to submit photos of him through my window."

Anna considered. "Darling, what you need is a diversion."

"What do you mean?" Veronica asked.

"You need to convince people that Bonkers has shuffled off his mortal coil. A tragic accident perhaps." Veronica - who has somehow figured out that I like Mexican food - slipped me a small chunk of her burrito.

"I'm not sure they'd buy it. The notice on the door didn't work very well."

"Well yes - you're going to have to close your curtains for awhile and make sure Bonkers isn't visible."

"I still don't see how we can make people believe he's dead."

"Ah, but that's where the diversion comes in," said Anna. "You need to create a grave."

"A grave?"

"Yeah - something for people to go to instead of your house."

"But how would people know?"

"Hello, have you ever heard of something called social media? It's what got you into this mess in the first place."

Veronica was skeptical. Still, she admitted that the idea was, if nothing else, perversely amusing; and since she and Anna had nothing better to do the next day they went on a tour of local sites that could, they thought, house the fictitious remains of Veronica's now-infamous pet.

To no avail: turns out - shock! - you can't just dig a hole in a city park, or create a do-it-yourself tomb in a public cemetery. Such restrictions were made vividly clear to them when they consulted the caretaker of one such cemetery in an upscale part of town. It was a high-class necropolis filled with an entire flock of obviously expensive marble angels in various dolorous poses. The fact that the cemetery was inhabited by the terminally idle rich might have had something to do with them not wanting to accommodate random dead pets; evidently wealthy folks want gated communities in the afterlife too.

"But it would just be a very, very small grave," said Veronica in her best little-girl voice.

"Yeah, a tiny little cat-sized one," added Anna. "You'd hardly notice it really."

The caretaker - a middle-aged woman whose arms were folded in a gesture of obdurate recalcitrance across her ample bosom - gave them an especially frosty look. "Girls, what you need is a *pet* cemetery. I don't s'pose you thought of that?" she asked derisively.

"Huh," replied Veronica and Anna, in stereo. They actually hadn't.

Back home over wine, an internet search revealed the existence of two such institutions in the Seattle area, and after reading Yelp reviews Veronica and Anna decided to make enquiries at one with the charming name of *Heavenly Paws*. I have no idea what these said to convince my human and her friend to check it out; they didn't share them with me, and the only morsel I got was Anna quoting a mysterious line from one of the reviews.

"What do you suppose 'Very strange combination' means?" she asked.
"Combination of what?"
"It doesn't say."
"Hopefully it's not combined with a fast food restaurant."
But what, after all, *does* one say about a pet cemetery? "Fluffy is mouldering away very happily there." "Fido just *loves* it here, he'll never leave." "A super-duper place to stick your dead animals in the ground!"

Heavenly Paws is located in lovely Kent, Washington, around twenty miles south of the city. It's not really the sort of place where you'd expect to find a pet cemetery - which I at least associate with rich old ladies mourning their dearly departed cats and dogs. Anna apparently agreed.

"It's in *Kent*? Seriously?"
"Why the surprise?" Veronica asked.
"Darling, this is a place that features numerous homes of the type that come with wheels. And many of those are inhabited by what one could euphemistically term, well," - she thought for a moment - "inexpensive blanched garbage."

Veronica stared blankly.
"Cheap white trash. Wake up, Vee."
"Ah. Clever. You're so good with words."
It's true - Anna is. Another reason I like her.
"Well," continued Veronica, "I suppose real estate in Seattle is just too expensive to devote to the permanent housing of dead pets, huh?"

The two of them agreed to drive down to Kent the following afternoon, after Veronica had completed a session involving a young man named Terence - *not* Terry, he emphasized - whose most earnest desire was to be kicked in the balls by an attractive woman in black stiletto heels. Veronica took him down into her dungeon, and thirty minutes and much screaming later the two of them reappeared. As he came up the steps into the living room, the man let go of his injured groin just long enough to fish a wallet out of his back pocket and hand Veronica four hundred-dollar bills. He limped his way to his car, but turned at the last moment to wave an incongruously cheery goodbye just as Anna walked up to Veronica's front door.

Anna looked over her shoulder at the guy, who was now gently easing himself into his car, uttering continual groaning noises as he did so. She kissed Veronica on the cheek in greeting. "What's his problem?" she asked.

"Oh, that's Terence," replied Veronica. "His balls had a few collisions with my feet."

"Ah, one of those," Anna replied knowingly. "Really Vee, I don't know how you do some of the things you do without laughing your ass off."

"Personally, I think it's a lot easier than what you do - pretending to enjoy it while some lame guy with a limp dick slobbers all over you."

"My clients never *slobber*," said Anna defensively. "Though," she added on reflection, "they do sometimes sweat. The fat, hairy ones are the worst."

Veronica shuddered at the image. "Ugh. Well, enough of that. Ready to go and check out *Heavenly Paws?*"

"Can't wait. In the past three days I've had a run of spectacularly boring clients who all needed Viagra to arouse their interest. It's enough to make a girl feel unloved. So," she added, "this may well turn out to be the highlight of my week."

Earl

Fortunately, Veronica decided to bring me along on their excursion to Trailerland. I hadn't had a walk in a few hours, and she told Anna she thought my presence might enhance her credibility as a caring pet owner.

We drove down in Anna's Mercedes convertible. Cute car, but not exactly built with a dog in mind. I mean, seriously - those stupid little bucket seats in the back are useful only if all your friends happen to be midgets. For quadrupeds, there's not enough space to place more than two paws anywhere; so maintaining your balance becomes a major challenge, and any attempt to look noble during the ride goes out the metaphorical window.

"*Moron!* Whoops - sorry, Jack!" Anna yelled, as her sudden braking to avoid a car that cut her off from the adjacent lane resulted in me being catapulted into the back of her seat for the tenth time.

I was missing Margo, Isaac's over-sized convertible.

After some arguments with the lady in the GPS - whose school-marm voice informed them, with frosty condescension, that Anna had taken the wrong turn twice now - we finally arrived at *Heavenly Paws*. The facility was situated down a dirt road - there are quite a few of these in Kent - just inside a small patch of woodland.

The dirt road led to a clearing and stopped just short of a double-wide trailer home. A hand-written sign pinned to the door announced that this was the office.

Anna parked the Mercedes next to a large dumpster and we all exited the car. One of us - the one who was stiff and bruised from being forced to be the ball in a pinball game on the interstate - tripped getting out and fell sideways onto the gravel.

"Jack, are you okay?" asked Veronica. "You really should be more careful."

Yeah, thanks for the advice.

Veronica walked up to the door of the trailer and knocked. There was no sign of life within. She knocked again, and called out. "Hello? Anyone home?"

Repetitions of this act did nothing to rouse anyone from the immediate vicinity.

"Shit," said Veronica, "I really hope we haven't come all this way for nothing."

But just then a man appeared, apparently out of nowhere from somewhere behind the trailer. He was in his 50s, with a paunchy belly, a head whose hair had seen much better days, and skin that was mostly bright pink. Disturbingly, he appeared to be wearing nothing except a towel.

"Hi there," he said cheerily. "Name's Earl."

Veronica and Anna stared blankly, not sure what to make of the middle-aged be-toweled vision before them. Earl filled in the slightly awkward silence. "Which're you two young ladies here for? Paws or Bears?" The girls continued to be at a loss for words. "See, who you need t' talk to depends on whatcha here for. I'm Bears, the wife is Paws."

Finally, Veronica managed to speak. "Bears?" she asked.

"Yep," replied Earl. "Bears." By way of explanation, he pointed to a high wooden fence. In the middle of the fence, next to a crudely carved life-size wooden bear statue that, inexplicably, none of us had noticed until that moment, was a large wooden gate, to which was affixed a rather inconspicuous sign. The typeface on the sign was sufficiently small that Veronica and Anna both leaned forward and squinted in an attempt to read it.

It was Anna who deciphered it first.

"You have *got* to be shitting me!" she exclaimed in disbelief.

"What?" asked Veronica. "I can't read it."

"Remember the Yelp comment about a 'strange combination'?"

"Yeah," Veronica replied, still squinting.

"Well, welcome to the Kent pet cemetery and nudist camp."

"You're shitting me."

"Nope. There it is - *Heavenly Paws* cemetery is joined to *Bares in the Trees* nudist camp. That's B-A-R-E-S," she added helpfully for the benefit of her short-sighted friend.

Veronica's mouth dropped at least an inch. "Oh my God," she said. She turned to Earl, whose towel had, worryingly, descended another couple of inches down his body. "Seriously?"

Earl was unfazed by the incredulity that currently held both women in thrall. "We believe here in multiple uses for the land," he said, as if that explained everything. "It's *very* sound, ecol-ogically speaking."

The girls had returned to a state of stupefaction.

"So," Earl reiterated, "Bares or Paws?"

"Um, Paws, actually," said Anna.

"Yes," echoed Veronica, "definitely not Bares."

"Ya sure?" asked Earl. "Two fine young ladies such as y'selves would be very welcome behind that there fence."

I can't be sure, but I'd bet my next can of dog food that the image of a prison compound was at that morning forming simultaneously in the brains of both girls. It was certainly occurring to me.

"Er, no thanks," said Veronica, a touch nervously. "We're here to enquire about a resting place for a pet."

"Ah, Paws then," nodded Earl. He looked down at me. "And would this be the pet?"

Fuck no it wouldn't, I thought, and backed away a little. "Jack?" said Veronica. "No no - he's very much still with us." Good to know.

"It's about my cat," said Veronica.

"Yes," added Anna. "Her *beloved* cat." It was obvious that Anna was going to try her best to make Veronica laugh in the ensuing conversation.

"Ah, I see," said Earl. "Well, you'll be wantin' the wife, then. I'll go get her."

Earl - whose towel had slipped even further south - retreated around the corner to wherever he had come from, leaving in our collective vision the distinctly distasteful image of a very hirsute butt crack.

Veronica and Anna turned to look at each other as he disappeared. There was a short pause as they processed the absurdity of the situation, then a pair of smiles spread slowly across their faces. Finally the two girls collapsed in gales of laughter and clutched each other as tears rolled down their cheeks.

"Well, fuck me!" said Veronica finally.

"I'd love to, Vee," said Anna. "Where do you want to do it - Bares or Paws?"

The Late Lamented

It was a good ten minutes before the curator of *Heavenly Paws* arrived. Which was good, because it took almost that long for Anna and Veronica to stop laughing. I, on the other hand, was bewildered: to a dog, the idea that running around without clothes on is special and somehow healthy is utterly idiotic. Almost as idiotic as those ridiculous little sweater vests that they put on poodles in winter.

I think we all half-expected the woman to show up in a towel, but when she finally appeared from the parallel universe behind the trailer home she was, thankfully, fully dressed. Between her unkempt hair, cotton flower-printed kaftan and the string of beads hanging from her neck, she looked disturbingly like Madame Lulu - enough so that I wondered whether she was one of Lulu's loopy relatives.

She smiled broadly, revealing unusually large teeth. She looked rather like a hippie tyrannosaurus. "Greetings, friends!" she gushed. "Welcome to *Heavenly Paws*! I'm Mirakel."

"Miracle?" said Veronica.

"No, no - MiraKEL," she said, "Common mistake," she added forgivingly, and helpfully spelled out the name. "The accent is on the *kel*, you see. *Kel* - like the Book of Kells. Only one. One Kell. Not really enough for a book, actually, ha ha!"

"I see," said Veronica, who didn't see, but also didn't care. "Well, nice to meet you."

"You too, my dear." She paused. "Um... names?" she asked.

Veronica started. "Oh yes, sorry. I'm Veronica and this is Anna."

"And this sweet little creature?" She pointed down at me.

"That's Jack," Veronica replied. "He's my dog."

"Ah," said Mirakel. "Jack. Nice name. Fits easily on a tombstone." I backed up again.

"We're actually here about my cat."

"Yes," said Anna. "Her *beloved* cat." Veronica shot her a look.

"Ah, poor thing," said Mirakel consolingly. "Is he - she - recently deceased?"

"Well -" began Veronica.

"Oh, *very* recently," interrupted Anna. "The pain she feels is still very raw."

"I'm sure, dear," said Mirakel, and patted Veronica's arm. "They're such *blessings* to us all, aren't they?"

"Yes," said Anna as Veronica was opening her mouth to say something. "That's *exactly* what Veronica was saying just this morning. Her poor little cat was such a *blessing*."

Veronica gave Anna another look, but she was obviously trying her best not to laugh.

"Such a full life," Anna continued. "You know, he was originally a boat cat - he lived on a sailboat on Lake Union."

"Really?" said Mirakel. "How sweet."

"Yes. Until the fire."

"The fire?"

"Yes. Fireworks, I'm afraid," Anna explained. "You know, they shoot them off from the park right there on July 4th. Well, one exploded on the boat and it caught fire. The poor little thing's owner was burned to a crisp."

"How terrible!" exclaimed Mirakel.

"Yes," continued Anna, who was clearly enjoying herself. "The only reason her pussycat survived was because he was such a good swimmer. From growing up on a boat," she explained.

"Oh marvelous," said Mirakel.

"Yes, marvelous," repeated Veronica, who personally thought Anna was going way too far in her account of her imaginary cat's life story.

"But such a *tragic* demise," added Anna. "In the end."

"Oh really?" said Mirakel, who was now clutching one of Veronica's hands and stroking it. "Yes," said Anna. "He was run over by a tram."

"A tram?" repeated Mirakel. Her other hand had now moved to Veronica's waist, and Veronica was beginning to look uncomfortable.

"Yes," said Anna, shaking her head. "Veronica lives on Capitol Hill," she added. "There's a tram."

"Oh how *terrible*," empathized Mirakel, who in her efforts to console Veronica was now pretty much openly molesting her.

"Quite," said Anna, with a sorrowful and ladylike sniff. "And after surviving the fire, too."

"Yes, terrible," said Veronica, who with difficulty managed to disengage herself from the tyrannosaur. "So you see, we need a safe spot to lay him to rest."

"And holy," added Anna. "A safe and *holy* place."

"Yes, yes, of course my dear," said Mirakel. "You've come to the right place. We pride ourselves here on providing the most tasteful resting places for our beloved and faithful companions. Would you like to take tour?"

"Yes, that would be lovely" said Veronica.

"Lovely," repeated Anna.

To our collective relief, the pet cemetery was not located on the other side of the fence that shielded an innocent world from whatever lay beyond in *Bares in the Woods*. Mirakel led us in the opposite direction, down a dirt path and through some trees.

We passed through a short section of dense forest and emerged into another clearing. There, we were suddenly confronted by a sizeable expanse of open land, filled with several rows of gravestones. A surprisingly tasteful white picket fence enclosed the cemetery.

Mirakel opened the small gate and led us down a path between the graves.

"We have everything here," she said as we walked. "Cats, dogs, hamsters, bunnies - you name it, we take it. Well, someone tried to bury a tarantula once, but we draw the line at big spiders."

I shuddered - and couldn't help wondering whether small spiders were okay.

Many of the graves were accompanied by laminated photos, or even small statues. One grave had a photo of a cat that looked remarkably like Bonkers. I resisted the urge to pee on it.

As we wandered the lanes of the departed, I glanced at each photo and ruminated on the lives that these animals had led. All too brief, I thought - but it seemed that this lot were at least loved. After all, any human who spends cold hard cash to inter her pet - some of the graves were obviously not cheap - must do so because they cared a lot for the critter concerned. It was actually very touching to see these small monuments to love.

At the end of one row was a particularly large grave with a sizeable tombstone, on which was inscribed a date of death and, in large letters, the name HOTÉ.

"What's this one?" asked Veronica, pointing.

"Oh," replied Mirakel, "that's a donkey."

"'Hoté'?" queried Anna. "Strange name."

"It's pronounced 'HO-TAY'," explained Mirakel. "You know, because it was a donkey called 'Ho-tay.' Donkey Hotay. Get it? Ha ha." She laughed, exposing her disturbingly large teeth. "Quite clever, really. Pity he was hit by a truck in the end," she added sadly.

"Huh," exclaimed Anna, closely followed by Veronica, who took a couple of seconds more to get the dreadful literary pun.

"So anyway," said Mirakel, "what would you like us to do with your sweet pussy?"

Veronica's eyebrows shot up and she looked distinctly startled, until she realized that the molesting tyrannosaur was actually enquiring about her cat.

"Oh," she said, "I hadn't really thought about it. Something simple, I suppose."

"Yes, okay. And what was his name, dear?"

Veronica's face suddenly went blank. Evidently she hadn't given much thought to whether she should use Bonkers' real name. There was an awkward pause which made it look as if Veronica was temporarily unable to recall the name of her beloved feline - the one who was such a *blessing*.

Anna stepped in. "Actually, his name was Demon Cat," she said. "Demon for short. D for even shorter. He was such a little terror in real life. A blessing, but a terror. Until the tram."

"Ah," said Mirakel. "And how old was he when he passed on?"

"Four," said Veronica.

"Twelve," said Anna at exactly the same time.

They looked at each other.

"Actually, nine now that I think of it," said Veronica, who apparently thought that splitting the difference would somehow not make the situation worse.

"I see," said Mirakel, who obviously didn't. "Well, we can show you some options for headstones back at the office. Now, were we wanting a ceremony for the interment?"

Again there was an unfortunately simultaneous response.

"No." Veronica.

"Yes." Anna.

"Yes?"

"Yes. His little Facebook friends would want that."

"They would?"

"*Yes*, they *would*," said Anna, pointedly.

Veronica looked at Mirakel. "Yes," she said. "A ceremony would be nice."

"But we can design that," said Anna. "No need to bother you."

"Oh it's no problem," said Mirakel. "We have an excellent minister on call - Reverend Steve. Well, he's not actually a real minister - he did one of those internet things. Church of the Infinite Cosmos, I think it's called. But he does a very nice job. Very moving."

"That's nice," said Veronica. "But I think we'd like to do something a bit more private?" She looked at Anna for confirmation.

Anna nodded. "He was a very private cat," she said, by way of explanation.

"I see," said Mirakel, who presumably had no more idea than I did of what a private cat would look like. "Well, let's go look at tombstones, shall we?"

"Yes, let's," said Veronica.

As we began to make our way back towards the trailer home, Mirakel looked down at me again.

"And we definitely don't want one for the doggie?" she asked hopefully. "We have a two-for-one discount running at the moment, and it's never too early to start planning."

"Er, no thank you," said Veronica. "I don't think Jack's ready to go just yet." No shit.

"Are we sure?" said the tyrannosaur. "I can throw in a free pass to the nudist camp."

Choices

As they entered the office in the trailer, they were greeted by the sight of Earl, still in nothing but a towel, sitting in an old armchair reading the sports section of the Seattle Times. His right leg lay atop the left at the ankle, thereby exposing enough of the area under the towel to leave little to the imagination. Mirakel was not amused.

"Earl, for heaven's sake! How many times have I told you not to sit like that when we have visitors?" She let out the sigh of a woman who puts up with a lot.

"Sorry," said Earl. "Was just catching up on Seahawks news," he added.

"Well go catch up on it somewhere else," ordered Mirakel. "Go on – shoo!"

Earl obediently shooed, flashing the girls a sheepish smile as he exited the trailer.

"I'm sorry," Mirakel apologized to the girls. "He scares people sometimes. He means well."

"No problem," replied Anna charitably. Having seen far more than her share of male genitalia, it took rather more to scare her than a middle-aged man inadequately covered by a beach towel.

The surfaces of the trailer office were populated untidily with papers and nick-knacks, and the walls held numerous photos of people and pets in various poses and life stages. There was a distinct bias towards youth in the images: kittens, puppies and babies cavorted together on the walls, cheek by jowl with photos of Mirakel and Earl smiling goofily at various locations around Paws and Bares. Prominent in the middle of one wall was a shot of Earl grinning broadly; he was dressed in what seemed to be the very same towel in which he had a few moments before exposed his nether regions.

Mirakel pulled a large three-ring binder off a shelf and placed it on a table cluttered with papers and pet supply catalogues. Since no living pet was anywhere in evidence, one did have to wonder why Mirakel needed so many catalogues of products that would be of zero use to the many deceased animals on the property.

She opened the binder and flipped through the pages of photos.

"Here's a lovely canine tombstone," she said with a glance down at me.

I looked around to make sure I had a clear path to the door.

"Yes, very nice," said Veronica. "But we need one for a cat."

"Ah yes, of course." She continued flipping until she reached the feline section. "Here we are. Just take a look through these and see if anything appeals to you. Have a seat, take your time," she said, unfolding an old and very uncomfortable-looking metal chair and placing it next to one of similar age and design already at the table. "I'll just pop out and make sure Earl's taken out the trash cans. The garbage men come tomorrow."

Veronica and Anna leafed through the pages of tombstones, which ranged from small and simple to larger than most human grave ornaments.

"God, who pays this kind of money for a headstone?" asked Veronica, shaking her head.

"Rich old ladies whose only true love in life was their pussy," replied Anna with a smile.

"Sick."

After more perusing, they settled on a simple design, mostly because it was the cheapest one available. And even that was hardly a bargain at $200 plus tax. The price included engraving of up to fifty words. However, it did not include another $200 fee for the plot of ground in which the dearly departed would be interred, nor another $100 for a simple casket.

"Five hundred dollars!" complained Veronica. "God, I had no idea this little ruse was going to cost me so much."

"You can't put a price on love," Anna replied. "Besides, think of it as an investment in a good story."

"You could always offer Earl a blow job in trade," Veronica suggested.

"No thank you, dearest – that particular penis shall remain unsucked, at least by me. Plus I rather doubt Mira-*kel* would approve. And anyway," she added, "it's not his side of the business. He's Bares, not Paws, remember?"

Etymology

Coil, (n.). In combination with *mortal* ("mortal coil"), the meaning is tumults or troubles [in life]. 16th century English, etymology in this sense uncertain. Most celebrated use is from Shakespeare's *Hamlet*, Act III, Scene 1: *For in that sleep of death what dreams may come, When we have shuffled off this mortal coil, Must give us pause.*

Substitute

Half an hour later, Veronica and Anna had concluded their business with *Heavenly Paws*. Veronica had paid cash for the tombstone and the plot, and had successfully resisted Mirakel's efforts to have her purchase a more splendid and expensive monument for the Demon Cat.

"Are we sure, dear?" said Mirakel. "This one is so magnificent." She pointed to the photo of a huge headstone that featured cherubs and heavenly cats flying happily together across a sky filled with cheerful, puffy clouds.

"Thank you, but I think we'd like the small one," Veronica rebuffed.

"He was a simple cat," added Anna by way of explanation.

After Veronica had agreed to provide Mirakel with suitable text for the headstone in due course, we all headed for the car. It was with general relief that we drove down the dirt road, with Mirakel waving a fond farewell. Earl, thankfully, was nowhere to be seen.

On the drive home, Veronica and Anna discussed the minor problem of what exactly they were going to bury now that they had secured a grave.

"We need something the same weight," said Anna. "How much does Bonkers weigh?"

"I don't know," Veronica replied. "Maybe ten pounds."

This was decidedly optimistic. Bonkers the pampered house cat is a good twenty pounds if he's an ounce, and half of that is fur.

"Hmm," pondered Anna. "Well I have a collection of old dildos in a box in my closet. I could assemble ten pounds' worth and put them in the casket."

"I don't know," said Veronica doubtfully. "The texture isn't exactly cat-like. What if they rattle around in there, or one of them accidentally gets turned on?"

They both laughed as they mentally conjured the image of a vibrating casket.

"Yes, p'rhaps you're right," said Anna. "Well, we'll think of something."

The next morning Veronica's doorbell rang, and she opened the door to find Anna on her stoop. She was carrying a plastic bag emblazoned with the logo of a prominent shoe store. The bag was closed at the top by a drawstring.

"What's in the bag?" asked Veronica as she ushered Anna into the living room.

"Guess."

"I don't know. Lunch?"

"Not exactly."

"So what is it?"

Anna handed the bag to Veronica, who with a quizzical look at her friend opened it.

"O my God!" she exclaimed. "It's a cat!"

"A dead cat," Anna corrected. "I found it on Jackson Street this morning. Hit by a car, poor thing. I'm afraid it's a bit, well, two-dimensional as a result."

Veronica laid the bag on the floor with an expression of distaste. "And you're bringing me this as what? Some kind of bizarre ritual offering?"

"No, no. It's a fake Bonkers. Now we actually have something we can bury."

"Seriously?"

"Yes, why not? Saves us the trouble of finding something of equivalent weight to shove into the little casket. Besides, it'd be nice to give poor pussy here a Christian burial, don't you think?"

"We don't even know his name. There was no collar?"

"Sadly not. He can be like the unknown warrior - buried with honor to proudly and anonymously represent every road-killed cat ever."

"Cute. You're sick, you know that, don't you?"

Anna smiled. "It's why my clients love me."

"Your clients love you because you have great tits and you could suck the chrome off a trailer hitch."

"Well yes - that too."

"Is it fresh?" asked Veronica, opening the bag again and peering warily into it.

"Well you couldn't exactly serve it with French fries and a garden salad, but yes, I think kitty only recently shuffled off his mortal coil."

"You're very fond of that expression, aren't you?"

"'Mortal coil'? Yes, I s'pose so. Though actually I have no idea what a mortal coil *is*."

She should have asked me. Isaac likes it too, and we'd been discussing its meaning a few days before. "Did anyone see you as you were scraping it off the road?"

"Just some Asian guy."

"That must have been weird."

"Nah. Asians think we white chicks are all nuts anyway."

Veronica continued to peer dubiously at the deceased feline in the bag. "Well, okay. I suppose we'd better hurry up and arrange the burial before he goes off," she said.

Anna raised her eyebrows. "Vee, he's going to go off awfully fast in this weather."

"So what do I do with him?"

Anna pointed to the fridge. "*Preserve* him, darling. That's why God invented freezers."

"O my God!" Veronica exclaimed. "You want me to put him in the freezer with the pork chops and the frozen peas?"

"Exactly. Otherwise you're going to have one *very* odiferous feline on your hands pretty damn quick. Besides," she added, "he won't mind – and neither will the frozen peas."

PHILLIP BOLEYN

Mystery Man

The next day I was sitting in Isaac's yard. He was updating me on Alice and Rachel. As he promised, Isaac had sent a cheap cell phone to the lake house, and Alice had called him to confirm she'd received it. She promised to call every day, and to remember to keep the phone charged.

How's Rachel? I asked.

"She's fine, Jack. Much happier now that she's living in the house and not having to catch her own dinner every day."

Did she mention me at all?

"You forget I can't talk to her - and neither can Alice. But I'm sure you're in her heart." He smiled.

I certainly hope so.

A couple of hours later I was wandering down the street looking for a place to poop. Veronica was busy with a client - I've no idea what his thing was, but from the thwacking sounds and screams coming from the basement it apparently involved some kind of whip - so I used the dog door she'd installed at the back to let myself out.

I crossed the street, and after some fifty yards of careful olfactory exploration, I detected the scent of dog pee under a bush. And not just any dog pee - this was the calling card of a particularly obnoxious Jack Russell that lived on the next block. As pretty much everyone knows, dogs pee and poop partly to mark territory; but beyond this, exerting dominance by literally crapping on the mark of a dog you dislike is a particularly sweet canine pleasure.

So there I am, giving vent to the processed remains of last night's serving of Purina Moist Meaty Burger With Cheese, when a human voice on the other side of the bush says, "O Jesus Christ! Did you have to do that right there?"

Still in the undignified crouching position in which dogs are forced to defecate, I turn my head to see a large telephoto lens poking through the bush. Behind it, through the vegetation, I can make out a man who is kneeling on the ground and holding his nose.

"Fuck off, dog!" he says from behind the bush as he swats the air in front of him in a futile attempt to disperse the admittedly potent butt fragrance hanging there.

Having finished my business, I am just about to go back to the house when Leroy Fawkes appears in front of me. Leroy ignores me most of the time, and right now his attention is firmly focused on the man hiding in the bushes.

"Hey, whatcha doin' in the bushes back there with that cam'ra?"

The man stands up. "I'm... I'm a birdwatcher," he says uncertainly.

"Birdwatcher?" repeats Leroy with obvious suspicion. "Birdwatcher my ass. What kinda birds you watchin' here? There ain't nothing but sparrows 'n' crows around here." Despite five years in Seattle, Leroy still sounds like he just arrived yesterday from Alabama.

"Well, I happen to like crows," says the guy. He's in his forties, with thinning hair and rather beady eyes. "Anyway, I'm not doing anything wrong. I don't see why I have to explain myself to the likes of you."

"Hmm," says Leroy. "Hidin' in the bushes with a camera could make a fella think you're some kinda pervert. Maybe I should call the po-lice."

"No no - no need to do that," the man says in a more conciliatory tone. "I'm just out for a walk. Not much to watch here anyway, so I'll be on my way."

"Hmpf," says Leroy, his suspicion clearly unallayed. With a scornful look at the stranger, he walks away. The stranger picks up a camera bag and a notebook from the behind the bush and starts to walk down the street. Suddenly he stops, picks up his right foot and examines the underside of his shoe.

"Oh *shit!*" he exclaims, and looks daggers at me as I hastily retreat back across the street to safety.

You're welcome.

Snuggle

I wish I could tell Veronica about the suspicious stranger in the bushes because on reflection I rather think that telephoto lens was pointed at our house. I could tell Isaac to tell Leroy to tell Veronica, but Veronica recently reiterated her fervent wish to avoid communicating with our redneck next-door neighbor at all costs. This was after he knocked on the door one evening to ask her if she wanted to go out with him for a beer. Veronica declined rather more politely than she wanted to; and when she'd subsequently exiled him to the other side of her front door, she looked at me and framed her refusal rather more bluntly.

"Jesus Christ, Jack, I swear to God that if someone offered me a choice between going on a date with that man and swallowing rat poison, I'd have to seriously think about which one to pick."

Anyway, later that afternoon, the client having been suitably beaten and dismissed, Veronica gave me a treat and then asked me whether I'd like to join her in bed for a snuggle. Of course, she didn't proffer the suggestion in a full sentence like that, because she believes I can't understand most of what she says; instead, she simply looked at me, made a cradling motion with her arms, and asked, *Snuggle?* in the exaggerated tone of voice humans use when they're talking to dogs, cats or babies. It's so cute when she does this, and even cuter that she tells her friends what an incredibly smart dog I am because - along with *sit, stay, come* et cetera - I can clearly understand the word "snuggle".

Veronica thinks I have a ten-word vocabulary, you see. I try not to be offended.

I've learned that the expected response to the snuggle question is to wag my tail and run enthusiastically up to the bedroom, jump on the bed, and wait for her to join me there. She means well, and it seems to bring her a childlike joy when I do this, so I'm happy to oblige.

Besides, I do love snuggling with her. Despite their fierce reputation, pit bulls are pushovers for physical affection; we love to be petted and held. Basically, we're total whores.

Twenty minutes later we were still there, happily spooning together, when the phone rang.

For reasons that have never been clear to me, Veronica's ring tone is Wagner's *Ride of the Valkyries*. I really wish she'd change it because it creeps the bejesus out of me every time it goes off. There's nothing like being abruptly awoken from a relaxing nap by music that accompanied the invasion of Poland.

Sleepily, Veronica reached for her phone and after a couple of uncoordinated stabs at the screen managed to connect the call. I could hear only one side of the conversation.

"Oh, hi mom. How are you? Uh-huh. Yeah, I'm fine. How's dad? Uh-huh... good... Yes, the weather's nice here... Uh-huh. What am I doing tomorrow? Nothing really, why?"

Suddenly she sat bolt upright and looked panicked. "Um... okay... what time...? No no, that's fine... Okay, see you then. Bye."

She put the phone down and gave me a distinctly deflated look.

"Oh, fucking hell!" she said. "My mother's coming to visit."

Secret

Veronica's mother Shirley lived with Veronica's father in a small town in the west - the actual name of which was not, as Veronica often liked to tell people, "Bumfuck, Wyoming". This was sufficiently far away to prevent regular visitations, but not so far that her mother couldn't just jump on a plane whenever she felt like it and be at Veronica's door in a few hours.

Indeed, her mother had a habit of showing up in Seattle on short notice. This happened two or three times a year, was never at a predictable time, and was usually inconvenient.

As Veronica bemoaned to Anna that evening, "Most mothers come on Thanksgiving or Christmas and arrange their visit weeks in advance, but not mine. For some reason, *mine* has to wait to tell me till the night before she descends."

Repeated requests to provide more warning for future visits inevitably produced a response that was a combination of vague excuse and maternal hurt. "But I thought you'd be *happy* that your mother was coming to see you," she said. "Besides, you know how *spontaneous* I am."

That's one way to describe it, Veronica would tell her friends. Another was *annoying*.

Every time her mother chose to drop in, it would inevitably happen when Veronica had a session with a client that she was forced to reschedule. This was because, like many sex workers, Veronica has never told her mother the truth regarding what she does for a living.

Around the time that she began work as a dominatrix and her mother had enquired, with predictable maternal concern, whether and how she was gainfully employed, Veronica had made the mistake of trying to convince her that she was an "entertainer". This is a euphemism commonly employed by sex workers in response to parental enquiries, but in Veronica's case it made absolutely no sense because she could neither play a musical instrument, tell a joke, juggle, do magic, nor indeed perform any act that anyone in their right mind might conceivably pay good money to see.

"An entertainer?" her mother had asked. The disbelief was very apparent in her tone of voice. "But darling, you can't sing a note."

Recognizing the implausibility of the lie, Veronica subsequently announced to her mother that she had given up her career as an entertainer and become an "organizational consultant" to businesses. This was brilliantly vague – after all, no one really knows what consultants do, including some of the people who hire them – and it seemed to satisfy her mother's curiosity.

It's not true that Veronica can't sing. She actually has rather a nice voice, and she often sings to me when we walk.

By the way, I'm nuts about the Beatles.

Digression: The History of Sewing

Before we continue, and in the context of Veronica's current occupation, it's worth bringing in a bit of the history of Seattle here. Specifically, the tawdry bit. The following is courtesy of Anna, who you will recall has a doctorate in history, and who remains a student of all things lascivious, whether past or present. It's worth noting that Anna's dissertation - *The Girls Upstairs: Prostitutes and Society Through the Ages* - remains popular reading at the university which conferred the exalted and gloriously useless degree upon the lovely Dr DeVere.

In the 1880's – so Anna told Veronica one day - Seattle was the center of a burgeoning lumber industry. The Pioneer Square neighborhood, which was one of two places where the first white immigrants had settled when they arrived in 1851, was home to lumber mills and the sprawling, unsanitary hodge-podge of ramshackle buildings that housed the men who worked in them. The well-to-do - the mill owners and other rich folks – lived up the hill in much more luxurious accommodation. Logs would be sent skidding down Mill Street - today called Yesler Way - to the Pioneer Square mills, earning the road, and the sleazy district at its bottom, the now-famous nickname of Skid Row.

The sex ratio in 19th century Seattle had never favored men. In the 1860's it was a whopping nine to one, and a woman named Asa Mercer famously undertook expeditions to New England to recruit girls willing to marry and settle in the Pacific Northwest. The abundance of lonely, sexually frustrated single men in the lumber industry and other occupations pretty much guaranteed the development of prostitution, and in due course Pioneer Square became the hotbed of local iniquity.

In those days, these Ladies of Negotiable Affection typically listed their occupation as "seamstress", although almost none of these fine women could be found in possession of an actual sewing machine. A census in the 1880's recorded more than 2,700 seamstresses living in Seattle.

Tired of being harassed by police and local officials, the local ladies offered to pay to the city a substantial tax on their considerable earnings in exchange for being left in peace. And substantial it was: the "sewing and entertainment tax" as it was called, was a whopping $10 a week per seamstress. According to Anna, this amounted to a small fortune at that time.

With occasional interruptions from those tiresome individuals known as reformers, prostitution continued to flourish into the new century, and gained new currency – literally – during the Klondike gold rush. By the time that the profession's most celebrated Madam, Lou Graham, was felled by syphilis in her early forties, she had become one of the wealthiest landowners in the northwest. Graham single-handedly staved off a local bank failure, and supposedly donated more to the education of Seattle's children than all of the city's other prominent citizens combined.

There's an amazing statistic wrapped up in all this, one which Anna loves to quote. In the late 19th century, prostitutes made up six percent of the population of Seattle, but contributed 88% of the city's revenue. Indeed, when the morality crowd at one point succeeded in clamping down on the carnal business, the city effectively went broke.

So, back then sex workers were seamstresses. Today they're entertainers or consultants. Times change.

Holly

holly (n.), evergreen shrub especially used for decoration at Christmas, mid-15c., earlier *holin* (mid-12c.), shortening of Old English *holegn, holen* "holly," from Proto-Germanic *hulin-*(source also of Old Saxon, Old High German *hulis*, Old Norse *hulfr*, Middle Dutch *huls*, Dutch, German *hulst* "holly"), cognate with Middle Irish *cuilenn*, Welsh *celyn*, Gaelic *cuilionn* "holly," probably all from Proto-Indo-European root *kel- (5) "to prick" (source also of Old Church Slavonic *kolja* "to prick," Russian *kolos* "ear of corn"), in reference to its leaves. French *houx* "holly" is from Frankish *huls* or some other Germanic source. Also a female name.

Veronica's mother was due to arrive the following afternoon, and so by maternal necessity Veronica temporarily reverted to being Holly. This was the name her mother had thoughtfully chosen for her at birth, and which Veronica had put aside the day she became a sex worker.

It wasn't that Veronica disliked the name; on the contrary, it was a rather lovely appellation. But it is not a good idea for a woman employed in the carnal professions to advertize under her own name, lest she is stalked by one of the numerous unhinged perverts that lurk in the dark corners of the Internet. Not that Veronica eschewed the run-of-the-mill perverts, of course - without them, she would have no business. It was the scary ones who were the problem.

All sex workers have experiences with these. They range from guys who are harmlessly obsessed with a particular girl to the creeps who are increasingly pushy in their sexual demands, or who try to do things that a girl has made clear are not on her menu of acceptable offerings. In the extreme case, a client could be sadistic and violent, relying on the fact that a sex worker is unlikely to report a case of assault or rape to the authorities. Indeed, in the prejudiced minds of many cops and much of Society in general, sex workers get what's coming to them for doing what they do in the first place. The general view seems to be that you can't *really* rape a sex worker.

All things being equal, Anna was more likely than Veronica to encounter one of these trolls. Any guy who wants to hire a dominatrix is usually submissive to begin with and therefore less likely to represent a threat. Veronica had certainly seen her fair share of clients with psychological issues: indeed, the desire to have a woman beat the crap out of you or do distinctly unpleasant things to your genitalia sometimes has its roots in past abuse - or so Veronica sometimes explains to a client. It's a little-appreciated fact that a good dominatrix is often as much a therapist as a deliverer of erotic stimulation. A domme can help a guy work out his abusive past in a manner that is constructive and (to him) pleasurable - albeit in a weird way with whips, restraints, and a couple of nipple clamps.

As a prostitute, by contrast, Anna attracted a clientele that was more likely to include nutcases of the worrying variety. Pretty much all high-end sex workers have a system of screens in place to minimize the chances of running into a dangerous client: these include references from other trusted escorts, and bulletin boards that post details of abusive men. Most girls will require at least two references and a copy of the client's driver's license or other identification.

But even then some creeps get through. Anna and Veronica both knew of girls who had been beaten up, or who had engaged clients who'd taken their pleasure and then cheated the girl of her fee.

A year or so before, Anna had encountered one of the latter, a smirking middle-aged guy who at the beginning of a session handed her a sealed envelope which supposedly contained cash. Unlike some girls, Anna doesn't trust *any* client, at least not the first time, so she discreetly took the envelope to the bedroom to inspect it. Inside, instead of several banknotes imprinted with the welcome face of Benjamin Franklin, she found pieces of newspaper cut into approximately the same shape and size.

The client in question presumably thought that the worst that could happen to him if he was caught was being yelled at and thrown out - this was a *girl*, after all - in which presumption he was very much mistaken. Thirty seconds later, Anna came running out of the bedroom wielding a baseball bat that lived under her bed, and with a well-timed upswing proceeded to direct it with uncanny accuracy to her intended target directly between the guy's legs. He howled, doubled over, and sank to the floor clutching his groin. Then, under a torrent of abuse from Anna and a threat that the next swing would connect with his head, he ran.

Perverts take note: for an appropriate fee, you can fuck Anna - but you definitely cannot fuck *with* her.

By the way, Anna's real name is Anna. But she exchanged *Brown* for the rather more exotic last name *DeVere* when she became an escort. And given that many men apparently find it a turn-on to have sex with a prostitute who has a Ph.D., Anna sometimes makes her clients call her "Dr. DeVere".

Veronica's own choice of professional name was not random. She had taken the name of one Veronica Franco, a courtesan in 16th century Venice who was, by all contemporary accounts, beautiful, cultured and highly educated. Franco wrote poetry and was a frequent contributor to Venetian *salons*. She counted some of the most influential nobles in Venice as her patrons, and these men apparently thought as much of her intellect as of her (presumably impressive) skills in the bed chamber. Most remarkably, Franco successfully stood up to the Inquisition when they attempted to try her for witchcraft.

And so, ever mindful of this noble lineage, Veronica - my Veronica - carried the name proudly in her chosen profession.

But for the next three days, with her mother poised to invade her little world, she was once again Holly.

Bullwhip

Veronica's mother arrived at precisely 2 pm on Monday afternoon, conveyed from Seattle Tacoma international airport in a bright pink taxi by an Indian driver named Manjeet.

"Manjeet's a Sikh," Shirley announced as she paid the fare. "His last name is Singh. Did you know that *all* Sikhs have 'Singh' as a last name?"

"Yes, mother. It means 'lion'." said Veronica. A sizeable chunk of the local taxi driver population was Sikh, and Veronica had spent enough time in Seattle taxis to have acquired a working knowledge of their culture.

"Well, fancy that," Shirley replied. "It must make things awfully confusing. I mean, what do they do when the phone rings and someone says, *Call for Mr Singh*?"

"Presumably the same thing happens at a Forman family reunion when there's a call for 'George'." Shirley stared blankly at her daughter.

"George Forman - the boxer," she clarified. "He has five sons and they're all called George."

"Really? Well isn't that sweet." She waved goodbye to Manjeet, who departed with a friendly honk.

"That's a very pink taxi," Veronica observed as she watched it disappear around a corner.

"I think it's adorable," Shirley replied.

Mother and daughter hugged, the former rather more enthusiastically than the latter.

Shirley suddenly noticed me sitting on the front step. "O hello, Jack. How are you?"

I dutifully wagged my tail in response.

"He's so *adorable*," Shirley said. Nice of her to say, though it must be said that, to Veronica's mother, half the world was adorable. The other half were Democrats.

Veronica picked up her mother's suitcase - which was also pink - and carried it into the house. "So, Holly dear... how are you? How's your business going?" The interrogation had begun.

"It's going fine, mother," she said.

"And is there a man in your life?" she enquired. "Someone special?"

"Not particularly, mother," she replied. Then, in an attempt to change the subject, she asked, "Would you like some coffee?"

"Well why not, dear? And no thank you." She continued, "I mean, you're a *very* attractive woman, and you apparently have enough of an income to afford a nice house. But you're not getting any younger, dear."

"Mother, I'm 29 years old - my sell-by date is a good few years off yet." Veronica was well aware that her mother's statement regarding her age was code for the fact that she desperately wanted grandchildren - something that neither Veronica nor her younger sister Kate had so far shown any signs of producing.

"Well I know, dear, but one never knows what will happen in the future. One doesn't want to foreclose one's options. You and Kate never seem to have *boyfriends*. Are you just too busy, or what?"

Veronica sighed. The next three days were clearly going to be a trial if this was going to be the theme. Before she could think of a response, her mother suddenly articulated a worried thought.

"O Holly, dear, please tell me you're not one of those horrid lesbians?"

"Mother, if I ever become a lesbian I assure you I'll be a very nice one," Veronica said, and immediately regretted the joke. Her mother had no sense of humor on this topic.

"Don't make fun, Holly. I worry."

What Shirley did not know was that Veronica's sister actually *was* a lesbian, and was living happily in sin with another woman in San Francisco. Veronica wondered whether her mother would ever adjust to the truth about her two daughters if she found out. As she would later tell Anna, she fondly imagined her mother attending a social event in Wyoming - perhaps at a local meeting of the Republican Party - and saying proudly, "O yes, one of my daughters is a professional sex worker and the other's a lesbian! Isn't that *adorable*?"

For now, however, Veronica had a more immediate problem. A week ago she had booked a client for today. She had already rescheduled the client twice and, while he had agreed to conduct the session as an outcall at his house, Veronica now had to concoct some excuse for why she had to go out right after her mother had arrived.

She had asked Anna that morning whether there was any way she could take her mother to lunch for a couple of hours while she met with the client. But Anna was busy - very busy.

"Darling, I can't," she'd said. "I have four clients back to back - I'm going to be fucking my little brains out all day. Besides," she added, "I never know what to say to your mother - she always wants to talk about cows." This was true. Shirley was obsessed with cows, and much of her life in Bumfuck, Wyoming revolved around the two dairy cows that - on some bizarre random whim and very much against the wishes of Veronica's father - she had decided to buy two years before.

Anyway, the excuse wasn't really the issue - she would just say she had a business meeting. The *issue* was that she had to somehow leave the house carrying a substantial quantity of bondage equipment that was required at the session. This client had *needs*.

"Mom, I'm afraid I have to go to a business meeting shortly. Can you occupy yourself for a while?" Her mother looked hurt. "But dear, I just got here. How long will you be gone?"

"A couple of hours, I expect. I'm sorry, but it can't be helped. It's important for my business."

Since her mother had long been worried about Veronica's career, it was hard for her to argue with that. "Oh very well," she sniffed. "But try not to be too long."

"Thank you. I'll just put some things together I need for the meeting. Are you sure you don't want some coffee or something?"

"I'm fine, dear. Do what you need to do. P'rhaps I'll take Jack for a walk."

"That would be great! He'd love that."

Actually, I wouldn't. The last time Shirley took me out I bolted after a squirrel and dragged Veronica's mother into an azalea bush, after which she put me on a two-foot leash for the rest of the walk.

Veronica disappeared into the bedroom, and I followed, hoping to be spared what was likely to be an unpleasant outing. She quietly closed the door, then packed up handcuffs, rope, a flogger and a variety of small torture-related implements into a medium-sized duffel bag. She added a couple of corsets, some pantyhose and a pair of size 12 stiletto heels; the client liked to be forced to wear women's clothing. She also packed a change of clothes for herself - she could no more conduct the session in jeans and a conservative blouse than she could bid farewell to her mother in the black vinyl microskirt and low-cut skin-tight top that just went into the duffel bag.

All of this she could get by her mother in the bag. But then she reached up to the top shelf of her closet and brought down the piece of equipment that constituted the major problem: a large bullwhip. I mean, *very* large the kind you'd use for herding cows, if cows were the size of small elephants. This impressive item - which till now has not made an appearance here since the opening line of this book - was Veronica's pride and joy. It was made of rawhide leather and beautifully constructed, and it had been a very expensive acquisition. And the client had specifically requested it.

Try as she might, it did not fit into the duffel, and she cursed herself for not having a larger bag available. She would just have to try and effect a distraction and sneak past her mom.

Closing the door behind her, she walked back into the living room. "Mom, let's take your bag to your room. Then I'll have to go."

She picked up her mother's pink suitcase and carried it to the spare room. Her mother dutifully followed.

"You have such an adorable house, dear," she said. "I'm so glad to see your business going so well. Apparently." There was an obvious element of doubt in her assessment of her daughter's fortunes.

Veronica kissed her mother on the cheek. "I'll be back as soon as I can. You just rest. Help yourself to anything in the kitchen if you're hungry."

"Yes, thank you, dear."

Veronica hurried back to her bedroom, grabbed the bag and the bullwhip and, satisfied that her mother was safely ensconced in the guest room, made a beeline for the front door.

But she was only halfway across when the guest room door opened and her mother stepped out.

"Holly, dear, where do you keep the–" Her mother suddenly stopped mid-sentence, and her daughter froze. Shirley's eyes were as wide as saucers. "Oh my *God*, Holly - what on *earth* are you doing with *that* thing?"

"Oh, this?" said Veronica, as if she had only just noticed the giant bullwhip she was trying unsuccessfully to hide behind the duffel bag. She laughed. "Oh, this is just a little joke."

"A *joke?*" her mother repeated. "It's hardly *little* - it's *enormous*. Why in heaven's name are you taking that to a business meeting? Come to that, why do you have such a thing at all?"

Veronica desperately attempted to effect a casual demeanor. "Oh mother, it's just a whip. It's beautiful. I take it to meetings sometimes as a joke. I brandish it at the beginning and tell people that they had better not get out of hand or go over time, or..." She had run out of things to say.

"Really? What a strange sense of humor you must have here in Seattle."

"Yes," said Veronica. "It's a Democrat thing," she added vaguely.

Her mother said, "I see" - though she clearly didn't. "Where did you get it, dear? It's quite, well, terrifyingly extraordinary."

Suddenly a lightbulb went off in Veronica's brain.

"I borrowed it from a friend," she said. "He's a farmer. He uses it to herd cows."

Her mother's face lit up. "Oh, *cows!*" she replied. "Well now you're talking my language. Cows.... how *adorable*."

Catsicle

An hour later I was lying on my day bed in the living room warily watching Veronica's mother, who was lounging in an armchair and reading the copy of *Better Homes and Gardens* that Veronica had bought that morning in an effort to delude her mother into thinking she was Martha Stewart rather than a female reincarnation of the Marquis de Sade. She had carefully packed away any item that might raise questions, taken the framed print from the *Karma Sutra* off the wall, and had made sure that the dungeon in the basement was securely locked.

Her mother sighed, sat up and looked over at me. "Well, Jack," she said, "I'm rather hungry. Let's see what Holly has to eat."

She walked into the kitchen and idly opened the fridge door. Seeing nothing that appealed to her there, she turned next to the cabinets. These were not especially well stocked - Veronica had not had time to go shopping for a few days.

Shirley returned to the living room and retrieved her cell phone from her purse. She dialed Veronica's number and waited for her to pick up.

As Veronica later related to Anna, at that moment Veronica was standing in front of her client, who was dressed in silk panties, high heels and a rather classy red and black corset. She was about to wield the infamous bullwhip when the phone buzzed. She paused, irritated. She has forgotten to turn it off as she usually did during a session.

Veronica glanced at the screen and saw from the Caller ID that it was her mother on the other end. She sighed, and thought about ignoring the call, but decided she should answer in case there was some emergency.

"You stay here!" she ordered her client.

"Yes, Mistress," the client replied obediently. It wasn't as if the guy had a choice - he was currently handcuffed to a radiator.

Veronica took the phone to the next room and answered the call. "Mother, I'm kinda busy right now with this meeting. What's the matter?"

Her mother had put the phone on speaker and placed it on the kitchen counter while she continued to rummage through Veronica's cupboards.

"Well dear, I'm sorry to bother you, but I'm hungry and I was just wondering what you had to eat." Veronica gave an exasperated sigh. "Mom, look in the kitchen. I'm sure you can find something to snack on while I'm away. I'll make a nice dinner later."

"Well okay, dear. But don't you have something instant I can microwave?"

"Maybe," Veronica replied. "There might be some *Lean Cusine* in the freezer, I don't remember."

"Okay dear, I'll look." Shirley picked up the phone from the counter, walked back to the fridge and opened the freezer door. "Well, let's see... there's some pork chops here..."

At the mention of pork chops, Veronica suddenly froze.

O God, the cat.

She was about to tell her mother to go look in the cabinet above the sink - or *anywhere* to get her away from the fridge.

"Whatever is this?" Shirley asked, and I watched her pull the bag containing one (1) very deceased cat out of the freezer. "My, it's rather heavy," she said.

"*Mom, don't open –!*" Veronica yelled, but it was too late.

There was a scream, and the sound of a phone being dropped on the floor.

Call of Nature

A few seconds later, Veronica's mother picked up the phone. The catsicle - which had been dropped along with the phone - remained in its bag on the floor.

"Holly? Are you there?" She still had a look of shock on her face.

At the other of the phone, Veronica tried to think quickly. "Yes, mom, I'm here."

"Holly, you have a *dead cat* in your freezer!" She said this as if it might come as a surprise to Veronica, and for a brief moment Veronica considered responding with an outraged, "I have a *WHAT* in my freezer?!" But even at the height of her desperation to explain, she realized that this went far beyond the bounds of plausible deniability.

Instead, she tried to be calm. "Yes, mom, I do. Don't freak out - it's just... um..."

"It's what?" asked her mother pointedly. She was now poking the catsicle bag with her foot, as if to make sure that the contents were indeed dead.

Veronica said the first thing that came into her head. "It's... for a science project."

"A science project?"

"Yes," she continued, making this up as she went along. "There's this kid in the neighborhood... he has to do a science project for school. He needs a dead cat."

"He does? Whatever for?"

"It's... it's something to do with anatomy class. I found the cat a few days ago and promised him I'd keep it for him."

Shirley was obviously not convinced. "Really? Why couldn't he keep it in his own fridge? Presumably his parents have one."

Veronica didn't have an answer for this. "Um... he's doing this project as a surprise... for his mother." She realized even as she said the words that this sounded patently ridiculous.

"A surprise for his mother? What a *dreadful* thing to surprise your mother with. As I can attest," she added pointedly, poking the catsicle again. "I swear I almost fainted."

"I'm sorry, I forgot it was in there."

"What's the boy's name?" her mother asked.

"Um... Jeffrey," Veronica replied. It was the first name that had come into her head. There actually was a little boy named Jeffrey who lived down the block, and she hoped to hell her mother didn't run into him while she was here.

"Well, it's *terribly* unhygienic," her mother noted. "It was right next to some pork chops."

"Yes mom, you're right. I'm sorry. Look, I really have to get back to this meeting."

Her mother sniffed disapprovingly. "Very well," she said, "but between bullwhips and dead cats you're scaring me half to death."

Veronica was about to hang up, grateful that she had - barely - extricated herself from a very awkward situation with her mother, when a voice from the other room suddenly called out to her.

"Mistress!" the voice said.

The client. Veronica hoped to hell her mother hadn't heard that.

At my end of the conversation, her mother started. Yep, she'd heard, loud and clear.

"Holly, who is that calling you 'Mistress'?"

"It's no one, mother. I have to go." She took the phone from her ear and stabbed at the screen in a desperate attempt to cut the connection, but right before she succeeded the voice called out again, this time more loudly.

"Mistress, *please*! I really have to pee."

The Play's The Thing

An hour later, the session was over. Veronica had whipped the client particularly hard for his vocal transgression, a punishment which oddly enough garnered her an extra $100 as a tip. After she had changed out of her domme outfit and packed up her gear she left - though she was in no hurry to return home and face her mother's inevitable questioning. She figured she had about thirty minutes in her car to come up with a plausible explanation for what her mother had heard. For once, she was grateful for the horrendous traffic, which added another fifteen minutes to the drive. By the time she finally pulled into her driveway, she had a story.

It wasn't a very *good* story, but it was the best she could come up with. It would have to do. As she walked through her front door, she decided to be proactive.

"God!" she said to her mother as the latter was opening her mouth, obviously to frame a question. "Don't ever be a consultant to thespians."

Her mother stared at her blankly. "You're a consultant to *lesbians*?" She looked horrified.

"No no, mother - *thespians*. Actors. It was an acting troupe." She dropped the gear bag and the bullwhip with a put-upon sort of sigh.

"An acting troupe?" her mother repeated. "Really?"

"Yes. They're doing a play. You could hear some of them rehearsing in the background."

"They were rehearsing? But I distinctly heard someone say he had to, well, pee." She said this as if the concept of bodily functions was alien to her. "Was that part of the play?"

"Yes, mother, it was. It's an avant garde production," she added, hoping that would explain everything.

"I see," her mother replied uncertainly. "And what exactly do you do in your consulting with them?"

"Well," said Veronica vaguely, "the usual stuff. You know, organization, a business plan, that sort of thing."

"I see." She didn't.

"Anyway," continued Veronica, "that's done. Now, what would you like for dinner?" She walked towards the kitchen, petting me as she passed.

"Well," her mother called after her retreating figure, "certainly not pork chops or anything in your freezer." From around the corner in the living room, I could see Veronica standing in front of the fridge. She was staring at something on the floor.

"O Jesus!" she exclaimed under her breath. "For Gods' sake, Mother!" she said loudly. "You could have at least put the cat *back!*"

Interlude: Dream

I know I said before that when dogs dream, it's always about chasing squirrels. Well, almost always.

A wise old sheepdog once told me that if a boy dog ever dreamed about a girl dog, it meant he was in love with her.

I dreamed about Rachel last night.

She was chasing a squirrel.

Purse

The following day, Veronica took her mother sightseeing, which activity included a visit to the famous Space Needle. Allegedly the views of the city, the Sound and the mountains are spectacular, but since they don't allow dogs up there I can't verify this claim. Which is fine; being that high would scare the crap out of me, and while I wouldn't mind having the distinction of being the first dog to defecate 500 feet above Seattle, I doubt I'd win any popularity contests by doing so.

As they ascended to the observation deck, Veronica wondered what her mother would say if she knew that, two years before, Veronica and Anna had, on a dare, together delivered a blow job to the operator of the staff elevator. The staff elevator traveled at half the speed of the public one, giving the girls precisely 82 seconds to complete the task they had assigned to themselves. The operator, an African-American friend of Anna's, held up his side of the arrangement with remarkably efficiency, and between his enthusiasm and their oral skills the girls arrived at the top still having several seconds to fix their hair and ensure that neither had bodily fluids as an unwanted decoration anywhere on her person.

Veronica smiled at the memory. She doubted that her mother had ever given a blow job in her life. Afterwards, they had lunch downtown and then went shopping. This traditional mother-daughter activity was one that Veronica endured, and typically involved her mother spending vast amounts of time trying on outfits before declaring to the increasingly irritated store clerk that everything was just too expensive to consider actually *buying*. Veronica had been known to slip a twenty-dollar bill to clerks on the way out to compensate for her embarrassment.

That evening over dinner, and while Veronica was desperately trying to think of something to do with her mother the following day, Shirley announced that she was going to visit her friend Margie.

"Margie? You mean Margie Vanderbilt?" asked Veronica. Margie Vanderbilt was an old college friend of her mother's whose principal achievement in life had been marrying rich and producing the requisite three perfect - and perfectly obnoxious - children.

"Yes dear. She was forced to move here with her husband recently, poor thing."

"Forced?" Her mother made it sound like living in Seattle was equivalent to a stretch of five to ten in the local penitentiary.

"Yes. Her husband is doing something with Boing. Lobbying or something," she added vaguely.

"Boing?" Veronica was mystified.

"Yes, dear - Boing. You know, the plane company."

"*Boeing*, mother." Sometimes her mother's lack of connection to the real world amazed her.

"Whatever. Anyway, poor Margie was uprooted from Laramie and now lives... well, here." Well, thought Veronica, that makes *two* Republicans currently in Seattle.

"Where does she live?"

"I forget, dear. Hang on."

Obtaining the answer to this simple question was not easy: a process was required. Shirley rummaged through her large red Louis Vuitton purse, pulling out various items in an effort to expedite the search for whatever it was she was looking for. Veronica watched in amazement as a parade of unrelated items were placed on the table in front of her. First, there was a mirror, a cell phone, a makeup kit, a flashlight, and a can of Mace.

"Mace?" said Veronica. "Why on earth are you carrying Mace?"

Her mother looked up, surprised. "Rapists, dear," she said, as if the answer was too obvious to be worth stating.

Given the clutter in her mother's purse, it occurred to Veronica that by the time her mother managed to actually *find* the can, any rapist would be done and probably back at home watching TV.

This first round of wonders was followed by a second which included dental floss, deodorant, lip gloss, hand sanitizer, a small bottle of perfume, a checkbook, a wallet, nail clippers and a nail file, a hairbrush (pink), some loose change, a theater ticket from two years ago, a crumpled photo of her two cows, a receipt for cat food, and several expired coupons for miscellaneous cleaning products.

Finally, from the bottom of the purse she produced a small notebook with a picture of a smiling Ronald Reagan on its cover. Then she plunged back into the bag, and after some more rummaging fished out a glasses case. She opened this and carefully adjusted a pair of reading glasses on her face.

She consulted the notebook, then looked up. "Madrona," she announced. "She lives in some place called Madrona."

Madrona is a neighborhood of contrasts. One half of it abuts Lake Washington, and features very expensive waterfront houses with views of the mountains. The other portion becomes increasingly seedy as one drives west, and eventually merges into the Central District which - although it is slowly becoming gentrified - is still known for drug dealing and the occasional drive-by shooting. Veronica had no doubt in which half Margie was to be found. Anna had a client in the rich part, a chemist who had made a small fortune helping to develop Viagra, and who now needed large doses of the stuff to successfully copulate.

"Nice area," was all Veronica said in response. She was still marveling at the quantity of things arrayed before her on the table, and wondering what else was lurking in the depths of her mother's still-by-no-means-empty purse.

"Is it far?" Shirley asked.

"No, it's quite close," her daughter replied. "I'll drive you over there. What time are you meeting her?"

"Oh, she's coming here, dear. She's picking me up at nine and we're going to spend the day together."

"The whole day?"

"Yes. Apparently I'm staying for dinner too. It's with some fellow Republicans," she said, adding "You wouldn't understand."

Veronica raised her eyebrows and sighed. Her mother's political views were a source of constant friction between them.

"No, mother," she replied, "I probably wouldn't."

"You don't mind me leaving you, do you dear?" her mother said in what was an obvious afterthought.

"No, mom, I don't. You go off and have a good time - Republicans in Seattle have to stick together." Her mother frowned disapprovingly.

"Anyway, it's fine," continued Veronica. "I have something to do with my friend Anna."

At Anna's name, her mother's face brightened somewhat. "Oh yes, how *is* Anna? Lovely girl. Does *she* have boyfriend?"

Anna did in fact have not one but three boyfriends, none of whom were aware of the existence of the other two, and only one of which knew that Anna made her living satisfying the sexual needs of other men. Needless to say, Veronica spared her mother any of this, but she couldn't resist teasing her.

"No mother, she doesn't," she said. "Like all of us women in this city, she's a lesbian too."

Her mother's eyes widened. It was apparent from her expression that there was some part of her that thought her daughter might actually be serious.

After all, this *was* Seattle.

Buzz Buzz

Later that night Veronica went into her bedroom to call Anna and ask if she was free the following day.

"Yes, sweetie. I have a client at 9 o'clock but am free after that. Besides," she added, "he's a preemie, so it never takes long."

Preemie is escort slang for 'premature ejaculator'.

"Okay, good," Veronica replied. "I was thinking it's time to lay poor pussy to rest. The pork chops are beginning to complain."

She then proceeded to tell Anna the story of her mother discovering the dead cat in her freezer, which prompted much laughter from the other end of the phone.

"Poor Shirley!" Anna said. "At least it wasn't a whole dead cow in there. I know how she feels about cows."

"I don't know," Veronica replied. "She'd probably like that."

"What's your mother doing tomorrow? Are you abandoning her?" Anna said.

"No - she's actually abandoning me. She's spending the day with an old friend at some sort of Republican love fest."

"There are enough Republicans in Seattle to have a love fest?"

"Apparently. I don't know - maybe they fly them in from Idaho."

Veronica agreed to call *Heavenly Paws* the next morning and see if they could arrange to bury Fake Bonkers. "I suppose we need to produce some suitable text for the headstone," she said. "I still haven't done that."

"Let's give it some thought," said Anna. "I'm sure we can come up with something good."

After the phone call to Anna, Veronica returned to the living room, where her mother was flipping through *Better Homes and Gardens*. Bonkers was patrolling the edge of the room; he was clearly bored and looking for something to do.

"How are the cows, mother?" Veronica asked. She didn't really want to know, but after the various events with the bullwhip, the client and the dead cat, she was being cautious in her conversation. Cows were a safe subject.

"Oh, they're wonderful, dear! We're thinking of getting Daisy pregnant." The cows' names were Daisy and Tuppence.

"Really?" said Veronica, trying to feign interest in her mother's odd obsession with all things bovine. "Who's going to do the honors - dad?"

"Don't be crude, dear. We're talking to a local rancher."

"The rancher's going to inseminate her? That's dedication."

Her mother sighed. "*No*," she said with considerable restraint, "the rancher has a prize bull he's looking to breed."

Meanwhile, Bonkers jumped onto a chair. From there he somehow propelled his overweight body up to a shelf on which sat various random items, including a black rectangular box.

Shirley then proceeded to regale Veronica with various facts about cows. "Did you know that a cow chews fifty times a minute?" she asked. "And that its jaw moves more than 40,000 times a day?" She was warming to this, her second-favorite subject in life. Her first was usually what Jesus would think of certain politicians - who coincidentally all happened to be Democrats.

Bonkers was now contemplating the various objects on the shelf, and I could see that his little cat brain was trying to decide which one to knock off first. This was not going to end well.

"And did you know," she continued, "that you can walk a cow upstairs but not down?"

Veronica raised her eyebrows. "Really? I wonder who was the first to find *that* out - and whether their cow is still upstairs."

Bonkers had apparently settled on trying to move the black box, partly because it was already perched rather precariously partway over the edge of the shelf. The shelf was behind Veronica so she was unaware of her obnoxious pet's nefarious intentions. I was tempted to bark and alert her to what he was doing, but then that would have deprived me of the opportunity for some fun - and to see my beloved house mate reprimanded.

"Yes, that's rather funny, isn't it?" Shirley said, smiling at the image of a cow permanently stranded in someone's upper-floor bedroom. "I can just imagine Daisy--"

At that moment there was a loud noise as the black box fell off the shelf, propelled by Bonkers' left front paw. It hit the ground with a thud. This was immediately followed by a loud buzzing noise from within the box, which suddenly began to move its way across the floor towards Veronica's mother.

"O God!" Veronica exclaimed. In her efforts to remove incriminating objects, she had completely forgotten this one.

Before Veronica could stop it, the box had shimmied its way to Shirley's feet. She stooped to pick it up. "What on earth is this?" her mother asked. Veronica reached over in a futile attempt to grab the still-buzzing box from her mother's hands, but it was too late. Shirley was taking off the lid.

Inside was a large purple vibrator complete with ribbed sides and an extension piece that presumably was intended to be inserted in, well, a secondary orifice. This was a serious piece of equipment: judging from the power of the vibration it might well have been rated industrial strength. The impact with the floor had accidentally turned it on; I don't know if Veronica had left it on maximum vibration the last time she used it, but any more power and the windows would have been rattling.

Shirley looked at the giant sex toy, and then handed it, still vibrating, to her daughter with a look of pity on her face.

"Oh Holly," she said sadly. "You *really* need a boyfriend."

Epitaph

epitaph (noun), "inscription on a tomb or monument," mid-14c., from Old French *epitaphe* (12c.) and directly from Medieval Latin *epitaphium* "funeral oration, eulogy," from Greek *epitaphion* "a funeral oration, words spoken on the occasion of a funeral," from *epi* "at, over"+ *taphos* "tomb, funeral rites," from Proto-Indo-European root *dhembh-* "to bury." Among the Old English equivalents was *byrgelsleoð*.

The next day, Veronica called *Heavenly Paws,* and Mirakel confirmed that she would be delighted to "send your pussy to his eternal rest", as she put it.

"This woman seems obsessed with pussy," said Veronica as she relayed this to Anna. "Maybe she's a closet lesbian."

"Can you blame her, married to Earl?"

"Good point."

At precisely nine a.m., Shirley's friend Margie appeared on the doorstep. She looked like a woman who had just arrived via time machine from the early 1960's.

Hovering above red pumps and a sensible tweed skirt there were, in vertical order of appearance, a red belt with a buckle in the shape of a Scottie dog, a pink cashmere sweater, enough pearls to sink a battleship, crimson lipstick, cat-style eyeglasses and a beehive hairdo that probably took most of the contents of a can of hairspray to hold in place - and which could probably have remained in place in a force eight gale. As she opened the door, Veronica was almost knocked over by the quantity of perfume radiating from her body.

"Oh hello, Holly," said Margie brightly. "Nice to see you again. You always look so lovely."

"Thank you, Margie," Veronica responded, and tried her best not to cough from the perfume cloud that enveloped her as she accepted a peck on the cheek. "It's nice to see you too."

"Hello dear!" beamed Shirley as she pushed past her daughter and gave her friend an affectionate but tentative hug.

"Ready to go?" asked Margie.

"Yes, let's," replied Veronica's mother. She turned to Veronica. "Goodbye dear. Have a nice time with Anna. I'll see you tonight." And with that, the two of them headed towards the white Cadillac that Margie had parked rather inexpertly on the street. Veronica sighed as she looked at it; attached to the rear fender was a BUSH-CHENEY bumpersticker.

Having thus despatched her mother for the day, Veronica awaited the arrival of her friend. Anna showed up just after ten.

"That was quick," commented Veronica. "Was he done that fast?"

"A ten-minute blowjob - during which I had to be very careful not to get him off - and then a two-minute fuck. Easiest $500 I've made this month."

"Don't you - I don't know - give him tea or something afterwards? I mean, the poor guy's paying for an hour, right?"

"Yes, but he never wants to stick around. I think he's a bit embarrassed, to be honest. And anyway, I always give him a break on the fee because of his, well, *brevity*."

"Well okay. Ready for *Paws* and *Bares*?"

"Ready for the former, not so much the latter," Anna said. "Got the cat?" she asked.

"O God!" Veronica exclaimed. "I almost forgot!" She went back into the house and emerged a moment later holding up the infamous shoe store bag. It was apparent that Veronica hadn't bothered to arrange the cat when replacing it in the freezer, because a very rigid tail was sticking straight up through the opening.

"Poor pussy," said Anna. "How's he doing?"

"Well," said Veronica, "he's still dead, if that's what you mean."

This time we drove down in Veronica's Subaru: two women, a dog and an increasingly dead cat. During the drive the main topic on conversation was what should be inscribed on Demon Cat's tombstone.

"P'rhaps it should be a poem," ventured Anna. "There was a young pussy named Demon," she began.

Veronica considered. "What rhymes with *Demon*?"

"Semen."

"You *would* think of that."

"Occupational hazard, darling. In more ways than one." Anna had lost count of the number of times she'd had to dry clean her clothing - and often wondered why Monica Lewinsky hadn't done the same thing.

The two girls tossed around ideas, and by the time we began bumpily driving our way down the now-familiar dirt road they had settled on an epitaph - a cheesy poem that Anna had somehow disgorged from her mind en route. Coincidentally, it was exactly fifty words, the maximum allowed on the headstone.

Veronica had thought the poem was pretty dreadful, but she couldn't think of anything better. Anna had scribbled the final version down on a cocktail napkin, which was the only thing they had to write on.

Mirakel was apparently expecting them because she was standing at the open door of the trailer office. She was wearing a purple sarong.

As we got out of the car, she approached us, flashing the tyrannosaur teeth in a wide and slightly predatory-looking smile.

"So nice to see you both again," she said. She open her arms and advanced for a hug, but - remembering the previous molestation - Veronica forestalled this by extending her hand.

"And how is little Jock here?" she asked, looking down at me.

Why does everyone keep calling me Jock? And while I'm no great Dane, I'm really not "little", thank you very much.

"Jack," Veronica corrected her. "He's fine."

"So," said Anna, "can we do the internment today?"

"Yes, dear," Mirakel replied. "We're all ready for you."

"Great," said Veronica. "We just have a simple ceremony planned."

"And we don't want Reverend Steve?" Mirakel asked. "He lives just down the road in a very nice double-wide. He can be here in a jiffy."

"No thanks," said Veronica. "Neither of us is very religious."

"Oh, neither is Reverend Steve," Mirakel assured them. "Actually I think he's an atheist. He's got one of those Internet minister certificate things."

"Yes," said Anna. "You told us."

"Anyway," said Veronica, "we'd like a private burial, if you don't mind."

"Of course, dear. I understand."

"So how does this work?" Anna asked.

"Oh well, you give us the... deceased, and we see to the burial arrangements. His little casket is all ready."

"Okay," Veronica said, "but do we do the ceremony first, or what?"

"Ah," Mirakel replied, "I see. No, we've dug a hole... I mean a *grave* - we've already prepared a plot, it's right next to a very nice chihuahua - and then we give you the casket with the deceased, and you do your thing. Say words of parting and consolation, recite a poem, lay a wreath - whatever you have planned."

Veronica and Anna looked at each other and realized they should have brought some flowers. They really hadn't planned anything.

"Then when you're done saying goodbye, we bury him for you and make everything nice and neat and ready for the headstone." She paused. " Talking of which, do you have some text for the epitaph?"

"Oh yes, we do," said Veronica. She fished the cocktail napkin out of her pocket and handed it to Mirakel, looking rather sheepish. Inscribing deeply meaningful words that commemorate a beloved pet on something that had recently sat under a gin and tonic seemed somehow inappropriate.

"Sorry," Veronica said. "The epitaph was sort of a last-minute thing today."

Mirakel took the napkin and held it at arm's length; evidently she was in denial that she needed reading glasses. She read the epitaph aloud.

> *Beneath this stone there rests a Demon*
> *Who started out his life with seamen*
> *Beloved pet and Youtube star*
> *Much admired from near and far*
> *We hope that kitty heav'n is nice*
> *And overrun with big fat mice*
> *Now you shall be - though we must part -*
> *Evermore within my heart*

"Very nice, dear," said Mirakel when she was finished. Her appreciation of Anna's poetry didn't sound very sincere.

"The seamen part is because he was born on a boat," Anna reminded her.

"I see," said Mirakel. "What's this bit about being a Youtube star?"

"Oh, he had quite a following," Anna explained. "Lots of funny kitty videos."

"One in particular," added Veronica darkly; she wasn't about to supply details. She and Anna exchanged glances.

"I see," said Mirakel again. "Well, everyone is on the Internet these days, aren't they? Even my granddaughter's hamster has his own Facebook page."

Catsicle II

"So," Mirakel said after a pause, "where's your pussy?" She seemed genuinely oblivious to the double meaning that screamed loudly from this question, and Veronica resisted the strong temptation to respond that her pussy was in its usual location between her legs. From the strained expression on her face, it was apparent that Anna was having difficulty suppressing the same thought.

Instead Veronica said, "He's in the back of the car. Shall I get him?"

"Not just yet, dear," Mirakel replied. "Let's get the casket first." She motioned for them to follow her into the trailer office.

They entered the trailer, which if anything was more cluttered than it had been before. They were relieved to see that there was no sign of Earl.

"Now where on earth did that man put the casket?" Mirakel asked irritably. "Earl was tidying up yesterday," she explained. All evidence to the contrary notwithstanding.

"Is that it?" asked Anna, pointing to the top of the fridge.

Mirakel looked up, put her hands on her hips, and sighed loudly. "O good heavens, why on earth did he put it up there? That's no place for a casket. I'm so sorry," she added, looking at the girls. "He means well."

"No worries," replied Anna. "I'm sure Veronica's pussy won't mind." Veronica shot her a look.

Having retrieved the casket from the fridge, where it was precariously perched on top of a pile of old magazines, Mirakel led us all back outside and over to Veronica's car. Veronica opened the back hatch and picked up the bagged catsicle, which in the warm summer weather was now a bit less of a catsicle than it had been an hour ago. The associated smell appeared to be getting stronger by the moment, and a person didn't have to look into the bag to know that there was all kinds o' dead something lurking inside. Despite the slow thaw, the tail was still rigid and sticking out.

Mirakel put the casket down in the back of the car, then took the bag from Veronica and peered inside. "Oh dear," she said sadly. "He's rather squashed, isn't he? It was a tram, you said?"

"Yes," said Anna, who was simultaneously trying to fake tears and suppress laughter.

"I'm so sorry, dear," Mirakel said, looking at Veronica. "This must be so upsetting to you." Veronica tried her best to appear upset, but the expression on her face just made her look like she was having trouble initiating a bowel movement.

Mirakel gently put the catsicle down, then opened the casket. It was a simple box, rectangular and made of pine, with a lid that slid into place via grooves on the inside edges of the sides. The interior was lined with white satin.

From some mysterious location inside her sarong, Mirakel produced a pair of latex gloves. After pulling them on with some difficulty - they were at least a size too small for her hands - she picked up the cat rather gingerly and attempted to place it into the casket.

Unfortunately, it wouldn't fit. More specifically, one of its frozen front legs was stretched out, and then there was the problem with the tail, which continued to be stubbornly oriented perpendicular to the catsicle's back legs.

"Oh dear," said Mirakel. "I hadn't anticipated this. He's still rather frozen, isn't he? Did you have him in freezer?"

"Yes," said Veronica.

"With some pork chops and frozen peas," added Anna, supplying completely unnecessary detail.

Mirakel frowned. "Well I suppose we could wait for him to thaw out a bit," she suggested.

"How long do you think that's going to take?" asked Veronica.

"Well, I'm not sure, dear. It's a warm day. Let's give it fifteen minutes or so. We'll put him in the sun." And so for the next quarter of an hour everyone sat around, making polite conversation and trying to ignore the un-ignorable stench emanating like an invisible cloud from the frozen cat corpse that was stretched out on top of the Subaru's hood.

Every few minutes Mirakel would take hold of the front leg or the tail and attempt to move it, but neither appendage showed any signs of budging.

After the allotted period had passed, it became clear that the recalcitrant catsicle was not going to cooperate any time soon. Rigid it remained. Finally, Anna ventured a suggestion.

"Do you have a microwave? P'rhaps we could put him on 'defrost' for a few minutes, you know, just to soften him up a bit."

"Or an oven," added Veronica helpfully. "If we baked him at 350 for a little while I'm sure that would do the trick."

Mirakel looked suitably appalled. "I don't *think* so, dear. I mean, I love pets as much as the next person, but I don't think I want a dead one being cooked in the same place Earl heats up his frozen burritos. Besides, he wouldn't fit in a microwave, I'm sure."

Presumably she was referring to the cat and not Earl.

There was a cogitative pause, then Anna said, "Well, what about a hairdryer?"

"O, *that's* a good idea!" beamed Mirakel. "Yes, that might work. I think I have one in the office, I'll just go and get it." She wandered off in the direction of the trailer.

"Poor pussy," Anna said as she surveyed the catsicle. "He's actually harder than some of my clients." "You're sick," said Veronica. In response, Anna gave her sweetest smile.

A few minutes later, Mirakel emerged from the trailer holding a large hair dryer, to which was attached a long orange extension cord. The cord didn't quite reach, however, so Veronica was required to get into the car and drive a few yards closer. As she did this, the catsicle was still stretched out in front of her, like some grotesque hood ornament from *The Munsters*.

And then, for the next few minutes, we were all treated to the distinctly novel sight of a middle-aged woman in a purple sarong blow-drying a dead cat.

"Now there's something you don't see every day," Veronica said to Anna.

Mirakel tested the leg and the tail periodically, and it was now apparent that poor pussy was slowly being revived from his glacial state; unfortunately, this decrease in rigidity was accompanied by a corresponding intensification in smell. Finally, both appendages relented sufficiently to be moved, and the catsicle was coaxed into assuming a more compact form.

Mirakel placed the corpse into the casket, and asked Veronica if she wanted to deliver a last kiss to the putrefying feline - admittedly she didn't use quite those words, but that *was* the reality of it - before the lid was closed forever. The look of horror on Veronica's face forestalled any repetition of the question.

"So, that would be a No, then?" Mirakel said, and slid the lid shut.

Putting the Fun in Funeral

"Are we ready, dears?" Mirakel asked.

"Um... ready for what?" asked Veronica.

"For the burial ceremony, dear," Mirakel replied.

"Oh yes... yes, I suppose so," Veronica said uncertainly.

"Perhaps you'd both like to be pallbearers," she said, pointing to the casket. "It's a bit large for one person, and I'm not as young as I used to be."

"Um, sure."

Veronica and Anna took hold of the wooden casket, which had a single brass handle attached at each end.

Veronica was again trying unsuccessfully to look sad.

They dutifully followed Mirakel on the path through the trees with me trotting along behind, and we emerged in the clearing with the cemetery. At the far end of one row was a freshly dug grave. As promised, it was located next to another recent internment, a chihuahua whose name - according to the freshly erected headstone - was Waffles.

Another stupid dog name. Seriously, I'd ask if you people would be so inconsiderate when naming your kids, but then I've heard enough stupid kid names - Norbert, for one - to realize that this particular affliction isn't confined to dogs.

They laid the casket on the ground next to the grave.

"Now," said Mirakel, "I assume you've prepared some words for the ceremony?" They hadn't.

"Actually," said Veronica, "we decided not to do anything elaborate. I think we're just going to stand here and remember him quietly."

"He was a simple cat," added Anna.

"So... if you could give us a minute," Veronica said.

"Oh, of course, dear," Mirakel replied. "I'll just leave you to it. I'll be in the office when you're done. I must say you're bearing up very well, considering." She smiled the tyrannosaur smile and discreetly wandered away.

Veronica and Anna looked at each other, then at the casket.

"Poor pussy," said Anna. "I suppose we should say something nice to send him on his way."

"Sorry you got squashed," ventured Veronica. "I hope you had a nice life - up to that point."

"Sadly we'll never know."

"He didn't have a collar. Maybe he was a stray."

"Poor pussy," Anna repeated.

"We really should have prepared something. You know, brought flowers, or a teddy bear."

"A teddy bear?"

"Yes, people put all kinds of toys and things on graves."

"Vee, he was a stray cat, not a six-year-old."

"Cats like teddy bears too."

"Does Bonkers have a teddy bear?"

"Not any more, he shredded the last one."

There was a pause.

"I just feel like we should do more," Veronica said.

"Hail Mary, full of grace," Anna began, "the Lord is with thee, blessed art thou amongst kitties. Hail Mary, mother of God, pray for us pussies, now and at the hour of our death, Amen."

"Where did *that* come from?"

"Like many in the business of professional fucking, I'm a good Catholic girl. When I was a kid we had to say that every night for about four million years. Though not the pussy version."

"Yeah, I got that part," said Veronica. "You're going to Hell - you know that, right?"

Anna smiled sweetly. "Yes," she said. "But at least I'll be in good company."

They looked back down at the casket.

"Poor pussy," said Veronica.

"Hang on," Anna said. She pulled a smartphone out of her purse, entered something into a search engine, and a moment later held the phone up. It began to play *Taps*.

"Nice touch," said Veronica. "Pussy would like that."

"I try," Anna replied. "It's the least we can do."

The two girls stood at attention, hands respectfully together in front of them, while the song played dolefully to the end. When it was finally done, they looked at each other, then at the casket.

"Bye bye, little kitty," said Veronica. "I hope there are mice in Heaven."

"How do you know he's going to Heaven?" asked Anna. "For all you know he could have been an evil cat."

"Well yes, I suppose. But I prefer to think of him as angelic." There was a pause.

"Okay then, that's that," said Anna. "Shall we go and find the Saronged One?"

"I suppose," Veronica replied. "Time for me to look distraught. How's this?"

Anna regarded her friend. "Actually, you don't look distraught, darling. To be honest, you look rather..."

"What?"

"Well... constipated."

The Fab Four

After we returned to the office, Veronica concluded her business with Mirakel, who said that the headstone would be ready and in place within a week. Veronica promised she would come down soon after to see the finished product and pay her respects at the completed grave.

"You get to look constipated all over again," Anna said, as we all got into the car and prepared to leave.

"Very funny. Maybe I'll squirt you with lemon juice so you're the one who's crying hysterically."

As we drove away from the trailer with a smiling Mirakel waving goodbye behind us, we heard giggles and splashing noises coming from the other side of the fence that separated the nudist camp from the rest of the world. Apparently there was a pool somewhere over there.

"Hmm," Anna said. "That explains why we didn't see Earl. He must be cavorting with the bares."

Veronica groaned. "Thank you for that image."

"My pleasure."

"Let's have some music," Veronica said later as we turned onto the interstate.

Anna connected her phone to the car's Bluetooth system and flipped through her extensive music collection. "Let's see," she said, perusing. "Adele, Beyonce, Abba..."

"Abba?" said Veronica. "Seriously?"

"Guilty pleasure," she replied. She continued reading choices. "Dido, Fiona Apple, Jackson Browne, Norah Jones, Rolling Stones, the Beatles..."

I barked.

Anna turned around. "Beatles, Jack?"

I barked again.

"Yeah," said Veronica, "Jack loves the Beatles. Go figure."

"No kidding," she said, smiling at me. Anna has a lovely smile. "Okay, Beatles it is."

She hit play and a few seconds later a song started. And then we were driving down the highway with all the windows down and *A Hard Day's Night* blasting out of the car.

> *It's been a hard day's night*
> *and I've been working like a dog...*

Veronica and Anna sang along loudly, smiling at me as they belted out these lines. Me, I put my head out of the window and enjoyed the music and the breeze.

Dogs don't work - well, sheepdogs, guard dogs and greyhounds excepted. But we all appreciate a nice car ride on a perfect summer day.

Confession

Late that evening, Veronica's mother returned from her meeting with what Veronica would later jokingly term the Ronald Reagan Dick-Lickers' Club. Shirley was, she said, happy to have been with "her people" for an evening.

"That's nice, mother," Veronica replied. "Tomorrow you can go home and be back with lots of your people in Wyoming. We only have a few of them here, mostly for the novelty value."

Her mother frowned. "Very funny, dear," she said, then added, "Senator Rumor was there."

"Who?"

"Catkins Rumor. The state senator."

Veronica stared blankly.

Her mother sighed. "He's a state senator," she repeated. "Very influential. Don't you keep up with local politics?"

"Not really," Veronica replied. "I just assume they're all assholes."

"Don't be vulgar, Holly. Anyway, he's a charming man. Such fine conservative principles."

Veronica rolled her eyes. "That's what they all say," she said. "And then you find out that they've been screwing girls on the side - or boys."

"Holly! That's not true!"

"Really? Let me give you a list. Herman Cain - sexual assault allegations. Chris Meyers - paid a gay prostitute. Newt Gingrich - had an affair. Chris Lee - sent sleazy photos of himself to a girl after responding to a Craigslist sex ad. Mark Sanford - I love this one - went off to Argentina to screw his mistress and then tried to claim he was hiking the Appalachian Trail. Oh, and let's not forget Larry Craig - the gay-bashing senator from Idaho who was playing footsie in an airport bathroom in the hope of getting some gay action. Shall I go on? There are lots more."

"Well," her mother said defensively, "the truly Christians Republicans don't do any of that."

"Really?" Veronica now had her hands on her hips, and was just hitting her stride. This was a sore subject. "Don't get me started on the fundamentalists. All those bloated tele-evangelists who rake in the money and preach about how the Bible hates gays and adulterers and other sinners - and then end up being caught doing any and all of that. Jimmy Swaggart - regularly hired prostitutes. Ted Haggard - major scumbag - hated gay people and yet hired rent boys for sex and for good measure bought crystal meth from them. Jim Bakker - another winner, remember Tammy Faye, his wife and her five pounds of make-up and addiction to drugs? He screwed his secretary and then paid her to keep quiet about it."

"Holly, stop. I take your point."

"Do you, mother? I'm sorry, but I'm just so sick of hypocrites."

"Well, Democrats certainly have their own share of scandals. Look at Bill Clinton."

"One bad thing doesn't justify another. And Bill Clinton never preached hatred to gay people and then screwed a rent boy. He just had terrible taste in mistresses."

"You have a lot of anger, dear, don't you?"

"Generally, no. About this, yes."

Her mother suddenly looked worried. "Holly, you're not a lesbian, are you? I mean, that would explain a lot. I don't mean to pry, and I'd love you whatever you are, but... well, I just need to know."

"You'd love me no matter what? Really?"

"Yes, of course," she said, though not without a trace of uncertainty. "You're my daughter."

"I'm not a lesbian, mother."

Her mother gave a sigh of relief.

"I'm a sex worker."

Confession II

She really hadn't meant to say it, she told Anna later. It had just come out. She was sick of hypocrisy, and her rant about Republicans and fundamentalists had primed her. And she was tired of hiding and living a double life.

Whatever the motivation, the effect of Veronica's confession on her mother was dramatic. Shirley stared at her, her eyes as wide as saucers. "You're... you're a what?" she asked, stunned.

"A sex worker, mother. To be precise, I am what they call a professional dominatrix." Her mother continued to stare, her mouth open.

Having jumped off the cliff, Veronica kept going. "I make my living dominating men. Men who pay me to do things to them - inflict pain or humiliation or other... other *things*. They actually pay me very well for this. I don't think you want the details," she added.

Her mother looked faint, and she wobbled her way into an armchair.

Finally she managed to speak.

"This... this isn't a joke?" she said. "Because if it is, it's in very poor taste."

"No, mom, it's not a joke. I"ve been doing this for a few years. I'm actually very good at it."

Her mother was still staring, but now her gaze was fixed somewhere in space. "You're... good... at it," she repeated.

Veronica knelt on the floor in front of her mother and put her hand on her knee. She looked up at her, sympathy in her eyes. She didn't regret having told her, but she knew this that stark truth about her daughter would be very difficult for her mother to assimilate into the fabric of her life.

"I know," she said, "this is a shock and a lot to take in. I'm sorry, but I don't want to live a lie with you." Her mother was staring blankly into space, and for once she was speechless.

Veronica wasn't sure what to do, so she defaulted to what she called "the British solution" for absolutely everything.

"Tell you what," she said, "How about I make some tea?"

Her mother continued to stare. "Yes," she whispered, as if awakening from a trance. "Yes, tea would be nice."

Veronica went into the kitchen and busied herself putting the kettle on and preparing the teapot. She opened a cabinet and surveyed the wide array of choices before her. There were various kinds of herbal teabags as well as several varieties of loose leaf tea; Veronica's a bit of a tea snob, so the latter are always of high quality (and correspondingly high price). Finally she decided on chamomile, partly because the label on the box prominently advertized the primary effect of this variety as "calming" - and she figured that if anyone needed to be calmed at that moment, it was her mother.

Anyway, in the absence of an injection of sedatives, chamomile tea would have to do.

When the tea was ready, and with not a little trepidation, she returned to the living room. Shirley was no longer staring into space, which was potentially a good sign.

She served the tea, and looked at her mother.

"So," she said. "I'm guessing you're confused and probably not happy right now." Her mother took a careful sip of the tea and returned her daughter's gaze.

"Holly, I don't know what to say." She paused. "Does this mean that you're..." She couldn't bring herself to complete the sentence.

Veronica knew what she wanted to ask. "A prostitute?" she asked. "No, I'm not. I don't have sex with my clients."

"Well, I suppose that's something. But I thought..."

"What did you think, mother?" Apparently Veronica was going to have to drag questions out of her.

"I thought... *sex workers*... were all... well, exploited."

Veronica gave her a sardonic smile. "No, mom, they're not."

"They're not?"

"No. Some are, for sure. There are girls who are forced into sex work by unscrupulous men..."

"Pimps."

"Yes, pimps. Some of those girls are under age. There are women who aren't exactly forced into prostitution, but who do it as a sort of last resort because they're desperate. Financially, I mean. But there are an awful lot of sex workers like myself who have actively chosen this line of work, and who - for the most part - enjoy what we do. That applies to all the dommes I know."

"Dommes?"

"Short for dominatrix. Pro domme, professional dominatrix," she explained helpfully.

Her mother nodded to show she had understood.

"It's also true of a lot of escorts."

"You mean prostitutes?"

"Yes, though they don't like that term." She didn't tell her mother that, in private, Veronica's escort friends frequently referred to one another as *ho*. It was usually a term of affection. Usually.

Shirley raised her eyebrows and uttered what was clearly a sigh of disapproval.

"I really don't know what to say," she repeated. "What on earth am I going to tell other people when they ask me what my daughter is doing with her life?"

"That's entirely up to you, mother. Tell them the truth, or tell them I'm doing something else, I don't care."

"You mean, something like you're a 'consultant'?" The sarcasm was obvious.

"Yes," Veronica sighed. There was no point in rising to the bait.

"Did I do something wrong raising you, Holly?" her mother asked. This time the tone was self-pitying.

"Oh for God's sake, mother, don't pull that one. You did nothing wrong, and this is not anything bad. It's my life, and my choice. And it's a choice I have willingly and enthusiastically made."

"I see," Shirley replied. Frosty tone now.

"So," Veronica said, "the part about you loving me no matter what I did - you didn't mean it?"

This caught her mother rather off guard, since she clearly couldn't confirm her daughter's accusation. "Oh Holly, of course I love you no matter what. I'm just having difficulty processing this. When you asked me that, I had no idea that *this* is what you meant."

Veronica relented. "I know, mom," she said. "I'm sorry, but you have to believe me that this is something I choose and enjoy doing."

Shirley sighed, then nodded, as if she had come to some internal decision.

"Well, I suppose I'm going to have to learn to live with this," she said. "But it's hardly what I expected. I thought you'd say you were... I don't know... a socialist."

Veronica couldn't help laughing. "Well, I'm that too. Sorry. But," she added, "if it helps, all my clients are Democrats."

Her mother sniffed. "Well, *that* doesn't surprise me." She paused, then asked, "Are any of them famous?"

"No, mother, they're not famous. They're just ordinary guys who have secret erotic needs - and vote Democratic."

As it turned out, she was wrong on both counts.

Mystery Man II

As Veronica would say later, she loved her mother but was usually glad to see the back of her when she left - and never more so than this time. After the Coming Out discussion, mother and daughter had passed a cordial but rather strained hour in what remained of the evening before bedtime.

The following morning, Veronica kissed her mother goodbye as another Mr Singh lifted her pink suitcase into the trunk of his taxi. This one was yellow.

Her mother's parting remark to her daughter was to instruct her, rather too loudly, to not become infected with "one of those new sex diseases"; she didn't specify which disease she was thinking of. The taxi driver pretended not to hear.

Veronica watched the taxi drive off, and heaved a sigh of relief. She looked down at me. "God, Jack, it's ten in the morning and I think I want to drink heavily. That's bad, right?"

I wagged my tail and nuzzled her hand. She laughed. "You goof," she said. "Whatever would I do without you? You know how to cheer me up, don't you?"

It's true, I do.

Two hours later - Veronica hadn't started drinking, yet - I was sitting in the window watching for squirrels when I saw Isaac talking to a man in the street. I squinted... was that...? Yes - it was the same man I'd seen hiding in the bushes before.

The two of them talked for a couple of minutes, and then the mystery man - who was again holding a camera walked off down the street. Isaac watched him go, then headed for our front door. Isaac knocked, and Veronica opened the door. "Oh hello, Isaac," she said. "What's up?"

Isaac looked serious. "Hi Veronica. Look, I don't mean to be alarmist, but I think you're possibly under some kind of surveillance."

Veronica frowned in surprise. "What? You'd better come in."

"Thank you. Hello, Jack."

Hello to you too. I wagged my tail enthusiastically to show how pleased I was to see my best friend.

"Would you like some coffee?" Veronica asked.

"Thank you, that would be nice."

"Latte okay?"

"Just a shot of espresso would be fine, thanks."

"Okay. Come into the kitchen and tell me what this is all about." We all wandered into the kitchen, and Veronica began preparing the very expensive Italian espresso machine on the counter.

"Well, I'm not sure. But I noticed this man today who was - well, he was pretty much hiding in the bushes, and he had a camera."

Veronica was beginning to look worried as she ground the coffee beans. "Why do you think he was interested in me?" she asked.

"Because I went over to talk with him. I didn't want to confront him, so I just pretended to be casual and say hi, and commented on the weather. I wanted to see if I could learn anything from him."

"And?"

"And - once he'd decided I wasn't suspicious - he asked me if I knew anything about you. Gave me some line about meeting you the other day and finding you very attractive, and he was hoping to approach you for a date."

"And you didn't believe him?"

"No. The guy had a very expensive camera and a notebook. He held up the camera and said he was an amateur birdwatcher."

"Maybe he's telling the truth," Veronica said hopefully. It wouldn't be the first time some guy had followed her home in hopes of getting a date.

I know this guy, I said in the pause that followed. *I saw him the other day, and Leroy came out to confront him. He got spooked and went away - and he told him the same story about being a birdwatcher.*

Isaac glanced down at me as I was saying this, and he paused for a moment; apparently he was trying to figure out a way to tell Veronica this.

"Well, yes, but I don't think so. And apparently Leroy saw this guy a couple of days ago and confronted him, and he left."

Veronica was looking more worried now. "So what did you tell him, when he asked about me?"

"I said you were a consultant and a very nice woman," Isaac replied.

"Well, thanks," Veronica said, as she handed him the espresso. "I'm not sure what to make of this. I mean, I don't know why anyone would want to keep watch on me."

Privately, she was terrified that this was somehow related to her business. Maybe it was a law enforcement operation targeting vice. She sighed.

"I don't know either," Isaac said, "but I thought you should know." He smiled as he sipped his coffee. "It's probably nothing."

The conversation changed to more routine matters. The weather, politics, and everyone's local religion - the Seattle Seahawks.

Twenty minutes later, after Isaac had left and she had glanced at a clock to satisfy herself that it was past noon, Veronica went back to the kitchen.

This time she got out the vodka.

But two days went by with no further sightings of the Mystery Man, so Veronica relaxed and optimistically hoped that perhaps it had all been innocent after all.

And, just after she'd said to Anna that she could really use a distraction, one landed squarely in her lap.

Refunded Refund

Surprise of the day for Friday: a letter from Oliver, the client whose genitalia Bonkers attempted to shred two weeks ago.

Almost as surprising as the letter's contents was the fact that this was an actual *letter* - not an email or a Facebook post or an instant message or an item on Instagram or any of the hundred other completely bewildering ways in which you humans seem to fritter away half your days. This quaint anachronism plopped through Veronica's mail slot this morning and proceeded to lay patiently on the mat, forced to keep company with the usual collection of coupon books, credit card offers and other random junk mail.

When Veronica finally picked it up and saw the sender's name, she experienced a brief moment of panic. O God, was this a lawsuit? But the anxiety quickly passed; the address on the outside had been hand-written, and when she turned the envelope over she found that it had been sealed with a little red heart sticker. You don't get too many lawyers sending little hearts to defendants - or, for that matter, to the lawyers' wives. Besides, no guy is going to pursue a lawsuit which requires him to reveal his sordid erotic proclivities:

Judge: *And while the cat was raking your penis with its claws, you were at that point naked and strapped to the, er* (adjusts reading glasses, consults notes)... *St Andrews cross, is that correct?*

Man: *Yes, your honor.*

Not happening.

Now very curious, Veronica opened the envelope. Inside was a check for the $2,000 fee that she had refunded to Oliver that night, and an apology. More out of astonishment than anything else, Veronica read the letter out loud.

Dear Veronica,

I am very sorry if I gave you the impression during our last meeting that I was traumatized by what happened regarding your cat. The fact is that since that night I have been consumed by the thrilling memories of that evening, and the intense pleasure which I received from the incident. To be so helpless in the face of such exquisite suffering was the very essence of erotic bliss, and the wounds I received were a small price to pay for the unique nature of that pleasure. If I seemed distant or annoyed while you were tenderly ministering to my injuries, it was only because I was attempting to process this unexpected realization of an unimagined fantasy.

I would very much like to make amends to you - <u>and to repeat the experience as soon as possible</u>. I am prepared to offer you a substantial bonus in addition to your regular fee if you can arrange to duplicate the exquisite pleasure I was lucky enough to experience that night.

It was very wrong of me to accept the refund of your fee, which I herewith return now with apologies and thanks. I hope to hear from you very soon.

Affectionately, Oliver

Veronica roared with laughter. My own reaction to this development was more along the lines of *You've got to be kidding*.

She turned to look at Bonkers, who was at that moment sitting on the couch studiously cleaning his fur. "Well, Bonkers, it seems you've redeemed yourself. And you can finally earn your keep."

Uh-huh. Apparently the obvious problem with this idea had not occurred to her: that its success would be entirely dependent upon a cat actually doing what its owner wanted.

Yeah, good luck with *that*.

Of Beastly Pursuits

bestiality (noun), late 14c., "the nature of beasts," from bestial + -ity. Meaning of "indulgence in beastly instincts" is from 1650s; sense of "sexual activity with a beast" is from 1611.

Related:
zoophilia (noun), "attraction to animals involving release of sexual energy," 1899, in a translation of Krafft-Ebing, from zoo- "animal" + -philia.

It is a matter of public record that until March of 2006, bestiality was not a crime in the great state of Washington. For the fact that it is now a Class C felony, punishable by up to five years in jail, the four-legged among us may thank a gentleman by the name of Kenneth Pinyan. Unfortunately, the gratitude must be delivered posthumously, because Mr Pinyan died of peritonitis after - sorry, but there is really no more subtle way to put this - being fucked in the ass by a horse.

Mr Pinyan was by profession an engineer employed by the mighty Boeing Corporation, but by night it seems he had other interests. According to the Wikipedia entry for the case - yes, there's a Wikipedia entry for absolutely freaking everything - a motorcycle accident left him without the ability to experience "certain sensations". Wikipedia doesn't specify what these sensations were, but you can probably at least vaguely imagine. Thereafter, he engaged in increasingly extreme sex acts, and was a member of a group of men who snuck around farms - other people's farms, mind - to have sex with horses.

On the night of July 2nd, 2005, Mr Pinyan and a similarly inclined friend were pursuing their favorite hobby at a farm in Enumclaw (which town's strange name sounds like it should be either a palindrome or an anagram, but is in fact neither). After spraying the stallion's nostrils with some sort of pheromone to make him aroused, Mr Pinyan duly impaled himself on the animal's impressively large penis while his buddy videotaped the act. Unfortunately, the horse proved to be *too* aroused, and apparently thrust rather too enthusiastically into Mr Pinyan's rear end. Reportedly his last words were, "Uh, I think something broke."

The something was, unfortunately for Mr Pinyan, his colon.

Following this terminal case of coitus interruptus, the buddy - one Michael Tait - thoughtfully dumped his friend at the nearest Emergency Room and fled into the night. By the time medical staff examined Mr Pinyan, he was already dead.

In the investigation which followed, the police managed to track down Pinyan's animal-lover friends and unearthed a large quantity of videotapes documenting their nocturnal equine couplings. For me, the funniest aspect of this case lies in the fact that detectives sedulously scrutinized these tapes in an effort to figure out what charges they could bring among the surviving members of the group. Bestiality not being illegal at the time, they were apparently left with only criminal trespass - recall that the happy horse sex was going on without the knowledge of the farms' owners - and animal cruelty. After dutifully poring over the copious video evidence, the police concluded that in fact no animals had been harmed during the commission of these unfelonious acts.

Which conjures up the delicious image of a pair of detectives sitting around a table watching horse porn and debating about how the animals themselves felt about what was happening.

George, does it look to you like he's suffering cruelty here?
Fuck, Frank, I dunno. But Jesus, that's a big dick.
Look at the expression on the horse's face... what d'you suppose that means?
Fuck, I dunno. Maybe we should show this to a horse expert.
Yeah, maybe. Know any?
Nah. Well, my sister knows some chick in Tacoma who trains thoroughbreds. But she's kinda nuts.
Your sister or the chick?
The chick. Well, both. (Laughs).
(Pause).
I dunno, look at his expression. Maybe he's enjoying it?
Well, he's certainly hammering away up there.
God, look at that dick. How the hell can you take that up the fucking ass?
Practice, I guess.
I guess. Practice and about a gallon of lube. Shit, I can't tell if this is animal cruelty.
Me neither. Let's look at another one.
Okay. I'll get the popcorn.

To make a long story short, Mr Tait agreed to a plea bargain and was given a one-year suspended sentence, a $300 fine and a single day of community service. The latter punishment does make one wonder what kind of service was involved, and how he presented himself on the day in question.

"Hi there! I'm Mike. I fuck horses and I'm here to paint the 3rd grade classroom."

Anyway, acting with uncharacteristic efficiency, it took the Washington State Legislature less than a year to pass a law criminalizing bestiality. According to one observer, reading the language of the statute - RCW 16.52.205 - "is very much like reading hardcore porn."

I will here refrain from once again commenting on the exceedingly bizarre nature of what you humans do to satisfy your sexual needs.

Dogs don't do any of this weird crap. It's just hump, hump, thank you ma'am, have a nice day and we're on our way.

Moral Dilemma

Veronica and Anna are having coffee at a café named The Station on nearby Beacon Hill, where Anna lives. Like much of Seattle, The Station is what is termed "dog-friendly" - note that there is no such thing, anywhere, as a "cat-friendly" café - so I am lying patiently on the floor next to Veronica's table. I am hoping that Veronica will remember that this particular café has a treat jar on the counter, but so far she's not showing any sign of movement despite pointed looks in that direction from me.

The Station is run by a charmingly lecherous and politically incorrect Mexican named Luis and his sweet, long-suffering wife Leona, who is black. It's the kind of cosy neighborhood joint where everyone knows everyone, and the café's Facebook page has photos of customers' dogs, all identified by name. It's my favorite café, and I wish Veronica came here more often.

Veronica is seeking Anna's advice on the dilemma of whether it is morally reprehensible to consider impressing one's cat into the service of a client's erotic pleasure.

Anna - who knows the story of Bonkers attacking Oliver's nether regions the first time around - snorts as Veronica asks her this. "God, that story is freaking hysterical," she says. "It will never die." She takes a sip of her latté. "So the client wants a repeat performance?"

"Uh-huh."

"Jesus! I will *never* cease to be amazed by what gets some men off."

"I know, right? I mean, I've had some weird requests in my day, but this one kind of tops the lot."

Anna nods. "I once had a client who wanted me to arrange for a large dog to do his girlfriend while he watched."

"Really? And did you?"

"No, of course not."

"Why not?"

"I don't know anyone with a large dog."

"Ah. Well, plus it's illegal."

"Yes, there is that."

"I do worry about that actually," Veronica says. "I don't know if what Bonkers did qualifies as bestiality." At the word *bestiality*, a middle-aged female customer at the next table glances over at Veronica with a frown, then returns to chatting with her companion.

"I don't know either," says Anna, "but it isn't like anyone's likely to find out. I mean, it's not something the client is likely to go around bragging about around the water cooler at work. *Hey, guess what I did last night?*"

Veronica laughs grimly. "No, I s'pose not." She pauses reflectively. "But do you think it's wrong to have a cat mixed up in sex work?"

The middle-aged woman looks at Veronica again, this time for rather longer; her brow is furrowed and she's obviously trying to make sense of the bizarre conversation that's happening at the next table.

Anna notices, and decides to effect a distraction. "Jack, what do you think?" she asks.

I think I'd like a treat.

And just like that, Anna rises and walks over to the treat jar. She returns a few seconds later with a handful of small dog biscuits, breaks them into pieces, and gives them to me one by one. I love this woman.

"Look," says Anna in a low voice as she continues to feed me, "it sounds to me like Bonkers had a good time with it, so where's the harm?"

Veronica sighs. "I suppose."

"Besides," continues Anna, "you could always add it to your list of special services for an extra fee. *Flogging, feminization, and furry feline fun.*" She laughs at her own alliteration, but the woman at the next table is now staring hard.

"Er," says Veronica, looking around a bit nervously. "Perhaps we'd better continue this little chat elsewhere."

Furry Feline Fun

After some more debate Veronica decided that, since her psychotic cat had apparently enjoyed himself lacerating Oliver's genitals the last time, it was okay to let him do it again.

The session occurred just four days after the arrival of Oliver's letter. Apparently he was *very* eager to renew his acquaintance with Bonkers.

This time I actually got to witness the event, which is odd because as I mentioned previously I am usually banned from the dungeon. Perhaps Veronica felt that the suggestive nature of a dog being present in the room added to the thrill for the client. Which is sort of okay, I guess - but if she takes it any further and expects me to actually *do* anything with the dude, I'm leaving home.

Oliver arrived promptly at six and politely declined Veronica's offer of a glass of wine and some pre-bestial hors d'oeuvres - apparently he couldn't wait to get on with the business of adding fresh scars to his genitals. I have no idea how he explains this to whatever woman he might be dating at the moment.

After Veronica had insisted that Oliver take two Viagra, we all trooped off to the dungeon, Veronica carrying Bonkers in her arms. The fact that he began this little enterprise annoyed at having his latest cleaning routine interrupted might have played in role in what happened next, but you can never tell with cats. They get pissed off at anything they don't like - which is pretty much everything.

Down in the dungeon, Veronica instantly transformed from tasteful wine-serving hostess into scary über-bitch, though in truth elements of both are often simultaneously evident in her persona. Think Martha Stewart in thigh-high boots, corset and black leather miniskirt (on second thought, don't).

After depositing the star of the show on the floor, she selected a whip from the array of such equipment affixed to the wall, and brandished it menacingly while ordering Oliver to remove his clothes. Meanwhile, Bonkers briefly surveyed the room and then lay down in a corner and resumed preening himself.

Five minutes later, Oliver was firmly affixed to the St Andrews cross, a ball gag in his mouth. His penis was already erect. This was partly as a result of Veronica raking it with her nails, but he needed neither external stimulation nor chemical enhancement to produce a boner that was well developed in anticipation of what was to come.

Veronica teased him for a while, whipping him and digging her nails into his balls as she verbally abused him. The theme of this abuse centered largely around his desire for sexual contact with animals.

"You're a cat fucker, aren't you, you filthy pervert?" she demanded as she wielded the bullwhip across his chest.

"Mmmph!" Oliver grunted through the gag, though whether this guttural sound denoted admission or denial wasn't clear.

This torture continued for a while, until Veronica decided it was finally time to unleash Bonkers on Oliver's throbbing member. She tied a leather thong tightly around his balls and let it dangle enticingly below them. Then she attempted to summon Bonkers, who was, incredibly, still cleaning his fur.

"Bonkers! Here, kitty kitty."

No reaction, lick lick.

"Bonkers! Come here, Bonkers!" Louder this time.

Bonkers looked up from his unending toilet long enough to shoot a contemptuous glance at Veronica, then went back to cleaning one of his hind legs. Lick lick.

With a sigh, Veronica picked him up and dropped him in front of the cross, then flicked the leather thong to make it move.

"Come on, kitty - play with the toy. You like this, remember!" She flicked the thong again.

Bonkers looked bored and turned to walk away. Veronica grabbed him, eliciting an annoyed miaow. She once again attempted to stimulate interest in the thong, but it was to no avail. Instead, he fixed her with a look which clearly said - and perhaps I'm over-interpreting here but I don't think so - *You-want-me-to-do-something-and-for-that-reason-I-have-no-intention-whatsoever-of-doing-it-and-wouldn't-even-if-it-was-the-most-interesting-thing-in-the-world-so-fuck-you*. Again, he started to walk away.

Veronica was now annoyed. She was also becoming rather desperate at the thought that she might miss out on the "substantial bonus" that Oliver had promised her for a repeat performance. She again bodily moved Bonkers back to the spot just below Oliver's genitals and jiggled the thong. But the only reward she received for her efforts was an irritable miaow.

"Come on, sweet little kitty - play with the nice toy! *Please* play with the toy! Please please please!"

Now it must be said that, from a client's point of view, seeing the woman you're paying to dominate you reduced to pleading pitifully with a small animal doesn't do much to enhance the erotic atmosphere. And indeed Veronica suddenly realized that she, the arch domme, had in effect just become a submissive. To a *cat*.

Angered by this unacceptable reversal of the domestic hierarchy, she grabbed Bonkers by the scruff of the neck and dragged him ignominiously to the door. There, she held him suspended, hissing and paws flailing, in front of her face at a distance that put her just out of reach of his claws.

"Now you listen to me, you little shit," she said in a terse whisper between clenched teeth. "You do what I tell you to or I'll throw you out into the street and make you catch mice for your fucking dinner."

For the record, Bonkers is crap at catching mice. He's just too fat and lazy.

Still clutching the cat, Veronica returned to the other side of the dungeon. By the time she arrived at Oliver's genitals Bonkers was thrashing about and emitting a series of increasingly shrill sounds that recalled the Demon Cat Incident. In a desperate attempt to enforce compliance to her will, Veronica thrust the flailing feline at the erect penis directly in front of him.

Now a cat is rather like a guided missile: when it's annoyed, it will lash out at pretty much whoever or whatever it's pointed at.

So, to the soundtrack of a screeching cat and the muffled screaming of a naked man, razor claws met turgid flesh.

The penis at the center of this melé jerked around wildly as it was repeatedly scratched and raked. Some eighteen inches farther up, the sounds emanating from the organ's owner duly increased in volume.

Bonkers was now sufficiently livid with rage that Veronica had to grip him with two hands, and it was clear that she would not be able to restrain him for much longer. But it mattered not, because Oliver was so aroused by the vicious assault on his penis and testicles that things rapidly came to... well, to a climax.

Remember the Squirrel Incident? I said at the time it was the greatest moment of my life. Not true. Indisputably the pinnacle of my entire existence now involves the incomparably glorious memory of a cat being blasted in the face by a wave of semen shooting like a volcanic eruption out of an injured but perfectly functional penis.

Dogs don't visibly laugh, but we do inside. And God, I almost peed myself at that moment. Poor Bonkers: he'll probably still be cleaning himself this time next week.

A few seconds later, Veronica could restrain Bonkers no longer and was forced to drop him onto the carpet. With a stentorian howl, he promptly rushed for the open door, his face a contorted mask of rage and, well, matted fur.

As he passed me, I wagged my tail to show him that I had greatly enjoyed the show.

Had fun? I asked sarcastically. *Love the new hair gel!*

In response, he spat at me and disappeared rapidly up the stairs.

Yep, I called after him, *I love you too!*

Afterbath

So that was that. The whole thing had lasted less than five minutes. The client was ecstatic despite his wounds, Veronica's bank account was supplemented by $3,000, and Bonkers - whose head seems to attract bodily fluids - got a cum bath.

Regarding the question of whether shoving a cat into a guy's genitals qualifies as either criminal bestiality or animal cruelty, I leave to the reader to judge. Personally, I think that - and I make no apology for the dreadful pun here - Bonkers had it coming.

Extending the pun, I don't know where Veronica comes out on this issue, but she was obviously feeling guilty afterwards about what had been done to her beloved cat, and tried to compensate him by serving him a plate of fresh tuna. I was a little annoyed that I didn't get an extra special treat too - after all, I had to *watch* this sordid little tableau, and for all Veronica knows it's scarred me for life.

Oh well. Since I'm not the one whose face was turned into a vagina substitute, I guess I really shouldn't complain.

The King

While these sordid happenings were going on with the real Bonkers, progress was being made on the Fake Bonkers Project, as Veronica had started calling it.

We were in Anna's apartment on Beacon Hill; she had managed to sneak me in, despite the rules. At a side table, Veronica was staring at a large bowl, in which swam three small goldfish.

"When did you get goldfish?"

"Oh, awhile ago. Those are the Furies."

"The what?"

"The Furies." She walked over to the table and pointed. "That's Alecto, the pinkish dude is Tisiphone, and the small one's Megaera."

"This is not becoming any clearer, darling."

"The Furies were Greek deities of vengeance. They pursued you if you'd done something really bad, like disobeying your parents or offing your mother."

"Offing?"

"Yeah, killing. That's what happened to Clytemestra after she'd killed her husband Agamemnon following the Trojan War - her son Orestes grew up and whacked his own mother in revenge. But then he was pursued by the Furies."

"They don't sound like fun."

"Yeah, they were serious bitches, those three. They had snakes for hair, dog's heads, black bodies, bat's wings, and blood-shot eyes... and they carried around brass-studded whips."

"And you named your goldfish after them."

"Yep."

"You couldn't just call them Tom, Dick and Harry or something?"

"Too mundane."

"You're braver than me, then. I mean, what happens if one of your goldfish dies? You've basically killed one of the Furies. Do bad things happen?"

"Nah," Anna said, "you just get another goldfish."

They sat down at the dining room table. Anna poured some tea.

"So anyway, we have a website?" Veronica asked.

Anna had mentioned earlier that she had a client who was a web designer. Remarkably, the domain name *demoncat* was not taken, so he'd registered it and constructed a slick-looking website devoted to Bonkers and his fan club. He followed this by somehow creating so many links to the website on social media - including many hitched to the original Youtube video - that within a few days it was getting hundreds of hits, and had quite a following.

"Remarkable," said Veronica. "But what about the grave?"

"Ah well, we wait until the headstone is done, and then we put some fake messages on the site - and on the Youtube video - announcing his very tragic demise, and noting that he has been buried with full military honors in a pet cemetery in lovely Kent."

"You're very good at this."

"Thank you. I try."

"So what else is new?" Veronica asked.

"Oh, nothing much," Anna said. "I was just advising my young cousin on matters of a sexual nature."

"Seriously?"

"Yes. She's 19 and one of those rather timid creatures who's terrified to give a blow job, so she's never actually done it. She says she doesn't know how to do it, and she's afraid the recipient will be gravely disappointed."

"Jesus, no guy gives a crap as long as you have his dick in your mouth."

"Exactly."

"So what did you tell her?"

I said, 'Darling, giving a blow job is like eating bacon - no matter how inexpertly you do it, it's still pretty fantastic.'"

Veronica laughed. Then she said, "Talking of bacon, I'm hungry. Do you feel like getting something quick to eat?"

"Sure," Anna replied. "We could go grab a hot dog from Vlad the Impaler."

Veronica looked blankly. "Who?"

"Vlad. He runs a hot dog cart near the Light Rail station. Loves Elvis. He's Russian - or Romanian. Or maybe Bulgarian. I can never remember which."

"Is he a vampire?"

"Not so far as I know."

"Then why is he called 'the Impaler'?"

"Oh, you'll see. Let's go."

We walked a couple of blocks to the Beacon Hill Light Rail stop, passing The Station café on the way. Leona, one of the owners, was standing by the door and greeted us. "Hang on, Anna," she said, and disappeared inside, returning a few seconds later with a treat for me. I love this place.

A short while later we saw a food truck parked on a vacant lot. As we approached, we could hear the owner loudly belting out an Elvis Presley song in some sort of eastern European accent.

Eet's now or ne-verrr
come hold me tight
keess me my darrr-lingk
be mine tonight
To-morrow vill be too late
Eet's now or ne-verrrrrrrr
My love von't vait!

"My God," said Veronica. "You weren't kidding."

"That vas Rrrussian," he said, as the girls applauded his performance. "But I do this, any accent you vant. English, French, Deutsch, you name it."

"Really?" Veronica said.

"Sure, lady. It's Elvis. Elvis, he's the King in any language."

"Can't argue with that," Veronica said.

"Now," he said, "vot you pretty ladies vant to eat?"

They ordered two hot dogs with the works - or "vorks", as Vlad put it. He busied himself preparing their food.

"I still don't get the 'impaler' part," Veronica said.

"Just wait," Anna replied.

A few minutes later, the two hot dogs were ready.

"Watch," Anna instructed.

Vlad picked up a large two-pronged fork, raised it high above his head, and then with a blood-curdling scream that sounded like a Samurai going into battle - *"Hiiiii-YAAAAA!"* - brought the fork down and perfectly skewered one of the hot dogs. He lifted up the impaled meat, inserted it into a bun, added the fixings, and handed it to Veronica. She looked slightly terrified.

"Wow!" was all she could manage to say.

Vlad repeated the performance with the other dog and gave it to Anna.

"Thanks, Vlad," she said, handing him a $20 bill.

"Can I contribute?" Veronica asked.

"Nope. My treat. Dinner and a show." She broke off a chunk of her hot dog and fed it to me.

"Thanks," Veronica replied. "Oh, talking of money, do I owe you something for the web designer? What did he charge?"

"Nothing. I promised him a couple of free blow jobs, and he was happy with that."

"God, men are such simple creatures."

"Amen to that, sister," Anna said. "It's what keeps the lights on in my house. And yours."

Typo

Two days later, Mirakel called to say that Demon Cat's tombstone was finished and had been placed tastefully at the head of his grave.

"It looks lovely," she said. "I added some flowers, dear, so it'll look nice when you come to visit him. They're plastic," she added, "but very life-like."

"Very thoughtful of you," Veronica replied. "Thank you."

Veronica and Anna drove down the following afternoon with the primary purpose of taking some photos of the grave for the Demon Cat website. When we drove up, Earl was sitting in a plastic lawn chair outside the trailer. He was, as usual, half-naked.

Veronica raised her eyebrows as we approached. "Well," she said, "at least he's in a different towel this time."

Earl stood up to greet us as we got out of the Subaru. "Hello, pretty ladies," he said cheerily. "Guess you're here to see your kitty's final resting place."

"Hello Earl," Veronica said. "Yes, we are." She stopped short of saying *Nice to see you again*.

"Well go on back," Earl said, gesturing to the path. "It looks real nice now the headstone's done. I'll go find Mirakel and tell her you're here."

"Nice towel," said Anna as we set off. Earl grinned.

It was a lovely afternoon, the summer air warm and fragrant with the smell of pine. On the other side of the trees we entered the cemetery and walked down the relevant row, past Donkey Hoté, three cats, a Jack Russell named Ripper - that's right, Jack the Ripper - and finally Waffles the chihuahua.

We all stood in front of the grave of the fictitious Demon Cat.

"Poor pussy," said Anna.

"It's actually rather tasteful," Veronica commented.

There was a respectful pause as we all contemplated the headstone.

"Did you remember the camera?" asked Veronica.

"Right here," Anna replied, producing a small point and shoot from the leather purse slung over her shoulder. She shot a few images from different angles, then inspected them on the camera's display screen to see if they were acceptable.

Suddenly she frowned. She peered more closely at the image, then leaned forward to examine the tombstone. Finally she let out a howl of laughter.

"What is it?" Veronica asked, staring at the headstone.

"Read it," Anna said. "Read it *closely*."

There was a pause while Veronica read the inscription, word by word. Then suddenly she too roared. "Oh my God!" she said. "That's hysterical!"

Anna read the first two lines aloud:

> *Beneath this stone there rests a Demon*
> *Who started out his life with semen*

Veronica laughed harder. "My God," she said, "that is one motherfucker of a typo."

Anna took some more photos, including close-ups of the epitaph. When the two girls were satisfied that the Demon Cat shrine had been suitably documented for an adoring internet public, we returned to the trailer. Mirakel was standing outside, exposing her impressive dentition in a welcoming smile as we approached.

"So, what do you think of the grave?" she asked. "Isn't it nice?"

"Yes, it's lovely," Veronica replied. "But we couldn't help noticing that, well, there's a *typo* in the epitaph engraving. A rather epic one, actually. Last word of the second line. It's supposed to read *seamen* but it actually says, well, semen. You know - *semen*." She gestured with her hands, as if this would somehow help to clarify the meaning.

Mirakel's expression changed suddenly. She sighed heavily and nodded. "Yes, I know," she said sadly. "Earl noticed it yesterday - he has an eye for that sort of thing."

"For semen?" asked Anna.

"What?" Mirakel looked confused. "No, no - for typos," she said. "They just leap off a page at him."

"Or a tombstone," Anna said. "Funny when you think about it. Semen leaping off a tombstone at someone."

Mirakel failed to register the humor. She was wringing her hands nervously, as if she'd just been caught performing a shameful sexual act in public. "Yes well," she said. "I called the engraver this morning, and he said he had some trouble reading your handwriting, dear. I think when you gave me the poem it was written on a napkin."

"A cocktail napkin," Anna clarified, unnecessarily.

"Uh-huh," said Mirakel. "Anyway, I'm *very* sorry. We were actually rather hoping you wouldn't notice - which is terrible of course. I feel terrible about it. Terrible," she repeated. "Of course, we'll have the headstone redone for you."

Veronica thought for a moment. "No," she said, "you really don't need to do that. It's okay the way it is."

"Actually," added Anna, "it's perfect."

Le Chat C'est Mort

Ten minutes later, we were heading back home, leaving a rather baffled Mirakel in our wake. She had tried to insist that the error on the tombstone be corrected, but Veronica had assured her it was unnecessary. She had said that her pussycat had always had a good sense of humor.

"Besides," added Anna helpfully, "it's quite accurate, biologically speaking." Mirakel had stared at her blankly.

"Darling, we *all* start out our lives with semen."

"Unless you're Jesus," Veronica noted.

The grave having been duly immortalized in pixels, all that remained was for Veronica to write a notice for the website announcing Demon Cat's untimely death.

We dropped Anna at her apartment, and shortly after we were back at the house. Bonkers looked up from his perpetual cleaning and gave me a glare. I sighed; he's such a tedious creature.

Veronica poured herself a large glass of red wine, opened her laptop computer and arranged herself comfortably on the couch. She began typing, and after various edits produced what she hoped was a suitably sorrowful death notice.

It is with great sorrow and deepest regret that we must announce the death of our beloved Demon Cat. His life was recently cut short in a tragic accident involving a tram on Capitol Hill. The end came quickly, and he did not suffer. He will be remembered fondly by the legions of fans who came to love him through his now-infamous Youtube video (click here for the link, and here for his biography).

Our little Demon was laid to rest in a moving private grave-side ceremony at the charming Heavenly Paws Pet Cemetery in Kent, Washington (link here). There he lies in a woodland setting of utmost tranquility. Farewell, sweet kitty! May you miaow in peace eternally in a heaven full of mice.

(Visits to Demon's grave are welcome, but in lieu of flowers we are asking that a donation be made to Homeless Cat Rescue of Washington State - link here).

Satisfied with the final version, Veronica emailed it to Anna, who sent it on to the web designer. Four hours later, Anna called to say that the death notice was already up on the website, complete with tasteful photos of the grave and a Google map giving directions.

"Well, Fake Bonkers is officially a go," she announced. "The dead cat is live."

Shrine

It took less than a week for the first pilgrims to show up at Heavenly Paws to pay their respects to Demon Cat. Veronica knew this because shortly after the visit she received a phone call from Mirakel.

"Hello, dear," she said. "We had this awfully nice couple come by today to visit your pussy. Two young women, very sweet they were. I thought perhaps they were friends of yours but it turned out they were complete strangers. I didn't realize how *famous* your pussy was..." - Veronica was now so used to Mirakel talking about her pussy that she didn't even smile at this - "...and then I watched the video. They told me about it, you see. O my! That was one funny video! I had no idea."

Veronica said she hoped it wasn't going to create a problem, but Mirakel assured her that they were always glad to have visitors. "Although," she added, "if more people come I'm going to have to ban Earl from lounging around in his towel."

And more came indeed. Two weeks later a small but steady stream of nutcases were heading to the backwoods of Kent to worship at the grave of Demon Cat. Many of the pilgrims wrote tributes in the comments section of the Demon Cat website - surprisingly few said anything about the typo - and at one point Veronica was worried that this was getting out of hand. Feeling rather guilty, she called Mirakel to say that she was sorry for all the attention.

"Oh don't apologize, dear," Mirakel said cheerily. "It's rather nice to be famous. And business has been booming thanks to you. We've had lots of burial enquiries from people who didn't know we existed. It's raining cats and dogs - dead ones, unfortunately, but well, one can't complain. And Earl's had so much interest in the nudist camp he can barely keep up."

"'Barely'? Pun unintended?"

"What? O yes! Ha ha! I didn't realize! That's funny."

The ramifications of the Fake Bonkers Project were surprisingly extensive, and went beyond the impact on *Heavenly Paws*. The following summer one of the local tourist outfits would include the grave on its tour of the Seattle area; apparently they showed the video on the bus on the way down to Kent. What's more, Homeless Cat Rescue of Washington State - which until then had been a rather small local charity - would see donations skyrocket.

At the suggestion of a friend, Veronica and Anna would later design some "I ♥ Demon Cat" T-shirts and coffee mugs and sell them on the website. Although this little capitalist enterprise would never make them rich, it would bring in enough revenue to significantly increase their shoe budget.

To summarize: the visits to our house by demented cat pilgrims ceased, a website begun as a joke flourished, and the whole thing resulted in the welcome support and enrichment of some local businesses.

So, it turns out that cats can have their uses after all. Just not when they're alive.

Sleazebag

Professionals In Pleasure

It is 10 a.m. on a Wednesday morning in September, and we are sitting in the rather cramped apartment of a woman who goes by the name of Desirée Divine. Her real name, as Veronica notes later, is the considerably less exotic Julie Smith. As you might guess from her adopted appellation, Desirée/Julie is a prostitute - and occasionally also a stripper. She is also the president of the local chapter of Professionals In Pleasure (PIP), a trade association - sort of - that promotes the rights of sex workers and seeks to educate a skeptical public about the legitimacy and benefits of the world's oldest profession. PIP is duly recognized by the Internal Revenue Service as a legitimate non-profit organization, which could be construed as odd given the current illegality of its members' occupation. I mean, it's not like you hear about a tax-exempt outfit representing the rights of burglars or the local Mafia.

Not that I'm equating what Veronica and Anna do for a living with occupations that are unequivocally criminal in nature. Which topic is in fact the reason for the current gathering. Apparently there exists a concerted effort by the Washington State Legislature to pass a bill that would impose harsh penalties upon those caught either offering or procuring sexual services in exchange for cash, and Desirée has called the meeting to discuss PIP's strategy in attempts to fight this latest assault upon the carnally employed.

That discussion, however, has not yet been initiated; we are still in the social portion of the meeting, which features coffee, some stale muffins and a couple of bottles of wine for those who find cheap chardonnay to be an indispensable part of a balanced breakfast.

The gathering consists of a dozen or so women, two gay men, one transsexual and an individual whose gender is not determinable - at least it isn't to me. The transsexual and two of the women are black; everyone else, including Desirée, is various shades of white, from pasty to tanned. The room features a wide range of hairstyles. At one end of the scale, a rather surly-looking woman with a nose ring and a neck tattoo is sporting a close-cropped butch cut that would not be out of place in a U.S. army unit. At the other is a redhead whose wild hair is sprung from her head like a shrubbery and thereby occupies a very significant chunk of the space around her cranium.

The range of body types on display – tall and slim to short and rotund - is, presumably, testament to the varied desires of men.

There's also another dog, a Corgi named Max, but after a quick greeting and a perfunctory mutual ass-sniffing we ignore each other and settle beside our respective humans. I lie between Veronica and Anna. Anna is feeding me bits of a cranberry muffin when she thinks no one is looking.

Much of the conversation inevitably revolves around recent work experiences.

"So," announces a pretty white escort who is known to everyone as Skinny Marie, "I finally got to see a micropenis."

"Really?" says the transsexual. "So how small was it?"

"Tiny. Poor guy really got screwed in the genetic lottery." Everyone nods in sympathy.

"So how'd it go?" the other gay man enquires.

Skinny Marie sighs. "Not well. I mean, it woulda been fine, but after some very lame foreplay he takes me from behind and I start moaning even though I'm not entirely sure he's actually *in* me, and he has to go and say..." Marie stops and giggles.

"What did he say?" someone asks.

"Well there I am, moaning and doing the *O yeah, fuck me!* thing, and suddenly he says, *That's right, baby, TAKE IT ALL!*"

The room erupts in laughter.

"O my God!" says Anna. "Don't tell me you *laughed*?"

Marie bursts into another fit of giggles. "I couldn't help it! And I didn't exactly *laugh* – it was more of an involuntary guffaw. I tried to cover it up with a cough, but it was no good – the damage had been done. Instant de-erection."

"And he couldn't recover?" Desirée asks.

"Nope, it was hopeless. I mean, I *tried*, God knows. But it's not easy to get a guy back to form when you have trouble finding his dick – I mean, I must have spent a full two minutes rooting around down there looking for something to suck."

More stories follow, but finally Desirée calls the meeting to order. She explains the details of the proposed legislation, and notes that this bill, and the accompanying intensification of law enforcement efforts around prostitution generally, represents a major threat to the livelihood of those present.

"So which Republican with a stick up his ass is behind this?" asks Anna. "Because it IS a Republican, right?"

Desirée nods. "Yeah. It's Catkins Rumor. He's chair of the Senate committee that deals with this stuff."

"Catkins?" asks the nose-ring butch haircut. "What kind of a fucked-up name is that?"

"I don't know," Desirée says. "Apparently it's his nickname. The guy's a douche-bag. Christian fundamentalist, holier-than-thou type."

"Of course," someone says. "Aren't they all?"

Anna sighs. "I'm really tired of these people trying to save us from ourselves."

"Yeah," says Veronica. "And I bet half these men are screwing other women on the side."

"Or boys," adds the black transsexual, whose name is Cassandra.

"Huh," Veronica says, remembering something. "My mother met Rumor recently." Then in response to several surprised looks directed her way she adds, "She's a Republican." There is a general hum of disapproval and sympathy.

The group discusses whether there is anything that PIP can do to influence this issue, but no one can think of any strategy that's likely to hold back the unstoppable tide of evangelical morality.

"We could pray to the good Lord," jokes a young woman with hair that's dyed blue. "Who's the patron saint of prostitutes?"

"Saint Nicholas," answers Anna.

"Are you making that up?" Veronica asks.

"No. Fourth-century Greek saint."

"I'm assuming he was persecuted like all the others at that time?"

"Most were, but not Nicholas. As far as anyone knows, he didn't suffer the usual ghastly martyr's death by shooting/torture/crucifixion/hanging/disembowelling/toasting/roasting at the hands of the Romans/Turks/Moors/Saracens/random rival Christian faction. Delete as appropriate."

"You're a fount of useless knowledge, darling," Veronica comments.

"Thank you. I try."

"What we need is a better education outreach program," says a tall brunette in a black leather miniskirt.

"No," says Anna. "What *we* need is a photograph of one of these morons in congress with a donkey."

Desirée nods. "Yeah, that would be nice. I know it's a long shot, but I thought I'd show you all pictures of the senators on this committee on the off-chance that one of you has one of them as a client."

She opens a laptop and begins to flash photos on the screen, working her way one by one through the mostly male members of the Senate Committee on Law and Justice. Since the photos are culled from the Senators' websites, they all show smiling men who are clearly trying their very best to project an image of trustworthiness and responsibility.

Six photos go by and no one says anything. But just as Desirée flips onto the next image, Veronica speaks up.

"Wait – go back to that last one."

Desirée hits the backspace key and an image of a handsome, impeccably dressed man reappears on the screen.

"Jesus!" Veronica says. "I think I know that guy."

Desirée's eyes open wide. "You know *this* guy? You mean he's a client of yours?"

Veronica nods. "Yeah, pretty sure. He's a serious masochist - I've done sessions with him half a dozen times. I mean, when I've seen him he's had a moustache and what must be a wig, but I'd recognize those eyes anywhere. Who is he?"

"Holy fuck," says Desirée, her eyes still wide. "*That*, my dear, is Catkins Rumor himself." There is a collective intake of breath in the room.

"Wow," exclaims Anna admiringly. "Jackpot!"

"Seriously?" Veronica says, as stunned as everyone. "When he's with me he goes by the name of 'Mr Lincoln'."

"As in 'Continental'?" Cassandra asks.

"As in Abe, presumably," Anna responds. "Apparently the guy fancies himself as the reincarnation of the sixteenth president of these United States."

"Sixteenth?" says Skinny Marie. "How do you know this shit?"

"I read."

"Plus she has a Ph.D.," adds Veronica.

"You do?"

"I do."

Although she hadn't known his identity, Rumor had been a regular client of Veronica's for around six months, and during that time his anonymity had been adequately protected by both the disguise he wore when he visited and Veronica's general disinterest in state politics. As Veronica informed the PIP meeting - and like a surprising number of men holding positions of great corporate or political power - Rumor was secretly a masochist. He liked to be tied up and feminized, and he had a particular fetish that involved being ordered to kiss a girl's stockinged feet, and to suck her toes.

Somewhat nervously - this *was* blackmail, after all - Veronica agreed to try to somehow obtain incriminating photos of the next session, although quite how she was going to achieve this wasn't entirely clear. She assumed that there would indeed *be* a next session; but given that Rumor had reliably visited her once a month for the past half year, this seemed a reasonable expectation.

She left the meeting duly voted as the Great White Hope of Professionals In Pleasure.

Interlude: The Troy Boys

After the PIP meeting, Veronica and Anna walk with Cassandra the transsexual to the nearest Starbucks for coffee.

"Small latté please," says Veronica when it's their turn to order.

"Same for me," Anna says.

Cassandra steps up to the counter. "I'll take a venti iced half-caff ristretto four-pump sugar-free cinnamon dolce soy skinny latte," she says.

Veronica and Anna both stare at her, eyes wide; the girl behind the counter doesn't even blink.

"How could she possibly get all that?" Veronica asks as they wait for their drinks to be made.

"She probably didn't," Anna replies. "My guess is that when people order shit like that the barista produces some vaguely exotic version of a latté. It's like

Dave Barry - you know, the humorist - says about Chinese restaurant menus: three thousands items, but no matter what you order you're just going to get some random combination of whatever happens to be sitting on the stove."

We sit at a table by the window, and the conversation returns to the topic of how to combat punitive legislation against sex workers.

"Blackmail's great," says Anna, "but we really *do* need to do a better job educating the public about sex work. Most people seem to fall for the misconception that all sex workers are exploited or coerced."

"Yeah," Veronica agrees. "Sure, there are girls who are forced into sex work by pimps, or who do so reluctantly as a desperate way of making ends meet. But as we all know there are a lot of sex workers who actively choose this occupation, and who enjoy it. For the most part, anyway - I mean, when it doesn't involve creepy politicians."

Cassandra nods. "I *try* to tell people these things, but they never believe me!"

"She said, with not a trace of irony," comments Anna with a grin. Cassandra stares at her blankly. "You know... Cassandra? Greek mythology, Trojan War. Ring any bells?"

"Not really," Cassandra says.

"Really, darling, you should know the origin of your name," Anna-the-historian berates her, then proceeds to deliver a potted lecture on the Trojan War.

"Cassandra was this Trojan princess who was courted by the god Apollo. He wants to fuck her, so he gives her the gift of prophecy in an effort to seduce her. But in the end Cassandra refuses to sleep with him, and Apollo gets angry. So he tells her she can keep the gift, but that now no one will ever believe her prophecies. And when the Greeks leave a giant horse outside the gates of Troy, she's the ones yelling at everyone not to bring it inside. But no one believes her - and the rest, as they say, is history."

Cassandra and Veronica are both genuinely impressed. "Hmm," the latter says, "I had no idea the story was that interesting." It's apparent that some other people at nearby tables have been listening to Anna's little mythology lesson.

"O God yes," Anna replies. "The Trojan War has everything: murder, betrayal, abduction, war, human sacrifice and matricide - you name it. Oh, and a beauty contest to start the whole thing off."

"Matricide?" asks Veronica.

"Yeah. Clytemestra, the wife of Agamemnon, murders him when he comes back from the war because ten years before he'd sacrificed their daughter Iphigenia to appease the gods and get them to change the winds so the Greek fleet could sail to Troy. The younger daughter - Electra - hates her mother for murdering dad. And then finally her kid brother Orestes grows up and murders Clytemestra in revenge. Then *he's* followed around by the Furies - who are kind of this divine police force always out for blood."

"Your goldfish!" Veronica exclaims.

Cassandra looks at the two of them blankly. "Goldfish?"

"Not important," says Anna.

"How does it end?" asks Veronica. "I've forgotten."

"Well, eventually Orestes prays to the goddess Athena, and she intervenes and basically slaps the shit out of everyone to stop the cycle of revenge."

"Sounds pretty fucked up," Cassandra says.

"Yep. Modern dysfunctional families have nothing on the Greeks and Trojans."

"Is there a short, you know, popular version of this story I can get without having to read the entire *Odyssey*?" Veronica asks.

"Actually, it was the *Iliad*. The *Odyssey* is about Odysseus' voyage home after the war."

"Whatever."

"Well yeah, there are about a billion retellings of this story, but if you want I can sum it up in a poem I wrote."

"You wrote a poem?" Veronica asks.

"Don't look so surprised, dearest. I do have some literary talents - albethey buried rather deep."

"I'm sure - I sometimes forget you're the intellectual among us. Is the poem long?"

"Nope. It's actually written sort of in headlines, as if the tabloids had been around at the time and were reporting on the war."

Aware that she has something of an audience, Anna stands, and pauses to collect herself. "This is called *The Troy Boys: A Tabloid Tragedy*," she says, then begins to recite.

Beauty contest - bribe suspected!
Queen abducted, spouse dejected.
King's best buddies vow revenge
(Sidebar: Centaurs built Stonehenge!)
Fleet's all set but wrong winds blow,
Troy invasion's big no-go.
Goddess angry, someone sinned,
Army's hopes gone with the wind.
King in daughter slaughter shocker!
Mom: He's off his royal rocker!
Off they trot to seek and slay -
Helen's Troy boy-toy must pay.

Ten years later, we're still here,
Resolution's nowhere near;
Gods and mortals still debating

JACK

Helen's tragic Trojan mating.
Townsfolk watch behind the wall
As battles rage and big names fall.
Ajax, Hector and Patroclus
Doomed by sword or hocus-pocus.
Even Paris bites the dust
Paying heavy price for lust.
And Achilles? All is sorrow:
Heel today, gone tomorrow.
It doesn't matter what you say,
Propheteering doesn't pay:
Just ask Cass, divining dancer
(Not that you'd believe her answer).
When one morning Troy awakes -
Greeks all gone, for goodness sakes! -
It's party time at Priam's place...
'Cept for Cass, still long of face.
When her warning all deride -
"Don't let that damn thing inside!" -
They learn, too late, the woes you get
From messing with the horsey set.

King comes home and wife will host;
Cassy: Agamemnon's toast.
Clytemnestra's out for blood
Aided by her live-in stud;
Husband, girlfriend both are slain.
Think it's over? Think again!
Now Electra's in a mood,
Whining, pining, off her food.
E to C: You done dad wrong!
That's why we don't get along.
End of mother-daughter spat:
Son grows up, kills mom - that's that.

Even though he had the testes
To commit the deed, Orestes
Guilty is of crimes injurious;
Gods and goddesses are Fury-ous.
Furies chase, demanding death
O. calls goddess, out of breath,
Prays that if his woes be seen

She'll divinely intervene.
Yo, Athena, cut me slack -
Get these bitches off my back!
Goddess: O. has had it rough;
OK, ladies - 'nuff's enough!

So our little tale is done:
Lots of bloodshed, not much fun.
Those left standing are a mess,
Struck with post-traumatic stress.
Wonder what's to be their lot...
Happy ever after? Not!

When she's finished, Veronica and Cassandra are joined in their applause by several others in the café. A group of hipsters at a nearby table claps particularly loudly. "That was cool, man," one of them says.

Veronica smiles. "My my, Dr DeVere, you never cease to amaze."

"Thank you," Anna says as she stands up and gives an exaggerated bow to the room. "I have my moments."

"Well," says Veronica as Anna resumes her seat, "I suppose we'd better think about how to tackle Senator Rumor. I guess I should get in touch with him and see if he wants to do another session."

Unbeknownst to Veronica, however, her plans for blackmail were about to be overtaken by events.

Senator

Senator Dick "Catkins" Rumor represented the good people of the 50th legislative district in Washington State, to which position he had narrowly won election eight years before. That he did was due in large part to the fact that his Democratic opponent was a philandering twerp with the IQ of a house plant. The opponent's lack of either intelligence or morals did not automatically disqualify him from office, but when he was photographed one Sunday afternoon in a bar wearing a San Francisco 49ers shirt and loudly rooting against the Seahawks, everyone knew he was electoral toast.

Rumor was handsome, smart and charismatic, three qualities that allowed many voters to overlook the fact that he was at heart a right-wing Republican who enthusiastically preached the conservative gospel on God, guns and gay marriage. He kissed babies and opposed abortion, gave lip service to equal rights but fought same-sex unions, and claimed to be a man of the people while quietly working to pass tax breaks for the wealthy folks who had been the major funders of his election campaign.

Rumor was gaining increasing attention in national political circles, and it was well known that he intended to run for national office in a couple of years.

Although Richard was the name that appeared on his birth certificate, he had gone by his odd nickname since childhood. As a little boy, he had exhibited a fondness for the hanging flowers of the hazel tree. When one day he brought some to his mother as a gift, she began calling him her "little Catkins". For better or worse - personally, I think worse - the name stuck.

His tenure in the State Senate had seen him rise to the chairmanship of the Committee on Law and Justice, from which lofty perch he dispensed wisdom on the virtues of clean living and family values as an antidote to criminal ways. The intended audience for these homilies was ill-defined, but was widely accepted to consist principally of minorities and others of the Less Fortunate Persuasions.

Senator Rumor was fond of quoting the Bible, and professed Jesus to be his inspiration in all things. He was the head of a perfect nuclear family consisting of a prim, frostily flawless wife and two beautiful teenaged children - one of each sex - who both looked as though they had been freshly plucked from Mount Olympus. The family faithfully attended Sunday services at their local Episcopalian church, gave generously to several missionary societies, and were sometimes to be seen at well-publicized events at which they performed Good Works for local charities.

All in all, Senator Rumor was a pillar of Society, a stalwart Christian, a shining role model for the nation's youth.

And, secretly, a flaming pervert.

Digby Again

The following afternoon, Veronica opened the front door in response to a loud knocking. There on the step was the familiar and distinctly unwelcome figure of Digby James from the Investigations Channel. He was accompanied by a new cameraman, one who was Not Jimmy.

Given the problems that he had caused her after his last visit, Veronica was in no mood to be civil. "*You* again!" she exclaimed. "Are you here to interview my cat this time?"

"No," Digby replied, I'm here to--"

"Fuck off!" Veronica interrupted, and slammed the door shut.

From the other side, an unfazed Digby loudly completed his sentence. "–get a statement from you about your affair with Senator Rumor." Receiving no response, he continued to yell through the door. "You have to come out sometime! We're going to stay right here till you do! You know he's married, right?" he added after a pause.

In the living room, Veronica was suddenly on the verge of panic. "O Jesus!" she said aloud to herself. "What the fuck is this about? Please don't let someone have found out he's my client!"

She phoned Anna. "So now I've got this moron outside my house laying in wait to ambush me. Somehow he's found some connection between me and Rumor and wants to announce it on his stupid TV show."

"Have you checked the Internet?" Anna asked.

"For what?"

"For anything about him... maybe there's a news story or something. This must have come from somewhere."

"A news story? O Jesus!"

She hung up and logged onto her computer. It took only thirty seconds to find something.

On the website of a left-wing blogger was an article whose headline sported an obvious pun:

RUMORS ABOUT RUMOR

We have just learned from a trusted source that Richard "Catkins" Rumor, the Washington State Republican Senator so beloved by right-wing conservatives, may not be such a paragon of virtue after all. The good Senator, who chairs the Senate Committee on Law and Justice and is widely expected to run for national office in a couple of years, has lately been observed visiting the house of a very beautiful young woman on Capitol Hill – in disguise!

Is Senator Rumor having an affair? Could it be that the lily-white evangelical Christian who espouses conservative positions on everything from gay marriage to abortion, is himself a hypocrite with twisted "family values"? And who is the mysterious siren who has claimed his heart?

We hear that a team from TV's Investigation Channel is following up on this developing story. Watch this space for updates...

Just as she finished reading, the phone rang. It was Anna, who had found the same website.

"I wouldn't worry yet," she said. "This is obviously some fringe blogger, and the mainstream media don't pay any attention to rumors promulgated in such places."

"Yes, but now I've got the poor man's Geraldo Rivera on my doorstep threatening to take this to television."

"He'll go away eventually. He can't exactly camp out there forever."

Anna's optimistic prediction appeared to be validated at midnight, when Veronica peered through the living room curtains and saw Digby James and his nameless cameraman packing up and leaving. But by 7 am the next morning they were back.

Worse, just before 8 am Veronica saw that they had been joined by Leroy Fawkes, and God only knows what he was telling them about her. Cautiously she opened the window and attempted to overhear the conversation.

"Nah, I dunno what she does for a living," Leroy was saying, apparently in response to a question from Digby James. "But," he added, "I'm pretty darn sure she's a lesbian."

"Why do you say that?" James asked.

"Cause I never see her with a man," Leroy replied, "and she won't date me. I tried lotsa times." Apparently when a woman inexplicably refused to go out with Leroy, the only conceivable explanation was that she was a homosexual. Which statement prompted Leroy to segue into his favorite conspiracy theory about the government secretly turning everyone gay.

Leroy continued to chat with the camera crew for another twenty minutes - Veronica couldn't hear much of the conversation thanks to a neighbor who had chosen that moment to use a leaf blower - and finally he drifted back across the street to his house. The camera crew looked relieved at his departure.

Four times during the day - at precisely 9 am, then again in the afternoon at 1, 5 and 8 pm, the dynamic duo knocked on Veronica's door in an attempt to flush her out of the house. Four times she ignored them.

Isaac came by during the afternoon and asked what was going on. Veronica hurried him into the house, but wasn't sure what to tell him.

"Well this is really embarrassing, Isaac," she said as Isaac patted me affectionately. "Apparently these people are under the mistaken impression that I'm having an affair with some married politician. They're waiting for me to come out and answer their questions. I'm not about to do that, but I'm afraid to go outside now."

"That's annoying," Isaac replied. "Can't you call the police or something?"

"Not really. I mean, they have a legal right to be there and anyway, what am I going to tell the cops? *Well, officer, these guys think I'm screwing some politician. Really, Miss? Which one?*"

"Hmm, I see your point."

"I suppose they'll give up eventually, but in the meantime I'm a prisoner in my own home."

"I see," Isaac replied. "Well look, Veronica, if they really don't go away - and if you have some spare time - why don't we head out of town to my lake house and enjoy some time at Chelan until this blows over? They'll give up eventually."

"Really?" Veronica said. The idea of a break-by-the-lake was very appealing to her. I of course was thrilled at the prospect of seeing Rachel again. "That sounds wonderful. But I don't want to be an imposition."

"Not at all. I'd love having the company, and I rather think Jack here would love to go back there. He has a lady friend in the neighborhood."

Veronica looked down at me. "Does he now?" she said, smiling. "I had no idea."

"Then it's settled," said Isaac. "Besides, I have other reasons for going back out there." I knew he was thinking about Alice.

Veronica hugged him. "Thank you, Isaac. But how are we going to get me out of here without Mutt and Jeff out there realizing I've gone? I don't want you to have to leave in the middle of the night."

"Oh, we'll figure something out."

"Great." Veronica sighed with relief. "If they're still here tomorrow, I'll take you up on your kind hospitality."

Tomorrow duly arrived. And there they still were.

What Could Possibly Go Wrong?

A dog is a man's best friend. If you don't believe this, try this simple experiment: lock your wife and your dog in the trunk of your car for an hour. Now, when you finally open the trunk, who's really pleased to see you?

For the record, I wouldn't much care for being locked in the trunk of a car: I'm mildly claustrophobic. But the joke is funny anyway, and has a kernel of truth to it.

Everyone knows that you humans have made some spectacularly bad decisions over the years. Everyone has their favorites of course; and Anna, as our resident historian, is no exception - she lectures on this from time to time, though in this case "lecture" is actually a euphemism for "rant". Some of her prominent examples include the following. First, Anna says, there's the US invading Iraq and thinking it would turn out well, with everyone singing Kumbaya and marching off hand-in-hand into a happy democratic sunset, with kittens and rainbows everywhere.

Indeed, brilliant military minds have provided an endless string of examples over the centuries - Napoleon invading Russia comes to mind. Hitler invading Russia. Hell, *anyone* invading Russia.

There's everyone's favorite from sports: the Red Sox trading Babe Ruth to the Yankees and then wandering in a titleless wasteland for more than eight decades.

From Stupid Product World, we have Clairol releasing its "Touch of Yoghurt" shampoo and wondering why an entire nation's worth of women went *"Ee-yuk!"*

Bad business decisions? Well, Anna points to Kodak Corporation clinging to film because they said digital photography was a dead end, and American Express turning down American Airlines' suggestion to start a new kind of credit card that gave mileage credit for travel awards. Oh, and Anna gives a special award to the twenty publishers who turned down J.K. Rowling's first *Harry Potter* book.

But other humans are hardly immune from this malaise, Veronica included. And when they write *The History Of Bad Ideas*, there's a good chance that what happened next will be right up there with the best of them.

Isaac and Veronica had agreed that the only way to sneak her past the camera crew camped on the street outside was for Veronica to enter Isaac's house by the backdoor and then be smuggled out in the trunk of Margo, Isaac's 1970 Oldsmobile Ninety-Eight convertible. They briefly considered the idea of having her hide under a blanket on the back seat, but decided that the risk of detection by the camera crew was too great. So the trunk became the default option.

Margo is a beast. She's 19 feet long and fits in Isaac's garage with literally an inch and a half to spare when he's pulled her up all the way to the front wall. A few years ago, he invested nineteen dollars and ninety-five cents in one of those laser do-dads that aim a red dot downward on a particular point on the front of the car so you know when to stop before you hit the wall - and was slightly annoyed when a friend pointed out that you could accomplish the same thing for free by hanging a tennis ball from the ceiling.

At one end of the beast is the 455-hp V-8 engine, housed under a hood that's longer than some Italian cars. All the way down at the other end is a trunk that's truly vast. Isaac describes it as a "two-body trunk" - to which Leroy Fawkes, in typical style, once added, "Yup - three if they're Asians."

The general idea was for Veronica to hide in the trunk, then climb out - preferably on a deserted street - once they'd gone a few blocks. But of course there had to be a complicating factor.

The problem was what to do with Bonkers. Normally he stayed with Anna any time Veronica was away. But Anna wasn't around this time: a wealthy client who was besotted with her was paying her a small fortune to accompany him on a trip to Hawai'i for a week of fun and fornication in the tropical sun.

So Bonkers had to come with us. Joy.

The *other* problem was that Veronica didn't own a cat carrier.

She and Isaac discussed this for a while, and both decided that Bonkers couldn't ride in the front of the car with no one to hold him (not to mention a dog making fun of him all the time, but we'll skip that part). It was at that point that Veronica uttered the statement that would never be forgotten.

"I guess I'll keep him in the trunk with me then."

Consider: a cat and a woman locked together in the trunk of a car.

I couldn't *wait* to see how this turned out.

The Return of Demon Cat

"Are you sure that's a good idea?" Isaac asked, partly in response to a sarcastic comment from me.

"Yeah, I'm sure it'll be fine," Veronica replied. "It's just for a few blocks. After that I can hold him, or we could leave him in the trunk. He'll probably just go to sleep in there."

I made another comment from the back seat - more of a gleeful prediction actually.

Isaac gave me a quick glance and a frown. "Okay," he said. "I suppose he should be fine for that distance." Now I fully admit that what I did next was unforgivably evil, but I just couldn't help myself. As Veronica picked up Bonkers, I told him in an obnoxiously self-satisfied way that I was going to be riding in the front of the car while he was locked in the dark of the trunk. I added a *Ha ha ha!* for good measure. He hissed at me as he was carried away.

Whether he would have reacted the way he did without me goading him is something we'll never know. But I like to think I can take a little credit for subsequent events.

So. Veronica climbs into the trunk holding a cat who is already pissed off at his canine house mate. Isaac and I make ourselves comfortable in the front, then he backs the Beast out of the garage into the street. The camera crew take note of the classic old vehicle, and one of them shouts "Nice car!" as Isaac closes the garage door. He smiles and waves back, puts Margo into first gear, and off we go.

The idea, as noted above, was to drive just far enough away to be safely out of sight of the camera crew. Three or four blocks perhaps, looking for a suitably quiet spot where the strange and suspicious act of a woman climbing out of a car trunk would not be witnessed.

It didn't quite work out that way. It took Bonkers precisely one block to freak out and unleash mayhem in the dark confines of Margo's trunk - which, while undeniably capacious, was not nearly large enough to allow Veronica any refuge from the feline fury happening next to her.

Our first hint that things were not going to plan was a loud miaowing coming from the back. The miaows rapidly escalated to yowls, and from the expression on the face of the old lady walking a Maltese terrier in the next block, it was apparent that what was happening in the trunk was audible to pretty much anyone within earshot. Isaac abruptly hit the gas, hoping to escape the woman, but he hit the accelerator rather harder than he'd intended, and this served to catapult Bonkers from the back of the trunk right into Veronica's head. Predictably, this did nothing to improve the temper of either of the trunk's occupants.

This was followed in short order by the sounds of the human occupant banging loudly on the trunk's lid, closely followed by muffled screaming.

All of which would have been bad enough, but perfectly manageable given that we were now three blocks from home, had it not been for the *extremely* unfortunate fact that, as the drama playing out in the darkness of the trunk was reaching its cacophonous climax of human screaming, feline screeching and trunk lid banging, a police car just happened to pass by going in the opposite direction, and of course because it was a hot day the officer inside had his windows down, and the next thing we knew he had effected a rapid U-turn and was coming up behind us with lights blazing and sirens raging, and Isaac was forced to pull over, and I thought this was the funniest damn thing I had ever seen but was just hoping that no one was about to get shot.

The cop did indeed have his gun in hand as he jumped out of the vehicle, and before he had even approached us two other police cars came screaming around the corner. Evidently the first officer had requested backup. Thirty seconds later we're surrounded by policemen pointing guns at us - well, at Isaac - and ordering him to put his hands in the air and stay where he was. Remarkably, Isaac managed to remain calm despite what could be termed a dangerously volatile state of affairs.

The same could not be said for the two life forms temporarily residing in the trunk. Veronica, having heard the sirens, had obviously figured out that Isaac had been pulled over - and why - and was no longer yelling or banging on the lid. Bonkers, on the other hand, continued to screech, and from the occasional yelp of pain emanating from the trunk it was apparent that he was continuing to take out his anger on random parts of Veronica's body.

The first officer approached the driver's side of the car and, continuing to point the gun at Isaac, demanded to know what was going on.

"Officer," Isaac began with a sigh, "I completely understand why you're concerned, and I will be the first to admit that this is a very unusual situation, but I can assure you there's a rational explanation here. Although," he added, "It's a long story."

"Who's in the trunk?" demanded the cop.

"It's a friend and her cat."

"A friend?" he repeated with obvious sarcasm. "You make a habit of locking your friends and their pets in the trunk of your car, do you?"

"No, but... well, it was a sort of a joke. Look, if you take the keys and open the trunk, the... occupant can verify that she is not in there against her will."

There was another screech, immediately followed by a scream from Veronica. Apparently Bonkers had just made contact with some particularly sensitive body part. There were quite a few to choose from, actually: I imagine that Veronica was by now probably deeply regretting the fact that she had entered the trunk wearing nothing but a pair of cutoff shorts and a tank top.

"It sure as hell doesn't sound like it to me," commented the cop.

"I know," Isaac said patiently. "Look, may I give you the key and have you unlock the trunk and verify this for yourself?"

The cop thought for a moment. "Okay," he said, "but keep your hands in the air." He motioned to one of the other officers, who opened the passenger side door.

"If your dog tries to bite me, I'll shoot him," he said.

Isaac looked worried. "He won't, he's a nice dog," he replied. Then he said to me, "Jack, hop in the back please."

Not wishing to be shot, I obediently jumped onto the back seat, and the cop carefully reached over and extracted the car key from the lock. He slammed the passenger door shut and walked around to the back of the vehicle.

He hesitated. "Ma'am, are you okay in there?" he asked.

From inside the trunk came Veronica's muffled voice. "No, I'm fucking well NOT okay!" she yelled. "I'm trapped in here with a psychotic fucking cat!" As if to emphasize the point, there was a muffled screech from Bonkers, followed by another scream of pain, and then Veronica yelling "*Jeeee-sus* Christ! Get me the fuck OUT of here!"

The policeman inserted the key into the lock. Another officer stood nearby with his gun raised. The first cop could have opened the trunk slowly, but he presumably decided that this would give the occupant too much time to do something bad if that was her intention. Instead, he threw open the lid... which was really *not* a very good strategy with which to release to freedom a terminally pissed-off cat.

A microsecond after the trunk was opened, the ballistic projectile otherwise known as Bonkers flew out of the compartment, claws fully extended, and with a terrifying screech launched himself at the first thing he saw in the daylight, which was of course the hapless cop.

Bonkers dug his claws into the officer's uniform, which - being summer issue - was not thick enough to protect him from the attack of an insane house pet. There was some screaming, followed by two police officers wrestling with the cat, until finally Bonkers was wrenched free and dropped to the ground. He ran to the kerb, still yowling, and then proceeded to initiate a furious bout of cleaning.

"Jesus Christ!" said the cop. The other policeman, trying unsuccessfully to suppress laughter, graciously helped Veronica out of the trunk. With scratches all over her and her hair a tangled red mess, she looked like she'd just been dragged through a thorn bush.

"Are you okay, ma'am?" the second cop enquired.

Veronica brushed herself down and straightened her clothing. She was calming down now. "Well, officer," she said, "let's just say I've had better fucking days."

Aftermath

Fifteen minutes later, sanity had been restored - sort of. Veronica had managed to convince the police that the whole thing had been the result of a lost bet, and that she really wasn't either an abductee or an abused woman. The local constabulary had duly dispersed, taking with them a story that, in the annals of police work, would never die.

As they drove off around the corner, Isaac suddenly erupted in helpless laughter. He was laughing so hard he couldn't speak, and for safety's sake he pulled to the kerb.

Veronica initially looked annoyed, and then closed her eyes, shook her head and smiled at the absurdity of what had just happened. Pretty soon she was laughing too, and then the two of them were shaking uncontrollably, tears rolling down their cheeks.

"That," she said when she finally managed to find her voice again, "was pretty fucked up."

"I know," said Isaac, who started crying again, "but - I'm sorry, Veronica - it was SO funny!"

Eventually the mirth subsided to a manageable level, and they thought about what to do next. After a suitable interval of time to give Bonkers a chance to cool off, Veronica rather gingerly picked him up from the sidewalk and, with an obvious touch of vindictiveness, cast him back into the trunk and slammed down the lid. The yowling resumed shortly afterwards.

"We *really* need a cat carrier," Isaac said.

"Yes," said Veronica simply.

No, I commented from the back seat. *What we* really *need is a tranquilizer gun and some bailing wire.*

Chelan Again

An hour later, we were heading out of Seattle and on our way to Lake Chelan.

Bonkers was on the back seat next to me, safely but unhappily confined to a cat carrier that Veronica had purchased at a pet store that we'd visited on the way out. It must be said that getting him out of the trunk and into the carrier had not been accomplished without the infliction of further injuries to his owner, who was still bleeding lightly from multiple scratches to her hands and arms.

"God," Veronica had said as we had finally secured the disposable pet and resumed our journey, "why on earth do we bother having cats?"

Um... can I weigh in here? I asked from the back seat.

Isaac briefly glanced back at me with the trace of a smile. "Well, I must say I've never found them very appealing," he said.

Veronica sighed. "Isaac, I'm really sorry for all this hassle I've caused you. And it's really kind of you to do this."

Isaac smiled. "Not at all, Veronica. I'm always happy to go to the lake, and it's nice to have the company. Besides, you just provided me with my entertainment for the week." He laughed.

"For the year, more like," Veronica replied with a sardonic smile.

There was a pause. We were out of Seattle now and driving through more rural areas. It was another lovely day.

"So," Veronica said, "I really should give you an explanation for all this."

"You really don't have to. It's none of my business."

"I know, but you just rescued me. Besides, I trust you, Isaac - you've always been a good friend to Jack and I."

"Well, thank you," he said. "I'm very fond of you both."

"So," she said, pausing for a moment. "I'm going to share a secret with you I wouldn't confess to too many people."

Isaac knew what was coming, but responded only with a comment that he appreciated her trust in him and that he would never tell anyone what was told to him in confidence.

Veronica took a deep breath, as if she was about to take a plunge into cold water.

"I already confessed this to my mother, so you may as well know too. I'm... Well, I'm actually a sex worker. I hope that doesn't shock you." She looked at Isaac apprehensively.

Isaac smiled reassuringly. "Not at all. In fact I'd guessed something of the sort."

Veronica looked surprised. "Really? How? I thought I've always been very discreet."

"Oh, you have, I'm sure. But I've noticed different men coming and going from your house, and sometimes they seem to emerge... well, how should I put it? Injured, perhaps? Between that and hearing what I thought was muffled screaming a couple of times, I couldn't help wondering whether I was living next to a dominatrix." Isaac omitted to mention the minor detail that he knew this about Veronica because her dog had told him, a point I noted from the back seat. He ignored me.

Veronica was obviously impressed with his apparent perceptiveness. "That's exactly right, " she said slowly. "Either I've been very careless, or you're remarkably insightful."

"I don't know about the latter," Isaac replied, "but the former certainly isn't true. I don't think anyone else knows - and I'm sure Leroy would have made some remark to me if he'd figured it out."

At this mention of our vile next-door neighbor, Veronica snorted grimly. "Leroy's as dumb as a raccoon in a coma. He could have an elephant living in his basement and not know it."

Isaac laughed. "So is the good Senator a client of yours then?"

"*Was*," Veronica replied. "Except that until this week I didn't know who he was. He would always wear this stupid little fake mustache and glasses when he came by. I suppose I should pay more attention to politics." She sighed, and gazed out at the Cascade Mountains that were looming ever larger ahead of us.

"Anyway," she continued, "I'm guessing from the mystery guy who was hanging out in the bushes across the street that someone - maybe his opponent in this election - got a private detective to follow him around to see if he was as morally pure as he claimed, and the guy caught him going into my house a couple of times. So whoever is behind this concluded he was having an affair. And if his wife knows about this, then she probably thinks *I'm* the affair. And then that moron from the Investigations Channel got involved and decided to camp out outside my house so he could confront me for his stupid TV show."

Isaac sighed sympathetically. "It's quite the little drama," he said.

"Yeah, though it's pretty funny in one sense... If his wife knew the real story - that her super-conservative husband likes being tied up and having strange things done to his nether regions - she'd probably have a fit."

Isaac laughed. "She'd probably kill him," he said.

Veronica nodded. "She might anyway, given what's happened. I can't say I'd blame her."

"Well," Isaac said, "this will probably blow over in a few days. The news cycle will move on to the next thing. Besides, they can't camp out there forever."

"I guess. Let's hope so, anyway."

They were silent for awhile, then Veronica asked, "So this house by the lake - your dad built it?"

"Yes," Isaac said. "Back in the 30's, after the dam raised the water level on the lake."

"How long since your dad died?"

"Oh, almost forty years now. He was 82."

"And your mom?"

"She died on a beautiful day in the summer of 1989, at 86. She was a wonderful woman."

"Wow. I was born that summer."

"Really? When's your birthday?"

"June 6th."

Isaac started. "You were born on June the 6th, 1989?" His surprise was obvious.

"Yes, why?"

"That was the day my mother died."

"Wow. That's really freaky."

"Do you know what time you were born?"

"Yes. 5 pm. Please don't tell me your mom died at 4:59?"

"Well, as a matter of fact, it was pretty close. If I recall, she passed away just before four in the afternoon."

"You don't suppose..." She didn't finish the sentence.

"Who knows? Maybe you're my mother reincarnated."

"Well, *that* would be a little too weird."

Isaac laughed. "Should I start calling you 'mom'?"

Veronica raised her eyebrows. "Please don't," she said, smiling. "I mean, I deal with some pretty bizarre situations in my profession, but I'm not sure I'm psychologically equipped to handle being the reincarnated mother of a guy in his seventies."

"There are more things in heaven and earth, Horatio..."

"Shakespeare, right?"

"Yes - *Hamlet*. The origin of half the cliches in the English language. I once met a woman who worked for the Royal Shakespeare Company who told me a story about an American tourist who said she didn't like *Hamlet* because it was too full of cliches."

"Really? I haven't read it since high school," she said. "What was your mother's name? If you tell me it was Holly, I'll probably freak out."

"Why Holly?"

"That's my real name. Veronica is a stage name, so to speak."

"Really? I had no idea."

"All sex workers have pseudonyms. It's about protecting yourself from the weirdos. So when I got into this business, Holly Ann McKenna became Veronica Delacroix."

"I see," he said. "But no, my mother's name was Audrey." He paused. "So do I call you Veronica or Holly?"

"Either." Veronica smiled. "I answer to both."

For the next hour, Isaac and Veronica exchanged details of their respective lives. Some of this I knew, much of it I didn't. Isaac was independently wealthy, the result of some patents he had taken out on inventions. Apparently these had solved a couple of the more challenging problems facing the oil industry's attempts to extract petroleum from beneath the sea floor.

"Wow," Veronica exclaimed. She was impressed. "I had no idea. You'd make a great sugar daddy for some lucky girl. But no," she added quickly, "I'm not hinting."

Isaac laughed. "I'm a bit old for all that, I'm afraid. And I'm not exactly rolling in money - I have enough to live comfortably."

"And you grew up in England?"

"I spent some of my childhood there, yes. My father was a diplomat. He was posted there and stayed on for some years after he retired, though he divided his time between England and the U.S. He loved both, but ultimately he settled here until he died. Had a place in Seattle, and the Chelan house too."

"And you went to school here?"

"University? I was in England for undergrad, but I did my Masters at Scripps in San Diego. I needed to be by the sea, always. I fell in love with it from an early age."

"You're quite the romantic," Veronica commented.

He smiled. "Yes, I suppose I am," he said. "It's how I ended up working with the oil industry in deep ocean drilling - not very romantic, but quite lucrative, as it turned out."

There was a pause, then Veronica asked, "Were you ever married, Isaac?" The question mirrored the one I had asked before in this same car, and on this same road. The question that had led to the whole Rowan story.

"No," he said. "I was very much in love years ago, but... well, it didn't work out." I could tell he was not about to offer more details, and was not going to mention Rowan, or their daughter. It was too complicated to explain in any terms that would be believable by someone else.

"What about you?" he asked, changing the subject.

"Me? God no. No marriage, and only the occasional boyfriend. They don't usually last long - my profession tends to put men off."

"I suppose it would," Isaac laughed. "Well, I hope you find someone worthy of you. You deserve that."

Veronica sighed. "Thank you, Isaac. If one ever shows up who doesn't run screaming, I hope they turn out to be half as decent as you."

We drove on, the two of them in easy conversation. We stopped for lunch in Leavenworth, an old forestry community that had recast itself as a fake Bavarian village when logging failed and the railroad moved elsewhere. Isaac and Veronica bought sandwiches from a café, and ate them on a bench while a man in lederhosen and a feathered cap serenaded passers-by with an accordion.

On the last leg to Chelan, Isaac told Veronica about Alice, and how worried he was about her situation with Sal Kaufman.

"Why did he even volunteer to take her on if he dislikes kids so much?" Veronica asked.

"Because Alice has a trust that she inherited when her parents died, and he gets paid quite well to look after her. Of course he spends most of it himself - he won't even buy her books, and I see her wearing the same old clothes all the time."

Veronica sighed. "This guy's really bad news, huh?" she asked.

"Yes, he's a real redneck."

"So he's like Leroy?"

"Worse."

"Worse? Seriously?"

"Yes. Imagine Leroy with a drinking problem and a shotgun."

A little over an hour later Margo pulled up outside Camp Fishless. I was hoping Rachel would be there to greet us, and she was. Alerted to our arrival by the sound of the car engine, she bolted out of the dog door at the back and ran up to me, tail wagging.

"Hello, Jack" she said.

I was wagging too. I was about to go around back and sniff Rachel's ass, but thought better of it.

Did you miss me? I asked.

"A little."

Only a little?

Rachel gave me a cynical look. *"O my dearest darling,"* she said, *"I have been pining for you day and night, counting the hours until you return."* Her tail was still wagging, albeit a little more slowly. *"Is that better?"*

A little, yeah.

Then Veronica walked up, holding Bonkers.

"O, nice!" Rachel said to me. *"You brought lunch."*

Off The Menu II

Half an hour later, Rachel is staring at Bonkers, who is stretched out on the deck, sunning himself.

"So when do we get to eat the cat?" she asks.

We can't eat the cat.

"Why not?"

It's not allowed.

"I repeat, why not?"

Because he's Veronica's pet.

"She can always find another one. There are plenty of cats out here."

Yes, but she actually likes this one.

"Why?"

I've no idea.

"He's so fat - he'd make a great meal."

Listen, you can't eat the cat, okay?

"Don't tell me you're defending him?"

No, I say, but it occurs to me that I'm finding myself in the odd position of protecting Bonkers. Is there really a kernel of affection buried deep beneath the mutual contempt that has defined our relationship?

"O my God, you actually like *him*, don't you?"

No, I don't like *him*. But if you want to stay on good terms with Veronica I strongly suggest you leave Bonkers alone. She wouldn't take kindly to her beloved pet being murdered. It's a human thing, I add.

She continues to stare at Bonkers, then says, "Okay, suit yourself. If he stays out here, the coyotes will probably get him anyway."

She's not joking, actually. There are indeed coyotes here, and they like nothing better than to pick off any hapless house cat that's dumb enough to wander into the woods.

A little while later, when Rachel is busy elsewhere, I approach Bonkers. With tedious predictability, he hisses at me when I cross the invisible line that marks the imaginary boundary of a distance that his furry little brain has decided is Too Close.

Listen, I say to him. *I don't like you, but I need to tell you something.*

He looks at me suspiciously, and his tail twitches.

You need to stay around the house while you're here. There are coyotes in this area - and they see all cats as snack food.

Bonkers turns his head and gazes serenely out onto the lake. His disinterest in anything I have to say is palpable.

I'm serious, Bonkers. Deadly serious. I don't much care if you end up as coyote bait, but I don't want to have to deal with Veronica being upset if you disappear. So please - pretty please - don't go out into the woods. Stay close to the house, okay?

Bonkers continues to stare at the lake for a while, his tail continuing to swish from side to side; then finally he turns and meets my gaze.

"Okay," he says.

And that, dear reader, is the one and only word you'll hear from the cat in this entire book.

Alice's Restaurant

Meanwhile, Veronica was wandering around the house in a state of unexpected bliss. In the time it had taken her to walk from the front door to the deck, she had fallen in love with Camp Fishless.

"God, Isaac, this is the most beautiful place I've ever seen." She meant it.

Isaac was touched. "I'm glad you like it," he said. "My mother loved it here too."

Veronica settled into a chair on the deck and uttered a deep sigh of contentment. "It's divine," she said. "I may never leave."

Isaac smiled. "You can stay as long as you like. Now, would you like some lemonade?" Veronica hesitated.

"Or would you prefer some wine?"

"Well, to be brutally honest I'd prefer a gin and tonic, but I'm probably pushing my luck on that one."

He laughed. "No, I think we can manage that. I have some gin around here somewhere." Veronica moved to get up but Isaac gestured for her to remain seated. "It's okay - I don't need help. Just relax and enjoy the afternoon."

Rachel - who had been inside the house - joined us on the deck. Veronica smiled. "Hello... Rachel, isn't it? Nice to meet you." Rachel moved to Veronica's side and sniffed the proffered hand. Seemingly satisfied with this inspection, she sat next to Veronica, who began to caress her head. "So you're Jack's girlfriend, eh?"

Rachel looked over at me. *"Girlfriend, huh? What have you been telling her?"*

I haven't been telling her anything. I can't talk to Veronica.

Rachel looked skeptical. *"So she's your human?"*

Yes.

"She seems nice. Except for liking that stupid cat."

Nobody's perfect.

Isaac reappeared and handed Veronica a tall glass. "One gin and tonic," he said.

"Thank you, Isaac. You're a girl's best friend." She sipped the drink, and sighed. "It's perfect."

Just then Rachel suddenly jumped up and ran down the steps from the deck to the path, barking. We all looked up, and a few seconds later Alice emerged from the woods, carrying a shopping bag. She stopped to greet Rachel, then the two of them walked up to the deck to join us.

Veronica stood up. "You must be Alice," she said warmly. "I'm Veronica. I've heard a lot about you." She put out her hand, but to her surprise, Alice gave her a hug. A long hug. And I suddenly realized that it had probably been a long time since this orphaned girl had been able to express any kind of intimacy with another female.

Finally, Alice stood back and looked at Veronica. "You're really pretty," she said.

Veronica smiled. "Thank you. So are you."

"I look alright, I s'pose. I don't have much of a chance to dress up out here."

"That's too bad. Do you like dressing up, Alice?"

"Yeah. I wish I had some nice clothes," she added wistfully.

Alice hugged Isaac next, and then bent down to pet me. "Hello Jack," she said. "Rachel missed you." I looked at Rachel, who was pretending not to notice my stare.

Alice looked up at Isaac. "Oh Isaac, can you ask Jack to ask Rachel what happened to her collar? She's lost it again."

Veronica gave Isaac a puzzled look, and Isaac shifted uneasily. He'd forgotten to tell Alice to keep our little chats a secret. "I'll certainly do that, Alice," Isaac said after a pause. He turned to Veronica. "We play a game where we pretend to talk to dogs," he said, not very convincingly. "It's rather like Dr Doolittle, you know?"

"No," Alice interjected, "I mean, can you find out..." Her voice trailed off at the pointed looks being aimed at her by two dogs and an elderly man. "I mean... uh, never mind," she ended lamely.

"So how much time do we have you for today?" asked Isaac, quickly changing the subject.

Alice's face brightened. "That's the thing! I told cousin Sal I was going to a friend's house for dinner, and... well," - she pointed to the shopping bag - "I thought I'd come make dinner for you. You know, as a sort of thank you for being so nice to Rachel and me."

Veronica raised her eyebrows. "You're going to make dinner for us?" Alice nodded. "How old are you, Alice?"

"I'm eleven."

"Well, you must be just about the most thoughtful eleven-year-old in the entire world."

Alice grinned. Then her expression became more serious, and she turned to Isaac again. "*Actually,*" she said, "I told Sal that I might be... um, sleeping over. You know, just in case I could spend the night here with you and Rachel." Her eyes held a look of hope, poignant and fragile.

Isaac smiled. "Are you sure your cousin isn't going to be suspicious?"

"Yeah. He's happy - means he can go out drinking tonight without having to think about the stupid kid. And he didn't even care enough to ask where I was going, or get a phone number."

Isaac looked like he was about to say something in response to this sad statement, but suddenly Veronica clapped her hands. "Wonderful!" she exclaimed. I know *just* what we're going to do!" She took Alice's hands in hers. "Oh Alice, we are going to have *so* much fun!" She twirled Alice around on the deck, both of them laughing.

After a few turns they were both dizzy and a little breathless. "Now," Veronica said, still laughing, "let's go to the kitchen and make some dinner for Isaac. I'll be the chef's assistant."

And without further ado, Veronica led Alice by the hand to the door into the living room. A few seconds later the sound of giggling came from inside.

We all stared at the house for a few seconds, taking in the moment. Then Rachel turned to me; on her face was a look of canine contentment.

"I *love* your human," she said.

I'm glad, I replied. *I trained her myself.*

For the better part of the next hour, Veronica and Alice danced around the kitchen as they prepared dinner under Alice's direction. The meal was just hamburgers, peas and mashed potatoes, but Alice had brought everything necessary, with ice cream for dessert. And, bless her, she cooked some beef liver for Rachel and I.

Isaac opened a good bottle of wine, and set the table. Then he sat in his favorite armchair and drank some wine as he looked over at the two girls who were alternately chatting, laughing and singing together. He petted me and smiled. "It's been a long time since I've seen so much energy in this house, Jack. Does my heart good to watch them."

And Alice seems very happy - that's nice.

"It's wonderful," he said. "Veronica is wonderful."

Finally, the two cooks served dinner with a flourish, and Isaac made much of their efforts. The burgers smelled good, and the beef liver was delicious.

After dessert was done and copious praise had been delivered to Alice, Veronica stood up. She stared at Alice, then very theatrically pointed her index finger at her. "You," she said, her voice deep and drawn out. "Come... with... me!"

Alice giggled. "Where are we going?" she asked.

Veronica approached her slowly, then suddenly grabbed her hand. Alice squealed. "Never you mind," Veronica said, "you'll see. We're going to *transforrrrrm* you." She followed this with a sinister laugh, and dragged the giggling girl off in the direction of the guest bedroom. Just before she entered she looked back over her shoulder at Isaac, threw her head back and raised one eyebrow in a dramatic gesture. "We'll be *back*," she said, and with another demonic laugh pushed Alice into the room and closed the door behind her.

For the next half hour Rachel, Isaac and I sat patiently in the living room and listened to the muted sounds of laughter coming from the bedroom. At one point a high-pitched shriek rent the air, followed by more laughter.

What are they doing *in there?* I asked.

"Maybe they're torturing the cat?" suggested Rachel. Bonkers had retreated to the bedroom before dinner and had refused to come out; evidently he didn't trust this strange new dog with whom he was being forced to co-exist. Honestly, I couldn't say I blamed him.

Finally, the door opened and Veronica stepped out, wearing a lovely blue silk dress with an orange sash tied around her waist. But before Isaac had a chance to comment on her appearance, she gestured dramatically to the doorway.

"May I present to you the Princess Alice Von Dogsbody," she said. Hesitantly, Alice emerged from behind her, shy but giggling. She was indeed transformed: gone was the tomboy with dirty feet and unkempt hair. Veronica had attired her in a gorgeous dress, also silk, in shimmering green; Alice wore a peridot necklace and earrings to match. She was fully made up, and her blonde hair hung in curled waves that cascaded over her shoulders. She looked stunning.

Isaac stood up and applauded. "Alice, you look *so* beautiful," he said. "So do you, Veronica. I'm truly a lucky man, to have the two prettiest girls in the world in my house tonight."

Alice blushed and grinned from ear to ear. Veronica bowed. "I thought it was time the wild girl of the woods came out to society," she said. She turned to Alice. "You can't always be Tarzan, darling."

"Where did you get those dresses? Do you always bring your finery to rural areas?" Isaac asked. Veronica smiled.

"Oh, I usually throw a couple of nice dresses into my bag just in case."

"In case of what?"

"Well, you never know when the Queen might visit."

Isaac laughed. "Fair enough - you certainly put them to good use tonight." He paused to look appreciatively at Alice once more. "Let's go and sit on the deck and have another drink."

We all trooped outside, dogs following humans, and arranged ourselves in chairs or on the floor, according to our station. I watched Alice pull her chair close to Veronica's, and without even a glance in her direction Veronica automatically reached out and took Alice's hand in hers as the little girl settled into her chair.

We all gazed at the moon, which was almost full. I thought of Rowan, and knew Isaac was thinking the same thing.

After some idle chat, Veronica said, "So Alice, it's your night. What do you want to do now?"

Alice pondered for a moment. "Can we watch a movie?" she asked.

"Well, I don't know. Isaac, do you *have* any movies?"

"I have some in the bedroom. I'm not sure what we have for kids, but we can check."

Perusal of the various DVDs on a shelf showed nothing appropriate until suddenly Alice squealed. "Oh, you have *101 Dalmatians*! Can we watch that?"

And of course we did. Because the DVD player and TV were in Isaac's bedroom, his large bed soon became host to two female humans and two medium-sized dogs - both of whom were very curious to watch a canine-inspired movie. Isaac politely declined the invitation to join us, and retired to the living room to read his book.

Two hours later the movie was finished, and Rachel and I had been suitably scared to death by the whole concept of Cruella de Vil wanting to skin her puppies to make a fur coat. I mean, seriously - where do you people come up with these ideas?

I stood up, stretched, and climbed down from the bed to check on Isaac. I looked up to see him standing in the door frame; he was gazing at the bed scene and smiling fondly.

Alice was asleep and curled up against Veronica, with Rachel stretched out snoring next to them.

Veronica opened her eyes and yawned. "I guess I'd better get this girl to bed," she whispered.

"No no," Isaac replied. "Stay where you are. Don't disturb her. I'll sleep in the guest room tonight."

"Are you sure, Isaac?"

"Absolutely," he replied. "I hope she has sweet dreams - and you too."

As he turned to go, Veronica said, "Isaac?"

"Yes?"

"Thank you."

He smiled. "No, thank you - for making a sad little girl very happy."

Veronica looked at Alice, who was fast asleep in her arms. "She's a wonderful kid," she said.

"She is," Isaac agreed. "And you'll make a wonderful mother some day."

Veronica raised her eyebrows. "Hmm, I don't know. I've never thought of myself as a mom."

"Well maybe you should start." He smiled. "Good night, Veronica. Sleep well."

I followed Isaac into the living room. He looked down at me. "Don't you want to sleep with them? With Rachel?" he asked.

Yes, but I want to sleep with you too.

"Really, it's fine, but thank you for thinking of me."

What, and leave you all alone? No, I can't do that. Besides, I added, *if I'm not there who's going to push you to the edge of the bed in the middle of the night?*

Isaac laughed. "Good point - I'd hate to miss that. Okay then - let's go to bed."

Introductions

The next day, after a leisurely breakfast on the deck, Veronica, Alice, Rachel and I went for a walk in the woods. Veronica and Alice walked hand in hand. As one would expect, Rachel and I were sniffing and peeing on things.

Alice was happily telling Veronica about her favorite music, when suddenly she froze. Veronica looked up and saw a man twenty yards ahead of them. He was tall and lanky, and was wearing old, stained overalls. He had a shotgun slung over his left shoulder. Veronica instantly knew who it was.

Sal Kaufman stood in the middle of the path, blocking the way. He was chewing something - gum or tobacco - and looking Veronica up and down with pretty much open lust.

"Well, well, what have we here?" he said. "I don't b'lieve I've had the pleasure." *Nor will you,* I thought. *Ever.*

Veronica said nothing, but Kaufman continued undeterred. "My little girl here never told me she had such a pretty friend."

"I'm not your little girl," Alice said sharply. Kaufman didn't respond, but I could see that he wasn't pleased by her contradiction.

"Anyway, who might you be?" he asked.

"I'm just a friend," Veronica said. She was being civil, but no more.

"An' does the friend have a name?"

"Veronica."

"Well, Veronica, nice to meet you. I'm Sal." he glanced at me. "That your dog?"

"They're both mine," Veronica replied. She knew the story of how Kaufman had threatened to kill Rachel.

Kaufman raised his eyebrows. "Huh. That one there" - he used the shotgun to point at Rachel - "looks a lot like the one Alice used to have. Got lost in the woods it did. Very sad." I could sense Alice's anger, but she said nothing.

"They're both my dogs," Veronica repeated.

"You live here?" Kaufman asked.

"No, just visiting."

"Too bad. Sure could use a pretty girl like you in these parts."

"Well, I'm afraid you'll just have to do without," Veronica replied. "Besides, I'm married," she added.

Kaufman whistled. "Well, yer husband's one lucky guy, yessir. Where is he, by the way? I don't see you wearin' no wedding ring."

Veronica bristled. "Are you always this nosy?"

"Easy, girl. I don't mean nothin' by it. Just makin' conversation."

"Yes well, we're just out for a quiet walk. And it's time to go back." She turned around, closely followed by Alice.

"Alice, baby, you come with me," Kaufman said.

There was an awkward pause. Alice didn't move.

"Come on now, girl. It's time to go home."

Still Alice didn't move. "I want to stay out with Veronica some more," she said.

"Well you can't, baby. I need you back at the house. You been neglectin' your chores."

Veronica put her head to Alice's ear and whispered. "You'd better go. We'll check in later, okay?" Reluctantly, Alice walked over to Kaufman, who put an arm around her. She immediately stiffened at his touch.

"There's a good girl." A smile, almost a sneer, was on his face.

As he turned to walk away, Veronica said, "What did you say your name was?"

"Sal. Sal Kaufman."

"Is that Sal like Salvatore?"

"Yes ma'am." He was still chewing, and staring at Veronica, obviously curious about her enquiry.

"Got a middle initial?"

"Yeah, A - middle name's Anthony. Why?" He was frowning.

"Just curious. I figured I'd have a friend look you up when I get home."

"Look me up where?"

"In his database at work."

Kaufman now looked, if not exactly worried, at least slightly concerned. "What *database*? Who'd he work for?" he asked.

"Child Protective Services," she said, and walked away.

Promise

Alice returned to the house that evening. Veronica jumped up from her chair and hugged her tightly.

"Are you okay?" she asked.

"Yeah," she replied. "He was pretty pissed, but that thing you said made him worried, I think. He decided to show what a good guy he's being, so he let me come over again. But," she added sadly, "I can't stay the night."

Isaac came out onto the deck and looked concerned. Veronica had described the encounter with Kaufman, including what she'd said to him at the end of the conversation.

"I hope everything's okay, Alice," he said.

Veronica sat down again and motioned for Alice to sit in her lap.

"I think you'd better be a good girl, Alice," she said. "I know it's not easy, but I don't want him creating problems for you."

Alice nodded sadly. "I'll try," she said. "But I *hate* him - that thing he said about Rachel today!"

"I know," Veronica replied, stroking Alice's hair. "But sometimes you just have to play the game. Unfortunately, he has all the power here, legally speaking."

Alice looked sad. Rachel was licking one of Alice's knees, attempting to console her with her tongue. It's a dog thing.

"Come on!" Veronica said suddenly. "Let's go cook!" She pushed Alice off her lap and the two of them stood up. Alice laughed, then suddenly became serious again.

"Veronica?"

"Yes, my love?"

"How long are you staying here? I mean, when are you going to leave and go back to Seattle?"

"I don't know, sweetie. In a few days, probably."

She looked downcast. "It's just that... well, I don't want you to leave."

If there is an expression associated with a breaking heart, it was the one on Veronica's face at that moment. She took Alice's face in both her hands and kissed her on the forehead. Then she looked at her intently and said, "Alice, listen to me. I will never abandon you. Never. I'll come back out here again as soon as I can, and we'll talk every day in between. You're my girl, and I will always, always be here for you. I promise. Okay?" Alice threw her arms around Veronica's neck and hugged her tightly. Finally the hug ceased, and Veronica smiled.

"Okay, now get your ass into the kitchen and start getting things ready. We're going to cook up a storm tonight!"

Alice skipped happily into the kitchen, and was followed by Rachel. The three remaining life forms watched them go.

Isaac turned to Veronica and put his hand on her arm. "You," he said, smiling, "just became my favorite person."

Disgrace

Things continued more or less normally for a few days. Alice came down to the house every day, occasionally sleeping over. She said she was being well behaved with Kaufman, and doing additional work around the house to keep him happy. Or at least as happy as that "miserable piece of shit" - as Veronica referred to him - could be.

"Good girl," she said to Alice. "The better you behave, the less chance there is he'll try to ruin our fun here." The daily routine included walks, boating, swimming and cooking, all accompanied by much laughter. In the evening Veronica and Alice curled up together in bed with a movie. Sometimes they read to each other from one of the innumerable books that filled the house.

Me, I trotted alongside Veronica in all of this, happy that everyone was happy.

But one morning Veronica received a phone call from Anna.

"Okay, Vee, the coast is clear - you can come home now."

"You mean those morons are no longer camped out at my house?"

"Oh, I think they left a couple of days after it was clear you'd flown the coop."

"Yeah, but they might come back as soon as I return."

"Unlikely, sweet pea. Your friend Digby has been screwed over, and good. I don't think he'll be doing much incisive reporting from local doorsteps any time soon."

"Really? What happened? Screwed over how? And by who?"

"By *whom*," she corrected. Good grammar is important to Anna.

"Whatever."

"Well," she continued, "from what I can gather from the Internet, his former cameraman - you know, the guy named Jimmy who filmed the Demon Cat episode - was fired by Digby, presumably for not sucking the great reporter's dick with sufficient enthusiasm. So Jimmy retaliated."

"Really? How?"

"He released the entire tape of Digby trying to get Jack to talk, suitably edited and annotated with sarcastic commentary. It's pretty funny, actually - you should watch it. I'll send you the link."

"And that got him fired?"

"Demoted. Apparently this wasn't the first time he'd made an idiot of himself - something to do with an exposé of pig farming and the Russian mafia. Management at the Investigations Channel was apparently concerned that Digby's earnest and now very public attempts to communicate with Dogkind compromised their credibility. It's sweet that they think they had any in the first place, but there you go. Anyway, the intrepid Digby is henceforth and for the time being relegated to Assistant Peon in the Production Department."

"O God, does this mean we're going to get yet another run of cat freaks coming by?"

"No, but I think the grave might. Don't worry - I already had my guy link the shit out of the new tape so avid fans are taken in the right direction."

"Thank you, darling, You're a life saver."

"All part of the service," Anna said. "Anyway, Lassie come home. I miss your stupid face."

"Okay, I'll come back. But--" She paused and looked over at Alice, who was playing with Rachel.

"But what?"

"It's complicated."

"Ooo... does this involve a *man*? I hope."

"No," Veronica replied. "I'll explain when I get there. But, well... I seem to be turning into a surrogate mother."

An Offer She Can't Refuse

We left two days later. There were long hugs and some tears between Veronica and Alice, and solemn promises by the former to return soon.

Rachel gave me a farewell lick on the nose, which I took as an encouraging sign. I'm still not entirely sure where I stand with her.

Shortly after we returned - the street was thankfully devoid of camera crews or creepy men hiding in the bushes - Veronica was sitting in the living room when her cell phone rang.

"Veronica?" enquired the voice at the other end.

"Yes?"

"This is Mr Lincoln."

Veronica frowned, and after a short pause said, "Hello Mr Lincoln. Freed any slaves lately?"

"I'm sorry?"

"Let me try again. Hello *Senator*."

"Senator? I don't understand."

"O yes you do. I know who you are now, and over the past couple of weeks you've caused me no end of problems. Not to mention loss of income. Because of you I had a fucking camera crew camped out outside my house, and I had to leave town to avoid them."

There was a long pause. Apparently the person on the other end of the call was trying to come to some decision. Finally he said, "Veronica, I apologize. My opponent in the upcoming election apparently decided to have me followed, and well, this was the result. It's been most unfortunate, and I'm sorry you got dragged into this little mess."

"Not so little."

"You must appreciate that a man in my position cannot afford to have, well, rumors of this kind in the public domain."

"Rumors - funny. And *you* must appreciate that a woman in *my* position is extremely vulnerable. Because of you I could well have had my photo and my profession plastered all over the fucking cable channels."

"Yes, that would be unfortunate. I'm sorry."

"Unfortunate - yeah, that's one way of putting it," Veronica said acidly. "And what about your vaunted relationship with Jesus, by the way? Is he okay with your perverse little extra-marital hobbies?"

There was silence at the other end of the phone. Finally Veronica spoke again.

"Why are you calling me, Senator?"

"Well, because... I know this will sound odd given what's happened, but... well, I was wondering if we could... could set up another session."

Veronica thought quickly. On the one hand, this guy was potentially poison, with the ability to ruin her if someone was still following him. On the other, the Senator's request presented an unexpected opportunity for her to become the unsung heroine of PIP. She really couldn't pass that up.

"Are you out of your mind?" She decided that playing hard to get would be more credible than agreeing outright.

"I know. I know it's been difficult for you, and I understand why you wouldn't want to continue our relationship. But..."

"But what, Senator? Give me one good reason why I should risk being seen with you again."

"Well, my dear, I can offer you... five thousand reasons."

It took Veronica a few seconds to process this. "I'm not your dear," she said with annoyance. "But do I understand you're offering to pay me five grand for a single session?" she asked.

"Yes. I think that's fair given that these... troubles... have impacted you financially."

"Okay, I'll think about it," Veronica said.

"Please do. Thank you, Veronica. I'll call back tomorrow."

The next day, the phone rang promptly at 9 a.m. She knew it was Rumor because the ID of the incoming number was blocked.

"Good morning, Veronica", he said. "So, can we come to some arrangement?"

"Yes. But the only way I'm willing to do this is if you come in the middle of the night to make sure you're not being followed or observed."

There was a pause. "Okay, yes. I think I can arrange that."

They agreed to conduct the session two nights later. As soon as she hung up, Veronica called Anna and enquired if she wished to participate in the felonious compromising of a leading local politician.

"Well, *duh*," Anna replied. "I wouldn't pass that up for anything. What did you have in mind, anyway?"

"I haven't really thought about it beyond tying him up and taking some lurid photos. Why don't you come over for coffee and we'll conspire together."

One hour, two pastries and four lattés later, the girls had a plan.

"Oh," said Anna as they concluded their plotting. "We'll also need a French maid."

"We will?"

"We will," she confirmed. Then added with a smile, "And I know just the guy."

Interlude: Divination

haruspication, noun, 1580s. The art of predicting the future by means of examining entrails.

haruspex, noun. From Latin *haruspex* (plural *haruspices*) "soothsayer by means of entrails," first element from Proto-Indo-European *ghere- "gut, entrail" (see *yarn*); second element from Latin spic- "beholding, inspecting," from Proto-Indo-European *speks "he who sees," from root *spek- "to observe" (see *scope*). The practice is Etruscan.

The next morning finds me sitting on the sidewalk outside our house, in a melancholic mood.

I am currently tearing bits off a squirrel carcass. It's the dog equivalent of *She loves me, she loves me not*. Rather messier than the daisy version, I grant you, but then you can't convert a daisy into a snack after you've exhausted its predictive potential.

I'd like to be able to say that I caught this squirrel, but actually it was hit by a car, mowed down in the prime of life by a very old Fiat. Such an ignominious end; 'tis a lesson to us all.

So: does Rachel love me, or am I just a vaguely pleasant but forgettable diversion in her little universe? Sigh.

And is this what my life has come to? Rooting through intestines for portents of romance?

There has to be more to life than seeking enlightenment in squirrel guts.

Oh well, time for lunch.

Blackmail

The Republican senator for Washington State's 50th legislative district arrived at Veronica's front door at 2 a.m. The street was deserted. As usual, he was thinly disguised with a mustache, glasses and a wig. Since Veronica now knew his true identity, he took these items off once he was safely inside the house.

Veronica didn't waste time with pleasantries or chit-chat. She handed Rumor two Viagras and a glass of water.

"I don't need Viagra," he said.

"You'll do as you're told, Senator," Veronica replied. "And you'll refer to me as 'Mistress' for the duration of this session."

"Yes, Mistress," he said contritely, and obediently swallowed the pills.

She held out her hand. "My fee?" she said.

"Oh yes." He rummaged in his jacket pocket and produced a plain white envelope. "Five thousand dollars, as we agreed."

Veronica took the envelope, glanced briefly inside to make sure it contained an approximately sufficient quantity of $100 bills, then placed it in a drawer.

Then, without further ado, she led Rumor to the basement. I followed, and for some reason Veronica didn't stop me. I hoped her plans didn't include bestiality.

In the dungeon, she ordered that he undress, and reinforced this command by brandishing a particularly large flogger.

"Please, Mistress, don't leave any marks on me."

"Don't worry, Senator, I'll be careful."

A moment later the Senator was standing naked before her. His penis was already standing up in anticipation of what was to come.

Veronica handed him a corset and some frilly lace panties in a rather garish shade of pink, and ordered him to put these items on. He complied, and then stepped into the size 12 high heels she produced next.

Satisfied that he was suitably attired, Veronica ordered Rumor to stand against the St Andrews cross and spread his legs. He did so, though not without some hesitation.

"What are you going to do?" he asked, with what sounded like a mix of trepidation and excitement.

"Punish you," Veronica replied. "I won't leave marks - which is why I'm using the flogger - but I'm going to whip a certain part of your anatomy to within an inch of its life as punishment for what I've had to put up with recently because of you."

Rumor literally shivered with anticipation.

"Thank you, Mistress. I haven't done anything like this in a long time. My wife doesn't..."

"I don't want to hear about your wife," Veronica interrupted. "For the next two hours, you belong to me."

"Yes, Mistress. I'm sorry."

"Now get back up against the cross."

Rumor did as he was told, and Veronica secured his wrists and ankles with rope. Then she placed a ball gag in his mouth. The gag was pink. Given Veronica's keen fashion sense, I have no doubt she selected it to match the panties.

She stood back and surveyed her client. He looked ridiculous, which was exactly what she intended. Then, after whipping his penis for a few minutes - during which groans that could have been either of pleasure or pain emanated from behind the ball gag - she informed him that she was going to leave him for a while so that the Viagra could take full effect.

Veronica and I headed back upstairs. She went to her bedroom, inside which Anna and a gay man named Kevin had been quietly chatting. Anna was giving Kevin make-up tips.

"Okay," she said. "You can come out now."

Downstairs, Veronica went to the kitchen and came back with a chilled bottle of white wine. She poured three glasses.

"How's our boy?" Anna asked.

"Exceedingly aroused," Veronica replied. "He really didn't need the Viagra, but I want him so hard he's fit to burst. When he sees you two and realizes I'm photographing what comes next he'll probably get very nervous and resist." She raised her glass to Anna. "And that, darling, is where your legendary skills come in."

Anna smiled seductively.

"And what do I do?" asked Kevin. "Don't I get to pleasure the royal cock too?"

"It's not royal," Anna corrected him. "He's a senator, not a king. We were a republic the last time I checked."

"Don't worry," Veronica said to Kevin. "I have a special role for you to play, dear."

To general amusement, she explained the plan as the three conspirators enjoyed the wine. After twenty minutes of chat, she looked at her watch, then at Kevin.

"Okay, sweetie," she said. "Time for you to get dressed. You'll find an outfit laid out for you on the bed in the guest room." She pointed to the appropriate door.

"Oooh!" Kevin exclaimed, and immediately rushed off in that direction. From the squeal of delight that came from inside a moment later it was apparent that Kevin approved of the chosen attire.

Anna and Veronica continued to chat, and five minutes later the door to the guest room opened and Kevin emerged, transformed into a French maid, complete with cap and feather duster.

Anna snorted with amusement. "Oh my God, Vee! It's perfect! Kevin dear, you look delicious!"

Kevin did a twirl, followed by a curtsey. "Ooo, ooo, can I keep it, *pleeeeeze*?" he asked.

"Of course, sweetie," Veronica said, smiling. "I have another for clients - this one's a spare."

They finished the wine. Veronica put down her glass and glanced over at the clock on the wall. "Okay," she said, "that ought to be enough time for our friendly neighborhood political pervert to be ready to roll. Time for some fun."

She retrieved her camera from a cabinet, and opened the door to the basement. "Shall we?" she asked the others.

"A moment, please," Anna said. She took off her sweater and skirt, to reveal some extremely sexy black underwear, with stockings and a garter belt to match.

Both Veronica and Kevin whistled appreciatively. "My God, girl," said Veronica, "you are one hot little bitch."

Anna bowed. "Thank you. Let's hope the Senator thinks so."

Then Anna did a strange thing. She picked up the backpack she had brought and pulled out a small plastic container with liquid inside. I knew instantly from the divine smell that it was the juice from cooked liver. My absolute favorite. What on earth was she doing with this?

Veronica looked at her quizzically. "What's that?" she asked.

"You'll see," Anna replied mysteriously. "Just a little extra touch I'm going to add to the proceedings." They descended to the basement, with me bringing up the rear. I was going to come anyway, but Anna specifically encouraged me to join them. Hmm. Oh well, I did want to see what happened, and anyway I'll follow beef liver pretty much anywhere.

It is an understatement of the first order to say that Senator Catkins Rumor was surprised to see Veronica leading into the dungeon a beautiful woman and a cross-dressing dude in a French maid's outfit. At first he was confused, and probably excited by the spectacle of Anna in killer black lingerie.

But then he saw the camera.

We couldn't hear what he was trying to say, of course, but from the size of his eyes he was clearly entering full panic mode. From the context, it was pretty obvious that the sounds coming from behind the gag - had the gag not been in place - would have translated to a demand to not take photos, with probably a few threats thrown in for good measure.

Veronica ignored him. Anna approached him and began by rubbing her breasts against his body. Veronica's camera clicked and flashed happily away.

Then Kevin replaced Anna on the floor in front of the cross, and posed for some particularly juicy images involving oral gratification of a prime portion of the Senator's anatomy. The anatomy cooperated rigidly.

The two alternated for a while, until Anna took matters in hand - literally - and decided to step up the pace.

She was clearly enjoying herself, which is not something that could be said for the Senator.

Or rather, for *most* of the Senator.

See, that's the thing about a penis - it's really not under a guy's control. It's its own man, so to speak. I mean, here's a guy who clearly doesn't *want* to engage in the act currently being perpetrated upon him because he knows he could face public humiliation and professional ruin as a result. And yet there's his penis, hard as a rock and happy as the proverbial clam because a pretty girl is doing fun things to it. It's like the brain is screaming "No! No!" as it's starved of blood, while two feet further down his tumescent member is going "Yes! Yes! Vo-dee-do!" and having the time of its life.

Finally, as things, well, *came* to a... conclusion, Kevin replaced Anna at the critical moment, which was immortalized by a perfectly timed click of Veronica's camera.

With the good senator still yelling unintelligible obscenities through his gag, Veronica and Anna reviewed the images on the camera. They lingered over a wonderfully graphic shot from the climactic moment.

"Huh," Veronica said. "I didn't notice before, but he's got that big crucifix dangling from his neck. It shows up rather nicely in this shot."

"Wow," Anna replied. "Gives a whole new meaning to the expression 'coming to Jesus'."

"Yep," Veronica said with a self-satisfied smile as she looked through a few more images. "That oughtta do it."

"Not quite," Anna said. Veronica looked at her questioningly. Anna picked up and opened the plastic container with the liver juice in it. She proceeded to smear some over Rumor's thighs.

Anna turned to me. "Here Jack! Come get a treat!"

You can't be serious.

Veronica erupted in laughter about the same time the Senator gave what sounded like a scream from behind the gag.

I thought about it for a few seconds.

The perversity.

The shame.

The indignity.

The taste... ah, the taste!

Oh, what the hell.

A couple of minutes later, Veronica turned to Rumor and held up the camera for him to see. On the screen was a perfectly exposed, perfectly focused image of the gay-bashing conservative politician being terminally pleasured by a hairy guy in a French maid's outfit.

"The feather duster's a nice touch, don't you think?" Anna said.

More muffled obscenities erupted from behind the gag.

Veronica flipped through to the next photo, an image of an obviously still aroused State Senator being licked with shameful enthusiasm by a pit bull. She held up the camera again so he could see the screen.

"Woof!" said Anna. Rumor blanched. "Nice tongue, Jack!" she said to me.

I do have a freakishly long tongue.

"Now, you hypocritical piece of shit," said Veronica. "Let's talk about your career."

Senator Rumor remained tied up while Veronica downloaded the images from her camera. She selected the best ones, then copied them onto a flash drive that she gave to Anna. She wasn't taking any chances. She didn't *think* he'd pay a burglar to break into her house and erase everything from her computer while she was out, but you could never tell with politicians. Better to play it safe and have backups elsewhere.

Finally she and Anna returned to the dungeon. Kevin stayed upstairs and busied himself dusting.

Apparently he was taking his role as a maid very seriously.

"Now," said Veronica, "we are going to be a very good boy, aren't we?" She didn't wait for a response. "We're going to have a little chat. After that I'm going to release you, and you're going to calmly put on your clothes and leave. Do not pass Go, do not collect $200. Got it?"

The senator remained motionless; there was no nod of agreement, and his eyes continued to radiate anger. Veronica sighed. She picked up a pinwheel device, designed to be run over the flesh and leave little red tracks in its wake.

"If you do not agree, I will put some marks on your body with this that you will have a very hard time explaining to your long-suffering wife - and Anna here will throw in a few hickeys for good measure." Anna, who was standing with her arms folded, nodded enthusiastically.

"Do you understand, Senator?" Veronica asked.

Finally, Rumor nodded.

"Okay. Here we go."

She removed the ball gag from his mouth.

"You fucking bitch!" he yelled. "You'll never get away with this!" Veronica sighed again. She and Anna exchanged glances.

"He really doesn't get it, does he?" Anna said. "Oh well, time for some embarrassing marks." She advanced towards his neck as Veronica placed the pinwheel against his chest.

"Stop! Stop!" he said. "Okay, okay, you win. Fuck!"

"That's better," Veronica said. "Good boy."

"I suppose you're going to blackmail me now. Is that what this is about?"

"Well, yes," Veronica admitted. "Sort of. But we don't want money."

Rumor looked confused. "You don't? What else do you want then?"

"We want a religious conversion," Veronica said.

"You want *what?*"

"Senator, you have a dismal track record regarding the rights of women and gays. That is going to change." Rumor rolled his eyes.

"You are going to suddenly have an epiphany, and start supporting gay rights, and a bit later we're going to talk about legalizing sex work in this state."

"You're out of your mind," Rumor said. "That's never going to happen."

"And," Veronica continued, ignoring his response, "you have some legislation that's before your Committee right now - it's a bill about further criminalizing sex work. I'm suggesting to you that it would not be in your personal interest for that legislation to leave your Committee and see the light of day."

"*Strongly* suggesting," Anna clarified.

"You're both crazy," Rumor said. "As soon as I get out of here I'm going to call the police and tell them you're blackmailing me."

Veronica sighed. "Seriously? That's your best response?"

"So lame," said Anna.

Veronica held up the camera again. "I really don't think you're going to do that, Senator. Look," she said patiently, "you have a choice between blocking some shitty legislation, *and* becoming a lot more civil in your stance on gay rights, or waking up one day to find photos of yourself all over the Internet - and possibly on the front page of the *New York Post -*"

"Oh, I *love* the *New York Post!*" Anna interjected. "They have such funny headlines. I can see it now: *THE RUMORS ARE TRUE.*"

"- photos showing you dressed like a drag queen," Veronica continued, "and cavorting with a dog and a guy in a maid's costume." She turned to Anna. "Does that sound like a difficult choice to you?"

"It does not," Anna averred.

"Now, if you agree to this, you have my word that those photos will never see the light of day and you can continue your disgustingly hypocritical political career."

Rumor laughed grimly. "Your word? That's rich. Why should I trust the word of a whore?"

She ignored the insult. "Because, Senator, unlike you I am actually an honorable person, and I keep my promises. But," she added breezily, "it's your choice. If you feel like embracing personal and political ruin, go right ahead. I'm sure your wife will love the pictures."

Rumor was obviously weighing the consequences of his options. Finally he said, "If I start supporting gay rights and legalization of prostitution, that's political suicide anyway for me."

"I doubt it," Anna replied. "If you were some state senator from Alabama, probably. But you're not. By some fucking miracle - delivered by a god with a sick sense of humor - you got elected here in the liberal Northwest. By a very slim margin, if I recall."

"Yeah, and only because you were running against a moron," Veronica added. "A more liberal stance on certain issues would probably do you the world of good in the upcoming election - not to mention two years from now when you run for national office. God help us."

Rumor considered; the logic did actually make some political sense. "I suppose I have no choice, do I?"

"Not really," said Veronica. "And who knows, you might actually turn into a human being in the process."

"I doubt that," Anna said.

"Just think of us as lobbyists," added Veronica. "Except instead of playing golf or taking you out for expensive dinners we save you from yourself."

Rumor scowled, and thought some more.

"Okay," he said finally.

"Okay?" repeated Veronica. "Does that mean you agree to pull the bill?"

"Yes."

"And promote legalization of sex work?"

"It's not that easy. But yes, I can set up a task force to look into it - or something like that."

"Do I have your word, Senator?"

He sighed. "Fuck. Yes, you have my word."

"Thank you. You have seven days to make good on your promise." She paused. "Now, when I release you, don't get any ideas. Anna here is a black belt."

This was a lie - Anna had taken a single karate class a couple of years back, but quit because she didn't like how it messed up her hair. Still, when she's mad Anna can be pretty freaking intimidating - and you already know how good she is with a baseball bat.

"And," added Veronica for good measure, "my pit bull here is attack-trained."

It's lucky dogs can't laugh. Either this was a patent bluff, or Veronica was still deluded by the memory of me "rescuing" her from the mugger in the park. As noted previously, that was based upon chance and a misunderstanding; but Veronica didn't know that - and neither did Rumor.

"Okay," he said. "Just let me go."

She untied him from the cross, legs first, then wrists. He stretched and flexed his muscles to restore the circulation to his limbs, then began putting on his clothes, pants first.

When he was fully dressed, he lost no time in heading upstairs. We all followed. As he opened the front door and was about to leave, he turned and looked at Veronica.

"You people are sick," he said. "You disgust me."

Veronica remained calm, and smiled. "Glass houses, Senator. Glass houses," she said as he walked out the door.

Three days later, Senator Dick "Catkins" Rumor surprised both the press and the Republican caucus with an announcement regarding the bill to increase criminal penalties for sex work. He said that, after much reflection and searching of his heart - and after consulting the "timeless wisdom of the New Testament" - he had decided that the bill was "misguided" and that he would not permit it to pass out of his Committee. After all, he said, Jesus was beloved by a prostitute, and his compassion for her was something we could all hold up as an example. In fact, he added, he was going to initiate a fact-finding task force to examine whether a more enlightened approach to the world's oldest profession was perhaps better than criminalization.

When asked by a stunned reporter whether that meant he thought prostitution should be legalized, he demurred. "I believe we should look at all sides of the issue," was all he would say.

"Well, it's a start," Veronica said over margaritas later that day.

"The Jesus part was a nice touch," Anna noted.

"Jesus my ass," replied Veronica. "What a scumbag."

"And Mary Magdalene wasn't a prostitute, by the way," Anna - ever the sexual historian - pointed out. "Common misconception. Still," she added, "the guy kept his word."

"Amazing."

"And they say that the common folk can't make a difference in the political process."

Veronica raised her glass. "Here's to participatory democracy," she said.

Comings & Goings

The Winter Of Our Content

So, to review. In the past three months, we had: been ratted out by a psychic, repelled numerous crazy people, buried one cat, turned another into a sex object, horrified Veronica's mother, blackmailed a politician, heard the ultimate faery tale, and fallen in love with a little girl and her dog. Did I miss anything?

And so, not surprisingly, by the time October rolled around we were all ready for some peace and quiet. And things indeed became sweetly uneventful for awhile. Winter slowly descended, and with it a pleasant domestic tranquility (and, inevitably for Seattle, rain).

Veronica conducted several sessions a week with various clients, earning herself a considerable sum, and her bullwhip a growing reputation. She even gave it a name; and soon the masochists who gathered at *Pussy Whipped* - the local BDSM club where Veronica would occasionally show up to troll for clients - began to whisper in awed tones about *Franz* and the alluring dominatrix who wielded him. The name, Veronica averred, had to be Teutonic.

Meanwhile, Anna surprised us all by summarily ditching her three existing boyfriends and replacing them with a single substitute. His name was Tom. A local architect in his late 30's, he exhibited no obvious signs of derangement, was good to Anna, and was enough of a pervert that he was actually very turned on by the idea of having a prostitute for a girlfriend.

To say that he and Anna were sexually compatible was an understatement: whenever Veronica called that winter, it seemed that Anna was in bed with her new boyfriend.

"God, are you two fucking *again*?" asked Veronica one day when it was obvious that Anna was being pleasured as she chatted.

"You're just jealous."

"Yes, probably," she admitted.

"When's the last time you got laid, anyway? I've been meaning to ask."

"You don't want to know."

"Yes I do - I'm naturally nosey."

"Six months ago."

"*Seriously,* Vee? God, I worry about you sometimes."

"Maybe I can borrow Tom some evening."

"Fine with me. And I'm sure fine with him too - he says he's never had a redhead."

"Anyway," said Veronica, "are you pre- or post-bonk right now?"

"Just post," Anna replied. "But Tom's still being *very* attentive." Suddenly she said, "O shit, is that the time? I have a client coming in under an hour!" Then, apparently to Tom, she added, "Yes, dear, we can come back to bed later. Now shoo - someone else needs to use my vagina."

In other news, visitations to the Demon Cat shrine - and presumably also to *Bares in the Trees* - declined in direct correlation with the falling temperatures. Veronica, Anna and Tom drove down one afternoon in early November to "pay their respects to Veronica's pussy", as Anna put it.

Mirakel greeted them warmly, eyeing me in the process. "And how's the doggie?" she asked, a touch too hopefully, I thought. "He looks a bit under the weather."

She accompanied us down to the grave site, enthusiastically pointing out new arrivals. "In the past month we've had eleven cats, six dogs, two parakeets and an iguana named Charlie," she enumerated.

We approached Demon Cat's grave. "Wow!" exclaimed Veronica and Anna together; it was awash in flowers, both real and plastic.

"Gosh," said Anna. "Dear puss has been venerationally inflorinated."

Veronica looked at her askance. "One of these days I wish you'd learn to speak English, or at least use words that us common folk can understand." She turned to Mirakel. "Sorry," she said, by way of explanation, "she has a Ph.D."

"Ah," replied Mirakel, "I see."

There were various cards and little signs accompanying the small mountain of flowers. Veronica picked up random examples and read them aloud. "We'll miss you." "Forever in our hearts." "You gave us so much joy in life." And - rather less charitably - "I hope you ripped that dog's balls off."

Earl appeared as we were leaving and proffered a cheery hello. Presumably in deference to the changing weather, the towel had been replaced by a terrycloth bathrobe. One did have to wonder whether Earl possessed any actual clothes.

"Gotta thank you," he said to Veronica. "Membership in the camp is up fifteen percent! Your pussy gets a lot of visitors."

"So does Anna's," Veronica replied.

"Oh, you have a cat too?" asked Mirakel.

"No," Anna said, and left it confusingly at that.

As usual, I spent part of every day with Isaac. In the afternoons we went for a walk, or if the weather was poor we settled down in front of the fire and he read to me. He began by reading *The Incredible Journey*, mostly because I asked for a book about dogs. I enjoyed it, though I could never understand why they didn't eat the Siamese cat somewhere along the way. I mean, they were hungry and they were in the Canadian wilderness for God's sake - no one would ever know. Lately we've moved on to *Harry Potter*.

Veronica and Alice talked or texted every day, and we drove out to the lake almost every weekend. Sometimes Isaac joined us; in late January Veronica essentially dragged him out there for a surprise birthday party that she and Alice had conspired to arrange. There was often snow on the way on these trips, but Veronica refused to let weather be an obstacle to her commitment;

and anyway, her all-wheel drive car negotiated even the back roads of Chelan with comparative ease.

With each visit, Veronica and Alice became closer - as did Rachel and I. In an encouraging sign, I started openly calling Rachel my girlfriend, and she didn't object.

The situation with Sal Kaufman appeared to be, if not good, at least stable. He continued to drink and occasionally yell at Alice for no good reason, but for the most part - as long as the support checks kept coming in from her trust fund - he cared too little about his young charge to place much restriction on her movements. So when she announced each Saturday night that she would be having a sleep-over with a friend again, he didn't object or even bother to ask who she was visiting. He was happy not to have her around, since that meant he could drink with his redneck buddies every weekend. On Sunday evenings when Alice returned, the house was always a mess, and it usually fell to her to clean it up.

Saturdays became everything to Alice, and she would spend the entire week planning a meal or some fun activity for Veronica for that sacred night. For her part, Veronica always brought some small special treat for her: a toy, a favorite food, or - more often - a new book. Alice was a voracious reader.

Isaac watched all this with growing affection for both of them. "Ah Jack," he said to me one day as Veronica and Alice were busily making a meal together in the kitchen, accompanied by seemingly unending laughter, "I do so wish there was a way to take that disgusting man out of Alice's life."

Remember the demi-gods? Apparently they were listening again - and this time, in a rare moment of magnanimity, they decided to do something that was actually useful.

But now your narrator is getting ahead of himself. Bad dog!

Visitor

And so a snowy winter passed slowly into a soggy spring. It is now April in my story, and for want of anything better to do on a drizzly Friday I am gazing out of our living room window to the street beyond. No squirrels.

I am about to desert my rodent monitoring station and think about giving Bonkers a good lick - he's fast asleep and he hasn't had a frenzied ritual cleaning session in a couple of weeks - when suddenly I see Isaac walking down the road, arm in arm with a young woman I don't recognize. She has red hair like Veronica, and is clothed in a long blue dress made from what looks like velvet. It's an unusual dress - one that belongs to another age, a more romantic one than this.

Isaac is smiling as he approaches his house; he looks very happy. The woman briefly glances in my direction and I catch a glimpse of her eyes. Green. Then she and Isaac disappear through the front door.

I debate whether to go over to Isaac's house. I don't want to intrude, but I'm very curious about his beautiful, mysterious visitor. Could it really be...? No - surely she is too young to be Rowan.

Half an hour later the suspense is killing me, and I exit the house through the dog door and walk over to Isaac's back yard. I bark - the signal that I'd like to be let in - and twenty seconds later the back door opens and Isaac admits me.

"Come in, Jack," he says. I walk with him into the living room, expecting to see the woman there too, but strangely there is no trace of her except for a lingering fragrance of wildflowers hanging in the air.

Um, what happened to... I begin.

"Ah, you saw her then?" Isaac replies.

Yes, I saw you walk into the house. Was that...? I hesitate.

"Rowan? No, Jack. Rowan can return only once more now. The woman you saw was Gwyn."

Your daughter? I'm stunned.

"Yes, my daughter. The first time I've seen her in many years."

But she's so young.

"Yes, but remember that she is part Fay, and Fay do not age in the Summerland where they live. She is actually 51 years old now."

She looks barely twenty.

"As you will recall, she was sixteen when she left. She has aged little since then, at least physically."

You must have been thrilled to see her.

"Well yes, but it's rather a case of good news, bad news, I'm afraid."

Why bad news? I'm concerned now.

He sighs. "You may recall from my story that Fay sometimes have premonitions of things that are about to happen."

Yes. What's about to happen? I realize my heart is beating faster now, because I fear the answer to the question.

"Gwyn's appearance... well, it signals that I am not long for this world, I'm afraid."

No!

"Don't be sad, Jack. I don't want to die, but this means that I will - I hope - finally be reunited with Rowan and Gwyn."

You really believe this? Confronted with the reality, I realize that I have never quite believed it till now.

"I have to believe, my friend."

You can't leave me! What am I going to do without you?

"You'll look after Alice and Veronica - and terrorize a lot of squirrels, I imagine."

But...

Isaac kneels and holds me close. "I'm sorry, Jack. I don't want to leave you, I really don't. I'll miss you greatly - you're really my best friend here. But I'm old and weary, and it's time for me to move on."

I know he's right, but I can't help feeling a huge sense of impending loss.

When is this going to happen? I ask, after a pause.

"I don't know. Soon, I guess. I just need to make sure all my affairs are in order, as they say." Suddenly a ridiculous thought occurs to me.

But you can't *die.*

"Why not?"

Because we're only on book three of Harry Potter.

The Perils of Pastries

Death does not take Isaac immediately. However, it does stalk him - and it's nice enough to give him a warning shot as it does so.

A week after Gwyn's visit, we are alerted by sirens to the rapid approach of an ambulance, which stops right outside our house. Veronica stares out of the window with curiosity and detached concern... but I know with a heavy heart what its arrival portends.

I run into the street, and as soon as Veronica realizes that the ambulance has come for Isaac she hurries out to join me. The crew rushes into the house, and a few moments later re-emerges with Isaac on a stretcher. He is conscious, but it's clear that he is very ill indeed.

He smiles weakly as he passes Veronica and I, and murmurs, probably to me, "Heart attack... too many cream puffs."

"O God, Isaac," Veronica says. "Please be okay!" Then she turns to one of the crew and asks where they're taking him.

"Harborview," the man says abruptly, and barely two minutes later the vehicle is screaming down the street, sirens wailing, with Isaac inside.

Some time later, Veronica calls Harborview hospital, and they give her an update. I can't hear this because she doesn't have the phone on speaker, and since I can't talk to her it's impossible for me to ask how he's doing. But she calls Anna a little later, and tells her that Isaac has had a massive heart attack, and that he's in intensive care.

Veronica goes to visit him the next day. I desperately want to see him, and talk to him; but needless to say dogs are not welcome in the hyper-sterile atmosphere of a modern hospital. And without Isaac's presence, I realize how much I rely on my conversations with him, how much a part of my daily routine they have become. Without that conduit to the outside world, I'm suddenly lost.

Veronica returns two hours later, and she is very somber. In another call to Anna, she relays what they told her at the hospital: that while Isaac is stable for now, the chance of a second heart attack is high.

A second one that - and here I am still in denial - will in all likelihood kill him.

The Passage Home

"The world is but a bridge: pass over it, but build no house there. He who hopeth for an hour may hope for eternity. For the world is but an hour: spend it in devotion - the rest is worth nothing."

Inscription, Fatehpur Sikri, India

Two weeks go by. Isaac returns from the hospital, weak but stable. I spend much time with him in his house, and Veronica insists on coming over every day to cook and clean. After awhile, things take on the illusion of the normal, and I'm quietly hopeful that he will make a slow recovery after all.

But the following month I am lying on my day bed on a Friday afternoon, thinking about nothing in particular and watching Veronica, who is stretched out on the couch reading a book.

And suddenly I am gripped by terror, and by the certain knowledge that something bad is happening to Isaac. I don't know how - I don't hear his voice, inside my head or out, but I just *know*. I know also that I must go to him, *now*.

I jump up and bolt to the dog door at the back of the house. Behind me, I hear Veronica call my name. "Jack? What the hell's the matter with you?" she yells, then adds, "Leave the squirrels alone!"

I run to the house and find the back door slightly open. Squeezing inside, I check the kitchen, then the living room. There is no sign of Isaac. I call out to him, then bark - something I rarely do. I hear a faint voice from the small spare bedroom where Isaac sometimes sits and reads. Running into the room, I see him stretched out on the bed, a hand on his chest. I stand by his side, and he puts a hand on my head.

Isaac! What happened? But I know.

He has difficulty speaking, but smiles at me weakly. "Hello Jack. I'm afraid this is the second heart attack they promised me." He pauses to catch his breath. "But how did you know? I called out to you, but in my mind only."

I don't know. I just knew suddenly that something was terribly wrong, and I came.

"You're a very remarkable dog," he says. He is struggling to get out the words. "And I'm so very glad you're here with me now. Thank you."

Isaac, please tell me you're going to be okay. I can try to get help.

With an effort, he shakes his head. "I'm afraid it's too late for that, my friend. It's time for me to go."

No! Don't leave me!

Isaac strokes my head. "Don't worry, Jack. You'll be fine. Look after Veronica. She's a very special woman."

But what am I going to do without you? Who will I talk to?

"It's okay, Jack. We'll meet again one day, I hope. Death is just the beginning of another phase in the journey."

So you're sure there's really life after death?

"Yes, I am."

You mean Madame Lulu was right?

He manages a smile. "Madame Lulu is an idiot."

We sit in silence for a while. His breath comes weakly, and I am gripped with a rising sense of loss as my best friend slowly slips away from me. It's paralyzing.

He puts his hand on my head and with an effort turns to look at me. "Jack, my dear friend. It has been a great privilege to know you," he says. "But I must go now. They are waiting."

No! Please don't go! Not yet, not yet!

He squeezes my paw, and some animal instinct deep within me knows that this is the moment it all ends.

I lick his face, willing him to stay. In response, there is the faintest trace of a smile.

One more breath, and then he is gone.

Rowan

Dogs don't cry, but we do feel a keen sense of grief.

I look at Isaac, now peaceful in death, and I think how strange it is that this body remains; yet the man, the spirit that was Isaac, is gone. He looks exactly the same as he always did, and he has that Isaac smell that I now realize I have always found somehow oddly comforting; yet he himself is no longer inhabiting this familiar shell.

I press my muzzle against his face and feel the warmth of his skin.

Where have you gone, my friend?

"He has gone home. Do not be sad." A woman's voice.

Startled, I turn towards her. And there, standing by the window, framed in light, is the most beautiful woman I have ever seen. She is wearing a long dress of forest green, and she looks like she just stepped out of a Pre-Raphaelite painting. Her red hair cascades over her shoulders, and even from here I can see that her eyes are a striking shade of green. She is quite literally radiant, outlined by a soft, faint glow.

You're Rowan? I ask, although I know the answer.

The woman nods, and smiles. "Yes, I am Rowan. And you are Jack. He has told me about you."

So this is her. The woman I have heard so much about, the woman Isaac loves, is standing here before me, finally. She really isn't a figment of Isaac's imagination.

Is he... with you now? I ask.

"Yes, Jack, he is here. Not in this room, but he has passed into my realm."

And where is "here", exactly? I ask.

"Here is the Summerland. What humans call Faery. It is my home - and his now."

Does everyone go there when they die?

"No, Jack. Humans can enter the Summerland only if they are invited, and only when they die. It is quite rare."

What about dogs? I realize this is a blatantly self-interested question, and I feel a little guilty for asking.

Rowan smiles. "Yes, dogs too. If invited." She pauses. "But I think we can make room for you, when the time comes."

I feel an overwhelming sense of relief, and joy, at the knowledge that I will one day be reunited with Isaac, and that I will in some form live on. I am tempted to enquire whether there are squirrels in the Summerland. Or cats - the idea of sharing an afterlife with Bonkers isn't especially appealing. But I refrain. Instead, I ask a more serious question.

Why did you choose him? Why a mortal human?

"Because of the wood," she replies. "Long ago, when he was a boy. Because he believed. Among humans, such faith is very rare, Jack. Some children have it, but most lose their faith when they grow up. Isaac never did. He always believed in Magic."

Some kids believe in Santa Claus too, but I suppose he doesn't really exist.

"No, I'm afraid he doesn't," Rowan replies. She pauses. "But the Easter Bunny is real."

Seriously?

She laughs mischievously. "No, of course not."

But what about the child? Gwyn?

"She is here too. He will see her again soon." This makes me very happy, knowing that Isaac will soon be reunited with his daughter.

"When she was young, Gwyn could come and go between worlds," Rowan continues, "because she is half human and half Fay. But now she spends most of her life with us, on this side. Coming here has a cost, even for her." I remember what Isaac told me, and understand.

We are silent for a while, and I look at Rowan more closely. It is easy to see why he fell in love with this woman. She is strikingly beautiful; but more than that she clearly has a keen intelligence, and she exudes kindness and warmth.

Rowan?

"Yes, Jack?"

Tell him.... tell him that I love him.

She smiles warmly. "He knows. He loves you too."

I know. I miss him already. I'm so used to having someone to talk to, you know?

Rowan nods. "Well, perhaps I can help with that."

I look at Isaac's body again. And I suddenly realize that no one outside this room knows that he is dead.

I suppose I should try to somehow tell someone that he's gone, I say.

"No need," Rowan replies. "The someone has already been summoned."

What, did you just dial 911 when I wasn't looking? I realize this is flippant, but the practicality of a real live faery managing to call Emergency Services is hard to get my head around.

Rowan laughs. "No, I didn't do that. But someone will come - you'll see."

And sure enough, a moment later there is a hesitant knock on the front door. There is a pause, and the door opens slowly, as if the person entering is fearful of invading Isaac's privacy.

"Is anyone home? Isaac?" I am surprised to see Veronica poke her head around the bedroom door. Then she sees Isaac on the bed, and cries out in alarm.

"Isaac! Oh my God! Isaac! Jack. O Jack!"

She kneels by the bed and puts her head on Isaac's chest, crying. I nuzzle up against her, wanting to tell her that it's okay, that he's gone to a better place. But of course I can't.

She raises her head and wraps her arms around me. "O Jack," she sobs. "I'm so sorry."

We remain in this embrace for a while, she petting me and I gently licking her face. From the corner, Rowan watches and smiles. A sad smile, but a fond one, full of affection.

Veronica wipes her eyes, heaves a deep sigh, and looks around the room.

"O God. I'm not very good at this," she says. "I don't really know who to call."

I find it strange that she is now looking directly at Rowan, but not acknowledging her presence in the room. I address Rowan. *Um, look, I can't exactly make the introductions here, and anyway what would I say?*

"Veronica, this is Rowan. She's a faery - not the kind we have here on Capitol Hill - and she's borderline immortal. You know, nothing you don't run into every day in the produce section of the local Safeway."

JACK

"You're very amusing, Jack." It's Rowan speaking. And I suddenly realize from Veronica's lack of reaction that she can't see her standing there.

She can't see or hear you, can she?

"No, Jack, she cannot. I can make myself effectively invisible at need."

Yeah, I remember - the trick in the woods. Isaac told me about that. You scared the crap out of him.

She laughs. "I remember." There is a pause. "Look, I have to go now, Jack. But I must do something first. A little gift for you."

Meanwhile, Veronica stands up, wipes more tears from her face, and sniffs. "Okay, I guess I'll call 911 or something."

And while she is standing there trying to collect herself, Rowan walks over and puts a hand on her head. Veronica suddenly freezes, her eyes closed; though I sense that her reaction is not because she feels Rowan's touch. Rather it is as if Time is suddenly paused, the moment suspended.

Rowan bows her head and whispers some words I cannot catch. Then she releases Veronica. Her eyes open abruptly, and she shakes her head. There is a sharp intake of breath.

Rowan smiles at me. "Goodbye, Jack," she whispers. "I give you my blessing." She blows me a kiss as she fades, and then she quite literally disappears into thin air.

And I am left with Veronica, who looks around nervously, as if seeking the source of the sudden, very strange discomfort she is feeling.

Finally she exhales loudly and announces, to the room in general, "Jesus Christ! I don't know what just happened, but I feel *very* fucking weird."

Insane

"There is a pleasure sure in being mad which none but madmen know."
  - John Dryden

A few moments later, Veronica and I are in the bedroom waiting for the ambulance that she has just called for. Veronica is sitting on the edge of the bed; she looks at Isaac and starts to cry again.

"O God, this is so *unfair*. He was such a wonderful man. And," she adds bitterly, "fucking Dick Cheney is *still* alive."

The continued and unwarranted existence on the planet of the former Vice President when so many good people die is a source of frequent complaint on Veronica's part. During the George W. Bush administration she drove around with a bumper sticker that read *IMPEACH BUSH - TORTURE CHENEY*. And she has widely let it be known that "when that bastard finally croaks, I'm going to throw a gigantic party and invite every liberal in Seattle."

I am touched by how fond she was of Isaac, and I desperately want to comfort her. I am so used to talking to Isaac that, without thinking, I look at her and say, *"It's okay, Veronica. He's gone home."*

Veronica suddenly sits bolt upright. She stands, looking nervously around the room. "Who said that?" she says, startled.

O my God. *She can read my mind*, just like Isaac! Really?

And then I understand: Rowan's gift.

I carefully consider my next move. After all, I am about to lead my human to the dramatic realization that her dog can talk to her. This is not something to be taken lightly: the news, and the shock, must be delivered gently, with great sensitivity and compassion.

But then, as I watch her pacing, a wicked thought occurs to me, and despite the dark solemnity of the occasion I can't help myself.

Veronica, sit! And then, for good measure, I add, *Stay!*

Veronica's head whips around, and there is a look of total confusion on her face. Now I feel guilty, and a little sorry for her.

Hi, Veronica. It's okay.

She looks down and sees me staring at her in what I hope is a friendly, comforting way. I wag my tail encouragingly.

Despite my efforts, she looks horrified. "Jack? What the fuck?!"

Yes, it's me. Jack. Your dog. By the way, I add, *you're looking very lovely today.*

Her mouth drops open and she puts a hand to her face. "O my God," she almost wails. "I'm going crazy. My dog is talking to me."

Don't be alarmed. It's very normal.

"NORMAL? What the hell? I can *assure* you that this is *very fucking far* from anything *remotely fucking normal*."

I have to concede the point. *Well okay, it's not normal. But it's real, and you're not crazy. It's... well, it's rather complicated.*

"Complicated? It's fucking insane, is what it is. I am going batshit crazy insane." She now has both hands to her face, and she covers her eyes.

You know you really shouldn't swear so much. You're much too classy for that.

She opens her hands and looks down at me. "What, now my dog is giving me lectures on morality? What are you, Miss fucking Manners? Oh my God, I'm going nuts. I'm hearing voices. And I'm *talking* to them!"

Veronica, you're not crazy. Calm down and I'll try to explain.

I am trying to think of how to tell her about all this, about Isaac and Rowan and the whole crazy reality of it, but suddenly there is the sound of a siren in the distance. The ambulance is arriving.

Um, well, I say uncertainly. *Maybe we should postpone the explanations until later.*

"Yeah," she replies. "And maybe I should just take a handful of Valium, go to bed and hope that when I wake up in the morning this will all have been some weird fucking dream."

The ambulance pulls up outside and Veronica tries to collect herself. She starts to walk towards the hallway to open the front door.

I suddenly feel great affection for this woman who swears like the proverbial sailor and essentially tortures men for a living, but who really does have a heart of gold. On an impulse, I say, *Veronica... Thank you for looking after me. I'm grateful, and I love you.*

She looks down at me and bursts into a fresh set of tears.

"O God," she says. "O my fucking God."

Explanations

Two hours later, we are sitting in our living room. Isaac's body has been taken to a funeral home, and the necessary phone calls have been made. Veronica has a large bottle of Russian vodka in front of her, a sizeable portion of which is currently sloshing around in her gastrointestinal system and is well on its way to poisoning her liver.

I have just finished explaining to her the whole story. Isaac, Rowan, their child. The connection with Alice and Rachel. She gets the whole shebang, magic and mystery and all. And all told to her by her dog, a fact which continues to disturb her only slightly less than it did a couple of hours ago.

When I have finished, Veronica pours another drink and looks down at me with furrowed brow.

"So let's see... I'm supposed to believe - from my talking dog, mind - that Isaac has gone off to live with some magical chick in Fairyland? A sort of happy-ever-afterlife? Seriously?"

Honestly, is that really any weirder than the fact that you're currently having an extended conversation with your dog?

"No... I mean yes, yes it is. O God, I don't know. This is insane." She knocks back another shot.

You're going to regret all this vodka in the morning, I admonish.

"Screw that. I already do. But drinking myself into a stupor may be the only rational way for me to process the uber-weird events of this very memorable day. May the tenth - the day Veronica officially went nuts."

I put a paw on her knee and look up at her. *Veronica, other than all this, do you feel insane?*

Veronica considers for a moment. "Well, no, I suppose not." Then she adds, "But you have to admit that talking with a dog is a pretty powerful argument for crazy."

I decide to try another tack.

Do you want to have sex with Leroy?

"What?"

Leroy Fawkes, our charming next-door neighbor - would you have sex with him?

She looks insulted. " No! Ugh! Of course not!"

Well then, you're probably not insane.

At this, Veronica actually manages a laugh. She shakes her head in continued disbelief, but she is smiling. "You're a pretty funny dog," she says. "Quite the canine comedian."

Thank you. I have my moments.

"Well," she says after a pause. "If all else fails, I suppose we could run away and join the circus with a magic act. The Amazing Veronica and Her Telepathic Dog."

Or we could write a book about a dominatrix and the homeless dog she rescued. We could call it "Fifty Shades of Stray".

She is still smiling. We are, it seems, over the hump.

True Confessions

It is now the following day, and things have calmed down. Except that Veronica had to break the news of Isaac's death to Alice, who sobbed uncontrollably in response. Veronica promised to come out to Chelan as soon as she could.

In terms of what might be called her New Reality, Veronica seems to be slowly accepting the wackiness of the situation, to believe the unbelievable without feeling the need to check herself into the nearest nut house.

"Please tell me you haven't been wandering around the greater Seattle metropolitan area telling every dog, person or passing squirrel the sordid details of what goes on in my dungeon?"

No, of course not. I do have some sense of discretion, you know.

"Well, that's a relief."

Suddenly her eyes widen as she remembers something, and a realization hits her.

"Oh my God! The talking dog! You *were* the talking dog!"

Um, yes, I admit. *In a manner of speaking, anyway.*

"So those morons from the TV station were actually right?"

Well, not exactly. I explain, telling her the story of Madame Lulu, how the version of events that she apparently passed on to dear Digby James was exaggerated, but with a kernel of truth at its core.

Isaac felt pretty bad about what happened actually, especially afterwards with all the Fans-of-Bonkers.

"As well he should have!" she replied, but with a smile.

While I'm at it, I also explain why I peed on the cat.

This detail produces much laughter as Veronica recalls Bonkers and his little wet head. "I don't think he's ever forgiven you, you know."

Look, Bonkers is a cat. He's never forgiven me for anything, starting with the inexcusable crime of my being a dog. If you hadn't noticed, cats think everything and everyone in the known universe is beneath them. Besides, you're the last person who should be criticizing - because of you he ended up covered in, well, other bodily fluids.

She laughs again. "O God yes, I'd forgotten about that! Poor Bonkers."

Since we are in honesty mode, I decide it's time to finally set the record straight about something else.

Um, Veronica, I have a confession to make.

"Another one? And what, dearest dog, would that be?"

Remember the day we met?

"When you rescued me from the mugger? Of course I do - you saved my life."

Um, yes. Well... about that... Now that I've started down this road, I'm finding that it's rather awkward.

"What about it? I'll always be grateful for what you did."

Yes, well... there's something you should know about that night.

And I proceed to tell Veronica the true story of what really happened, and how my rescuing her was not heroic at all, just the happy coincidence of hunger and accident.

I hope you don't think less of me because of that, I say when my confession is complete.

Veronica stares at me blankly for a moment, and then she erupts in laughter. "O my God. You were going for the *sandwich*? That is fucking hysterical. And all this time here I was thinking you were the intrepid rescue dog."

My heart sinks; I drop my head and my ears, and look as ashamed as I suddenly feel. To mix mammalian metaphors, I am a hang-dog being sheepish.

Veronica sees my discomfort, and smiles. Then she gets down on her knees, puts her face close to mine and strokes my head. "O Jack," she says. "I could never think less of you. You're my best friend." At this, I look into her eyes, and I melt.

Of Beef and Bequesting

A few days after the funeral, Veronica received a phone call from Isaac's lawyer asking her if she could come to his office, where, he said, "you will learn something to your advantage." They arranged an appointment for the following morning.

"And I believe you are the guardian for Jack," the lawyer added. "Is that your child?"

"In a manner of speaking, yes," Veronica replied, without further explanation.

Ignoring the ambiguity in her response, the lawyer said, "Good. There's something in Mr Rosenberg's will for him too."

Veronica and I arrived at the lawyer's office promptly at ten a.m. the next morning. The lawyer looked at me and frowned.

"We don't usually allow dogs," he said. "But I suppose we can make an exception. Please sit down, Miss McKenna."

Veronica sat as instructed; I sat next to her.

The lawyer, whose name was Ernest Woodford, picked up a document from his desk. "Mr Rosenberg was quite a wealthy man, Miss McKenna. Apparently he had some rather profitable patents on inventions."

"Yes, he mentioned that to me once, though I didn't know he was wealthy, exactly."

"Oh yes. He also invested very wisely, apparently."

"That doesn't surprise me. He was a very smart man - and a wonderful person."

"Yes, indeed," Mr Woodford replied. "And after this morning you may well regard him as all the more wonderful."

Veronica gave the lawyer a curious look. "I will?"

"Yes." He flipped through the document in his hands. "This is his will. Mr Rosenberg left some small bequests to a few individuals, and also provided for a couple of his favorite charities."

"Oh. So is that why I'm here? I mean, am I getting one of the small bequests? That was awfully nice of Isaac, if so."

"Oh no, Miss McKenna, you're not one of the small bequests."

"I'm not?" Veronica looked a little disappointed. "So what am I doing here?"

"Because, my dear, after the charities, the funeral expenses and the minor bequests... well, he left the rest of his estate to you."

Veronica stared blankly. "I don't understand," she said.

Mr Woodford smiled at her from across the large oak desk. "I'm not going to enquire regarding the nature of your relationship with Mr Rosenberg, but he apparently thought very highly of you. And you are about to become a very wealthy woman."

Veronica's eyes were now stretched wide with genuine shock. "What? He left everything to *me?* Seriously?" she asked, stunned. She paused to take this in, then asked, "Um, how... wealthy, exactly?"

"Well, the investments alone are currently valued at close to two million dollars. And then there are the two properties in Seattle and Lake Chelan."

Fuck me! I said from down on the floor. I don't usually swear, but when you live with Veronica it's hard not to pick up bad habits. And if ever an item of news deserved an expletive-laden exclamation, this was it.

"No kidding," Veronica replied, glancing down at me.

"Excuse me?" asked Mr Woodford.

"Oh, nothing," Veronica said. "I... I honestly don't know what to say. This is a complete surprise."

"Yes, I imagine it is. A very pleasant one. Of course there is some paperwork to deal with, which I'll give to you before you leave. Oh, and he left this for you too." He handed Veronica a sealed envelope. "This will explain things, perhaps."

"Thank you," Veronica said as she took the envelope. She was still reeling from the knowledge of her impending change of fortunes.

"One more thing. There is a bequest for Jack - your child or ward or whatever he is."

"Really? What is it?" She looked down at me again.

"Mr Rosenberg specifically designated a bequest of a hundred dollars for him, with a rather odd stipulation attached to it."

"What was the stipulation?"

"That it be used to buy..." He studies the will, then says, "Well, I originally thought this must be a typo, but if it is I can't imagine what it's actually *supposed* to say."

"What *does* it say?"

"Well, to be honest, it says that it must be use to buy, well - beef liver." Veronica roared with laughter.

Mr Woodford smiled. "I take it from your amusement that the bequest makes some sort of sense, then? Perhaps you'd be good enough to explain," he said.

"Yes. Yes it does," she replied. Then she pointed down at me. "This," she said, "is Jack."

A Farewell

Veronica waited until we returned to the house to open Isaac's note.

"Well, Jack," she said, "I'd better pour myself a stiff drink for this. Get ready for waterworks."

She poured herself a shot of bourbon on some ice, sat in her favorite armchair, and slit open the envelope. Inside was a single sheet of ivory-colored paper, folded into three. She opened it; on it was a page of text written in Isaac's rather elegant hand.

Can you read it to me? I asked.

"I'll try," she replied, "though I suck at this sort of thing. I doubt I can get through it without making an idiot of myself."

She took a deep breath, and began to read.

My dearest Holly:

If you are reading this note, it means that I have left this life. For reasons that will become apparent later, I am not unhappy to do so, and I am hopeful that I shall continue to exist elsewhere; but now, as I write this to you shortly after my heart attack, I have no way of knowing whether that optimistic prediction will indeed come to pass. But do not grieve for me: if I'm right, then - as clichéd as it will sound - I am now in a much better place.

As you will know by now, I have left you almost all of my earthly possessions. They are of no use to me any more, and I have no children or close relatives to whom I can bequeath my wealth, such as it is. It may seem strange to you that you have become the beneficiary of my estate. It is strange to me too, in a way; but I have my reasons for this rather capricious act in my old age.

In your looks - and your kindness - you remind me of a woman I loved long ago, an extra-ordinary woman named Rowan to whom my heart will always belong. At the lake house you will find, in a large box on the top of a bookshelf in the living room, her story - our story. I ask that you read it without judging me as mad; you will understand why I say this when you have heard the tale. Do not make the mistake of thinking it is fiction: I assure you that it is all true.

When you have absorbed that strange narrative, you will perhaps understand why I am a firm believer in the seemingly impossible. And in that regard, I am probably foolish to entertain, even briefly, the preposterous idea that you are the reincarnation of my mother. That you were born an hour or so after she passed away is probably just a remarkable coincidence; but I would be lying if I said that this coincidence did not play at least some minor role in my decision to leave my estate to you. After the things I have seen in my life, I do not discount even the most bizarre occurrences as being something other than the product of mere chance.

Anyway, these ramblings of an old man aside, I hope that you can make good use of the bequest. I ask of you only two things. First, that you keep a close eye on Alice at Chelan. I know that you will: your kindness to her over the past months has moved me greatly, and I have watched with pleasure as the friendship between the two of you has grown under your care. I'm not sure you realize just how important you are to Alice now. I fear for her safety under the guardianship of that odious man, and hope that you can help her and guide her in her future life.

Second, take good care of Jack. I know this is a silly request, because you are already devoted to him, as he is to you. More than you know, actually. Jack is an extraordinary dog - I wish I could tell you just how extraordinary, but I fear that that revelation would push your opinion of me well over the edge into one where you regard me as certifiably insane. Anyway, I am most grateful that you loaned him to me so often: his friendship was a source of great comfort in these last years of my life. Hug him for me from time to time. And I hope he enjoys the little gift I've left him in my will!

As for you, Holly/Veronica, I wish you a long and happy life. You are a wonderful woman, deserving of good fortune and the true love I hope you find one day - as I did long ago.

Farewell now. It has been a privilege to know you.

With much love,

Isaac

Crying, Veronica put down the note, then lay down on the floor next to me and hugged me tightly. I licked her face.

"O Jack," she sobbed, and buried her face in my neck.

A little while later, she picked up the note again, and realized that there was a short postscript on the other side. She read it to herself, laughed loudly, and then turned to me.

P.S. I know this is going to sound utterly ridiculous - put it down to the eccentricity of an old man - but I'd like to ask one more favor of you. Could you please read the Harry Potter *books to Jack? You can start with book four.*

Snuggle Chat

Half an hour later, Veronica and I were curled up in bed together, snuggling. Her tears were exhausted.

"Was he really reading *Harry Potter* to you?" she asked.

Yeah. He read lots of things to me. Last winter we did Lord of the Rings.

"Seriously? *All* of it?"

Yes. I loved it. It's Alice's favorite too, by the way.

"Really?" She paused, thinking. "Do you know anything about this manuscript that Isaac referred to?" she asked.

Yes. He read me the whole thing. It's wonderful - a great love story.

Veronica pondered. "I'm very curious to read it. I mean, I know the basics from what you've told me..." She shook her head. "God, I still can't believe this."

What? The story about Rowan?

"No - the fact that my *dog* told me about this."

Well, if you think that's weird wait till you read the story.

"Okay. We'll go out to the lake house in a couple of days. And check on Alice and Rachel. I'd better make sure there's enough dog food in the house."

Talking of which...

"What?"

I believe that, as the beneficiary of Isaac's estate, you have an important job to do.

"I have quite a few of those right now. Which one were you thinking of?"

The most important one of all - the one where I get beef liver.

Chelan Again, Again

Two days later, we were back on the road, driving to Camp Fishless. Alice was at the house when we pulled in, and she immediately ran out from the back door and almost bowled over Veronica as she stepped out of the car. The two of them enjoyed a long hug, and when they finally separated I could see tears in Alice's eyes.

Veronica knew why she was crying, and she began to tear up too.

"I know, sweetheart," she said. "I can't believe Isaac's gone. He was such a wonderful man."

"It's so *unfair*," Alice said between tears. She looked up at Veronica with red eyes. "I really loved him," she said. "He was so good to me and Rachel."

"I know. I loved him too."

"And now," Alice continued, "it's really sad because we have no way to talk to Jack and... um, I mean..." She trailed off.

Veronica looked at her and frowned. "Wait - you *know* about that?"

"Um, about what?" asked Alice, who was suddenly trying her best to feign innocence.

"You know that Isaac and Jack could talk to each other?"

Alice looked at me. Since I can't talk to Alice, I wagged my tail instead.

"Um... yes?" she said, hesitantly.

Now it was Veronica's turn to look at me. "Jack?"

Veronica? I paused, she continued to stare, her hands on her hips. Finally I said, *Yes, yes - she knows.*

"Jesus Christ," Veronica said. "How many other people know I have a talking dog?"

Just you and Alice, that's it.

"Just me and Alice and a freaking TV crew," Veronica said. It was sweet that she moderated her swearing in front of a child.

Well yeah, but no one believes them.

"Thank God."

Now it was Alice's turn to be surprised. Despite the fact that she could hear only one side of this exchange, it was obvious to her that Veronica wasn't talking to herself, and she was looking back and forth between us as we talked.

"Wait," she said, "*you* can talk to Jack too?"

"Yes."

"Always?"

"No - just since Isaac died. It's a long story."

Well, I said, *I'm glad we cleared that up. By the way, where's Rachel?*

Veronica sighed. "Well, since you now know that I'm crazy too" - she raised her eyebrows and shook her head - "Jack wants to know where Rachel is."

"Oh," Alice said. "She's off in the woods somewhere. She'll be back soon."

And indeed, a moment later Rachel came tearing around the corner. She launched herself at my shoulder and knocked me flat, then proceeded to lick my face.

Veronica and Alice stood over us, laughing. "Well, well," said Veronica, "apparently Rachel missed Jack."

Rachel stopped licking and looked up. *"Yeah,"* she said. *"A little."*

Yes, I said to Veronica. *She says she can't live without me.*

Teeth in my butt. Ow!

"Why did she do that?" Veonica asked with a laugh.

Who knows? It's all part of being a bitch.

Rachel was about to nip me again, but then she stopped.

"Wait - you can talk to Veronica now?"

Yes.

"Since when?"

Since Isaac died, I said. *It's a long story.*

Poesy

We returned to Seattle a few days later, for there was much to be done. Veronica brought with her Isaac's story of his romance with Rowan, and read it over the next few days. She was in tears long before she finished the last page.

"God, this is amazing," she said to me. "It's so beautiful, and so sad. This really happened?"

Yes. Rowan is real - as I told you, I met her when Isaac died. So did you, sort of - she's the reason I can talk to you.

"Yeah," she said with a frown, "I'm not sure I'll ever completely adjust to that little wonder."

Veronica spent much of the next few weeks dealing with the legal and other necessities that followed Isaac's death and her new-found status as a woman of independent means. She conducted the occasional session with preferred clients - "more as a social service than anything else", as she told Anna - but for the most part she focused on various post-mortem tasks.

She decided to keep the lake house but sell Isaac's Seattle home. This was not difficult to do: the Seattle real estate market had been the hottest in the country for some time. When the house hit the market two weeks later, it sold in five days in a typical pattern: on the market Thursday, open house Sunday, accepting offers Monday. And indeed, at 5 pm on a Monday afternoon, the offers flooded in. Despite Veronica's realtor pricing the house high to begin with, it became the focus of a bidding war among buyers desperate to buy prime property on Capitol Hill, and sold for $150,000 over the asking price. Veronica was now even richer.

Before the sale, Veronica had to clear out the house - a not inconsiderable task, and one which had a somber beginning. She had that day collected the death certificate, which she took into the house and decided to set aside. She opened the drawer of Isaac's writing desk, and placed the paper certificate inside. She was about to close the drawer when suddenly she noticed that next to the document was Isaac's birth certificate.

A chill ran down her spine. Here was an entire life: 79 years of experiences and memories, from birth to childhood, through adulthood, work and various relationships, into old age and finally death; a life with all its innumerable sorrows and joys - all of it bracketed between two pieces of paper. Life is brief, she thought grimly, but bureaucracy never dies.

She closed the drawer and over the next two days sorted through Isaac's possessions. She kept a few that seemed to have some special significance, and donated the rest to charity.

Among the items she saved was a gold ring that Isaac had worn. She had noticed it while he was alive but had never enquired about it. It had been returned to her from the funeral home in a small envelope. She picked it up and examined it. It was a pretty ring, very unmasculine, she thought. The outside edge was engraved with a floral pattern within which was set four words in a language she did not recognize. *T'vyezh et ez vesta* the ring proclaimed.

An internet search of various translation engines came up blank. Curious, she showed the ring to Anna. "You're the historian," Veronica said. "Any idea what this says?"

"I'm a historian, darling, not a linguist."

"Yeah, but you have a Ph.D. Doesn't that make you an authority on everything?"

"Sadly not. Only on how to make yourself both useless *and* poor with a graduate degree." Anna examined the ring. "It's a poesy ring," she said.

"What's that?"

"Poesy rings were popular in the Middle Ages. They were given by lovers to each other and were inscribed with some sort of romantic sentiment. One of my clients gave me one a couple of years ago, actually - he was rather obsessed."

"What did it say?"

"It was cute, sort of. *I have wished for thee with all my heart.*"

"Did you accept it?

"Nooo! I told him he could wish all he wanted but my heart wasn't available, and my body was still $600 an hour. He was crushed, poor thing."

"You're a heart-breaker. Any idea what this inscription says?"

"Well, I don't know what the language is. But I'd guess that the first two words are *You and*. It's pretty similar to some other languages."

"Hmm, interesting. Are you making all this shit up?"

"No I'm not, for once." Anna has a habit of giving complex and completely specious answers to questions that come up in random conversations, and because she lies convincingly and has a doctorate people tend to believe her.

"Anyway," she said, "go talk to a linguistics person. Someone will know."

Later, when we were alone, Veronica looked again at the ring. "So who am I going to ask?" she said, aiming the question in my general direction. "Just any old professor of language?"

Try someone who speaks Basque, I said.

"Basque?"

Yeah.

"Why do you think that?"

Because I'm your super-smart dog. She shot me a cynical look. *Look, Isaac wore that ring always, which means it must have something to do with Rowan. She must have given it to him. So if it's that true, it's probably in her language. And I remember Rowan saying something in the story about that language being close to Basque.*

"That's remarkably insightful of you."

Yes. Probably I deserve some more beef liver.

"Ugh, I hate cooking that stuff. It smells vile."

Ignoring my desire for cow parts, Veronica returned to the computer and, after a quick search, sent an email to three academics in Europe who all listed Basque as their area of specialization. The first reply came back later that day. She read the email aloud.

Dear Miss McKenna. Thank you for your email. I do not recognize the language from your inscription, but you are correct that it is somewhat close to Basque.

"Ha, you *are* a super-smart dog," Veronica said.
And yet I still don't have any beef liver.
"Hush. I'll give you some later." She continued to read.

The first word is very different, but overall the wording is similar to the Basque phrase "Duzu eta es beste", which translated into English would be "You and no other."

"You and no other," Veronica repeated, and gazed wistfully into the distance. "That's so romantic." She sighed. "I really wish I could have met this woman." Then added, "Or whatever the hell she was."

See Spot Run

So in my little story it is now mid-July. And, after various short visits to Chelan following Isaac's death, we have recently returned here for an extended stay. Summer is in full swing, and the weather is gorgeous.

Alice comes to the house as often as she can, and is a frequent overnight visitor. Today, however, she has been tasked by Sal Kaufman with cleaning the house - a task made particularly arduous by the fact that the man is a total slob. Since he regards Alice as free labor, he sees no particular reason to be tidy or clean, and leaves pots, pans and dirty clothes lying around for her to pick up and wash. Alice resents this, of course, but knows that if she serves as his unwilling but compliant housemaid, he's less likely to stop her from spending lots of time with us.

It's a beautiful afternoon, bright and shining. I am stretched out on the deck, absorbing the warmth of the sun and simultaneously being cooled by a delicious breeze that is wafting in from the lake. I'm totally relaxed.

Veronica appears on the deck and fixes me with a sardonic gaze.

"My my, don't you look comfortable," she says.

I am indeed, thank you.

"I'm going to get some groceries for tonight," she announces. "Want to come with me?"

I ponder for a second, then say, *No thanks. I think I'll stay here. It's too warm and cosy to budge.*

She looks at me derisively and snorts. "So I suppose you're content to let your slave go off and shop for your dinner?"

Pretty much, I respond.

"Okay then," she says with a smile. "I'll be back in an hour or so. Try to stay out of trouble while I'm away." A moment later, I hear the sound of the car pulling out of the driveway, then lay my head back down and close my eyes.

What a wonderfully relaxing day. Maybe I'll take a nap.

Thirty minutes later, I am still sunning myself on the deck, wondering whether Veronica will remember to buy beef liver, when I look up to see Rachel approaching down the path at an astonishingly high rate of speed. Man, that girl can move.

"Jack!" she almost yells, leaping onto the deck in a single bound.

What is it?

"Where's Veronica?" There is an obvious urgency to her question.

She's not here. She went into town to buy food. What's wrong?

"It's Alice. Kaufman's really mad at her. He found her cell phone and read the things she was saying about him in all the texts she was sending to Veronica every day. He was swearing at her and threatening her, it was really bad. Then he banned her from ever seeing Veronica again. She sneaked out and was on her way here. But he came after her and caught her, and now he's dragged her off into the woods to punish her somehow. I'm really worried he'll do something bad."

What can we do?

"Well we can't wait for Veronica. We have to find them. Hurry!"

And without waiting for a response, Rachel takes off down the path into the woods, with me behind her, trying hard to catch up. I do, finally, but I can barely keep up with her. She is tearing along the path, which now ascends the side of a hill in a series of switchbacks. We run for a good half mile, heading in the general direction she thinks Kaufman has gone.

Suddenly, in the distance, we hear the unmistakable sound of a girl screaming. We increase our pace up the hill; Rachel is now ignoring the switchbacks and running directly up the slope between them. I have no choice but to follow her, but my lungs are burning.

Finally we burst through a dense cluster of oak trees and emerge into a semi-open area, at the far side of which a cliff drops steeply down into the woods below. And suddenly we both stop, shocked by the sight before us.

Sal Kaufman is standing at the top of the cliff. He has Alice by her ankles and is suspending her, upside down, over the edge.

Enter the Cavalry

As we approach, Alice continues to scream.

"Now see, this is what happens to bad little girls who don' do what they're told, see?' Kaufman says. "You ain't never gonna see that fucking bitch again, you hear? You do that shit again and maybe next time I'll just find myself lettin' go, and tellin' the world what a tragic accident just happened to my little girl."

Beside me, I can feel Rachel's fury, which exceeds even mine. She growls menacingly and bares her teeth.

Kaufman turns, and looks at us with a sneering contempt.

"So what do we have here? The fuckin' cavalry?" He pauses, swings Alice back from mid-air and drops her in a heap on the ground.

"It's time I fin'lly fixed you two once an' for all," he says, and moves to pull out the handgun that is lodged behind him in the waistband of his pants.

"No!" Alice screams, jumping up from the ground and hurling herself towards him. He turns, grabs her by the throat with one hand, and hits her across the face with the palm of the other, knocking her back to the ground.

"You little bitch!" he yells. "I'll deal with you later." Again he moves to retrieve the weapon at his waist. And three seconds later, the loaded gun is in his hand.

It is pointed directly at Rachel.

That Other Isaac

Upon every moment hangs a choice, upon every choice a different path, a diverging narrative.

A man, late for a meeting, crosses a street in a hurry and is hit by a car he does not see; abruptly, his narrative ends, the future snuffed out in an instant by a careless twist of Fate.

Or: he his not late, he takes more care, the car passes before he reaches the kerb; and his narrative duly blossoms. A wife, children, grandchildren; a long life and a prosperous future.

In a moment frozen in time, a man points a gun at a dog. Three paths, three possibilities.

One: the man changes his mind, and puts the gun away. He relents, perhaps even sees the folly of his anger and the meanness of his life. The chance of this narrative becoming reality: in this case, pretty much zero. Although Sal's brain possesses the same evolutionary architecture as every human, he himself is all reptilian core.

Two: he shoots the dog, then turns and shoots the other. And this specific narrative ends in mid-sent --

Three: some external force stays his hand.

Well, we have already ruled out Possibility One. And since I'm still here, Possibility Two obviously didn't happen.

Which leaves only Possibility Three...

I will never know what possessed me in that moment, nor what I was thinking. Actually, it was probably the fact that I *wasn't* thinking that freed me to make the decision that would change all our lives, and allow our narratives to continue. At that moment, I was nothing but pure rage. Rage at the cruelty of this ignorant, sadistic man towards a sweet little girl. And terror that the unthinkable was about to happen, that this disgusting, worthless human being was about to murder this beautiful creature with whom I'd fallen in love.

That I was certainly going to be next in the firing line never occurred to me.

Suddenly, I was no longer the cowardly fraud, the dog who rescued a girl from a mugger in the park under false pretenses, entirely by accident. For one brief, glorious moment, I was transformed. I was Lassie rushing to the rescue. I was Super Dog.

As Kaufman leveled the gun and took aim at Rachel, I sprang forward. With a growl whose ferocity surprised even me, I leapt at him, oblivious to the danger that this act presented to myself. I saw the hammer on the gun cocked back, and a split second later I struck Kaufman full force in the chest. The gun went off, and from somewhere nearby I heard Alice scream.

Newton - another Isaac - and his third law of motion: every action has an equal and opposite reaction. By all rights, I should have plunged over the cliff, but instead - thank you, Isaac - as Kaufman reflexively stiffened to try to hold his precarious position I found myself bouncing off his chest, and I landed on solid ground a few feet back from the edge.

But Kaufman himself had been knocked backwards, towards the edge... towards the yawning gulf of empty air beyond.

He hung there for a second, his arms cartwheeling in a desperate attempt to regain his balance. He wavered for a moment on the brink, and then with a shriek he fell. Out of the depths came his last wail, *Precious!* and he was gone.

Okay, so I stole that last bit from *Lord of the Rings*; it's actually one of my favorite scenes in the book. And you have to admit that Kaufman did have some personality traits that were distinctly Gollum-like.

Did. Were. Past tense. As in - mercifully - no longer existing. At least not in this realm.

I have no idea where that mean, shriveled little spirit has gone, but it sure as hell isn't the Summerland.

Post-mortem

Two dogs and an eleven-year-old girl are standing at the edge of a cliff, staring down at the crumpled, broken mess that a few moments before had been Sal Kaufman.

"Think he's dead?" asks Rachel.

I don't think he's alive.

"He looks kinda messed up."

Yep. I think he landed on his head.

"Is that blood leaking from his head?"
Well, it's probably not ketchup.
"I don't see any brains."
That's because he didn't have any.
We all continue to stare downward.
"Yep," says Rachel, "I'd say he's dead."
Yep.
"Ugh!" says Alice.
I'm thinking we shouldn't say too much about this, I say, after a pause. *I mean, about the exact manner of his demise.*
"You mean, we should omit the minor detail that he died because you pushed him off a cliff?"
Yeah, that. That's what I'm thinking.
"I'm thinking you're right."
There's another pause as we all take in the moment. Then Rachel delivers a particularly wet, sloppy lick to my nose, and presses her muzzle into my neck. And I am suddenly flushed with the elation of knowing that she's proud of me.
"Well, shit," says Alice finally.
We both stare at her. Surely she can't be feeling regret.
"Shit," she repeats, and she bends down to hug me. "Now I'm going to have to pretend to be upset."

Post-Mortem II

Two dogs and an eleven-year-old girl are trotting along a woodland path. The girl starts to skip and whistle a happy tune.
Um, I say, *I really don't think she should be looking so chipper right now.*
Rachel stops, sits on the path in front and looks pointedly at Alice. Alice stops skipping and looks at her.
"What?" she says. Rachel continues to stare.
"O yeah," Alice says, looking contrite. "Look upset. I forgot. Sorry." She rearranges her face into a caricature of despair. "How's this?" It's pretty funny, but Rachel isn't amused.
"Tell her to take this seriously," she says.
I can't talk to her, remember?
"Oh, right. Well, tell Veronica to tell her to take this seriously. She has to play the distraught step-child for a while."
We continue, heading for Camp Fishless so that Alice can tell Veronica what's happened. But partway there Veronica emerges from the trees, running towards us.

"Are you okay?" she asks with a look of concern on her face. "I heard a gunshot." She's out of breath; Veronica needs to exercise more.

This is the part where Alice has to tell Veronica that she has just witnessed an event that has traumatized her deeply, one that will be burned into her memory forever - another scar from an already tragic childhood.

"We're great," says Alice, smiling broadly. "But cousin Sal just fell off a cliff."

Post-Mortem III

Two dogs, a woman and an eleven-year-old girl are standing at the edge of a cliff, staring down at the crumpled, broken mess that a little while before had been Sal Kaufman.

"O God," says Veronica. She turns to Alice and puts a hand on her shoulder. "Alice, are you okay?"

I suspect Alice is very tempted to say "Never better", but instead she just says, "Yeah."

"How did this happen?" Veronica asks her.

Alice tells Veronica the story of how Sal was holding her by her ankles over the edge and threatening to drop her.

"That son of a bitch," Veronica says in response.

"And then Rachel and Jack arrived, and he pulled out his gun and was going to shoot them both..." Veronica is openly horrified, and gasps.

"...and then I guess he just lost his balance and fell," Alice concludes. It's clear that she is trying her best to look sweet, innocent and truthful.

Well, I say, *that would be one way of putting it.*

Veronica looks down at me. "And what would be another way?" she asks.

"Jack!" Rachel says with some urgency. *"Don't tell her!"*

I have to. She's my best friend, and we can trust her.

Veronica looks confused. "Wait, who are you talking to now?" she asks.

I'm talking to Rachel.

"Rachel?" she says, and sighs. "I swear to God I'll never get used to this."

Rachel doesn't think I should tell you the truth. She's worried I'll get into trouble.

Veronica kneels and pets Rachel. "Rachel, I would never betray you or Jack. Or Alice. Never. I know what a horrible human being he was, and what he did to you."

"Okay," says Rachel simply.

Then I take the leap, and tell Veronica what really happened, how I charged at Sal and pushed him over the cliff.

Veronica stares at me, eyes wide. "You *attacked* him?"

Yes, I say proudly.

Veronica can't help but laugh. "I thought he was holding a gun, not a sandwich."

I try to look crestfallen. *That was uncalled for*, I say.

Still kneeling, Veronica pets me. "I'm sorry, Jack. You really pushed that worthless piece of crap over the edge?" She looks up at Alice. "Sorry," she says.

"No worries," says Alice breezily.

Yes, I pushed him.

"Wow. But how come you didn't go over too?"

I dunno - I kinda bounced off him, I guess.

She kneels and hugs me. "O Jack," she says. "That was incredibly brave of you. You could have died." She has tears in her eyes, and hugs me tighter.

Don't cry, Veronica.

"I can't help it," she says. "The thought of losing you is unbearable."

I lick her face, and then Rachel joins me in the face-licking, and then Alice kneels down to join us - just to be clear, she doesn't lick Veronica - and before we know it we're all having a gigantic group hug at the edge of the cliff, fifty feet above a mangled corpse.

Eventually Veronica disengages from the impromptu love-fest, stands up and looks down at Kaufman's body again.

I look too. *I don't regret doing it*, I tell her. *Is that bad?*

"Hell no," Veronica replies. "After what he did, I'd have killed the fucker myself." She looks at Alice. "Oh, sorry, Alice."

She grins. "No worries."

Two dogs, a woman and an eleven-year-old girl are sitting on the deck of Isaac's house, enjoying the afternoon and discussing what to do. Veronica and Alice are casually drinking lemonade.

Three options are being considered. None of them are completely truthful.

In Version One, Sal and Alice were out in the woods. Sal shot at a squirrel and the recoil - or something - knocked him over the edge of the cliff.

Version Two is closest to the truth. Sal was abusing Alice but fell over the cliff (somehow). Veronica doesn't like this one because it raises awkward questions and potentially provides a motive for foul play.

Finally, Version Three has Alice not being present at all, and after going out looking for Sal she finds him dead. No abuse, no squirrel.

After some debate - and more lemonade - we decide on Version One, which develops the additional refinement of Sal stepping back at the edge of the cliff to take aim at the fictional squirrel and plunging to his death.

Veronica nods approvingly, but directs a serious look at Alice.

"Alice, you realize you're going to have to lie to a police officer. And preferably you also need to look upset, something which - frankly - right now you pretty much suck at."

"I know," Alice replies, sighing. "But yes, I can lie."

"Just keep the story simple, okay? He was going after a squirrel, he fell, that's it. If all else fails, just try to look traumatized and don't say anything else."

"Okay."

"Can you do that?"

"Yeah."

"And can you look upset?"

"I'll try."

"Just keep thinking about what would have happened to Rachel if Jack hadn't pushed him off the cliff."

Alice nods. "That's a good idea," she says.

"Then after, you came running down here to find me."

"Got it."

Veronica and Alice take their time finishing the lemonade. They look out at the lake, which is blue and shining in the afternoon sun.

"It's a beautiful day," Veronica observes.

"It's a *great* day," Alice replies, grinning.

"Alice!" Veronica almost barks at her. "Upset, remember?"

She stops grinning. "Okay," she says. "Sorry."

"Okay," Veronica says. "I guess it's time to call the cops. Are you ready for this?"

Alice nods. "Yeah. Yes, I am."

Veronica rises from the Adirondack chair, smooths her hair, and takes a deep breath. Then she picks up her cell phone and dials 911.

"Hello," she says. "I'm afraid I have to report a tragic accident..."

Twenty minutes later, sirens announce the arrival at the house of the local police, closely followed by a fire engine and an ambulance. Alice is clutching Veronica and hiding her face. She isn't pretending to cry, but all in all she's doing a pretty good job of playing the traumatized child.

Veronica explains to the two police officers what she says Alice had told her, and then says she'd take them up the path to the cliff. Veronica tells Alice to stay at the house.

"I don't want her to have to see the body again," she says quietly.

"I understand, ma'am," one of the cops - the taller, rather dishy one - replies. "Honey, are you going to be okay staying here for a while?"

Alice nods but says nothing. In the absence of fabricated tears, she has apparently decided to adopt a blank, stunned look. It's surprisingly effective.

"You stay here, sweetheart," Veronica says. "I'll come back soon, I promise. Rachel will stay here with you." Alice nods again and remains silent.

"Who's Rachel?" asks the dishy cop, looking around for another person.

"Her dog," Veronica answers, and points to Rachel, who is sitting by Alice's side looking attentive.

"I see." He looks at me for the first time. "Is this her dog too?"

"No, that's Jack - he's mine."

I wag my tail and try very hard to look sweet, cute and not at all like a murderer.

"Poor kid," the cop says as we walk away. "She must be devastated."

Veronica leads the group of miscellaneous emergency responders into the woods. They're all men, several of whom are rather obviously ogling the very attractive woman at the head of the parade; even dressed casually in shorts and a tank top, Veronica looks stunning. I trot alongside my human.

As we walk, she tells the two policemen Alice's true sad story, about how her parents had been killed in a car crash, and how she has now lost her only other relative.

"God, that's terrible," the older, dumpier-looking cop says. "Such bad luck - it's not fair, is it?"

"No, officer, it's really not."

If only you knew, she thought. The demigods certainly tried to make up for the past today.

"Are you a friend?" Dumpy Cop asks.

"Yes - friend and neighbor. She's such a special little girl. So resilient despite all the tragedy."

"So she has no other family at all?"

"No," Veronica says. "What happens in cases like this?"

"Well, a court will have to decide. She'll probably have to go into foster care in the meantime."

Veronica considers as we walk. "Can anyone be a foster parent?" she asks.

"Pretty much," says Dishy Cop. "You have to take a class and get certified, but as long as you can meet some financial requirements and you have no criminal record, it's pretty easy. Would you do that for her?"

"Yes, I would," Veronica replies, surprising herself. She'd never thought of herself as the motherly type, but this was different. "She's a great kid."

"That's very cool of you," Dishy Cop says, and smiles - rather too warmly. Veronica suddenly realizes he's actually flirting with her. She also realizes that, even though this is completely inappropriate behavior given the circumstances, she doesn't mind.

She smiles back.

A woman, seven guys and a dog are standing at the edge of a cliff, staring down at the crumpled, broken mess that an hour or so before had been Sal Kaufman.

"O Jesus," says one of the fire crew. "*This* one's gonna be a challenge."

"Yeah," says another. "How the hell are we going to get him up here?"

"O shit," says a third guy, pointing down. "He's a FUBAR." This, we learn later, is emergency responder slang for Fucked Up Beyond All Recognition.

"O man, looks like there's brains to clean up." Guy number one again.

So Sal did have some vestige of a brain after all. Huh. I suppose something in there had to keep his limbs moving.

"Oh crap, not that again!" Guy number three. "It's my second one this month. I'm gettin' really sick of brains."

"Guys, guys!" admonishes Dishy Cop. "There's a lady present! Sorry," he says to Veronica. "They're a bit - you know - battle-hardened. They should be more sensitive." Guys one, two and three all look slightly sheepish, and there is a chorus of sorries.

"Don't worry, officer--"

"Call me Mike," he says. His partner gives him a look.

"Okay, Mike, " Veronica continues. "Don't worry - I'm not particularly invested in this. I barely knew the guy," she lies.

"What was he like?"

"I don't know. Bit of a redneck, really. To be honest, I didn't care for him much."

"Sure. Did the little girl get along with him?"

"Yeah," Veronica lies again. "Far as I know." She tries not to look at the cop as she says this.

They continue to chat while the fire crew works out how to get down to the body. Their conversation is easy and light; he's a nice guy, I decide from my position a short distance away. I'm gazing up into the trees, hoping to find a squirrel to chase.

Eventually Veronica sighs and folds her arms across her chest. This has the effect of pushing her breasts up, a phenomenon which does not go unnoticed by some of the men present.

She turns to Dishy Cop. "Do you mind if I go back to the house now, officer?"

"Mike."

"Mike, right. Okay if I go back?"

"Sure, that's fine... we'll take it from here. You go and take care of the little girl. I'll come by later and tell you what's happening and help you with the arrangements."

"Arrangements?"

"Well, yeah. For the... the body - you know, a funeral parlor. And for the girl."

"Ah, okay. Thanks."

Veronica calls to me and then walks away. She is very conscious that the cop is watching her go. She smiles - but only to herself.

A little later Dishy-Mike returns to the house. Veronica sees him coming down the path from the woods and shoos Alice into a bedroom so that she doesn't have to pretend to be sad; she had been singing happily to herself in the living room.

Veronica offers the cop some wine, which he declines, and some lemonade, which he gratefully accepts. They sit on the deck, and he explains to her the details of what needs to be done, and who she needs to contact to discuss arrangements for Alice.

"Where is she, by the way?" he asks.

"I sent her to bed to rest. She's pretty upset, as you can imagine."

At that moment the sound of giggling comes from the bedroom - Alice is apparently playing some rough and tumble game with Rachel - but if the cop notices he doesn't say anything. I bark a couple of times, and apparently both Rachel and Alice get the message, and silence descends once more.

Veronica and Mike chat some more on casual topics, Things Not Related To The Mangled Corpse Of Sal Kaufman. Finally, and with obvious reluctance, the cop rises from his chair.

"Well," he says, "I'd better be going. I have a report to write."

Veronica nods. "Of course. Thank you for all your help."

"No problem." He pulls a business card from his wallet and hands it to her. "My number is on there if you need anything."

"Thanks."

He turns to go, then stops and looks at her again.

"Really, call me if you need anything at all. Or--"

Veronica looks up from the card. "Or what?"

The cop looks rather sheepish. "Well, I was wondering if maybe you'd like to grab a cup of coffee sometime?"

Veronica cocks her head and smiles coyly. "Are you *hitting* on me, officer?"

He pauses, as if deciding what to say next, and glances over his shoulder to see if anyone else is around. Then to Veronica's surprise he gets down on one knee, gazes into her eyes, and says, "You are the most stunningly beautiful woman I have ever seen in my entire life. So yes, I'm hitting on you."

Veronica grins. "Thank you, Mike," she says, and puts her hand on his knee. "I'll call you. I promise."

Balls

I am grateful to Veronica for many things. For rescuing me in the first place. For housing and feeding me. For giving me lots of affection. For not beating me, even when I do things that annoy her - like chasing a squirrel through the house without regard to the consequences for valuable and unfortunately fragile objects.

And, perhaps more than anything, for not chopping my balls off.

I'm very attached to my balls, and very much wish to remain so. There was a brief discussion of this topic back when she adopted me. Several people, ranging from neighbors to complete strangers, proffered the annoyingly unsolicited advice that castrating a male dog was essential. A couple of people added darkly that this was especially important for a pit bull; according to one woman who accosted Veronica outside the local supermarket, no baby, cat or small child in the neighborhood would be safe until I had an empty scrotum.

Ironically, it was probably Leroy who decided the fate of my testicles. He intercepted Veronica one afternoon as we were headed out for a walk, and gave her a lecture on the importance of emasculating male dogs. "Ya just never know what they gonna do otherwise," he opined. "Even if they's not vicious, they's just gonna pee on everything in yer house."

For the record, I've never peed on anything in the house. Well, except for once on the cat, but there were extenuating circumstances there.

Veronica's distaste for our redneck next-door neighbor is sufficiently pronounced that, just on principle, she would probably do the opposite of whatever he told her to. Accordingly, it was lucky for me that he told her to have me neutered.

If he'd said the opposite, I'd probably be missing a couple of key body parts right now.

I mention the intact nature of my genitalia because I have been attempting to persuade Rachel to mate with me.

I'm not a virgin: I've had dalliances with several female dogs of various breeds. Not always successfully, it must be said. I once tried humping a mastiff. She was willing, but the logistical challenges of mounting a dog that's twice your height are not inconsiderable: it's like a dwarf trying to bonk a female basketball player without benefit of a step-ladder.

As was the case with the mating of my mother that produced me, dog sex is usually brief and unromantic. This is normal. Female dogs don't expect flowers, poetry or Purina dog chow served by candlelight. And while most females won't mate with just any male that comes down the road, as a rule they're usually pretty non-discriminating - any good-looking specimen with minimal fleas and a working penis stands a fair chance of getting laid.

But of course Rachel isn't most females.

My first attempt at seduction happened early on in our relationship, while Isaac was still alive. We were wandering through the woods together one afternoon when Rachel stopped to sniff some particularly interesting smell in the undergrowth. Confronted with the enticing sight of her rear end prominently elevated right before my eyes, I did what any self-respecting male dog would do and hopped onto her back. The reaction was swift and, well, not what I had hoped. Rachel jumped forward before I had a chance to connect with anything intimate, and turned to face me with an annoyed look.

"What do you think you're doing?"

Um... isn't it obvious?

"I don't recall giving you an invitation to mount me."

I've never needed one before.

"Well I don't know who you've been humping in the past, but I'm not one of your back-alley floozies."

I don't think you're a floozy. But we're friends.

"So what? I used to be friends with a parakeet but it doesn't mean I wanted to bonk him."

But...

"Look Jack, I like you and I really appreciate that fact that you've helped Alice, but I'm not ready to have sex with you yet."

But you might be one day?

"Maybe."

Encouraged by this, I tentatively broached the subject again a few times after that, but was again rebuffed. However, the interval between my suggestion and her refusal lengthened with each enquiry; I took this as a good sign.

The day after the demise of Sal Kaufman, Rachel and I were sitting on the deck alone. Veronica and Alice were cooking together in the kitchen; they were singing, and laughing a lot.

They seem very happy, I commented.

"Yes," Rachel replied. *"I'm so happy for Alice now that that monster's gone."* There was a pause, and then Rachel turned to me and wagged her tail. "Okay," she said, and I could see the canine equivalent of a smile on her face.

Okay? Okay what?

"Okay," she repeated. *"I'll have sex with you now."*

Revenge

"Vengeance is mine and I shall repay." - Leo Tolstoy, *Anna Karenina*

Rachel's sudden change of heart caught me a little by surprise. *Really?* I asked.

"Sure. I think you've proved yourself a worthy suitor."

Well okay!

I immediately walked around behind her and prepared to mount. This was not a popular move.

"*Jesus, not* HERE!" She quickly maneuvered away from me.

But you just said...

"Yes, but I didn't mean right here, in front of Alice. God, sometimes I wonder whether male dogs have another set of balls in their skulls where their brains should be." She emitted the sigh of the long-suffering. "Let's go into the woods."

We trooped off down the path, and walked until we reached the clearing where we'd met for the first time.

Rachel stopped.

Nice, I said. *The site of our first date. How sweet.*

She gave me a disdainful look. "Yeah, right," she said. "Okay, get on with it."

Get on with it? That's not very romantic.

Another disdainful look. "What d'you want - flowers?"

No, but... oh, never mind. Okay, hold still. I approached her and was about to hop up onto her hind quarters, when suddenly she moved away from me.

"Hang on," she said.

What's wrong?

"Fleas, I think." She raised a hind leg and vigorously scratched her ear for a good twenty seconds. Finally she stopped and turned around again.

Done?

"Yeah, I think so."

I moved into position again.

"Wait..."

Now what?

"I'm just checking to see if I need to pee first." There was a pause, presumably while Rachel consulted her bladder. "No, I think it's okay - go ahead."

You're sure now?

"Yes."

Finally I mounted her, and a few seconds later - after some fumbling and rather uncoordinated movements - we were conjoined.

I'll spare you the intimate details of what followed, but you've undoubtedly witnessed two dogs humping - there's not a lot of subtlety or variation in the procedure. The key element in dog sex is what's known as the *knot*, which is essentially where the male's member swells inside the female and locks the two of them into place. Once two dogs have knotted, it is neither easy nor a good idea to separate them until the male's excitement has, well, subsided.

Which made what happened next particularly unfortunate.

There I am, happily joined to my lover in copulatory heaven. This moment represents the culmination of months of waiting and anticipation, and the ultimate consummation of our relationship.

And, fuck me, a squirrel chooses this very moment to dart out from the trees and pass right in front of us at top speed.

I'd like to say that Rachel considered the consequences of chasing the squirrel before moving. I'd like to say that she hesitated out of concern for the fact that I was in a compromised, not to mention delicate, position. But she didn't, not for a second - her prey drive kicked in and suddenly nothing else mattered. And in that not-a-second I went from blissfully relaxed to painfully panicked as I was dragged across the clearing, against my will and mostly by my penis.

Trying to keep up with the dog you're glued to when you have only your back legs on the ground is, to say the least, challenging. I'm yelling *Stop! Stop!! STOP!!!*, but Rachel's ignoring me. And the most amazing thing is that, despite chasing this squirrel with a 60-pound dog stuck up her reproductive tract, she's actually *catching up to it*.

In a desperate attempt to improve my situation, I try lifting my back paws off the ground and clinging on to her back with my front legs, but that serves only to drag both our butts down. Hurriedly, I make contact with the ground again, and look up just in time to see the squirrel heading for...

No no no! Not those bushes!

As we rapidly approach a collision with the wall of vegetation before us, it becomes abundantly clear that Rachel - who is now only about a yard behind the fleet rodent - is not about to slow down. So, all I can do is to tighten my grip on her back, close my eyes, and hope for the best...

A minute or so later, we are on the other side of the bush, which now sports a dog-sized hole in its middle. We are no longer joined together, but we're both panting - and scratched to hell. The squirrel is safely up a tree, no doubt greatly enjoying the moment and thinking evil squirrel thoughts regarding how he has just taken revenge for every dog who ever chased him or his kind.

Rachel is gazing wistfully up at her escaped prey. Finally she turns to look at me, as if she had forgotten until that moment that I had been a central if unwilling participant in what had just happened.

I am licking my wounds. She, however, is wagging her tail with far too much enthusiasm. *"So, sweetheart,"* she says with a doggie smile, *"was it good for you too?"*

Visitors

Over the next few days, we had a series of visitors to the house, all in connection with the death of Sal Kaufman.

First there was a representative from the local funeral home, a tall, thin man named Mr. Larson with an appropriately lugubrious countenance; he was, inevitably, dressed entirely in black. Mr Larsen extended his condolences, and Veronica tried hard to look sincere when she thanked him. Then he enquired how she, as the temporary guardian of Kaufman's only known relative, wished to deal with the "remains".

Ask him if we can turn him into cat food, I said. Veronica glanced at me and frowned. Bonkers, who was curled up in a chair, glared.

"Something simple - and inexpensive," Veronica finally replied. "Until the estate is resolved, I'm afraid I'm the one footing the bill for this. I don't want to seem cheap, but... well, you understand."

Mr Larson nodded, and if he disapproved of Veronica's funereal thrift he kept that to himself.

"Will we be doing a viewing?" he asked.

It took Veronica a few seconds to understand what was meant, and then she said, "God no! He was quite a mess when they picked him up - I don't think anyone wants to see that."

"Oh, we can... *adjust* him quite nicely. Our morticians do a wonderful job. You'd be surprised at some of the cases they've had to deal with. Industrial accidents and such. We once had a man whose head was entirely removed by a steel cable - the cable broke, you see - and--"

"Yes, thank you," Veronica interrupted. She really didn't care to hear further details of a beheading. "But that won't be necessary. Besides, there's really no one to see him - he didn't have any relatives except Alice."

"Sad. So sad."

"Yes, tragic," Veronica replied with as much sincerity as she could muster - which wasn't much. "Anyway," she continued, "I think just your cheapest casket and cremation would be fine."

Mr Larson nodded again. "Of course." He produced some papers from a battered briefcase. "There are a few documents for you to sign," he said.

Twenty minutes later, Death's Caretaker departed. "Do give my condolences to the young lady," he said. "Such a tragedy for her."

"Indeed," Veronica replied as she closed the front door.

Next, Dumpy Cop - whose name, it turned out, was Bill - came by and went over details of Veronica's statement about the events of the day before. She signed it, and hoped that some nameless god wouldn't strike her down for perjuring herself.

"Ok, that's it, thanks," Bill said. "But Officer Pavone will probably be by later."

Veronica had no idea who this was. "Is this someone asking more questions?" The cop grinned.

"No, it's Mike - he's gonna make a *social* call."

And indeed, Mike showed up a couple of hours later. He asked how Alice was doing, and enquired if she or Veronica needed anything. He was out of uniform.

"We're fine, thank you," Veronica replied. "Though I'd like to claim that cup of coffee you promised me - but since there are no cafés anywhere within walking distance I suppose I'll just have to make it myself."

"I don't want to be any trouble," Mike said.

"Yes you do." She smiled. "Come on in."

They had coffee on the deck in the sunshine, and chatted. Alice appeared from somewhere in the woods, with Rachel trotting alongside her. She was singing as she walked up to the deck, but stopped and hurriedly tried to effect a sad look when she saw Mike there.

"You seem to be doing better, young lady," he said. "I'm glad to see it."

Alice seemed unsure how to react, but Veronica smiled and patted her thigh. Without hesitation, the girl plonked herself down in Veronica's lap, her head against Veronica's shoulder. Veronica stroked her hair.

"You two make a lovely couple," Mike said, smiling.

Alice looked up. "We do, don't we?" she said.

The last visitor was a social worker. She was a prim-looking woman in her forties; judging from the fact that she was constantly sniffing, she was apparently afflicted with a cold.

"You are" - she consulted a clipboard - "Miss McKenna?"

"Yes."

"I'm Priscilla Henderson. I'm the social worker assigned to the case of" - she again consulted the clipboard - "Alice Cavanagh. Is she here?" She sniffed.

"Yes, she's inside. Come in."

Alice was curled up in an armchair reading a book. Rachel was laying on the carpet next to her. "Alice, this is Miss Henderson. She's a social worker who's here to chat about you."

"Hello," Alice said uncertainly.

"Alice, how are you?" Miss Henderson asked - though the enquiry held no discernible sincerity or interest.

"I'm okay."

"Good. Miss McKenna and I are going to have a chat, and then I'll come and talk with you, okay?"

"Okay." Alice looked worried.

The social worker turned to Veronica. "Is there somewhere we can talk privately?" Sniff.

"Yeah, I guess. We can go into the bedroom." She showed the way, with me following. Veronica flashed Alice a reassuring smile before she closed the door.

The social worker sat in a chair and consulted her clipboard. "So," she said, "you're not a relative then? Just a neighbor?"

"I'm a friend," replied Veronica, who had seated herself on the edge of the bed. She was very aware of the fact that the bed was an unmade, rumpled mess. "Alice has no relatives," she said. "Not any more."

"Yes, I see. Her cousin, Mr" - another glance at the clipboard - "Kaufman... died in an accident, I understand."

"Yes. He fell off a cliff." Veronica glanced down and gave me a pointed look. I tried to look nonchalant.

"Well, it's nice of you to look after her here. It must be a bit of an imposition, I imagine."

"She's not an *imposition*," Veronica said, rather frostily. "She can stay here as long as she wants."

Miss Henderson sniffed. "Well yes, she can stay here for *now*, but given her circumstances she's effectively a ward of the state. Very soon we'll have to find a foster home placement for her. And eventually an adoption," - another sniff - "hopefully."

"Well, that's just it," Veronica said. "I'd actually like to be the one."

"The one? The one what? You mean a foster parent?"

"No - I'd like to... well, I think I'd like to adopt her."

Miss Henderson's eyebrows were raised. "I see. Have you discussed this with the child?"

"No, I haven't yet," Veronica admitted.

"You *think* you'd like to, you say. Is this something you're sure about? We wouldn't want to give her false hope."

Veronica nodded. "Absolutely sure," she said. "Though I must admit I'm a little surprised myself." She said this as much to herself as to the social worker.

The social worker frowned. "This is not a decision to be taken lightly."

"I'm aware of that, Miss Henderson." Veronica was finding the tone and general demeanor of her visitor to be rather cold and officious; she'd imagined that social workers were all warm-and-fuzzy people, full of empathy and the milk of human kindness. This one clearly was none of that. "I wouldn't say it if I didn't mean it," she added.

"Very well. If you're really sure then we should ask the child. She gets to have a say in this. Do you think she'd agree?"

"I don't know," Veronica replied. "I mean, I know she likes me." Now that it had come to the point, Veronica realized she was rather nervous at the prospect of being rejected.

The social worker walked to the door, opened it and looked out into the living room. Then she turned back to Veronica. "What's her name again? Alison?"

"Alice."

"Of course, Alice." She called out. "Alice? Can you come here for a moment?"

A few seconds later, Alice appeared, and was duly ushered by the social worker into the bedroom. Rachel followed. Alice looked even more worried now; she was very aware that her future was under discussion.

"Alice," Miss Henderson began, "as you know, we have to find a place for you, a family." Alice gave a slight, serious nod.

"Usually we'd put you into a foster home, and then eventually we'd try to find a family to adopt you. Permanently, I mean."

Alice stared at the social worker, and it was obvious that tears were beginning to form in her eyes as she took in the uncertainty of her future.

"But," Miss Henderson continued, "in this case we may have another option. Miss McKenna here has offered to adopt you. So I have to ask you what you would think of--"

She didn't get to complete the sentence. With a yelp and a *"YES!"*, Alice launched herself at Veronica, threw her arms around her and knocked her back onto the bed. "Yes yes yes yes yes!" She was smothering Veronica in kisses, and the two of them collapsed into a hugging, rolling, giggling mass. Energized by the excitement, Rachel and I started barking, then jumped onto the bed. There was more laughing as two dogs enthusiastically licked their respective humans and joined the joyful pile.

Miss Henderson sniffed, but now there was the slightest trace of a smile on her face. "Well," she said as she stood up and gathered her things, "I suppose that answers that."

To Conclude

And they all lived happily ever after. We hope.

IT'S NOW BEEN A LITTLE OVER A YEAR since Isaac died, and Veronica inherited the lake house and everything else besides. Except that she is no longer Veronica.

To the lasting dismay of masochists all over the Emerald City, Veronica quit the dominatrix business. Her legendary bullwhip no longer kisses male flesh, and her dungeon has been transformed into a home theater, where she and her friends gather whenever she's in town to eat pizza and watch movies on a gigantic wide-screen TV.

Upon retiring as a sex worker, she likewise retired her name and became Holly McKenna once again - though Anna hasn't quite adjusted, and still calls her Vee from time to time. She doesn't mind.

She's still dating Mike, the Dishy Cop. He's a great guy, kind and generous, and he loves dogs. He's very good to Holly and Alice, and I can tell that they both love having his strong, dependable presence in their lives.

A few months back, after all the paperwork for the adoption was done and dusted, and with great trepidation, Holly told him about her sordid past. She and I had long discussions about this beforehand, and with my characteristic canine wisdom I told her that she had to tell him, because if it was meant to be, it would be, and anyway she couldn't hide a secret like that forever.

And so she did. The confession came late one night on the deck under a full moon, after she'd cooked him an outstanding salmon dinner - and gotten herself good and liquored up in the process. He listened to her without saying anything; and when she was done and staring at him, anxiously awaiting his reaction, he leaned over and kissed her tenderly, and told her he found it all incredibly hot, and couldn't wait to hear the stories.

However, she hasn't told Mike about the unique connection she has with me, and probably never will. Confessing to your boyfriend that you were once a sex worker is one thing; telling him that you can talk to your dog is quite another.

The other day I walked in on Mike as he was hiding a small box containing what I'm pretty sure is an engagement ring. I won't spoil the surprise and say anything to Holly, but I really hope she says Yes when he proposes. I've no doubt she will. She deserves the love of a good man - though I can't wait to see the look on Anna's face when Holly tells her she's marrying a cop.

Talking of Anna, she's still dating Tom the architect. Since no boyfriend has ever lasted this long, or so well, we fully expect wedding bells from that quarter at some point. What's more, they've just bought a house together, and - much more important - Anna recently adopted a dog from an animal shelter. He's a pit bull, and his name is Ernie. Ernie is cute, affectionate and snuggly, and he continues a proud tradition among our breed by being utterly useless as a guard dog.

Alice is almost thirteen years old, with a bright future. Ironically enough, as the officially adopted child of Sal Kaufman, she inherited his house. She had no attachment to the place, indeed nothing but bad memories; and so, with Veronica's help she sold it, and banked the proceeds into a trust that will pay her college expenses a few years hence.

She is growing up to be a beautiful young woman: *smart, thoughtful, funny* and *kind* are some of the adjectives people use when describing her. She is a child of Nature, and there are days when I almost fancy she has Fay blood in her veins. In summer she practically lives in the woods by the lake, with Rachel constantly at her side.

Rachel and I are about as happy as two dogs can be, and just last week we found out she's pregnant.

Puppies! I'm not sure I'm ready for this.

Even though she doesn't need to, Rachel still chases squirrels, because that's what dogs do.

Holly's mother visits us sometimes. She still doesn't give more than a day or two's notice, and she still talks a lot about cows. Shirley and her daughter never mention Holly's past "situation", as her mother euphemistically puts it. She has become surprisingly close with Alice, whom she adores - and spoils her shamelessly on every visit.

When one day Shirley complained to her daughter about her failure to produce grandchildren, Holly threw her a reproachful look. "You *have* a grandchild," she said, pointing to Alice, who was reading on the deck in the sunshine. "Alice is every bit as much my daughter as anything that was to come out of my vagina."

Shirley grimaced. "Don't be crude, Holly. But yes, you're right." She gazed through the window at Alice and smiled.

As for me, my existential crisis is a small dot in the rear-view mirror of my world these days. Being so absurdly happy with Holly, Alice and Rachel, it's pretty easy to forget philosophy. When I'm stretched out with Rachel on the deck of the lake house, gazing up at the stars, I'll admit I still occasionally ponder the perplexing question of why I'm a dog and not something else, or give fleeting thought to the mysteries of the universe. But mostly I live from day to day, ever thankful for my good fortune, and loving every precious moment of this ephemeral, glorious life.

But I miss Isaac, and wonder if I really will see him again in another time, another realm.

What else?

Well, despite Holly's newfound financial independence, our days are hardly idle. You may recall that, back when she first discovered that she could talk to me, we joked about starting a circus act or writing a book. We've actually done both. The book is the one you are holding in your hand (though we ultimately decided not to title it *Fifty Shades of Stray*).

And we didn't join the circus either. Nonetheless, *The Amazing Holly and her Telepathic Dog* have given many performances over the past few months.

We don't charge - Holly doesn't need the money, and anyway she prefers to provide this service for deserving causes: mostly children's wards in local hospitals, or the occasional charity fund-raising event.

In keeping with the title of our act, we never cease to amaze our audiences. Indeed, we have become something of a minor legend in the secretive circles of amateur magic. Recently, a professional magician heard about our act and attended a performance, assuring everyone he could easily explain how someone could whisper a secret to a dog and have that secret faithfully revealed by the beautiful red-haired woman who had been sitting in the next room.

The magician was left as mystified as everyone else. When he pressed her, Holly reminded him of the old adage that when everything possible had been ruled out, then only the impossible remained.

He snorted. "The only impossible thing here would be you actually talking to your dog," he said, with a mixture of frustration and grudging admiration. "And we know that's not happening." Holly smiled sweetly, and said nothing.

But you, dear reader, who have witnessed the impossible, know different.

By now you know that dogs can talk, that faeries exist, and that sometimes bad people do get their just desserts after all. And that love eventually emerges triumphant, albeit sometimes not until a happy-ever-afterlife.

And I hope that you have also learned one other thing.

That in life, as in this book, it is most important that you believe in Magic.

Epilogue

In a city park on an overcast day in autumn, a woman and her dog are out walking.

The woman is in her early forties. She is strikingly beautiful, with green eyes and red hair that cascades over her shoulders. She is stylishly dressed in a black leather jacket and a crisp black skirt whose hemline falls well above her knees, and she walks the path in blood-red high heels that match her hair. She is the kind of woman who turns heads, both male and female, wherever she goes. Still, the wedding ring on her left hand marks her as unavailable to men.

The woman walks very slowly, because the dog at her side is clearly old. His muzzle is gray, and he plods along unevenly under the burden of arthritic hips. He stops to sniff something in a patch of grass, and remains there for some thirty seconds; his nose does not work as well as it once did. The woman waits patiently for him to finish, and eventually he moves haltingly on to the next patch, the next smell.

As they walk down the path, a squirrel darts out from behind a tree. The dog stops and stares, alert and focused, his ears erect and his tail wagging. But he stays where he is; the days when he chased squirrels are now long past.

A hundred yards farther on, the dog stops and looks up at the woman. She returns his gaze, and speaks to him.

"Time to go home?" *There is a pause, almost as if she is hearing an answer, and then the two of them turn around and begin to walk back along the path.*

Some time later, the dog stops and lays down on the grass, panting. The woman kneels and strokes his head.

"Need some help?" *she asks. A pause, then she nods.* "Okay."

With studied gentleness, she takes the dog in her arms and carries him the rest of the way home. As she approaches the house, a keen-eyed passer-by would observe tears in the woman's eyes, and would perhaps hear her whispering to the dog as she holds him close and presses her face to his.

"O my dear friend, I think it's almost time for you to go." *Now the tears come more freely.* "God, what am I ever going to do without you?"

She pauses, as if listening to a reply, then says, "Yes, it's true - it's not fair at all. Dogs don't live long enough - sixteen years is such a short time."

Another pause, then: "Yes, you're right - only fourteen for Rachel. I miss her too."

She allows herself a few more tears, then opens the front door and carries the dog inside.

The woman carries the dog upstairs to her bedroom and gently lays him on the king-sized bed. She wipes the tears from her face with the back of her hand, then tenderly covers him with a blanket.

Now she undresses. Leaving her clothes in an untidy pile on the floor, she climbs onto the bed and lays down in her underwear next to the dog. She curls up against him and drapes her right arm across his torso, holding him close, her head pressed against his. She feels the warmth of his frail old body, and the slow rhythm of his heartbeat in his chest. They remain like this for a while, the woman stroking the dog's belly and occasionally kissing the top of his head. Once, the dog turns his head and gently licks the woman's face.

The dog sighs audibly, and with an effort sits up and looks down at the woman.

"What is it, my love?" *she asks, staring at him with concern in her eyes.*

There is a long pause, during which the woman continues to gaze at the dog. Partway through the pause, she begins to cry again.

"Really? It's really time? Oh please, not yet! I'm not ready to let you go."

Another pause, and then the woman gives a great sigh, chokes back some more tears, and then collects herself.

"Okay," *she says with another sigh.* "Okay, my friend. I'll call Alice and tell her to come."

Two women sit on a bed with an elderly dog. The redhead has been joined by a pretty girl in her early twenties: she has long blonde hair that hangs in a braid down the center of her back.

The women hold hands, and both use their free hand to caress the dog. They lean over him, crying silently, their heads touching. The dog is obviously having trouble breathing: his chest rises and falls heavily, as if each breath requires effort.

"He knows it's time," *says the redhead. She says his name in a choking sob, and weeps as she lays her head against his.*

"Thank you, my friend. Thank you for everything."

"Yes," *says the younger woman through her tears.* "Thank you. Thank you for saving me, thank you for everything you've done."

The dog's breathing is shallower now, as if he is slipping away.

"Farewell, sweetest animal," *says the older woman, sobbing, and kisses his forehead.* "I will always love you."

"I love you too," *says the younger.* "So much. I hope what awaits you is wonderful."

For a moment the dog struggles to cling to life. He takes a few more labored breaths, and there is a brief instant of panic and fear; and then he wills himself to let go.

He feels as if he is falling, falling into a warm, comforting darkness, falling away from the only world he has ever known. There is the sound of two women weeping, becoming ever fainter as he descends. A final touch of hands against his body.

PHILLIP BOLEYN

And then he drifts away, floating effortlessly into an ethereal sleep; and he passes beyond consciousness, and into the void.

When the dog awakens, he is in a sunlit meadow. The air is warm and there is the sound of birdsong in the trees. The grass around him smells fresh and fragrant, and a breeze lightly caresses his body. Although he does not move yet, he is aware that he feels wonderfully strong and hale, as if all of the accumulated ailments of his old age have been banished. He knows without moving that his limbs are supple, and that there is no longer aching or pain.

At first he cannot make out detail; he is slowly emerging into whatever world he has entered, and his vision is clouded by a haze.

As he lays there quietly, he gradually becomes aware of someone talking. There are three voices, soft as a whisper. And, somewhere nearby, another dog is barking excitedly. A familiar bark.

As the haze slowly clears and his eyes begin to focus, the dog sees a man and two women standing over him. Both women are beautiful; both have red hair and green eyes. The man is old, but his eyes are those of youth, bright and clear. His face is full of kindness, and he smiles as he crouches down to place his hand on the dog's head.

The haze disperses, and the man's face finally comes into focus.

"Isaac?" says the dog.

The man lovingly pets the creature before him.

"Hello Jack," he says, smiling. "Welcome home."

THE END

Acknowledgments

It took me way too long to start writing this novel. But now that it has finally been expelled, spluttering and wailing, from the womb, I would be remiss if I did not thank a number of people - and dogs - for assistance with a few aspects of its birthing.

I am grateful to Mary Roach, best-selling popular science writer extraordinaire, for her encouragement. Mary read an early draft of *Jack*, and her enthusiasm for the story, and wise advice on some aspects of the writing, were greatly appreciated as I struggled to figure out where this tale was going.

Erin Falcone was my first reader, and I am grateful for her thoughtful comments.

Any student of faery lore will recognize that Rowan and her kind are largely a creation of my own mythology, which occasionally borrowed names from regional traditions. If anyone can be said to have fostered my love of folklore, it is Katharine Briggs, who was arguably the foremost expert on the topic. I was fortunate enough to spend time with her in the 1970's a few years before she died. Finding to my delight that she lived in my own village in England, I wrote to her, and she graciously invited this long-haired, unkempt 19-year-old into her home, where she served me sherry and patiently answered my questions about English folk tales. I remember her as a woman of considerable erudition, and one of great dignity and kindness; and I was always entranced when, in a soft, enchanting voice, she would lapse into recitation of some poem or quotation.

I have occasionally included words from other people in this book, simply because they were just too good not to use. Some are attributed in the text; others are not. In fairness to the latter individuals - all of whom are far better writers than myself - I herewith give credit where credit is due.

First, I should note that much of the etymology that is peppered through the book - for I, like Jack, love words and their origins - is either paraphrased or quoted directly from the wonderful online etymological dictionary at *www.etymonline.com*.

When Isaac contrasts Greece with Britain, he notes that "someone" once described the latter as being a land "with its narrows towns and narrow roads and narrow kindnesses and narrow reprimands." This perfect description of the country of my own birth originates with the actor Anthony Hopkins, who was talking about his first experience of America. The full quotation is as follows: "It created in me a yearning for all that is wide and open and expansive, a yearning that will never allow me to fit in my own country, with its narrows towns and narrow roads and narrow kindnesses and narrow reprimands."

The beautiful line that Isaac quotes to Rowan in Santorini after their first kiss - "I had been my whole life a bell, and never knew it until that moment

I was lifted and struck" - is from Annie Dillard's memoir *Pilgrim At Tinker Creek*. It is one of innumerable gems of writing in that wonderful book; and if you care at all about the beauty of language, you should run out a grab a copy and read it at your first opportunity. (To those who would point out that the book was written long after 1965 when the scene occurred: get over yourselves).

The tale of the thief and the promise to teach the king's horse to talk is not mine; as Rowan noted, it originated in the Middle Ages, and is said to have been told to Henry VIII by Jane Seymour, the only wife that that most odious of English monarchs claimed to have truly loved (and one of four he didn't execute - she died in childbirth before he could get around to lopping off her head).

There is no 50th legislative district in Washington State - or at least there wasn't when I wrote this book. If gerrymandering has created one since, I apologize to the current occupant, especially if his name happens to be Senator Rumor.

On similar lines, as far as I know there is no pet cemetery or nudist camp in Kent, Washington, so please don't go there looking for either.

On other matters, I'm grateful to my young friend Rachel for allowing me to name a major canine character after her. After her initial reaction ("What? I can't believe you made me into a bitch!"), I think she secretly liked being the namesake for such a cool dog as Rachel.

My wife and I are fortunate to count as friends one of Seattle's top pro dommes, Ms Savannah Sly, as well as Kathleen Ashford, the beautiful Proprietrix and Innkeeper of InnThrall, Washington State's only kinky bed and breakfast. I am grateful to both of them for supplying the basis for a couple of the stories that I wove into this book. They include the infamous scene with Bonkers and Oliver; something similar happened with one of Kathleen's clients and her cat, although I greatly embellished the original tale. I also thank Kathleen for allowing me to use, for Veronica, the tagline of "the sweetest bitch you'll ever meet".

Savannah has been a driving force behind the Sex Workers' Outreach Project (SWOP), which seeks to educate the public regarding sex work of all kinds, to debunk a lot of myths about the industry, and to advocate for legalization. Yes, sex work has its issues and bad apples, as does any industry; but far more sex workers than you'd imagine are just ordinary people like you and me who have actively chosen this occupation, and who enjoy it and fulfill a widespread need that is almost as old as sex itself. SWOP's website is *www.swopusa.org*: check it out.

The wonderful Station café on Beacon Hill, run by Luis and Leona Rodriguez, actually exists, and it has transformed the neighborhood since it opened in 2009. If you're ever in the area, drop by for a cup of excellent coffee and a warm welcome. As Jack notes, it's the kind of place where everyone knows everyone, and it's a favorite haunt of my own dog, Alice.

With her gender transformed, Alice is roughly the model for Jack. Like him, she's a mix of pit bull and something with a crazy prey drive. All our previous dogs were sweet as pie and dumb as rocks, but Alice has a brain, and I can easily imagine her giving a running commentary on human behavior the way Jack does. However, she would not do well around Bonkers: although we've never let her catch one and, like Jack, she's aware that they're unaccountably off the menu, she knows the addresses of all the cats in our neighborhood. When she's not trying to murder innocent rodents, Alice is the sweetest dog on the planet, and she has hugely enriched our lives. The spirit of this book comes in significant part from her, and from all the dogs I've ever loved.

Finally, I owe a great debt to my wife Yulia. I really have no idea what this extraordinary, smart, kind, drop-dead-gorgeous creature is doing with me; but I wake up every day and discover again that this was *not* a dream, that I actually *am* married to the most wonderful woman in the world. Thank you, my love, for everything - you are, and always will be, my Rowan.

-30-

ABOUT THE AUTHOR

The unacknowledged love child of a sordid tryst between Bigfoot and former Alaska governor Sarah Palin, Phillip Boleyn - not his real name - lives in resentful seclusion in a cold, damp and rather drafty cave somewhere in the Cascade Mountains, emerging only occasionally to check on whether the whales are still responsible for global warming. In a parallel, kinder universe, he is a retired marine scientist who until recently directed a large research program focusing on the biology, behavior and conservation of cetaceans. British by birth, he has lived in the U.S. since 1980, and holds a Ph.D. in zoology. Phil has published five books and more than 170 scientific papers about whales (about five of which are actually worth reading), and has been the recipient of several awards for achievements in science and conservation. He lives on a small island near Seattle with his absurdly beautiful Russian wife and a crazy, adorable dog named Alice. This is his first novel.

Made in the USA
Columbia, SC
08 October 2021